PRAISE FOR
PIG-STY HIGH

"David Mathews is indeed a master storyteller! Congratulations on a job well done. This book was an enjoyable read from start to finish! The author did a masterful job developing a wonderful story revolving around interesting characters, and you feel yourself being pulled into their lives throughout the book. It has just the right blend of small-town humor and inspirational faith concepts. I found myself contemplating these principles long after reading the last page. If you are looking for an enjoyable read with lasting life lessons, this book is for you!"

–Bruce Scifres,
Former Butler University football player, record holder, and MVP;
Twenty-seven-year career as a high school head football coach;
Seven Indiana State Football Championships;
Twelve-time Coach of the Year;
2018 Indiana Football Hall of Fame inductee

DAVID MATHEWS

PIG-STY HIGH

WHEN PIGS FLY

AMBASSADOR INTERNATIONAL
GREENVILLE, SOUTH CAROLINA & BELFAST, NORTHERN IRELAND

www.ambassador-international.com

PIG-STY HIGH
WHEN PIGS FLY

Hardcover ISBN: 978-1-64960-741-6
Paperback ISBN: 978-1-64960-621-1
eISBN: 978-1-64960-672-3

Cover design by Karen Slayne
Interior typesetting by Karen Slayne
Edited by Megan Griffin
Illustrations by David Mathews and M.W. Khoirul

Scripture marked ESV taken from The Holy Bible, English Standard Version. ESV® Text Edition: 2016. Copyright © 2001 by Crossway Bibles, a publishing ministry of Good News Publishers.

Scripture marked KJV taken from the King James Version of the Bible. Public Domain.

AMBASSADOR INTERNATIONAL
Emerald House
411 University Ridge, Suite B14
Greenville, SC 29601
United States
www.ambassador-international.com

AMBASSADOR BOOKS
The Mount
2 Woodstock Link
Belfast, BT6 8DD
Northern Ireland, United Kingdom
www.ambassadormedia.co.uk

The colophon is a trademark of Ambassador, a Christian publishing company.

To everyone who could use a good laugh about now.

"A joyful heart is good medicine."

—*Proverbs 17:22*

ACKNOWLEDGMENTS

I appreciate my high school history teacher and
football coach, Kermit Davis. His patience with me in the
classroom and on the field has not been forgotten.

I am thankful for a mother and father
who labored to instill in me a love for
God and a high regard for His Word.

I am truly blessed to be married to Donna,
my loving and supportive wife. She inspires me daily
to be more Christlike with her passionate heart for
serving the Lord and others.

I am most grateful for my Heavenly Father,
Who, because of His great love and mercy,
extended to me the privilege of becoming one of His children
(John 1:12; Ephesians 2:4-5).

CONTENTS

PROLOGUE 17

CHAPTER ONE 19
The Edge of the World

CHAPTER TWO 27
A Pig in a Poke

CHAPTER THREE 35
Blindsided

CHAPTER FOUR 41
Small Town Welcome

CHAPTER FIVE 49
Preparing for Battle

CHAPTER SIX 55
There's a Skunk in My Classroom!

CHAPTER SEVEN 63
The Mighty Misfits

CHAPTER EIGHT 71
The Feud

CHAPTER NINE 83
Unconventional Methods

CONTENTS
(cont.)

CHAPTER TEN 91
"What It Was, Was Football"

CHAPTER ELEVEN 99
Pig Wars

CHAPTER TWELVE 109
Whole Lotta Quakin' Goin' On

CHAPTER THIRTEEN 119
Home Field Advantage

CHAPTER FOURTEEN 131
Ineligible

CHAPTER FIFTEEN 143
The Letter of the Law

CHAPTER SIXTEEN 153
Getting to Know You

CHAPTER SEVENTEEN 161
Cousins

CHAPTER EIGHTEEN 173
Field Trip

CHAPTER NINETEEN 185
Super Bo and the Mighty Ferrell Hogs

CONTENTS
(cont.)

CHAPTER TWENTY 197
Unexpected Competition

CHAPTER TWENTY-ONE 209
The Raiders

CHAPTER TWENTY-TWO 223
The Aerosol Artist

CHAPTER TWENTY-THREE 233
Crossing the Great Divide

CHAPTER TWENTY-FOUR 243
Criminals and Convoys

CHAPTER TWENTY-FIVE 253
Senior Prank

CHAPTER TWENTY-SIX 263
The Runt of the Litter

CHAPTER TWENTY-SEVEN 275
When Pigs Fly

CHAPTER TWENTY-EIGHT 287
All's Well That Ends Well . . . ?

EPILOGUE 293

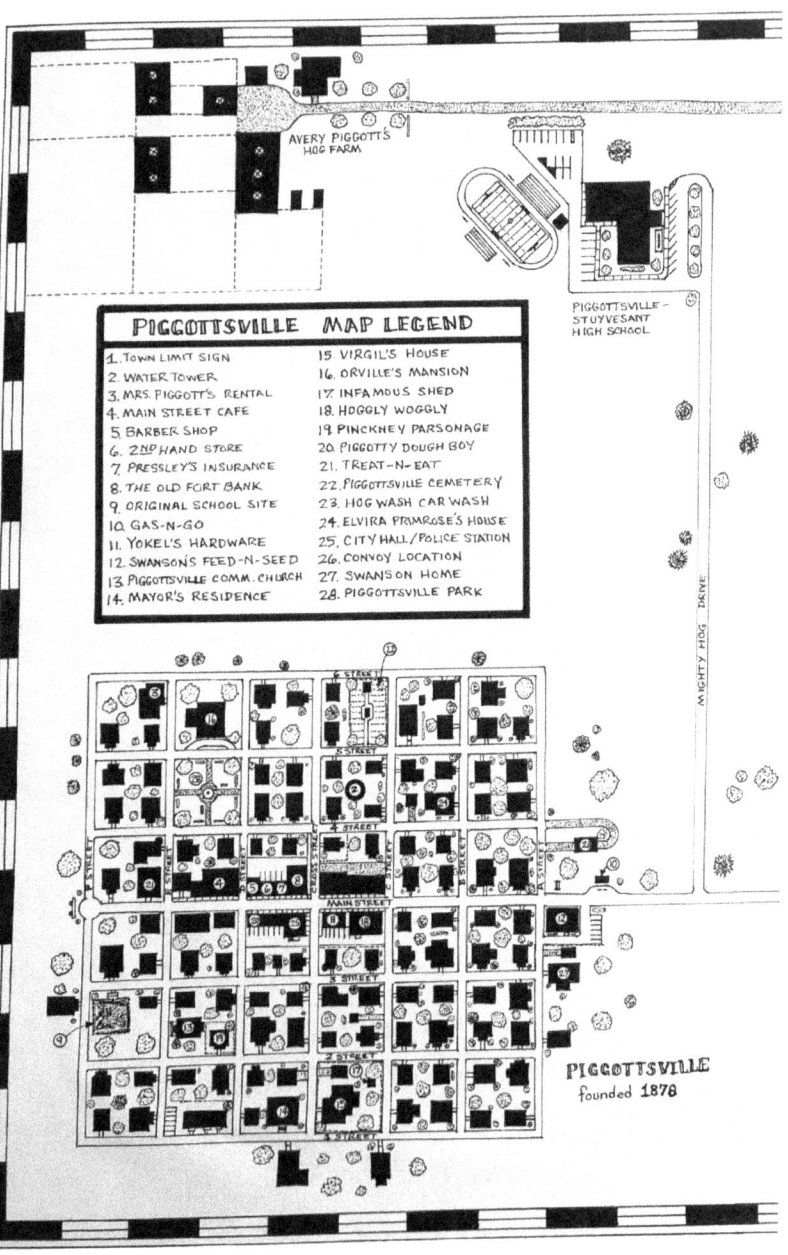

AVERY PIGGOTT'S
HOG FARM

PIGGOTTSVILLE-
STUYVESANT
HIGH SCHOOL

PIGGOTTSVILLE MAP LEGEND

1. TOWN LIMIT SIGN
2. WATER TOWER
3. MRS. PIGGOTT'S RENTAL
4. MAIN STREET CAFE
5. BARBER SHOP
6. 2ND HAND STORE
7. PRESSLEY'S INSURANCE
8. THE OLD FORT BANK
9. ORIGINAL SCHOOL SITE
10. GAS-N-GO
11. YOKEL'S HARDWARE
12. SWANSON'S FEED-N-SEED
13. PIGGOTTSVILLE COMM. CHURCH
14. MAYOR'S RESIDENCE

15. VIRGIL'S HOUSE
16. ORVILLE'S MANSION
17. INFAMOUS SHED
18. HOGGLY WOGGLY
19. PINCKNEY PARSONAGE
20. PIGGOTTY DOUGH BOY
21. TREAT-N-EAT
22. PIGGOTTSVILLE CEMETERY
23. HOG WASH CAR WASH
24. ELVIRA PRIMROSE'S HOUSE
25. CITY HALL/POLICE STATION
26. CONVOY LOCATION
27. SWANSON HOME
28. PIGGOTTSVILLE PARK

MIGHTY HOG DRIVE

PIGGOTTSVILLE
founded 1878

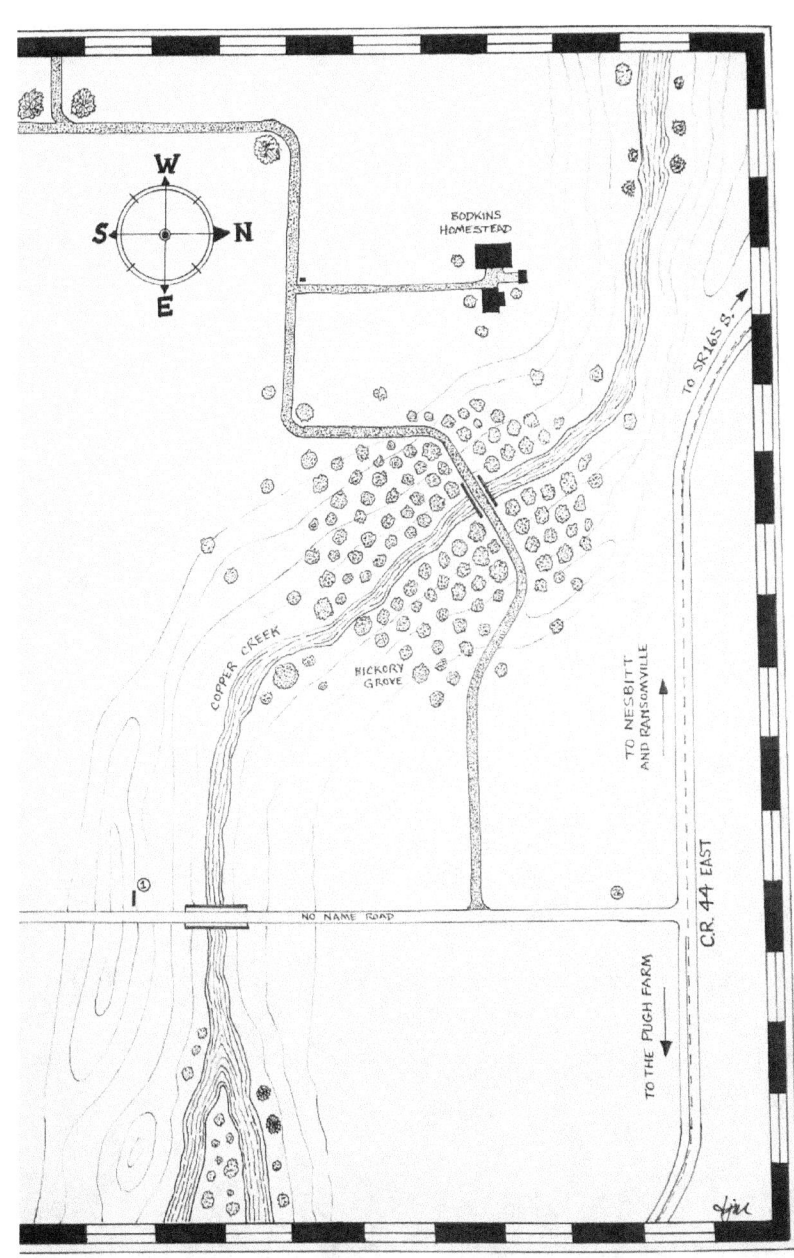

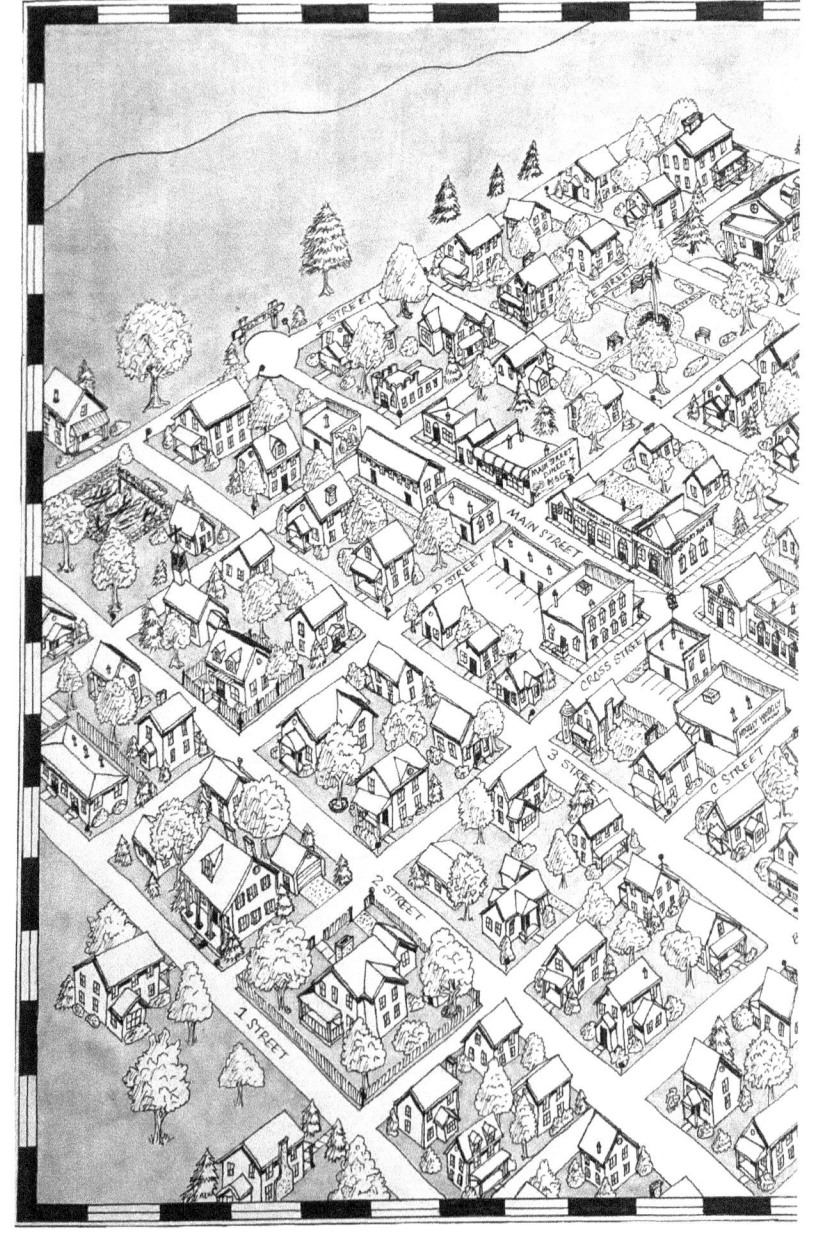

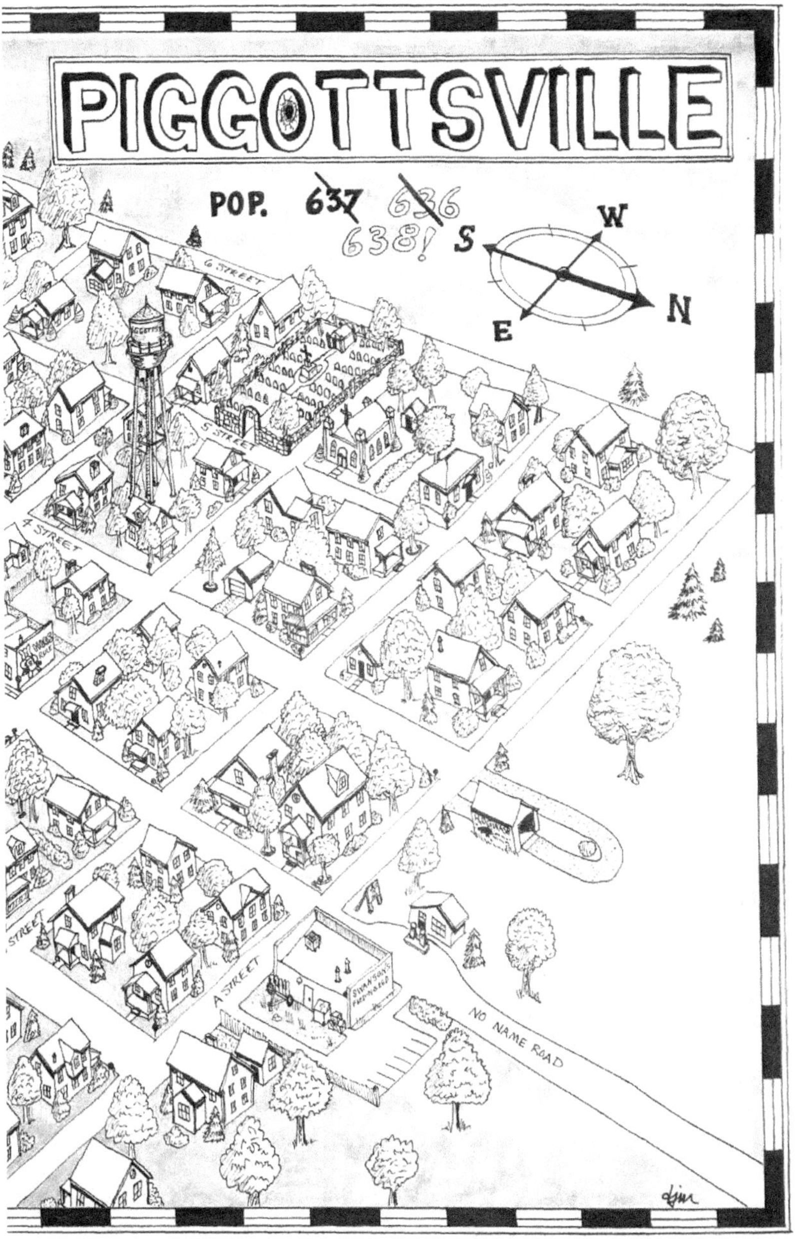

PIGGOTTSVILLE
POP. 637 636
638!
S
W
N
E
6 STREET
5 STREET
4 STREET
STREET
A STREET
NO NAME ROAD

PROLOGUE

There is an old adage that states, "When life gives you lemons, make lemonade." That sounds like pretty solid advice, don't you think? But I have discovered through personal experience that that is only true if life gives you *good* lemons—and plenty of sugar! What can be done when all you have to work with are bad lemons—and no sugar? Or worse yet, no lemons at all? You can't make something out of nothing, can you? Only God can do that. How can you begin with little to nothing and then mold and manipulate it into something meaningful, something valuable, something special? That would take nothing short of a miracle! Well, I just happen to believe in miracles. At least, I do now. "Why?" you might ask. Because recently I was part of one.

My name is Jason Wisniewski. I'm your typical twenty-four-year-old Midwesterner with traditional heartland values and ideals and all that. I have no extraordinary gifts or abilities to speak of—average-looking, average height and weight, mostly average grades, not part of the popular clique in high school, no outstanding athletic skills to brag about, and definitely no musical inclination whatsoever. In fourth grade, I flunked the recorder!

But in spite of that meager resume, I'm truly blessed to have something for which to be grateful. I am a child of God. That's my identity. I gave my life to Him in the eighth grade and have tried to live for Him since. Mind you, I'm nowhere near perfect. I've made plenty of mistakes and a few bad choices along the road, yet He has lovingly and patiently guided me to where I am today.

It's an indisputable fact that life is full of challenges. For example, I wasn't at all sure I'd even make it to college. Because of my rather anemic GPA and low SAT scores, my application was rejected by a number of larger state and private institutions. However, after committing the matter entirely to God, I was finally accepted by a very small Division 3 school, Wooster College. It took me five long, arduous years; but when the smoke cleared, I emerged with a Bachelor of Science degree in history and a minor in sports management.

Oh, did I mention that I'm a big football fanatic? I was even on my high school football team, believe it or not. During practices, I served as a tackling dummy for the huge, first-string defensive neanderthals; and during games, I mostly rode the bench. While the real jocks went about collecting their letters, I was collecting splinters. But I've always been fascinated with the game—the way it ebbs and flows, the physical and mental competitiveness of it, and the way a team must manage the clock and play as a cohesive unit in order to be victorious. So for those reasons, against my own better judgment—and that of a few highly respected mentors—I decided to try my hand at coaching high school football. Little did I know at the time what I was in for.

CHAPTER ONE
The Edge of the World

I eased my seventeen-year-old faded maroon Toyota Corolla off State Route 165 South and onto County Road 44 East and stole a glance at the dashboard clock. It was almost 3:00 p.m. I'd been up since five that morning and on the road since 5:30, when I'd left home for the nearly ten-hour drive to where my new life was about to commence. I'd had a whole day to contemplate my arrival in the little farming community of Piggottsville, Arkansas, a whole day to anticipate what was awaiting me. And I had absolutely no clue what to expect. You see, I'd never been to Piggottsville before. In fact, I'd never even heard of the place until that fateful first email from Mr. Herold popped up in my inbox. It's such a small town in such an out-of-the-way location that it doesn't even register on most state maps. With a listed population of under seven hundred residents, I figured it would turn out to be a mere wide spot in the road, an assessment that proved uncannily accurate.

Ten minutes later, I turned onto a stretch of pavement appropriately called No Name Road, a narrow, two-lane ribbon of crumbling asphalt that disappeared over a small rise about a mile ahead. It occurred to me that I hadn't passed a town or cluster of homes for nearly thirty minutes. Nothing but open, gently rolling hills as far as the eye could see. I was so far from civilization that if the earth were flat, I'd be in danger of falling off the edge about now. The uneven pavement growled beneath me, and I found myself bouncing painfully each time the tires discovered a pothole which had somehow managed to escape the attention of the county's highway maintenance crew.

One jolt was so severe that for a second, I thought I'd lost a contact lens. Even the lunar surface doesn't have craters *this* big! Risking a glance away from the deathtraps, I was relieved to see several farms in the distance on either side of me, but they were too far away to discern what sort of animals resided there. I breathed a sigh of relief. At least *some* traces of civilization remained in this remote part of the world.

As I approached the rise, I passed a rectangular green sign announcing the town's limit. I frowned, then slowed down and pulled over to the side of the road. *Did I read that right?* Throwing my arm over the seat and looking over my shoulder, I backed up until the sign was in front of me again. I stared incredulously, my mouth agape like a slack-jawed imbecile. It read, "Piggottsville, pop. 637." But there was more. Someone had crossed out the 637 with white paint and had handwritten the number 636 above it. That, too, was crossed out, and the number 638 was added with an exclamation point following.

Then I noticed the holes. Now, I've never been around guns all that much, but I do know a bullet hole when I see one. I counted six of them, with one dead center in the letter "O." I now had some inkling what the local yokels did for fun around here. Shaking my head, I muttered under my breath, "Nobody's gonna believe this back home!" Then I pulled out my cell phone and snapped a picture, in the event I should ever need irrefutable proof.

As I crested the rise in the roadway, a wide, shallow valley unfolded before me, dotted with numerous farms and homesteads all around. Immediately ahead lay the sleepy hamlet of Piggottsville, population 637. Make that 638. It was indeed not much more than a wide spot in the road. A cylindrical water reservoir towered above the small cluster of buildings like a Martian's spindly legged fighting machine in *War of the Worlds.*

Driving into town on what was now posted as Main Street, I passed a dozen or so large turn-of-the-century homes. That's the twentieth century, by the way. They definitely were showing their age, but most seemed to be well-maintained and were all nestled underneath a variety of mature, stately shade trees.

Three blocks later, I reached the center of town, which looked like a postcard from the past. This was the only intersection with a traffic light, a flashing four-way stop. At least they had electricity here. I could

only hold out hope for indoor plumbing. The cross street at the light was simply marked, "Cross Street." It must have taken someone with a lot of imagination to come up with that one. Straight ahead, Main Street ended at the far edge of town. I say far, but it's actually only six blocks from where Piggottsville begins. And by ended, I don't mean Main Street changed back to No Name Road; I mean it literally dead-ended three blocks past the center of town! In all my life, I'd never heard of a municipality whose main thoroughfare simply ceased to exist. This place was truly at the proverbial end of the line.

The side streets parallel to Main Street were all numbered consecutively "1, 2, 3 . . ."; and those perpendicular to it were lettered "A, B, C," and so forth. So much for the creativity of the town planners. I soon learned they only went up to "6" and "F" Streets. Honestly, I have no idea why they even bothered to mark them at all. If you can't count to six or remember *A* to *F*, you probably shouldn't be driving, anyway. Perhaps it was for the postman's benefit. However, in such a small community, the names on the mail should have been clue enough as to which mailbox the envelopes belonged in. The entirety of Piggottsville proper was only a quarter of a square mile: six blocks long and six blocks wide.

While stopped at the intersection, I checked my phone for the address where I would be living, half-expecting there to be no cell reception in this primitive wasteland. The rental property was located at 632 E Street and managed by Mrs. Mary Piggott, wife of the mayor. I had an appointment to meet her there in ten minutes, at which time I would sign a rental agreement and move into a furnished upstairs apartment.

I put down my phone and proceeded forward, but a sudden movement to my right caught my attention and caused me to hit the brakes. I sat there in the middle of the intersection in wide-eyed disbelief as a billy goat meandered past the front end of my car, completely unaware of or unconcerned with my presence. Once again, I felt compelled to grab my phone and capture the moment for posterity. Then I watched as the traffic violator continued across the road and sauntered on down Cross Street without a care in the world. Apparently, the creature believed he'd arrived at the light before me.

Two hours later, I was settled comfortably in my new home. It was a two-story clapboard residence from the 1920s with a wide veranda porch facing due west. The exterior could have used a fresh coat of paint a decade ago; but other than that, it was in pretty good shape. The interior had been divided into four separate furnished apartments, two downstairs and two upstairs. It reminded me of the off-campus housing I shared with eighteen other guys during my junior and senior years at Wooster, an experience that created pleasant memories and caused PTSD. I silently prayed that this residence had a significantly lower occupancy level.

Since I'd contracted to teach history and coach football for the upcoming school year, I went ahead and signed a twelve-month rental agreement. Mrs. Piggott, my landlady, was a short, petite woman in her early sixties with a very pleasant, although somewhat quiet, disposition. I'm afraid I peppered her with too many questions about the town, of which, I confided, I knew very little. But she politely answered them all while maintaining a kindly smile throughout the inconvenient inquisition.

"This town was founded by my husband's great-great-grandfather, Ferrell Piggott, in 1878," she informed me. "He was a larger-than-life character, I'm told. He owned the biggest hog farm in the county and became one of the wealthiest and most influential men in this part of the state. He purchased a tract of land and built this town from scratch, established the bank, created a volunteer fire brigade, and organized the chamber of commerce. He even built the first school with his own money."

"How long has your husband been the mayor?" I asked.

"Thirty-one years," she replied succinctly.

"Is he the founder's only descendant here in town?"

My landlady's eyes widened. "The only one? Oh my, no! There are plenty of Piggotts still living in this area." She suddenly chuckled and added, "Which might account for my husband's being elected mayor for so long. Most of the townsfolk are related in some way, either directly or by marriage. There's my oldest son, Orville, and his younger brother Virgil. Orville is president of the bank and head of our chamber of commerce; and Virgil is the town constable, county sheriff, and justice of the peace, all in one. And my brother-in-law, Avery Piggott, manages the huge family hog farm just outside the town limits behind the high school. Then there's a whole slew of children and grandchildren scattered about. You'll meet some of them when school begins. No doubt a good number will be in your classroom."

I could hardly wait.

Later that evening, after grabbing a bite to eat at the only diner in town, I plunked down on the well-worn, white-painted porch swing, exhaled slowly, and watched the sun settle behind the distant undulating hills. I was about to begin my new life. I have to admit, I had a few misgivings about the uncertainty of what lay ahead, and I justified them by surmising that even the finest thoroughbred college graduates must feel that way right out of the gate. But I also had a kind of deep-down peace. After all, I'd prayed about landing the right job all summer, and this seemed to be an answer to my prayers. Actually, it was the *only* answer to my prayers. Prior to commencement, I posted my resume online and began the process of contacting numerous high schools seeking a teaching/coaching position. I even had a half dozen in-person interviews and one follow up, but nothing came of them. Nada. Zilch. By mid-August, I had grown so discouraged that I felt as if I were riding the bench all over again—but this time during the all-important game of life.

Somewhere in that time frame, I turned to the Bible for encouragement and guidance and ran across Psalm 27:14: *"Wait for the LORD; be strong, and let your heart take courage; wait for the LORD!"* So I determined to do just that. And wouldn't you know it, not three days later, I received an email from a Mr. H. Herold, high school principal and school board member of the Piggottsville-Stuyvesant Consolidated School Corporation in southeastern Arkansas. That began a series of emails, phone calls, and video conferences, which culminated in him extending to me a one-year contract as history teacher and football coach. With the school year rapidly approaching and no other offers anywhere on the horizon, I readily accepted the position, sight unseen. And now, here I was on the cusp of the unknown. At 10:30 in the morning, I had an appointment at the high school with Principal Herold, the man who had offered me a new lease on life.

Stoked about the prospects that lay ahead, I inhaled the sweet, fresh, country air wafting all around me in this idyllic little corner of the world. I was convinced I would remember this moment for as long as I lived. Was I ever right. I breathed in again, this time as deeply as I could. And I gagged. The wind had suddenly shifted out of the west. With eyes watering profusely, I deduced that the overpowering stench must be coming from Avery Piggott's humongous hog farm on the outskirts of town. It was *awful!* I'd never smelled anything like it. Good grief! Only four-and-a-half hours had elapsed since I had taken possession of my new residence, and I was already entertaining the notion of moving to the other side of town. But that really wasn't an option, since I'd just committed to twelve months' rent. Besides, a six-block relocation probably wasn't going to diffuse the situation all that much, anyway. Grumbling to myself, I climbed the stairs to my new apartment and went to bed. Reality had come home to roost.

CHAPTER TWO
A Pig in a Poke

The following morning, I awoke with renewed enthusiasm; and the anticipation of the day ahead drove the previous evening's unpleasantness into the remote regions of my mind. I showered, shaved, and put on a pair of dress pants as well as a shirt and tie. It was imperative that I make a good first impression with Mr. Herold. Then I walked three blocks to the little diner on Main Street for breakfast. I planned to visit the town's only grocery store later that afternoon to stock up on food. When you're on a beginning teacher's salary, frequent dining out isn't such a smart idea, especially when the source of that salary is the parsimonious Piggottsville-Stuyvesant Consolidated School Corporation.

Leaving the diner, I spied a bank at the other end of the block. I figured it had to be the one managed by my landlady's son because how many banks could there possibly be in a place this size? Since my meeting at the school wasn't for another hour and since I would need to set up an account at some point, anyway, I walked down the sidewalk toward the intersection of Main and Cross Streets. I passed a barbershop, a second-hand clothing store, and an insurance agency not much wider than its front door. When I reached the bank, I glanced up at the sign painted on the building's two-story brick wall. "The Old Fort Bank" was printed in large black letters outlined in gold, along with a logo resembling a castle watchtower.

I did a double take. The sign had been slightly altered. Someone had spray-painted over the letter "O" in the word "Fort," making it an "A." I'm pretty sure I don't need to spell it out for you; but at that point, I burst into laughter, which drew the attention of a passing elderly woman in a floral-print dress. She threw me an unmistakable look of contempt before crossing over to the other side of the street.

After regaining my composure, which took some time, I wiped the tears from my eyes, adjusted my tie, and whipped out my cellphone to capture this latest sample of the local culture. Then I did my dead-level best to enter the bank as if nothing had happened.

With an account established and a new bank book in hand, I returned to the apartment, grabbed my briefcase containing my employment contract and other related documents, and headed off to my appointment. The high school was about a mile from the center of town at the end of a long entrance road that was straight as an arrow. Driving down the lane, I caught sight of a large farm across the open fields. As it turned out, this was the very same farm that was the perpetrator of my olfactory assault. I couldn't help but wonder if its proximity to the school might cause disruptions to the daily educational learning process. I parked in the lot out front and walked up the cracked sidewalk toward the building that would be the launch pad and proving ground for my new career as a high school history teacher.

I'm not sure I can adequately describe the mixed emotions churning in my gut in that moment; but the words exhilaration, anticipation, uncertainty, and terror come to mind. My place of employment for the next nine months was a two story, red-brick building with metal-framed windows protected by diamond-patterned screen mesh. It looked as if it had been resting comfortably there since the Dark Ages. The large sign that stood to the left of the main entrance appeared to be much younger than the edifice behind it: "Piggottsville-Stuyvesant High School / Home of the Mighty Ferrell Hogs." Another photo op.

No sooner had I opened one of the heavy wooden doors and stepped into the main hallway than my attention was drawn to the lone figure of a man with his back to me about twenty yards down the long corridor. He was operating a noisy, chrome-plated machine using sweeping motions to buff the faded tile floor. For some reason, the word "asbestos" flashed across my mind. Careful to avoid the long, orange extension cord that snaked down the hall, I approached the balding, gray-headed man.

"Excuse me, but can you direct me to Mr. Herold's office?" I had to repeat the question and crank up the volume. The man shut off the machine and turned to face me. He wore a faded blue janitor's uniform with a patch bearing the letters "PSHS" sewn on the front and sported a pair of oval, gold-rimmed glasses that slouched on the bridge of his nose.

"Come again?" he half-shouted as if the machine were still running.

"Can you direct me to Mr. Herold's office?" I asked for the third time. "I have a 10:30 appointment with him."

He silently studied me for a moment. "You must be the new history teacher."

"History teacher *and* football coach," I informed him with a smile.

A look of incredulity swept across his otherwise stoic face. "Football coach?" He suddenly began chuckling and shook his head as if in disbelief.

"What's so funny?" I asked, unsure of how to interpret his reaction.

"Exactly how much did Mr. Herold tell ya, anyway?" he inquired.

"You mean about the coaching position?" I shrugged. "Not much, really. We mostly discussed my teaching responsibilities and the history curriculum. All he said about the coaching job was that I'd be taking over the entire football program this season."

He quirked an eyebrow. "Entire football program, huh? Is that what he called it?"

"Um . . . yes," I replied, now totally befuddled as to where this conversation was heading. "Is there something more I should be aware of before I meet with him?"

The janitor shot me a cryptic grin. "Oh, I reckon you'll find out soon enough." He chuckled again before pointing down the hall. "Third door down on your right."

I wanted to question him further about his coy remark but thought better of it. "Well, okay then, thanks." I started in the direction he'd pointed but stopped and turned around. "Oh, by the way, I'm Jason Wisniewski." I extended my hand in a show of goodwill and grinned. "History teacher *and* football coach."

The man wiped his palm on the front of his overalls before grasping it. "Winston Banks. School custodian *and* grounds maintenance." With that, he turned his attention back to the machine, flipped the toggle switch to the "ON" position, and continued buffing his way down the corridor.

After locating the aforementioned door, which had the word "Office" stenciled on the translucent glass, I took a deep breath to steady my nerves and entered the inner sanctum. Facing me was a waist-high counter capped with a worn piece of black laminate about eight feet in length. Behind that sat a couple of secretarial desks, a bank of filing cabinets, a water cooler, and a copier, all so ancient that I wouldn't have been the least bit surprised to see a manual typewriter or mimeograph machine as well. No one was there, but I heard someone talking through a partially open door in the far wall.

I hesitated, unsure of how to announce my presence. Should I wait here until Mr. Herold came out to get me, or should I go knock on his door? If he was going to be a while, I might not be able to prove that I'd been on time. On the other hand, I didn't want to interrupt him if he was in a big meeting. My dad had always stressed the importance of punctuality; so with the minute hand on the large, round wall clock pointing due south, I chose to announce my arrival. Spying a silver call bell at the far end of the counter, I walked over and hit the shiny button with my palm. Maybe a little too forcefully. The conversation in the other room instantly ceased; and for a second, I didn't know what to expect.

Then, a very business-like voice bellowed, "Come in!"

I crossed the room and cautiously peered through the doorway. Mr. Herold was parked behind an impressive mahogany desk, firmly entrenched in an equally impressive high-backed executive chair, with a phone plastered to his ear. He glanced up and motioned me toward the only other seat in the room, an ugly orange monstrosity that was child-sized in contrast to the black leather behemoth already occupied.

"Can I call you back after lunch, Ed?" he asked into the phone. "My 10:30 is here. I'm confident we'll be able to wrap things up today." He paused. "Two o'clock? That's fine. Talk to you then." Without saying goodbye, he ended the call. "Mr. Wisniewski! Welcome to Piggottsville!" He stood and extended a hand across the broad, cluttered desktop. "It's so nice to finally meet you in person."

I sprang to my feet and grasped his hand firmly. "Thank you," I replied, mustering every ounce of confidence I had. "It's nice to meet you as well, sir."

"Please, call me Mr. Herold." He sat down and waved me back into my chair. "I take it you had an uneventful trip?" Before I could reply, he continued. "When did you arrive?"

"Yesterday afternoon, around three."

"Were you able to meet with Mrs. Piggott concerning the living arrangements I recommended?"

"I was! In fact, I've already signed a rental agreement and moved in. It's a very nice place. Thank you for suggesting it. I'm sure it's going to meet my needs just fine." I thought it best not to mention the little issue of the air quality in that part of town.

"I'm glad that worked out for you so quickly. Now we can focus on the upcoming school year." The principal glanced at his watch. "By the way, thank you for being punctual. That kind of personal discipline is fundamental to my administration's success. As I stated in one of our prior phone conversations, you'll find that I run a very tight ship here. Tight, but fair. It is my sincere belief that an effective academic environment cannot be established or maintained without the proper authoritarian structures in place."

I took note of the authoritarian structures in place around the man and was convinced that he believed every word he said.

He abruptly changed the subject. "Let's get down to the business at hand, shall we? Now, where did I put your file?" While he shuffled through the papers on his desk, I grabbed the opportunity to size up my new boss. Mr. Herold was not a large man, but he still cut an imposing figure. What he lacked in physicality, he more than compensated for by the way he dressed, spoke, and conducted himself. Even his business-style haircut suggested to the casual observer that this was a no-nonsense, take-charge person you'd best not challenge or cross. Authority and confidence oozed from every pore.

Then I noticed the nameplate on his desk: "Harold Herold, Principal." *Harold* Herold? That's what the "H" stood for? Seriously? It was all I could do to keep a straight face. To distract myself, I plotted how I might covertly use my phone to capture this latest "Believe It or Not" souvenir.

The principal eventually located the misplaced file; and for the next sixty minutes, he laid out his classroom disciplinary system and my responsibilities as the school's lone history teacher. I won't bore you with specifics, but I learned I'd be teaching three periods of U.S. History and three of World History. When every detail had been thoroughly discussed and every question answered to *his* satisfaction, he relaxed and sank back in his chair with a contented smile.

"Well, I think that about covers everything related to your teaching position," he stated with a note of finality. "However, being new to our school system and to the teaching profession as a whole, I'm sure you will have additional questions once the academic year commences. Please understand that my door is always open. I'm here to assist in any way possible."

"Thank you. I appreciate that very much." He really meant it, and so did I. I was going to need all the help I could get. But I suspected he already knew that.

He shifted in his huge chair and clasped his hands together. "Now, let's discuss your other responsibilities outside the classroom and on the football field."

"Yes, I've been very anxious to learn more about that. Being a first-year coach, I fully expect to have a steep learning curve, especially with the job coming on such short notice." I laughed nervously.

He gazed at the ceiling and nodded pensively. "I can pretty much guarantee that."

"So, what kind of staff will I have? An assistant coach? Offensive and defensive coordinators?"

"Well, we're currently in negotiations with your . . . ah . . . coaching staff, so I can't say much about that right this minute. We thought it important to fill the head coaching position first. But we expect an answer in the next day or two, so I'll let you know."

"I guess that will have to do. May I ask how the team performed last season? I'm eager to learn what kind of returning talent I'll have to work with this year."

Mr. Herold cleared his throat. "About that, Mr. Wisniewski," he hedged. "I'm afraid I must be perfectly honest with you. In our previous communications, I failed to mention a few, shall we say, 'minor details' regarding the football program here at Piggottsville High."

That didn't sound too good. But I was confident. "Well, I've already spent a fair amount of time prepping for the worst-case scenario, so I'm ready for just about anything."

"That's good, very good," he replied quickly, "because the truth is, Mr. Wisniewski, we didn't *have* a football team last year."

I was wrong. I wasn't ready. "Um . . . what about the year before that?"

"Actually, our football program is presently defunct. We haven't had a team for the past five years."

My stupefied mind began processing this latest news flash. The program wasn't defunct. It was *extinct*! Dead as a dinosaur! I managed a hoarse, "Why not?"

"I'm afraid there hasn't been enough interest among the student population to field a complete team." He sounded genuinely disappointed. Then he brightened. "That's why we brought *you* on board."

I shook my head. "But why me? I have no real experience."

"Because early in the interview process, you struck me as someone who is eager and willing. I know you have no coaching experience, but I feel your youth and enthusiasm for the game are exactly what we need to revive interest in the sport." He quickly held up a hand as if to ward off my protests. "Mind you, we don't expect a lot this year—or in the near future, for that matter. I speak for the entire school board when I say we just want you to give it your best shot. That's all we ask. Whatever you do and however you choose to do it, just know we stand behind you 100 percent."

A ray of hope pierced the looming clouds. I was being handed a blank check. They truly believed I was the right man for the job. And I believed it, too. I was ready for this. I could handle it. Sure, it was going to be a huge challenge; but they had the utmost faith in me, and I wasn't about to let them down. I mentally held the first pep rally of the season right there in his office. *You can do this; yes, you can! You can do it; you're the man!* Then I sought a final answer. Not that it mattered at this point. "Excuse me, but I'm just curious about one thing. Why didn't you tell me any of this during the interviews?"

Mr. Herold's reply was simple and direct. "Because I was afraid you wouldn't come."

In that moment, it dawned bright and clear just how much work lay ahead of me.

CHAPTER THREE

BLINDSIDED

When the meeting in his office concluded, my new boss took me on a grand tour of the building. He showed me the cafeteria and teachers' lounge and introduced me to my classroom, which was on the second floor. A whiteboard spanned the width of one wall in place of the well-worn green chalkboard I'd envisioned, and a canister of pull-down maps was mounted above that. The longer side wall contained two windows which overlooked the front parking lot and supplied the average-sized room with plenty of natural light. In addition to my desk, I counted thirty student desks arranged in rows of six. Overall, the room met my expectations and appeared adequate for my needs.

"How old is this building?" I asked as we headed downstairs toward the gymnasium.

"It was completed in 1962," Mr. Herold replied. "In the late fifties, the town was facing a severe budget deficit, so the council decided to merge with two other schools in similar crises. The plan was to build a new consolidated school in Nesbitt, the Stuyvesant county seat. But due to the significant clout of Ferrell Piggott's many descendants in this area, they finally agreed to move it here instead."

"Are we on the site of the original schoolhouse?"

"No, that's at the south end of 3 Street."

"I'd like to see it sometime."

Mr. Herold cracked a wry smile. "That might be a little difficult. It burned to the ground last year. The official cause was listed as teenagers shooting off fireworks."

Great. Not only did the local ruffians entertain themselves with guns and spray paint, but they also played with matches!

When we reached the far end of the hallway, he pointed to a solid wood door near a wall-mounted drinking fountain. "This will be your office." The placard on the door read, "Janitorial Supply." He must have noticed the expression on my face. "Oh, don't worry about that," he assured me with a wave of his hand. "The new one says 'Football Coach.' It's on order. Should be here any day now. I'd show you inside, but I'm afraid I left the keys in my desk drawer. I'll see that you have your own set, of course. I'm sure you'll want to check it out as soon as possible."

I wasn't so sure about that.

We stopped in front of a laminated oak curio cabinet resting against the wall beside the gym doors. It looked like an item you might be tempted to donate to Goodwill but probably not one you would want to buy from them.

"This is our main trophy case," the principal announced. I'd have never guessed. Behind the glass sat three anemic trophies, each one isolated from the others so that the cabinet appeared almost empty. He pointed to the one on the top shelf. "This is from the year our basketball team made it to the sectionals. And the one below it is when we had a cross country runner finish third in the county championship."

I noted the dates on the plaques, 1974 and 1998. Evidently, there hadn't been much to brag about since. Then he pointed to the smallest of the three sitting on the lowest shelf. "You'll be particularly interested in this one," he said, pride tingeing his voice.

Curious to see what could possibly evoke my excitement, I bent down for a closer look. Attached to a wood base was a clear crystal goblet with so much dust on the rim that it looked like salt on a margarita glass. I read the inscription: "Piggottsville-Stuyvesant High School / 2018 Football Season / 8-0."

So there *was* life in the Piggottsville athletic department after all! I straightened up and looked at him. "That's awesome! A perfect season?" Since then, I've become much better about jumping to conclusions.

"Well, that's how *we* like to think of it, anyway," he said, "but not for the reason you might expect. It's more of a participation trophy. The school board felt the team needed a little encouragement."

I was confused. "How much encouragement does an undefeated team need?"

Mr. Herold hedged his response again. "Well, they weren't exactly undefeated. The eight represents the first time the school was able to field a team for an entire eight game season."

I was almost afraid to ask my next question. "Then how many games did they actually win that year?"

"That's what the zero stands for," he replied sheepishly.

When the guided tour ended, Mr. Herold urged me to check out the football field on my own. He apologized for being unable to accompany me and excused himself, stating that he was due at a school board luncheon in fifteen minutes.

I returned to my car to drop off my briefcase and shed the coat and tie. It would be an understatement to say that August weather in Arkansas is less than ideal for suit wearing. As I followed the sidewalk around the building to the stadium out back, my excitement grew with every step. This was it—my ground zero! The epicenter for the start of my coaching career. I could picture the Friday night lights and the hard-fought battles to come. I could smell the hot dogs and hamburgers and buttered popcorn, feel the Coliseum-like electricity in the air, and hear the screech of the referee's whistle and the roar of the crowd.

When I reached the sideline, the whirling dervish in my mind came to a standstill. I gazed out across the field in dumbfounded silence. Talk about being blindsided! I had expected to see a well-manicured green surface with white stripes and yard markers. Instead, what lay before me was nothing more than an overgrown patch of pastureland. Weeds poked their heads above the uneven clumps of grass; and small, round spots of bare, reddish-brown earth dotted the untamed wilderness. I distinctly recall seeing a dozen or so mole hills as well as a few groundhog holes. Just terrific!

I wandered out toward midfield and immediately stepped in something soft. What I'd thought were bare spots of dirt were actually cow patties, some of them obviously quite fresh. I instinctively glanced around to make sure this pasture was not home turf to a two-thousand-pound bull. No bull, but I did catch sight of a lone black and white cow grazing contentedly in one end zone. Disgusted on so many different levels, I navigated back to the sideline as carefully as a soldier in a minefield. I grabbed a hold of the chain link fence that separated the stands from the field and made a gallant effort to scrape off the warm, gooey mess clinging for dear life to the soles of my shoes. It smelled pretty bad but not as bad as the odors emanating from Avery Piggott's hog farm. I wondered how many other scents my nose would be forced to identify by the end of the school year.

Having cleaned off my shoes as best I could, I climbed to the top of the stands to get a better view of the stadium. The goalposts were intact but showing signs of rust with one leaning to the right like the Tower of Pisa. Behind the far end zone stood the scoreboard, once bright red but now a faded pinkish hue. Two tall wooden poles, each topped with a bank of four lights, stood behind the bleachers on either side of the field. At least, the Friday night lights part of my fantasy was still alive. That is, providing they actually worked. Both grandstands were fairly small, and the wooden benches a weather-beaten gray with some sections sagging in the middle like a gangbanger's pants. The concession stand at the end of the bleachers was a low-roofed, cement-block structure with peeling white paint and a boarded up serving window. Suddenly feeling weak-kneed, I sat down to process what I was seeing; but I immediately leaped to my feet with a yelp. I fished around for a second or two and then dislodged a three-inch sliver of wood from the seat of my dress pants.

After making sure the coast was clear, I sat back down in a state of utter despair and began negotiations with myself. I'm fairly certain portions of the conversation were debated audibly—on both sides of the argument. Here I was, in a new place I'd never seen before, ready to start a new job I'd never done before—a job offered to me only because my employers were as desperate to fill the position as I was to find one. The situation was hopeless, especially the coaching part. To quote the Munchkin coroner who certified the wicked witch's demise, the football program was "not only merely dead," it was "really most sincerely dead!"[1] I looked at the carnage all around me. What was I supposed to do? Was *this* what Mr. Herold meant when he said the school board was behind

---

1 Victor Fleming, dir. *The Wizard of Oz* (Culver City: Metro-Goldwyn-Mayer, 1939), film.

me 100 percent? They'd given me nothing to work with! Why, even Michelangelo needed a block of marble to chisel a statue; Emeril Lagasse needed ingredients to make his famous chili; Dr. Ben Carson needed a brain to operate on. And here I was being asked to pull a rabbit out of a hat without being given the hat, to make lemonade without being given the lemons, to create something without being given anything! Who did they think I was, anyway? They were asking for a miracle, expecting me to do something only God could do!

A lightbulb suddenly exploded. I think it must have been the Lord smacking me upside the head with a heavenly sized two by four. *Something only God could do.* I rewound my memory to where He had answered my prayers and given me peace about this job not even two weeks ago. I recalled the verse that had encouraged me; and I suddenly felt ashamed for thinking that this was all up to me and then complaining about it. The truth was this *did* require a miracle, and it *was* something only He could do. But that was the point of it all. I needed to trust God. He was doing His part. Now, I just needed to do mine.

CHAPTER FOUR

Small Town Welcome

I had only one week to get all my ducks in a row, seven days to prepare for my dual roles as a high school teacher and football coach. That's not much time at all, especially for a novice. However, I was fairly confident about the classroom part. I'd enjoyed my practicum and student teaching at Wooster, and those experiences confirmed my decision to go into teaching. And while my four years as a student manager with the school's football team taught me much about the sport from a coaching standpoint, I still didn't feel adequately prepared to tackle the responsibility of being a head coach. I'd assumed that my initiation into the world of high school sports would be a gradual process, maybe starting out as the special teams coach or an assistant to an assistant and then working my way up to the top spot once my experience caught up with my enthusiasm. But when this lone opportunity had presented itself, I'd jumped at the chance, in part due to the pressure of the rapidly approaching school year. But also, I think because the offer appealed to my pride. "Head Coach" sure sounded more impressive than "Assistant" or "Staff Member." So now here I was, heading up an entire football program that didn't even exist. Yet I had to push ahead, to figure this thing out, to find a way when there appeared to be no way. And to trust God to help me do what seemed impossible.

The day after my appointment with the principal, Mr. Herold handed me the keys to my new office and promised to announce a meeting on the first day of school for all those interested in playing football. Most schools begin practices in early August on the first date allowed by the state athletic association, so I was already several weeks behind the eight ball. With the season schedule beginning in mid-September, I'd have less than three weeks to field a team and get it ready for the first game. Mr. Herold had instructed me to concentrate on my teaching role and not to worry too much about football, reminding me that his sole expectation was for me to try my best. But that was easier said than done.

When I went to check out my office, I was surprised to find the door standing open and the lights on. Someone was moving around inside, so I stepped in to see who it was. The room was small, about the size of a typical yard shed, approximately ten feet by sixteen feet. There was an old wood desk and chair with a chalkboard mounted on the wall next to it. A few metal shelves sat against the opposite wall filled with helmets and shoulder pads and large cardboard boxes. I glanced around the dwarfish room. Not much of an office. A more accurate door placard would have been "Coach's Closet." A number of boxes had been pulled from the shelves, and piles of jerseys and football pants were strewn on the floor. The smell of mothballs hung like a heavy cloud over the room. A man was rummaging through one of the boxes on the floor with his back to me.

"Can I help you?" I asked.

"I sure hope so." He straightened up and turned around. "But the better question is can I help *you*?" It was Winston Banks, the custodian.

"Mr. Banks! I thought it might be you. I knew it had to be someone with a key."

"I got keys to every room, nook, an' cranny in this place," he replied, jingling the large ring on his belt as proof. "Not to mention every locker, storage cabinet, an' electrical panel." He pointed to the jersey in his hand. "Hope ya don't mind me comin' in here like this, but I figured you could use a hand gettin' this stuff organized."

"Not at all. In fact, I could use all the help I can get." I glanced around at the equipment scattered across the room. "What have we got so far?"

"Well, the good news is I think we're gonna have enough equipment to outfit a team. But . . . " His voice trailed off.

"Let me guess. Not in the best of shape?"

"That's puttin' it mildly." He poked a finger through a hole in the mildewed jersey. "Most o' these are gonna need quite a bit o' mendin'—if they can be saved at all—an' some o' the pants don't have pads in 'em. A few shoulder pads have dry-rotted laces, an' a couple o' helmets are missin' chin straps. Could all use a new coat o' spray paint, too."

I tried masking my disappointment. "You're right, that doesn't sound good at all. But I guess it could be worse. I'll get that taken care of before practice begins. Somehow."

Propped up in the corner was a large duffel bag containing five footballs, two clipboards, a small whiteboard for diagramming plays, and a bunch of old mesh practice vests. Three of the balls were flat, and many of the vests were torn and tattered; but Mr. Banks promised to find a hand pump we could use to inflate the balls. I said I'd find a way to mend the vests or get them replaced. Setting the bag aside, I began helping him with the rest of the equipment. The poor condition of the uniforms reminded me of the sorry state of the field. "Has Mr. Herold said anything to you about getting the stadium ready for the season?"

The janitor glanced in my direction. "The stadium? Uh . . . not really. But I plan to mow the grass before your first practice, an' I'll have the field striped before the season opener. 'Fraid I can't guarantee much more'n that."

"What about the field lights? Do they work?" I held my breath.

He shrugged. "They did the *last* time we played a game."

That was not the answer I was hoping for.

I took the opportunity on Saturday to run a few errands around town. I filled my car with gas at the only place in Piggottsville, a small, two-pump establishment that made Goober's Mayberry filling station look like one of those mega truck marts out on the interstate. Then I stopped by Yokel's Hardware to see if I could find replacement laces for the shoulder pads and some foam pieces that might work for the football pants. I had no idea what to do about the missing chin straps. With those two stops checked off my list, I headed for the little barber shop on Main Street to get a trim before the start of school. A faded barber pole was mounted beside the door, and the name "A Close Shave" was painted on the window along with the hours of operation and a caricature of a sheep.

I entered the long, narrow room to find a single barber's chair, a couple of metal tables covered in old newspapers and magazines, and a row of well-worn wooden chairs lined up along one wall. Mirrored glass on both sides created the illusion of space. The proprietor wore a white smock over his clothing and was parked in his barber chair engaged in lively conversation with four men seated against the wall. When they saw me, the room fell silent; and every eye focused on the stranger who'd just walked through the door.

I hesitated, glancing between the men and the barber. "I'm sorry, I didn't realize you were so busy. I can come back some other time." I started to retreat.

"We're not busy at all," the barber insisted, breaking the silence. He jumped to his feet and motioned to the chair he'd just vacated.

I looked at the others. "Oh. I just assumed they were waiting in line."

"Who, them? Naw, we were just shooting the breeze, that's all. Not much else to do on a Saturday morning." I sat down in the chair, and the barber fastened a cape around my shoulders. He was a bland little man in his fifties with plastic-framed glasses and obviously dyed hair around his temples. He sported the worst comb-over I'd ever seen, which might have accounted for the no waiting.

"I don't believe I've had the pleasure of your acquaintance, son," he began. "You new in town?"

"Yes, I am, actually. Just got in Thursday afternoon. I'm the new history teacher at the high school." I thought it best not to mention the words "football" or "coach."

One of the men sitting against the wall spoke up. "So *you're* the young man who moved into the apartment on E Street. My wife told me about you." He got up with a grunt, waddled over to me, and extended a hand. "I'm Wilson Piggott III, mayor of this here town."

I shook his hand. "I'm pleased to meet you, Mayor. I'm Jason Wisniewski."

"How do you like it?" the barber interjected.

"Just fine, so far. What little I've seen of it, anyway. Seems like a friendly enough town."

"No, I mean, how do you like your *hair* cut?" He patted the top of my head. "A good scalping or just a little off the edges?" Apparently, those were my only two choices.

I laughed self-consciously. "Just a trim, if you don't mind. I want to look my best when school begins." With a silent nod, he set about his craft.

Assuming a master of ceremonies role, the mayor took center stage and introduced me to the others in the room. "This here's Rube Elkins," he announced, pointing to the barber. "Been in this shop nigh onto thirty years. And that's Phil Swanson, owner of Swanson's Feed-N-Seed; Darryl Pressley has that little insurance agency next to the bank, and my brother Avery Piggott manages that big farm back of the high school."

So *this* was the man behind the ghastly nasal attack my first night in Piggottsville! For the next five minutes, the mayor moderated the discussion, asking me a number of questions and telling me about his town. He was obviously comfortable being in the spotlight and accustomed to being in control. When his little performance ended, he pulled out a huge handkerchief, mopped his brow, and returned to his seat. The previous conversation gradually resumed; and in between the questions tossed my way, I was able to size up the influential townsmen seated against the wall.

Mr. Swanson was a small man with a slight build and looked to be in his late forties. Mr. Pressley was of normal height and weight and appeared to be six or eight years younger. It was the Piggott brothers, however, that drew most of my attention. They were as different as a double-breasted suit and a burlap sack. Mayor Piggott was—to put it mildly—quite rotund with his girth nearly that of his height. He had a white shock of unruly, Einstein-like hair sitting atop his beefy red face, which glistened as if in a perpetual state of perspiration. In spite of the heat and humidity, he wore a three-piece, light gray, linen business suit with a gold watch fob displayed across his prominent stomach and a pair of shiny, black, patent-leather dress shoes.

Avery, on the other hand, was the polar opposite of his brother. If Wilson Piggott III was a beefsteak tomato, then Avery Piggott was every bit a spear of asparagus. He was tall and lanky with short-cropped, light-gray hair and a chin puff resembling that of the billy goat I'd met at the stop light. He was dressed in a pair of denim bib overalls with a red plaid shirt underneath and wore scuffed brown work boots on his feet. He reminded me a little of Fred Ziffel in the old *Green Acres* TV show, a farmer who, if my memory serves me correctly, also had an affinity for swine.

It didn't take long for the barber to finish my trim. He unhooked the cape and whisked a few loose hairs off the back of my neck.

"How much do I owe you?" I asked, stepping out of the chair and reaching for my wallet.

Rube Elkins dismissed me with a casual wave of his hand. "No charge," he replied. "Didn't take but ten minutes. Consider it an introductory special."

"Why, thank you! In the future, I'll see that you have all my business."

Darryl Pressley chuckled. "Unless you cut your own hair, you don't have much of a choice. This is the only barbershop in twenty miles."

The men chuckled, and I couldn't help but join them.

Avery Piggott leaned back dangerously in his chair and thrust his thumbs under the straps of his overalls. "Good thing ya didn't ask fer a scalpin', young man. Come springtime, Rube's other job is shearin' all the *sheep* in the county!"

The hoots and howls of the five men followed me out of the barbershop and down the sidewalk.

On Sunday morning, I dressed in my finest and walked to the little white church at the other end of E Street. The building was an old clapboard structure with a small tower and spire straddling the steep roof line. A flock of pigeons had replaced the bell, which at some point in history had summoned parishioners to meeting. A plaque mounted beside the entrance read, "Piggottsville Community Church / Sunday Service 10:00 A.M." The minister and his wife warmly welcomed me at the front door, introducing themselves as Reverend Norbert and Nancy Pinckney.

Inside the small vestibule, I met several more members of the friendly little flock, including Orville Piggott and his wife, Jolene. When compared to his father Wilson and uncle Avery, Orville landed somewhere in between. Jolene was a very pleasant sort of person, much like Mary, my landlady, but more outgoing. She proudly informed me that she was head of the Women's Missionary League.

As I stood reading some notices on the bulletin board, a flurry of activity on the steps outside caught my attention. It was none other than Mayor Wilson Piggott III making his grand, last-minute arrival. He swept into the church with his wife in tow, greeting those already inside with a nod or a handshake and a "Good to see you!" He then marched ceremoniously into the sanctuary and down the center aisle to his seat up front, parting the parishioners like Moses crossing the Red Sea. Apparently, that was the signal for the service to begin because everyone else quickly found their places and Reverend Pinckney, bringing up the rear, ascended the dais.

It was a simple service beginning with the singing of old traditional hymns, followed by a few announcements, the reading of Scripture, and a solo by a woman with a remarkable soprano voice. Then the Reverend Norbert Pinckney preached a pretty decent sermon but not before embarrassing me by having me stand and introduce myself to the small congregation.

At the conclusion of the service as the people were filing out, I noticed an elderly woman in a floral-print dress frowning at me over her spectacles. When we met in the center aisle, I gave her a polite nod and a smile, which she failed to return.

"Young man, did you find anything humorous about the service this morning?" she huffed with a none-too-pleasant disposition.

I was taken aback. "I beg your pardon, ma'am?"

She shot me a familiar look of disdain. "I'm surprised you didn't break out laughing in the middle of the minister's sermon! Or do you reserve your outbursts strictly for bank buildings?"

Before I could formulate a reply, she turned and marched haughtily up the aisle and out of the sanctuary.

Stunned, I turned to the soloist, who was in line behind me. "Excuse me, but who was that lady?"

"That's Elvira Primrose, bless her heart." She gave me a puzzled look. "What was *that* all about?"

I felt the color rise in my cheeks. "Well, ah . . . the other day she witnessed my reaction to the sign on the wall of the bank. I'm afraid I may have offended her."

The soloist grinned knowingly. "Oh, I see. Well, I wouldn't take it too personally. She's like that with most folks around here—not happy unless she's got something to complain about."

I nodded with relief and thanked her for the beautiful musical number. Then I hightailed it out of there before anyone else could ask me any more questions.

CHAPTER FIVE
Preparing for Battle

The week prior to the start of school was a very busy one. I spent Monday through Wednesday setting up my classroom and working on lesson plans for the first quarter. I asked the principal if there was anything available on which to project images from my laptop; and to my surprise, he had Winston deliver an old thirty-six-inch flat-screen TV that had been sitting in storage somewhere in the building. On Thursday and Friday, Mr. Herold held teacher training sessions in one of the first-floor classrooms, where I was able to meet and get to know the other instructors. As the week drew to a close, I grew more and more excited about teaching; and by the end of the Friday afternoon session, I felt as ready as I'd ever be.

The same could not be said for coaching, however. By three o'clock that Wednesday afternoon, I still had not heard from Mr. Herold concerning my staff; so I walked down to the office and peeked in, anxious to learn who the school board had hired. The principal's door was closed, and I was greeted by a woman behind the counter.

"May I help you?" she asked politely.

"Is Mr. Herold in? I need to talk to him about my coaching staff."

Her eyes brightened. "Oh, you must be Mr. Wisniewski, the new football coach."

"Football coach *and* history teacher," I corrected her with a laugh. "And you can call me Jason."

She smiled and shook my hand. "Nice to meet you, Jason. I'm Claudine Cooper, Mr. Herold's secretary. Secretary *and* office staff." She glanced at the closed door behind her. "He's been in meetings all day and asked not to be disturbed. But I'll let him know you stopped by the first chance I get."

I thanked her and headed for the coaching office to see what I could do on my own to prepare for the upcoming season. Once again, I found the door open and Winston Banks inside, busily mending the uniforms using the items I'd found at the hardware store.

He glanced up from the shoulder pads he was relacing. "Thanks for pickin' up these shoelaces. Had to tie some o' the shorter ones together, but they'll do. Should hold up most o' the season, I reckon."

I rolled the chair out from under the small desk and sat down, almost tipping over in the process. It was missing a castor.

"Been meanin' to fix that," he said with a sheepish grin. "Got a spare wheel around here somewheres." He changed the subject. "So, what are your expectations for the season?"

"You mean, how many games do I think we'll win?" I picked up a pencil and began tapping the desk pensively. "That's pretty hard to say, not knowing what kind of team I'll have or how tough the competition is. It would be nice to win half our games, but that's probably unrealistic for a first-year coach and a first-year team. I'd say if we put two, maybe three, checks in the win column, we could call this season a success." I put down the pencil. "What do you think?"

"You're the head coach," he replied without looking up.

I watched him work for a minute or two. "I really appreciate all your assistance with the equipment, Mr. Banks. Every bit helps."

"No problem. An' the name's Winston. Mr. Banks was my daddy's name."

"Okay . . . Winston." I laughed. "But isn't this taking up a lot of your time? You've probably got a hundred other things to do before school starts. When the rest of my staff arrives, I'm sure they'll be able to take over here."

"Staff's already here," he replied laconically.

I carefully leaned forward in my chair. "You know who they are?"

"Sure do." He stood up and extended a hand. "Winston Banks. Custodian, grounds maintenance, *and* assistant football coach."

I was gobsmacked. "You mean you're going to be on my staff?"

"Well, not *on* your staff, exactly. Truth is, I *am* your staff!"

I was doubly gobsmacked. "Wait . . . you're it? You're all I *get*?" His raised eyebrows forced me to clarify that exclamation. "Sorry, I didn't mean it that way. I just thought . . . I mean, I was expecting to have several assistants, that's all."

Winston chortled. "I don't blame ya one bit. If ya want my opinion, I think ya got the short end o' the stick with this whole coachin' thing."

"Thank you for understanding." I gathered myself together as best I could and heaved a sigh of resignation. "Well then, it looks like it's going to be just you and me."

He pointed to the desk. "There's the schedule," he said without further ado. I picked up the typewritten page and gave it a look-see. There were five home games and three away games this season.

I glanced up from the schedule. "How much do you know about these other schools?"

"Know a little bit about 'em. Been workin' at Piggottsville High for twenty-six years."

"Do you know anything about football?"

He picked up a pair of shoulder pads and resumed threading the new laces through the eyelets. "A little. Been around the game for a while, back in the day."

"Ever play?"

He hesitated. "Some."

"What level? Pop Warner, middle school, high school?"

"Uh . . . I played a little college ball."

"Oh yeah? Where at?"

"Two years at Ole Miss."

The surprises just kept on coming. "Ole Miss? That's SEC ball, Division One! The big times!" He looked away as if upset that I'd wrung the information out of him. I back peddled. "Look, I don't mean to pry into your past, but I had no idea you had that much football experience. I played some in high school and was a team manager in college, but that was Division 3. And I've never coached on any level, as you're well aware. I don't understand why Mr. Herold and the school board didn't ask *you* to coach this team. You're obviously much more qualified and knowledgeable than I am."

He paused again. "They did . . . but I turned 'em down."

"They did? Why did you turn them down?"

My assistant jerked his head in the direction of the football field. "Have ya forgotten whatcha saw out there?" He held up the shoulder pads in his hands. "Or whatcha see in here?"

I grimaced. "I know what you mean. Boy, do I ever! But I still don't understand. If you didn't want to be the *head* coach, then why did you agree to become my assistant coach?"

Winston turned away, as if embarrassed. For a second, I thought he might not answer my question at all. When he finally looked at me, I saw something akin to compassion in his eyes. "I couldn't stomach the thought o' standin' around watchin' ya get hung out to dry," he replied.

In that moment, I had great respect for Winston Banks; and suddenly things started to look a little brighter knowing I wasn't alone in this crazy adventure.

Sunday night, I went to bed early. In the morning, I would begin my teaching and coaching careers; and I wanted them both to start off on the right foot. I'll admit to having some reservations and a few butterflies, but I knew this was what I wanted to do and where I needed to be. I just didn't know what to expect. What would my students be like? How would they behave in my classroom? Would they welcome this rookie from outside their little community with open arms, or would they test my resilience from the get-go? How many students would show up for the first team meeting? What kind of players and talent would I have to work with? My head was a hornet's nest.

When I finally fell asleep, I dreamed that I walked into my classroom only to be greeted by thirty helmeted hooligans in shoulder pads and jerseys seated at their desks clutching bazookas capable of launching spit wads the size of baseballs, spray paint cans the size of propane tanks, and flame throwers. Then they proceeded to trash everything in sight while I cowered behind my desk. It was morning before I knew it.

On the drive over to the school, I kept telling myself that the dream was merely a release of built-up tension rather than a harbinger of things to come; but I don't think I convinced myself of that. Upon arrival, I sat in my car and threw up a quick prayer of desperation, much as Peter did when he began to sink while walking on the water. *Lord, save me!* Then I entered the building and made my way up the stairs. The first thing I did when I reached my classroom was to take out a wooden-handled silver bell from my messenger bag and place it on my desk. My mother had given it to me the night before I left home as a token of her support. Then, after setting up my laptop and connecting the cable to the flat screen TV, I wrote my name on the whiteboard and sat down to await the inevitable.

CHAPTER SIX

There's a Skunk in My Classroom!

The squeal of brakes outside followed by the youthful voices of students pouring from their buses pierced my pensive thoughts. Soon, exuberant chattering filled the corridors; and as the cacophony neared its crescendo, backpack-toting students began trickling into my room. As I observed them sitting there conversing among themselves and tossing glances my way, I recalled what a college professor once told me about this very moment: "The first five minutes will set the tone for the rest of the year." I was about to test his theory. No pressure, right?

At eight o'clock sharp, the bell rang indicating the official start of the school day, the school year, and my teaching career. However, the signal did little to squelch the animated palavering among my students. The moment of truth was upon me. Taking a deep breath, I arose from my chair, sauntered out from behind my desk, and leaned against the front edge, not only to convey an air of casualness but also to steady my quaking knees. I surveyed the faces in front of me, and the room grew silent.

Just as I opened my mouth to speak, the door flew open; and a latecomer rushed in and threw himself into the last available desk. After one final glance at the door, I addressed my class.

"Good morning! Well, if that's everyone, why don't we get started? But before we do, would you all please pull out your schedules and check them one more time? It should say 'First Period U.S. History, Room 204.'

If yours shows something else, then I'm afraid you're in the wrong class." I paused as they looked at their schedules.

One boy let out a groan, grabbed his backpack, and hastily retreated to the snickers of the other students.

"Happens every semester," I said, throwing up my hands as if I'd done this a thousand times. "If you attended school here last year, may I see your hands?" Every hand went up. "That's what I figured. You all know each other, but I don't know any of you. And none of you know me. So allow me to introduce myself. My name is Mr. Wisniewski." I pointed to the whiteboard. "It's pronounced Wiz-new-ski. Let me give you a visual that will help you remember that." I walked behind my desk and picked up a single emerald-green water ski with a price tag hanging from it. I held it up before the class. "Now, does anyone want to take a stab at how this item helps with the pronunciation of my name?" I waited.

Finally, a girl in the second row timidly raised her hand. "Yes. What's your name?"

"Abby Crenshaw."

"Nice to meet you, Abby. So, what do you think?"

"Does the ski refer to the last part of your name?"

"Yes, it does!" I tossed her a piece of candy from the bag I'd set on my desk. "Any other thoughts?"

A boy sitting in the row closest to the windows raised his hand. "Your name, please?"

"Maynard McCoy."

"Okay, Maynard. What's your guess?"

"That thingy looks like a price tag, so, um . . . does that mean the ski is *new*?"

"Way to go! Wow, you guys are pretty sharp for this early in the morning." I tossed him a piece of candy also. "You've got the "new" and the "ski" so far. Anyone want to give the first syllable a shot?"

After a pause, another boy raised his hand and identified himself. "Is it because you 'whizz' across the water or down the slopes on your new skis?"

"I hadn't thought of that one, but that's a great guess. I like it! I think you deserve a reward, anyway." I gave him a candy. "Anyone else?" There were no takers, but I could tell I had their attention. "Nobody? I'll give you a clue. What color is this ski?"

"Green!" a voice near the back of the room blurted out.

"Brilliant observation!" I grinned wickedly. "Now I know you're not color blind. And you are . . . "

"Jackson Pressley."

"Pressley? Is your father the one who owns the insurance agency next to the bank?" I asked.

"Yeah, he's my dad."

"I met him on Saturday. So, Jackson, how do you think green relates to the first syllable of my name?"

He shrugged. "I dunno. Maybe you're an Irish leprechaun?" The class tittered.

"Nice try, but I don't think that'll earn you a reward." He grumbled in disappointment. "Anyway, Wisniewski doesn't sound very Irish, does it? Now, what shade of green might go with 'Wiz'? Any other guesses?" A girl in the front row raised her hand. I pointed to her. "Yes?"

"I'm Savannah Scott. Um . . . is it emerald green? You know, like the Emerald City in *The Wizard of Oz*?"

"Bingo! You nailed it." I tossed her a candy. "If you guys don't remember anything else about today's class, at least you'll know how to pronounce your new teacher's name. An emerald-colored new ski. Wiz-new-ski."

"What kind of name is Wisniewski, anyway?" Jackson wondered.

"It's Polish."

"You mean you came all the way from Poland just to teach in Piggottsville?"

I laughed along with the class. "No, not quite *that* far. I'm from central Indiana, just west of Indianapolis. Who can tell me something about Indianapolis?" Hands shot up all over the room. Teens really like candy.

"The Indianapolis 500 mile race!"

"It's home to the Colts and the Pacers."

"Isn't it called 'the Crossroads of America'?"

"It's got the word 'Indian' in it?"

I chatted with my students for about half the period, trying to put names with faces. I traded information about myself and my background for information about them and theirs. By the time we moved on to the lesson, I'd dispensed all the candy I'd brought for this bunch. When the bell rang signaling the end of first period, I let out a sigh of relief. I don't know what I'd been so worried about. These kids were no more abnormal than the ones from my student teaching. My first class was in the books, and it had gone remarkably well. I don't mind telling you, I was quite pleased with myself.

Then came second period.

I fully expected my next class to be a carbon copy of the first. But I soon learned what most parents of multiple children already know: no two are exactly the same. Their temperaments, thought processes, and behaviors are quite different; and it often takes some creative parenting to find out what motivates them. Or so I've been told.

Second period began on a slightly different note. Immediately following the bell, Mr. Herold's authoritative voice resonated throughout the building via the intercoms mounted on the classroom walls.

"May I have your attention, please? This is Mr. Herold. As your principal, I'd like to welcome each and every one of you to Piggottsville-Stuyvesant High School. I'm confident you will do your best to ensure that we have an excellent start to the academic year. Since you are adjusting to your new schedules, we will not count anyone late for class today. But commencing tomorrow, every student must be in their seat when the bell rings; or your teacher will mark you as tardy. This year we are anticipating some new and exciting things here at the high school. Let me share some of them with you."

He droned on and on about this and that, and I kind of zoned out while waiting for the one announcement I'd been so anxious to hear. Finally, it came.

"I am also very excited to announce that this year, we are starting up our football program again for which I know many of you have been eagerly waiting." I witnessed several students look incredulously at each other with raised eyebrows. "The season schedule is posted on the school bulletin boards and website, and our first game will be at home against the Elliston Eagles on Friday, September 22. That's less than three weeks away, so we need to get organized as quickly as possible. For those of you interested in playing football, there will be a meeting after school at three o'clock in the gymnasium. Let's all get behind the team and show some Piggottsville pride, shall we?" Then he uncharacteristically bellowed into the microphone, "Go Mighty Ferrell Hogs!"

He cleared his throat twice and resumed his droning. "The lunch menu for today is chicken croquettes, cooked carrots, apple sauce, and your choice of a brownie or cookie. Have a great day!" With that, Mr. Herold returned control of the classrooms back to his teachers.

As I was about to address my class, I detected a strange odor somewhere in the room. Avery's hog farm came to mind, but this one had a different, musky scent to it. I shoved the thought aside and began my introductory spiel using the emerald ski example. However, this group of stone-faced students wasn't as cooperative as the last bunch, so I ended up giving them the answers. Changing my plan on the fly, I decided to ask each person to give me their name and share something about themselves with the class. That was a huge mistake.

"My name is LeBron James, and I'm a basketball player."

"I'm Taylor Swift, and I think you're cute."

"Captain Marvel . . . and I love to go commando!"

So much for *that* strategy. I made one last-ditch effort to break the ice. If this attempt failed, I was going to dive headlong into the stream of history cold turkey. I held up the bag of candy and promised *two* pieces to every student who told me the truth. That seemed to do the trick. Starting with the front row, I stood beside each desk; and when that student gave me the information I'd requested, I gave them their bribe.

Sitting about halfway back in the middle of the room were two very large kids with flaming red hair and freckles. I figured them for siblings. They were so much bigger than the rest of the kids that they stood out like two zits on a beauty queen's nose.

"Okay, you're next," I said, stepping up to the huge boy's desk.

"I'm Isaiah Pugh. I'm seventeen, and I'm her big brother." He grinned and pointed to his even larger sister.

I laid two candies on his desk and turned to the other redhead. "Now you, sis."

"I'm Jeremima Pugh. I'm seventeen, and I'm Isaiah's little sister . . . by three minutes!"

I immediately felt sorry for their mother. "Did you say your name was Jemima?" I wasn't sure I'd heard her right.

"No, it's *Jere*mima."

"I don't believe I've ever heard that name before. Do you happen to know what it means?"

She shot me a grin similar to her brother's, only bigger. "Sure. It means my father wanted twin boys! See, my father's name is Ezekiel; my grandfather is Nehemiah; and my great-grandfather was Ezra. My father was hoping for twin boys so he could name us Isaiah and Jeremiah. But when *I* came along, he had to settle for Isaiah and Jeremima instead."

"You mean Porky and Petunia!" someone mumbled from the back of the room. The class cracked up.

Jeremima spun around in her chair and glared at the instigator. "You better be quiet, Willie Skaggs; or I'll come back there and whup the fire outta you! And you know I can do it, too!" She glared menacingly at him.

I quickly intervened. "No need for that, Jeremima. As for the rest of you, let's keep our comments positive, shall we? Now, where are we? I believe we're back to you, Captain Marvel."

"Jimmy Dean Tucker." The slouching teen sighed and rolled his eyes as if my request was an unreasonable imposition on his otherwise valuable time. "I'm a junior. I live with my grandmother. And I *hate* history!"

Since I was rewarding honesty, I had to give him his candies. It was then that I caught another whiff of that strange, musky odor. It was stronger this time. I couldn't begin to describe it—something between fresh manure and a dead animal. I sniffed to get a fix on the source. It was coming from the very back corner of the room.

"Does anyone else notice that?" I asked, sniffing again. "What's that smell?"

"It's Skunk!" someone blurted out.

"Skunk!" My adrenaline shot through the roof. "There's a *skunk* in here? Everyone, stay calm! I want you all to slowly get up and walk quietly out of the room. Leave your books and backpacks where they are." I waved them toward the door, but they weren't budging. Instead, they were laughing. "Quickly now! I don't want anyone to get sprayed or bitten. Wild animals can be dangerous!" They were rolling on the floor. I stopped and stared at my class. "What's going on here? What's so funny?"

"It's not a wild animal, Mr. Wisniewski," Jackson Pressley answered, laughing so hard he could barely form the words. "It's Willard!"

That was just swell! First guns, then paint, then matches. Now a skunk named Willard. In my classroom, no less! I was beginning to wonder if I'd ever make it to graduation alive. "All right, then; so where's

the skunk?" I demanded firmly. "Would somebody please tell me where this Willard is?"

"He's right there, teacher." Jimmy Dean pointed to a scrawny boy slunk down in the corner desk, which had been pulled apart from the others. His hair was a tangled, sandy-brown mop, and his face and arms looked like he hadn't bathed in years. He was dressed in a soiled T-shirt and filthy jeans full of holes that weren't meant to be fashion statements. His formerly white tennis shoes were a grimy gray color, and his untied, frayed laces posed a major tripping hazard. He eased up his hand and waved at me.

"*You're* Willard?" I asked, trying hard not to stare.

"Yup. Willard Bodkins. I live on a farm three miles outta town; I gotta do chores ever' mornin' an' evenin'; I hate takin' baths; and ever'body calls me Skunk." He grinned broadly and sat up straight in his seat. "An' I don't mind it one bit. That's who I am, an' I'm proud of it!" He held out his hand. "Now, where's my candy?"

I tossed it to him from a distance. Then I walked over to the windows, opened both sashes as wide as possible, and tried to salvage what was left of second period.

Like I said, no two classes are the same.

CHAPTER SEVEN
THE MIGHTY MISFITS

I made it to the end of the day intact and without further escapades. My World History classes could even have been described as normal. However, I was convinced that I'd come face to face with at least a few of the hooligans who had inspired my nightmare. The only additional surprise was meeting a foreign exchange student in fifth period named Nigel Oglethorpe, a junior from England who was in the United States for twelve months and who hadn't been here long enough to affect his clipped British accent. I wondered what his overall impression of Americans would be after spending the year in such an outlandish outback as Piggottsville.

Putting all thoughts of the classroom behind me, I refocused my attention on the upcoming meeting in the gymnasium. I stopped by my office to grab a clipboard with the signup sheet attached and took a few minutes to review what I planned to say to my new recruits. Mr. Herold had mentioned that many students were eagerly waiting for the football program to start. Did that mean he knew something I didn't? Would his announcement elicit such an overwhelming response that I'd be forced to hold tryouts and cut lesser-talented players? Would we need additional uniforms?

With my expectations spiking, I added two more sheets to the clipboard. When I strode out of the office and into the gymnasium, I was fired up. In a few minutes, I'd have my answers. Just then, my cell phone beeped. It was a text from Winston.

"CANT MAKE MTG BACKED UP TOILET FILL ME IN L8R."

No matter. I could handle this myself.

At three o'clock, the door opened; and two students walked in. Isaiah and Jeremima Pugh crossed the gym floor to where I was sitting on the first row of the bleachers.

"We're here for the football meeting," Isaiah announced. I heard the "we" but just assumed his sister had come to support her twin or to wait for a ride home. An assumption can be a mighty dangerous thing.

"Great!" I stood up and handed him the clipboard. "Go ahead and fill out your information on this signup sheet. We'll get started as soon as everyone's here." When he finished, I reached for the clipboard.

"What about my sister?" he asked with a puzzled expression. "Doesn't *she* need to sign up?"

A hundred thoughts raced through my mind in that millisecond, but I'd prefer not to share them. I was flummoxed, to say the least. I turned to his twin. "Jeremima, is that true? Do you really want to play football? It's a pretty rough sport."

She gave me the most determined look I've ever seen in a female. "I sure do! I can't wait to get out there on that field and *hit* somebody!" I believed her instantly.

Suddenly, the door flew open, and Nigel Oglethorpe came racing across the floor. He slid to a screeching halt in front of me.

"Awfully sorry, mates!" he panted. "Didn't mean to be late, but I couldn't get my locker open. Hope you don't think me a plonker!" He looked around the gym. "Is this the meeting for those who want to play football?"

"You've come to the right place," I assured the lanky lad.

While Nigel filled out the sheet, I asked the twins about their playing experience. Both said they had none; but they were quick to point out that they loved watching games, had a pretty thorough understanding of the sport, and were willing to be coached. I probably should have been more disappointed that neither had ever played a single down before; but when you're facing a pair of six-foot-something, 280-plus-pound teenagers with a passion to pulverize someone, you don't look a gift hog in the snout!

When Nigel handed me the clipboard, I glanced at the wall clock. It was 3:12. Since it was highly unlikely that *all* the latecomers were having similar locker troubles, I made a mental note to stress the importance of punctuality to the entire team at the end of the meeting. Then, I began with those present.

"Okay, thank you all for coming out for this first team meeting. I'm sure the others are on their way; but I don't want to hold you up, so let's get to it. I'm really excited to be coaching the Mighty Ferrell Hogs this year. I know you haven't had a team for a while, but everything has a beginning, right? Now, I know Isaiah and Jeremima don't have any experience, but what about you, Nigel? Have you played football before?"

"Aye, deffo! Played regular-like since I was six. I was on my school football team and on a club team as well."

"Fantastic!" I could barely contain myself. "What position did you play?"

"Oh, some right midfielder but mostly center forward."

I stared blankly at him. "Right midfielder, but mostly . . . "

"Mostly center forward. You know. Striker!"

My knees suddenly grew wobbly, and I had to sit down. Nigel thought he was coming out for soccer!

"How can we be expected to field a team with only two players?" I bemoaned, posing the question to Winston as we sat in the coaching office following the meeting. "There have got to be more kids interested in playing football in a school with an enrollment of . . . what, four hundred and fifty students?"

"Maybe, but don't forget Piggottsville's a consolidated school. Over half the kids are bussed in from surroundin' towns an' don't have no other transportation. Might not be able to stay after school for practices."

That was something I hadn't considered. "Yeah, but even so, only *two*?"

"Well," he replied, stroking his chin, "could be not everybody was payin' attention to the announcement this mornin'. Or maybe some couldn't make the meetin' for one reason or another."

"You really think that's it?" I asked hopefully.

"Nope," he replied bluntly, bursting my bubble. "Experience tells me there just ain't much interest in the sport is all."

"Then we're just going to have to change that, aren't we?" I stated resolutely.

Winston gave me a look of respect. "I admire your determination, Coach, an' I'm with ya 100 percent. Question is, how do we do that?"

I thought for a moment, then snapped my fingers. "We don't wait for them to come to *us*; we go after *them*. First thing tomorrow morning, we begin recruiting players!"

"How do ya figure on doin' that?"

"Let's start with Isaiah and Jeremima. They're both eager to play, so let's get them to convince some of their friends to sign up. And that British student, Nigel—we can still use him. A lot of teams have successfully converted soccer players into field goal kickers."

"That's a possibility," he admitted, nodding his head. "We could go after some o' the kids on the basketball an' baseball team, too. Most ain't that good, but now ya take that pitcher, Knox Piggott. He's got a purdy decent throwin' arm. Might be able to turn him into a quarterback."

"He sounds promising. But we don't have much time. We need to begin practices as soon as possible. I'll talk to the Pugh twins and ask around during my classes tomorrow. Can you talk to Knox for me?"

"I'll give it a try," he promised. "But we may hafta resort to some rather unconventional methods to motivate these kids to play."

"Unconventional methods? What do you mean by that?"

"Got a few ideas in mind. I know these students an' their families purdy good." He flashed a sly grin. "Leave that to me."

On Tuesday, I spoke with Isaiah and Jeremima after second period, and just as I had hoped, they were both eager to lend a hand with our recruitment efforts. I also approached several male students who appeared to be fairly athletic and who had the typical build of a football player, but they were either disinterested or non-committal. However, later in the day, I was able to convince Nigel to be on the team by telling him that successful coaches like Jim Harbaugh made it a point to pursue soccer players; and NFL stars such as Sebastian Janikowski, Adam Vinatieri, Chad Johnson, and Odell Beckham Jr. had excelled at soccer before they ever played a down of American football.

Wednesday, as I was beginning the lesson for second period, Jimmy Dean Tucker raised his hand. I stopped and called on him. "Yes?"

"I heard a rumor that you're gonna be the new football coach. Is that true?"

"Yes, it is. And practice will begin just as soon as we get the team organized."
He smirked at his classmates and snorted loudly. "That'll be the day. When pigs fly!"

That seemed to be the general consensus among the pupils in all six of my classes and throughout the entire student body. I not only was facing widespread apathy but also skepticism as well. Nobody cared or believed in what I was trying to achieve. Maybe this football fantasy of mine was nothing more than a pipe dream—the impossible dream. All that aside, I failed to take into account those "unconventional methods" Winston had alluded to.

That afternoon, I called another team meeting in the gym. Winston informed me that he had spoken with Knox Piggott; and when I asked how certain he was of Knox's commitment, all he said was, "Fairly." When we entered the gym from the coaching office right down the hall, we saw Nigel sitting alone in the bleachers.

"I'm here, Cap'n!" he said, standing up and saluting me. "I'm ready to play football for you. *American* football, that is. Going to give it a proper go, I am."

"Thank you, Nigel," I said to my punctual kicker. "You can just call me Coach. And that goes for Mr. Banks as well."

"Right-o, Coach!" He saluted again.

"Uh . . . you don't have to salute," I instructed him, hoping his skill set matched his enthusiasm.

Isaiah Pugh entered the gym, along with two other boys. "Mr. Wisniewski, I brought two of my friends with me," he announced proudly.

My spirits rose. In just forty-eight hours, our team had doubled in size! One was Clay Piggott, son of Virgil Piggott, the town constable, county sheriff, and justice of the peace. The other was Henry Panke, pronounced Pang-key. He was about five eight and 140 pounds and wore thick, black-framed glasses. Both were in my fifth period World History class. I greeted them warmly. "Clay, Henry, thank you both for coming out."

"We all call him Hanky," Isaiah informed me.

"Hanky?"

"Yeah, Hanky Panke!"

I eyed the boys skeptically. "How did he earn *that* nickname?" I turned to the bespectacled lad. "Do you have a reputation for getting into mischief or something?"

Henry/Hanky grinned broadly. "No, it's because I have bad allergies, and I always carry a hanky with me." He pulled out a huge, wrinkled handkerchief and held it up. I recoiled at the sight of the thing. Then, as if to substantiate his claims, he loudly blew his nose into the slightly discolored snot rag.

The door opened again; and Jeremima Pugh marched into the gym, followed by five young men of varying sizes. They crossed the hardwood floor single file like a brood of goslings following their mother. As Jeremima approached me, her entourage sat down on the first row of the bleachers without a word. Sitting in front of me with crossed arms and frowning faces were Maynard McCoy, Jackson Pressley, Willie Skaggs, and, of all people, Jimmy Dean Tucker. It was then that I caught a whiff of a familiar scent. Sitting off to the side by himself was Willard "Skunk" Bodkins.

"I told you I'd find more players for you, Coach!" Jeremima announced, beaming proudly. "I kept my promise, just like I said."

"I guess you did," was all I could think to say. "But how in the world were you able to convince this many to come out for football?" I turned to the five newest recruits, whose expressions ranged from defiance to fear. "I didn't know you all were interested in being on the team."

"We're not!" Jimmy Dean mumbled under his breath.

"We didn't come here 'cause we *wanted* to," Jackson Pressley added with a scowl. "She threatened to beat us to a pulp if we didn't join the team."

Willie must have seen the doubt written on my face. "They're not kidding, Mr. Wisniewski. You don't know Jeremima like we do."

"Yeah, she's beaten everybody at arm wrestling ever since third grade," Jimmy Dean informed me.

I looked at Winston. He confirmed that claim with a raised brow and a nod. I turned to the big girl standing beside me. "Did you really force them to come to this meeting?" I asked.

She stared at her big feet. "Well, not 'force,' exactly. Some of them needed a little persuasion, so I helped them make up their minds." She suddenly looked up with fire in her eyes. "You said to try my best, and that's what I did! Besides, how can I play football if we don't have enough for a team?"

I couldn't argue with her motives, but I had to address her methods. "Jeremima, I appreciate your enthusiasm, but you might want to work on your people skills a bit."

"All right, Coach." She flashed a sheepish grin and took a seat on the bleachers.

It was then that I noticed the bandage on Maynard McCoy's chin. "Maynard, did Jeremima do that to you?" I demanded, pointing to his face.

"What, this?" He touched his chin and suddenly blushed. "Naw, I cut myself shaving this morning."

"Yeah, and he got all three whiskers!" Willie quipped, softening most of the dour looks in the group.

I glanced at Jimmy Dean Tucker sitting beside Willie. He had an angry red knot on his forehead right between his eyes. "What's that bump on *your* face, Jimmy Dean?"

Jackson Pressley jumped in before he could respond. "He was eyeballing Lexi Rae Brannigan after third period and ran into the edge of a door!" That elicited a few laughs.

"Well, at least that injury is one of your own making," I joked. Then I grew serious. "Look, guys. I'm only interested in those who *want* to play on this team. If you don't want to be here, you don't have to stay. Do any of you want to leave?" Willie Skaggs started to raise his hand but quickly lowered it after a glance at "The Enforcer." They all shook their heads. "Are you sure? Are you absolutely sure?" They all nodded in unison.

Just then, Knox Piggott entered the gym and walked up to the group. Winston gave him a fist bump and patted him on the back. Suddenly, a dark scowl fell across the boy's face. "What's *he* doing here?" our potential quarterback demanded, pointing to his cousin seated among the other recruits. "I didn't know *he* was gonna be here!"

Clay returned his cousin's scowl. "Well, I didn't know *he* was gonna be here either," he retorted. "I'm not gonna play on the same team as *him*!" The two glared at each other.

"And I'm not gonna play football at all as long as *he's* on the team!" With that, Knox spun around and angrily stomped out of the gym. The room grew so silent, you could have heard a dead mouse. All eyes focused on me like I was supposed to do something about it. I stood there like a schnook at a complete loss for words.

Winston sidled up to me and lowered his voice. "Just to clarify one thing, Coach. I only said I was *fairly* certain 'bout his commitment."

"Do you know what just happened?" I whispered back. "You said you knew these kids and their families. What was that all about?"

Winston sighed. "Guess I shoulda warned ya first, but I thought I had it worked out. I'll give ya the full scoop in private."

I gathered what was left of my wits and resumed the meeting. As the newcomers filled out the signup forms, I counted heads. We now had ten players—one shy of a complete team—and I was hopeful that once we got to the bottom of the little tiff between the two cousins, we could get Knox back as our quarterback. But even with him on the team, if only one person got sick or missed a game for any reason, we'd have to forfeit. That's the State Athletic Association's rule. And unless we could double our membership again, they'd all have to play every down of every game—on offense, defense, and special teams. The situation was far from ideal, but at least, we were close to meeting the minimum requirement to be considered a legitimate high school football team.

After the meeting, Winston and I escorted the players to the coaching office to get them outfitted. There were a few issues with the equipment, and not everything fit the way it was supposed to; but we did the best we could. It was rather comical to watch Jeremima squeeze into the largest jersey and pants we had and to see Willard standing there like a helmeted Bobblehead doll with his jersey hanging down to his knees. Two of the helmets still lacked chinstraps, but we decided to duct tape them to the players' heads until we could locate the replacement parts. I'm fairly certain that's not one of the 1001 known uses for duct tape. To be perfectly honest, these armor-clad figures probably would have looked more at home on the Island of Misfit Toys than on a football field; but all I could see through my rose-colored glasses was a fully equipped army of warriors with me as their general. The Mighty Ferrell Hogs were about to burst onto the scene for the first time in five years. Watch out, world. Here come the Hogs!

CHAPTER EIGHT

The Feud

As soon as the last team member left the room, I turned to Winston, who was putting away the leftover equipment. "Okay, what's the scoop on Knox and Clay? Are they competing over grades, or are they interested in the same girl? It involves a girl, right? It always does."

Winston shook his head. "Nope, ain't nothin' like that. Goes much deeper than grades or girls. Goes further back to when their daddies was in their twenties."

I was all ears. "Go on," I urged him, sitting down in my chair.

"Well, as I recall, it was back in '06. I'd been here 'bout eight years then. I think Orville was twenty-four an' Virgil was twenty-three. One day, Orville went out an' bought himself a brand new four-wheel-drive pickup truck—bright red, chrome rims, top o' the line. Man, he was as proud o' that thing as he is of Knox today. Virgil was jealous, of course, 'cause he's a year younger an' always seemed to live in his brother's shadow. So he decided to play a prank on Orville just to spite him.

"One night, he snuck over to his brother's house an' jacked up that truck on blocks an' took the wheels an' hid 'em in a shed somewheres. In the mornin', Orville thought his pride 'n' joy had been vandalized, an' he raised a big stink all around town. Even took out an ad in the county paper offerin' a $500 reward for the return of his wheels an' another five hundred for the arrest an' conviction of the persons responsible."

I was on the edge of my seat. "Did he get the wheels back or learn who the culprit was?"

Winston straddled his chair and grinned. "A few weeks later, Virgil made like he just stumbled across the stolen wheels by accident an' returned 'em. Even collected the $500 reward! Then, 'bout a year later, somebody tipped off Orville that Virgil was the thief. Who it was or how they knew about it, I never did figure out; but you'd better know Orville blew his stack! He threatened to have his brother arrested an' even filed a lawsuit against him. When their daddy, the mayor, stepped in, Virgil reluctantly agreed to return the money; an' Orville eventually withdrew the suit. But he's never forgotten it. Still holds a grudge against Virgil."

"Sounds to me like a real old-fashioned family feud." I tried to make the connection. "So is that why Knox and Clay aren't getting along?"

"Oh, there's more." Winston seemed to enjoy the retelling. "Orville an' Virgil ain't been on good terms since. Still give each other the cold shoulder. You can imagine what goes on in the town council meetin's with both of 'em bein' on the committee an' their daddy tryin' hard not to take sides. If one of 'em brings up an item o' business, the other vetoes it. An' if one votes no, the other votes yes." He chuckled. "They say the wheels o' progress turn slowly, but them two act like the wheels in this town are still hidden in that shed!

"A few years ago, things quieted down some, an' it looked like the rift might be comin' to an end. But it all flared back up again when Orville bought Knox a new truck last year. Virgil pulled Knox over an' wrote him a hefty ticket for speedin' an' reckless drivin'. Orville claimed the whole thing was bogus an' retaliated by refusin' to give Virgil an auto loan so he could buy a used car for Clay." He held up one of the jerseys. "An' now the next generation's taken up the gauntlet."

Thursday, I was encouraged when the Pugh twins and Nigel wore their "new" moth-eaten, slightly-mildewed football jerseys to school. That simple show of team pride reinforced my optimism like nothing else. However, in second period, Jimmy Dean Tucker started to make a snide remark about their unusual apparel, but one glare from Jeremima shut him down in mid-sentence. So, while not everyone on the team felt the same way, I was confident that long-held attitudes were beginning to change. We just needed to figure out a way to get Knox to join the team.

That afternoon, as I awaited the team's first official practice, I sat at my tiny office desk fiddling with a little blue-suede container about twice the size of a ring box. It was a gift from my father, handed to me just before I embarked on this grand adventure. I opened the box and took out the highly polished chrome whistle with the initial "W" engraved on it. This was the symbol of my chosen profession, much as a baton is to a conductor, or a stethoscope to a doctor, or a gavel to a judge. I couldn't wait to use it.

While the players were suiting up in the locker rooms, Winston and I went out to the stadium lugging the bag containing the practice vests and five inflated footballs. Make that four footballs. One had already sprung a leak. He'd mowed the grass the day before with the riding mower, a fact evidenced by the tire tracks running through several cow patties, most of which had not fully cured under the early September Arkansas sun. The playing field hadn't yet been striped, but he'd leveled the mole hills and filled the groundhog holes. It was an improvement over the untamed jungle I'd witnessed during my first visit to the stadium.

"Where do you keep the practice equipment?" I asked, stepping onto the field. "We need to get it out before the team gets here."

"What practice equipment?" Winston wanted to know.

"Don't you have a blocking sled or some blocking pads?"

He gave me what could only be described as an amused look. "We ain't got nothin' like that. Too expensive. School board wouldn't spring for it five years ago, an' they for sure won't spring for it now."

I stared at him. "You mean, we have nothing at all to use for practice? But I just assumed that—"

"Nope," he cut me off definitively. "Not a thing. Figured ya knew that."

"No pads? Not even a few old tires to use for footwork drills?"

He shook his head. "We're gonna hafta improvise. But I might be able to pick up some old tires next time I'm over in Ransomville havin' the bus worked on. They got a scrap yard over there."

I couldn't believe it. This was something I should have anticipated and checked on before now. Chalk up another one to inexperience. I looked around. "With only ten players, we're going to need something to represent our opponent's team. Anything around here we can use for that?"

He scratched his head. "Well, there's some old foldin' chairs stored in the concession stand. Don't know how many exactly, but they might do in a pinch."

He unlocked the side door, and we entered the abandoned building. Everything inside was covered in dust and cobwebs and mouse droppings. It looked like it hadn't been disturbed since that award-winning eighth game of the 2018 season, if not longer. We hauled out eleven rusting metal chairs and carried them to midfield, where we set them up to approximate the defensive positions. I figured we would concentrate on basic offense for the first few days, and Winston was in full agreement. It was decided that I would run the offense and he would run the defense, since that's what he knew best from his days as a linebacker at Ole Miss.

When the last of the ten players straggled onto the field, I blew my new whistle and summoned them into a tight huddle. I gave a brief pep talk before having them line up in a basic offensive set facing the chairs. Without Knox in the lineup, it was more like the "missing man formation" you see at airshows; so I pulled Jackson Pressley from the left tackle slot and had him fill in at quarterback.

After explaining the role of each position and demonstrating the different stances, I handed a football to Maynard McCoy, whom I'd placed at center. "McCoy, I want you to practice hiking the ball to Pressley a few times." They dropped it five out of six snaps. "That's okay," I said. "I'll have you practice that exchange every day. You'll get the hang of it."

I then diagrammed a simple running play and had the offense walk through it in slow motion a few times. Then we tried it at full speed. They fumbled the snap twice and dropped the ball a third time when Henry Panke, whom I'd placed at running back, collided with Jackson. I glanced at Winston, who stood behind me chewing his lip to keep from laughing. On the fourth try, the ball stayed off the turf. I counted that as real progress.

We moved on to an easy pass play but not before chasing off two black and white Holsteins that had wandered onto the field in search of something to eat. Jackson was supposed to drop back and throw a short pass to Nigel, who was to run a straight fly route. It was basically a toss-and-catch exercise, but Jackson underthrew him on the first try and overthrew him on the second. On the third attempt, the quarterback found his target. There was just one problem. Nigel didn't even try to catch the ball. Instead, he bounced it off his chest and trapped it with his feet! I blew my whistle and ran out to explain the proper way to catch a football—American style.

"Terribly sorry, Coach," the Brit apologized, smacking the side of his helmet. "I must be daft! Deserve a proper dressing down for that one."

"No, Oglethorpe, you're not daft. You've just got a lot of soccer in you. But you'll develop new instincts over time." I patted his shoulder pads. "Chin up, old chap!"

When our first disaster of a practice wrapped up, Winston and I shared a few words of encouragement with the players before having them run a lap around the track and sending them off to the showers. Then we lugged the folding chairs back to the concession.

"We sure don't have much to work with, do we?" I grumped, feeling as deflated as that fifth football.

Winston shot me a questioning glance. "Ya talkin' 'bout the equipment or the team?"

"To be brutally honest with you, both!" I forced a pathetic smile.

He chuckled. "When it comes to the equipment, I couldn't agree more. As far as the team's concerned, only time'll tell."

We labored in silence for a few minutes before he turned to me. "Wanna hang around while I test the field lights?" he asked, stacking the last of the chairs against the wall.

"Field lights? You bet!" I followed him around the side of the building to where a gray electrical box was mounted on the wall. He pulled a small ring of keys from his pocket and removed the padlock. Then he grabbed the handle of the main breaker switch.

"Hold onto your britches," he warned before pulling the lever. There was a loud popping sound, followed by a huge explosion of multicolored sparks from one of the four light banks. Even the Fourth of July celebration in downtown Indy earlier that summer couldn't hold a candle to this grand display of fireworks. We stood there gaping up at the poles like two turkeys in a thunderstorm. The lights atop the one nearest us were completely burned out, and only one bulb on the opposite side was lit. At the far end of the field, two more bulbs were out.

I shook my head in disgust. "Go figure!" I muttered under my breath. I noticed the frown on Winston's face and tried to sound a bit more positive. "At least *some* of them are still working!"

He grunted. "That's better'n what I was expectin'. Guess now I'll hafta rent a scissor lift an' replace them bulbs." He shut off the power and snapped the padlock onto the electrical box. Then we walked back to the school in silence.

"Well, we survived the first practice," I remarked as we neared the building. "It's obvious none of these kids have ever played football before, but I saw glimpses of potential here and there." He didn't reply.

When we reached the door, he turned to me. "You still plan on winnin' two or three games this season?"

I grimaced. "After what I saw today, I'd be happy with just one! But it's all pointless without Knox. If we can find some way to get him to change his mind, then I think they might have one good game in them. What do you think, Coach? Give me your honest opinion."

He opened the door and entered the building. "I think you're bein' way too generous."

"Ouch!" I laughed as I closed the door behind us. "And *I* think you're being way too honest!"

The second practice didn't fare much better than the first. I added some conditioning drills and sessions where Winston and I split up the team to work on various components of the game. Then we came together to run the patchwork offense again. After multiple dropped passes, botched handoffs, and the occasional collision with a folding chair, I was beginning to wonder if these players would ever grasp the concept of teamwork. After all, this was, without a doubt, the most undisciplined, out-of-shape, ragtag, motley crew ever to grace a high school gridiron.

That being said, I would be remiss if I failed to mention the few positives I saw. They were making an effort—some more than others—but at least, they were trying. Additionally, I was surprised that none of the bad attitudes from the gym had carried over onto the field, at least not openly. However, I did have to address Jeremima's frequent complaints that she wasn't being given a chance to maul somebody, but my lecture on the virtues of patience seemed to temporarily quench her thirst for blood. I had a feeling this was going to be a very long season.

Saturday, I drove to the Hoggly Woggly to buy groceries for the coming week. The market, located at the corner of C Street and Main, was the only grocery for miles and was similar to the small IGA stores I'd seen in a few towns around Indiana. I was pushing my cart through the meat department when I noticed an extremely tall man transferring products from a wheeled cart to the refrigerated unit. He was every bit of six foot eight and had a deeply tanned, leathery face underneath a reddish beard. He wore a flat-topped straw hat and had a white apron tied around his waist. I mistook him for the grocer. When he turned to grab more packages, he looked me over so intently that I began to feel uncomfortable.

"You must be the new history teacher," he finally said, following the awkward moment.

"Yes, I am. I just moved here two weeks ago."

He extended a huge paw. "The name is Ezekiel Pugh."

I fumbled for his hand. "I'm Jason Wisniewski."

He shook my hand vigorously. "It is a pleasure to meet you. I believe you already know my children, Isaiah and Jeremima."

"I do! They're both in my second period history class." I glanced at his cart. "Do you own this store?"

He followed my gaze. "Own it? No, I'm just a simple farmer. I raise hogs and chickens, mostly. I supply the store with locally grown and processed pork and poultry." He held up one of the paper-wrapped packages.

Just then, a rather sturdy woman in a full length, robin's-egg-blue dress approached us, pushing another wheeled cart piled high with more meat. "This is the last of the ham," she informed the tall man. She was about five foot nine and had her long red hair pinned up in a tight bun. She had to be the twins' mother. The children must have inherited their height from their father and their heft from her.

"I would like for you to meet my wife, Naomi," Mr. Pugh said, placing a long arm around the woman's broad shoulders. "My dear, this is Mr. Jason Wisniewski, the children's new history teacher."

"It's so very nice to meet you," Mrs. Pugh greeted me warmly. "Where do you hail from?"

"I'm from Plainfield, Indiana, just west of Indianapolis."

"Oh, you're a Hoosier, then!" Her face lit up. "I have some relatives living in the southern part of the state, near Bloomington. Did you attend Indiana University?"

"No, ma'am," I replied, feeling the heat rise in my face. "I applied to IU, but I went to Wooster College instead."

Mr. Pugh cocked his head to one side. "I don't believe I have ever heard of that school."

I gave a nervous little laugh. "Not many people have. It's a small, liberal arts college in northeastern Indiana." He didn't look convinced. "*Very* small, I might add."

"In any event, we'd like to welcome you to Piggottsville, Mr. Wisniewski," the twins' mother said graciously. "Isaiah and Jeremima have told us so much about you this past week."

"It's a pleasure to have them as my students," I assured her. "They frequently participate in the classroom discussions, and I know they're both going to be a great asset to the football team."

"About *that* . . . " Mr. Pugh stroked his beard thoughtfully. "I must confess that, at first, we were opposed to Jeremima playing football, but we were not surprised that she wanted to be on the team. She is a very intense student of the sport, even more so than her brother. And she can be quite a headstrong young lady, as you will likely discover. But I am sure you will find her tenacity to be of great value in the long run, as you will find Isaiah's. You can count on them to do their best, Mr. Wisniewski, both on the field and in the classroom; for we have sought to raise our children according to what the Good Book says: 'And whatsoever ye do, do it heartily, as to the Lord, and not unto men.'[2]"

I smiled. "I can certainly appreciate that, Mr. Pugh. In fact, I agree with you whole-*heartily!*"

He either missed my intended pun or chose to ignore it. "You may call me Ezekiel," he granted. "And you may call my wife Mrs. Pugh." He picked up a package of meat and thrust it into my stomach. "Here, try some of my premium pork chops. Just tell them at the checkout Ezekiel gave it to you as a sample."

---

2 Colossians 3:23, KJV

I visited the little community church again on Sunday morning and was warmly greeted by those I'd met the previous week—with the exception of Orville and Jolene Piggott, who weren't in attendance, and Elvira Primrose, who was but who apparently was choosing not to associate with me. Before the service, I spied Clay Piggott off to one side, chatting with a few of his friends, including Savannah Scott, one of the girls in first period.

Then Reverend Pinckney grabbed my arm and introduced me to Clay's parents, Virgil and Ruby Piggott. Virgil was in his early forties, about six foot two, and two hundred pounds and sported a very serious flat top haircut. He struck me as the epitome of a law enforcement officer. I could picture him in a brown and tan sheriff's uniform with a wide-brimmed hat set squarely on his head, mirrored chrome glasses hiding his expressionless eyes, writing out a traffic ticket for his nephew with the new truck. His wife, Ruby, seemed very nice but excused herself after meeting me to join up with the choir.

A few minutes later, Mayor Piggott, followed closely by his wife, made his usual grandiose entrance, thereby signaling the start of the service. I can honestly say that never before had I been in a church with a call to worship quite like this one.

At the conclusion of the service, I was waiting in line to shake Reverend Pinckney's hand when I noticed a young lady standing near the back of the sanctuary talking with some other parishioners. Her name was Emily Davenport, the English and literature teacher at Piggottsville High. I'd met her during the training sessions, and I'd seen her in the cafeteria sitting with some of the other teachers. She was about my age, maybe five foot seven, slender, with long blond hair which she usually kept pulled back in a simple ponytail. She was quite attractive and someone I'd be interested in getting to know better at some point. But I really couldn't afford to pursue that. Relationships require a lot of time and attention and effort and money, and I had none of those luxuries. For the time being, I needed to concentrate on teaching history and coaching football. Besides, I didn't even know if she was married or not.

"Mr. Wisniewski, it's so good of you to come back!" Reverend Pinckney grabbed my hand with both of his. "Might we have the pleasure of seeing you on a regular basis?"

I smiled politely. "Yes, Reverend, I think you might. I've enjoyed the music and the preaching, and all the people have been so welcoming and friendly."

Okay, that last statement was a lie. I should have said *most* people, but I didn't want to rain on his parade. Anyway, I don't believe that one bad apple necessarily spoils the whole bushel. Mrs. Pinckney, who was standing next to her husband, asked me to join them for Sunday dinner, an invitation which, as a bachelor accustomed to eating frozen dinners and ramen noodles, I gladly accepted. Plus, I figured if I was going to be a regular at their church, it might not be a bad idea to get to know the preacher.

Once the last of the worshipers had left, Reverend Pinckney secured the building; and I followed the couple around the corner to the modest parsonage on 2 Street. The small bungalow, with two windowed dormers over the front porch, was surrounded by a well-cared-for lawn tucked behind a white picket fence running parallel to the sidewalk out front. When Mrs. Pinckney disappeared into the kitchen to prepare the meal, her husband and I sat down in the living room and chatted for a while.

He told me they were originally from Topeka and had come here five years ago after learning that the church was without leadership and in danger of closing. Rather than see the congregation dispersed and the church building vacated, they resigned their former ministry and, after leaving it in capable hands, moved to Piggottsville to carry on the Lord's work here.

Mrs. Pinckney announced the meal, and we adjourned to the dining room, where a juicy pork roast, steaming potatoes, cooked carrots, and buttered green beans awaited us. Oh, and homemade apple pie! Reverend Pinckney blessed the food, and then I dug in. I hadn't eaten this well since leaving home, and I had to constantly remind myself to watch my manners and not eat too fast.

"So, how was your first week at the school?" Mrs. Pinckney inquired politely as I stuffed my face with her incredible culinary concoctions.

"It went pretty well," I replied, wiping my mouth on the linen napkin. "I have six history classes, and they all got off to a good start. For the most part."

That caught the reverend's attention. He raised his eyebrows. "Hmmm. Sounds like it wasn't all smooth sailing. Did you experience a few rough seas?"

I chuckled. "Well, as a matter of fact, yes, I did. There were a few times I had to ask the Lord to still the wind and calm the waves." That elicited light laughter from my hosts. "I have a few wisenheimers who bear watching; but all in all, I'd say week one was a success." I decided it might be best not to share the Skunk story in such refined company, especially not at their dinner table.

The reverend propped his elbows on the table and clasped his hands together. "The mayor tells me you're going to be coaching football this year as well. I think that's wonderful! The sport is such a good framework for teaching character, discipline, and life principles. I'm all for it!"

His enthusiasm took me by surprise. At least, I had one ally in town besides Winston. "Thank you, Reverend, but I'm afraid football hasn't started off quite as well as history."

He looked at me over the top of his glasses and smiled. "Do I detect trouble in paradise?"

His unexpected wit put me at ease—so much so, I opened up about the difficulties I'd encountered with the facilities and equipment, the general apathy among the student body, and, without naming names, the personality clash that had left us one player short of a football team. Reverend Pinckney shared a glance with his wife.

"Go ahead, Norbert," Mrs. Pinckney urged her husband. "I think he needs to know what he's facing."

Reverend Pinckney chose his words carefully. "Am I correct in assuming that the two parties involved are members of a very prominent family in this town?"

I took a sip of my iced tea. "Yes, you are, Reverend. I've already been given an abridged version of the conflict, so I have a general idea of the root cause."

"The root cause is nothing more than pride, jealousy, and an unwillingness to forgive!" Mrs. Pinckney replied with feeling. Her candor surprised me even more than her husband's wit.

"Now, Nancy," her husband chided her gently, "be that as it may, let's not bring emotions into it." He glanced out the dining room window before resuming. "Mr. Wisniewski—"

"Please, call me Jason," I cut in, holding up my hand.

"Jason it is. Jason, I mean to avoid all appearance of evil here, and I don't wish to backbite or spread malicious gossip. But since you're now a part of this little community and have already been thrust into the middle of this thing, I feel it my duty to inform you of the scope of the situation. Besides, what I'm about to share, you will likely learn soon enough, so you might as well hear it from a neutral source.

"What began as a simple quarrel between two brothers nearly twenty years ago has spread to include not only their families but also the entire town as well. Most in this community are in some way related to the Piggotts, and many of them have chosen sides in this matter. Half the townspeople aren't speaking to the other half. Talk about a house divided! I've seen relatives cross the street just to avoid other relatives, and civic meetings often degenerate into verbal jousting matches. And don't think our little church is exempt from the hostilities, either. The two brothers and their families still attend here faithfully but not on the same Sundays. They alternate weeks, so they don't have to face one another.

"In spite of all that, you'll see their father, the mayor, in church every week. He tries his best to remain neutral, but even *he* hasn't been able to end the feud after all these years." The Reverend Norbert Pinckney's face sagged as he let out a long sigh. "And I'm sad to say, neither have I."

As I glanced at the distraught faces of the pastor and his wife, I realized it was going to be a lot harder to build this team than I thought.

CHAPTER NINE
Unconventional Methods

"I thought o' somethin' over the weekend that might get Knox to change his mind," Winston informed me as we prepared for Monday's practice.

I glanced up from the equipment bag I was packing. "This wouldn't be one of those unconventional methods you referred to earlier, would it?"

He cracked a smile. "Ya might call it that. Remember, I also said I knew these families purdy good. Well, I happen to know that Knox is as spoiled rotten as they come. He's Orville 'n' Jolene's only child, an' they've pampered him since he was in diapers! His daddy gave him that new truck he drives to school—you know, the one Virgil ticketed last year. An' his mamma dotes on him to no end."

"So how does that work in our favor?" I wondered.

He crossed his arms. "We use praise 'n' pastries."

"Praise and pastries?" I shook my head. "I'm not following you."

"That boy is used to bein' the center of attention. Loves the limelight. So when I tried recruitin' him last week, I played to his pride by remindin' him that the quarterback is the star o' the offense, the backbone o' the team, the one who gets all the press 'n' publicity. I thought that'd do it, but you saw what happened when he spied his cousin sittin' there in the gym. So, we gotta up the ante. He's used to gettin' most anything he likes. An' there's nothin' he likes better than maple-glazed donuts from the Piggotty Dough Boy."

"Piggotty Dough Boy?" I'd never heard of that.

"Yeah, the local donut hole over on Main and D Streets. They got amazin' donuts. Even the day-old stuff tastes good. I bet if we offered him a dozen maple donuts for every game he plays, we'd have our QB an' a full team for the entire season!"

I'm ashamed to admit it, but I gave his suggestion serious consideration. I had no better plan, and we were running out of options and time. "I don't understand one thing, though. If he already gets everything he wants, why would offering a dozen donuts make him change his mind?"

"That's the beauty o' livin' in such a small town," Winston pointed out. "Ya pick up a lot o' little details here 'n' there, an' I'm good at keepin' my head down an' my eyes 'n' ears open. One o' the few things his folks don't indulge him with is sweets. Both of 'em are on a diet an' think he oughta be on one, too, even though he's got an athletic build. So I'm purdy sure if we was to appeal to his pride *and* dangle a dozen donuts under his nose, he'd change his tune soon enough."

I realized I was dealing with a very shrewd man here. "But wouldn't that be going against the wishes of his parents?" I pressed, concerned that his suggestion was pushing ethical boundaries.

He scratched his chin. "Well, the way I look at it, they never expressed that wish publicly. Leastaways, not that I know of. I picked up that bit o' information by listenin' to certain conversations in the hallways. Besides, he'll burn off more calories playin' football than he'll ever gain eatin' donuts! Far as I'm concerned, it's a win-win solution all the way around."

I still wasn't fully convinced. "But what about Clay? He said he wasn't going to play if Knox is on the team. What do we do with him?"

"Ya think Knox is the only one I got the goods on?" His eyes twinkled mischievously. "Coach, you just concentrate on gettin' the team ready for the season opener an' leave the personnel problems to me!"

There is something to be said for unconventional methods. Sometimes, you need to think outside the box and say to yourself, "I wonder what would happen if . . . " and then follow through on it. Sure, failure is possible. Even likely. But isn't the reason you turned to unconventional methods in the first place because you already *failed* using conventional ones? And who's to say that you won't succeed this time?

I began practice Tuesday afternoon without Knox or Winston. It was not like my assistant coach to be late, so I was sure he had a good reason for not being there. My ten players were in the middle of warmups when Knox jogged onto the field in full gear. I thanked him profusely for his change of heart and welcomed him to the team with a warm handshake and a pat on the shoulder pads. I noticed he had sticky fingers and what looked like powdered sugar around the edges of his mouth.

After Knox joined his teammates, Winston came up beside me. I leaned over and whispered, "Wow, you really work fast!" He turned away but not before I caught the grin. "I hope it's enough this time. So, what did you do to make sure *Clay* doesn't walk?"

Winston continued watching the players stretch. "Ya don't wanna know!" he replied cryptically.

I moved Jackson back to his tackle position and had Knox take a few snaps from Maynard. Then, because Knox had missed the first three practices, I had to start over explaining the offense. It didn't take him long to catch on; and soon, we were back on track. Besides Isaiah and Jeremima, who hadn't had a chance yet to show me how well they could block or tackle, I'd say Knox was one of the more athletic players on the team. His hand-offs to Henry and Willie improved with each exchange, and his passes to Willard and Nigel were more accurate with each throw, although not much could be said for the receiving end of those throws. Feeling rather confident, I introduced a new running play involving a hand-off between Knox at quarterback and Clay at fullback. That's when things went slightly awry. On the first attempt, Knox turned and collided with his cousin.

"Watch where you're going!" Knox growled.

"I am! You're the one who ran into *me*!" Clay retorted.

"Run that again!" I interjected quickly. "And, Clay, remember to take a step to your right first. That'll give you more space for the exchange." He nodded and lined up again.

"See, told ya so!" Knox hissed before moving back under center. Their next attempt resulted in a fumble.

"You didn't put the ball in my stomach!" Clay complained loudly, gesticulating like an angry Italian.

"I did, too! *You* didn't secure it like you're supposed to," Knox shot back, balling up his fists and taking a step toward his cousin.

I got between them. "Guys, guys, it's okay! Let's walk through it in slow motion a few times. It'll come to you. Repetition is the key to getting better. What you're doing now is building muscle memory. Before long, you'll be running these plays with your eyes closed."

Knox scowled at his cousin. "He's *already* running like his eyes are closed!"

"Oh yeah?" Clay fired back. "And if you're building muscle memory, we're gonna be here a long, long time, you lamebrain!"

The wrestling season began a little early at Piggottsville High. Winston and I pulled them apart.

"I can't work with him!" Clay whined to me. "Can't we just run plays where we don't have to work together?" I was about to lecture him on the importance of teamwork when I caught Winston giving him a knowing stare. Clay wilted. "Oh, all right," he mumbled under his breath. "I'll give it another try."

We made it to the end of practice without any further tantrums.

"Well, *that* didn't go so well," I stated the obvious to Winston as we bagged the equipment. "Those two have more animosity between them than Aaron Burr and Alexander Hamilton!"

"Look on the bright side," Winston suggested.

I stared at him. "What bright side? I don't see one—unless it's the fact that in *this* duel, nobody got killed."

"Ya made a lotta headway with them two today." He chuckled. "At least ya got 'em talkin' to each other again!"

The attitudes during the remaining practices that week improved after Knox's first day on the team. There were a few exchanges of words and one shove; but other than that, the two cousins pretty much kept their hostility off the field. The team as a whole showed slight improvement by week's end, but that's not saying much. And it was not enough to warrant any confidence on my part that they would be anywhere near ready for their first game in just one week. The players had started so far behind that even if they were given an entire year to prepare, they would still be woefully lacking in every facet of the game. On offense, ball exchanges were still being mishandled; passes were off target or dropped on a regular basis; wide receivers often ran the wrong routes; and running backs frequently collided with the stationary chairs they were supposed to dodge. Nigel still trapped the ball with his feet, and Jeremima still complained about not being able to pulverize people.

Don't get me started on the state of the special teams. Nigel had a pretty strong leg, but he had great difficulty adjusting to kicking a ball that was not spherical like the one he was used to. Both his kickoff and field goal attempts usually failed to gain altitude and distance. The only bright spot I could see was that he was going to be a natural with the onside kick.

Over the weekend, only one incident is worth mentioning. Saturday morning, I stopped by The Old Fort Bank to deposit my first paycheck as an employee of the Piggottsville-Stuyvesant Consolidated School Corporation. The fact that it was generated on an ancient dot matrix printer, along with the anemic face value, testified to the frugality of my employer. As I waited in line at one of the two teller windows, Orville Piggott waved from his office and came out to greet me.

"Mr. Wisniewski, it's so good to see you!" He grabbed my hand firmly and then, without letting go, proceeded to engage me in some idle chit-chat before getting around to what I assumed was the real reason for his congeniality. "By the way, Knox tells me he's going to be the starting quarterback on your new football team."

"That's right. I'm really glad he decided to play." I opted not to tell him that his son was going to be the *only* quarterback on my new team or the reason *why* he decided to play. "He has a strong throwing arm; and with a little work on fundamentals, I think he'll make a decent quarterback."

"Oh, he's a very gifted athlete," his father informed me proudly. "He's the star pitcher on the Piggottsville baseball team and the leading scorer in basketball. On top of that, he's an excellent student and a mighty fine son." He beamed. "If you ask me, Knox is as good as gold! Yes sir, as good as gold!"

When I left the bank, I put two and two together. Orville was one of the wealthiest men in town and president of The Old Fort Bank. His only son, Knox, was as good as gold. Fort. Knox. Gold. Really? Was that where Knox got his name? After what I'd seen and heard since coming to Piggottsville, it wouldn't surprise me in the least.

It was the beginning of my third week at Piggottsville High. All history classes were going reasonably well. I had a firm grasp on the curriculum and a good rapport with most of my students. I had to lean on a few of the class clowns now and then; but other than that, there were no major problems. My biggest concern was what to do about Skunk once the weather turned too chilly to keep the windows open. I kept a can of air freshener in my desk drawer; and every day before and after second period, I used it religiously. That made things manageable for the time being, and I chose not to worry about later. After all, "sufficient for the day is its own trouble."[3]

At lunchtime on Monday, I went downstairs to the cafeteria, picked up a tray, and started through the food line. Teachers used the same facilities as the students but ate in an annex off the main lunchroom. I was famished and asked for extra portions at nearly every food station. I must have overloaded my tray because the person behind me commented on the mountain of manna.

"Why, Mr. Wisniewski! Is that lunch for the history teacher, or the football coach . . . or *both?*"

I turned around to see Emily Davenport standing behind me wearing a pixie grin on her face. Mine turned as red as the beets on my tray. "Oh, uh . . . hi!" I compared my tray to hers. "Yeah, well, since I've been asked to wear two hats, I think I should get two meals, don't you?" I know that makes me sound like a total cornball, but I honestly couldn't think of anything clever to say.

She smiled, revealing perfect white teeth. "Well, I think you deserve it. I heard you had trouble fielding a team. How are the practices going?"

I postponed my answer long enough for the lunch lady to plop a dollop of mashed potatoes onto the only space left on my tray. I heard myself address her in a pitiful, youthful voice a' la Oliver Twist: "Please, ma'am, I want some more." She gave me a frown before adding another scoop. Emily was laughing behind me. Apparently, she understood cornball. As we moved on, I answered her question. "Practices? Not as well as the classroom, I'm afraid."

"I'm sorry to hear that," she empathized. We reached the end of the counter and walked across the cafeteria to the teachers' room. "Do you

3 Matthew 6:34

mind if I join you today?" she asked casually. "I'd be interested to learn about your first impressions of Piggottsville High."

"Not at all," I replied, trying to hide my enthusiasm. I purposely chose an empty table on the far side of the room, eager to compare notes on our classrooms rather than the amount of food on our lunch trays. We sat down facing each other across the table. When she reached for her utensils, I glanced at her hand. She was not wearing a wedding ring.

The lunch period flew by like an old VHS movie on fast forward. I didn't even finish my meal. As I shared observations from my two weeks at school and my three-and-a-half weeks in town, I managed to learn a little more about the friendly teacher sitting opposite me. I asked if she was related to the Piggotts, an assumption not so far-fetched considering the proliferation of Ferrell's descendants in the area; and I was pleased to learn that she was an outsider like myself. She said she was from Elyria, Ohio, and had heard of the job opening from her great-aunt with whom she lived in town. Since this was her second year at Piggottsville High, she was able to share her knowledge of the present climate and culture of the school and town. Her insights jibed with what I'd experienced so far, which was reaffirming considering my propensity for exaggeration and embellishment.

We chatted a while longer until the bell rang. After taking our trays to the return window, we went our separate ways. Climbing the stairs to my classroom, I couldn't believe how enjoyable and effortless the conversation had been. To my surprise, I found myself longing for more.

On Wednesday following fourth period World History, one of my students lingered behind while the rest of the class filed out of the room. The boy timidly approached my desk as I was putting away my class notes. "Mr. Wisniewski?"

I looked up from my paperwork at the small, dark-haired boy standing in front of me. It was Danny Swanson, son of Phil Swanson, whom I'd met in the barbershop. He was the shortest, scrawniest sixteen-year-old I'd ever seen. He couldn't have weighed a hundred pounds if he were dressed in a full-length cement overcoat. The other kids had nicknamed him "Runt," not only for his diminutive size but also because he was the youngest of ten children. Yet, he was well-liked and didn't seem to mind the nickname.

"Yes, Danny. What can I do for you?" His face was at the same height as mine, even though I was seated.

"Well, I was wondering if you needed any more help with the football team."

His comment caught me off guard. "Let me get this straight. *You* want to be on the football team?" Visions of him being scraped off the turf flashed through my head.

"Yeah! I really like football."

My response could have been a tad more, shall we say, politically correct. "But *you* can't play football. You're too small!"

A smile broke out across his face. "Oh, I don't want to *play*, Mr. Wisniewsi." He giggled nervously. "If I did that, I'd get creamed off the map! I just want to be a team manager, that's all. You know, help with the equipment, keep the stats, be the waterboy. Whatever you want!"

I felt an immediate kinship with the lad and considered his offer for a moment. "Sure, Danny, I could certainly use your help with those things. Thank you for volunteering. Now I'll be able to concentrate more on coaching."

He looked as happy as a hound dog after treeing a possum. "I'll work real hard for you, Mr. Wisniewski," he promised. "I stock shelves and keep track of inventory at my dad's store on weekends, so I'm pretty good at organizing things. You can count on me!"

"That's great, Danny." I walked him to the classroom door. "Can you come by the coaching office after school today? While the others are suiting up for practice, I'll show you what needs to be done."

"You bet! Thanks, Mr. Wisniewski." He suddenly paused, his exuberance giving way to timidity again. "Do you think it would be okay if I called you Coach, even though I'm not really on the team?"

"Of course, you can." I placed a hand on his shoulder. "But remember, you're just as much a part of this team as any of the players on the field!"

As I watched the newest addition to the football program walk out the door, I truly began to get excited about the upcoming season.

CHAPTER TEN
"What It Was, Was Football"

Friday was finally upon us—the season opener. Game day! However, it felt more like D-Day to me. My soldiers were not ready to face an enemy; they were totally unprepared for live fire, and I was about to lead my troops into battle before they'd even completed basic training. When you scrimmage against eleven stationary folding chairs, your combat skills don't get much of a workout. Not only was I worried about their lack of preparation and knowledge but also their lack of conditioning and stamina. Two-and-a-half weeks was not nearly enough time to achieve any of those goals, especially when the recruits were as raw and undisciplined as mine. I was sending them out to attempt the impossible. And yet here I was, expecting them to do just that.

To instill team pride and generate interest among the student body, I'd asked the players to wear their jerseys to school that day. I'd found an extra one for Danny, but it hung like a full-length dress on his slight frame and looked ridiculous. At the beginning of second period, Mr. Herold's commanding voice came over the intercom to read the day's announcements.

"Good morning, PSHS students! Welcome to Friday. Congratulations for making it to the end of another week. Just to remind you, on Monday, the reading challenge begins in the library; and on Tuesday, yearbook pictures will be taken in the gymnasium. We want everyone to look their best; so please come to school dressed in the appropriate attire, or you will be sent home to change." He cleared his throat. "It has come to my attention that some students have been casually referring to me as 'Mr. H.' Let me remind you that the proper way to address your principal is to call me by my full last name. I am to be called 'Mr. Herold.' Let's get it straight, young people!"

The principal resumed his upbeat tone. "This is a very special day here at Piggottsville High School. Tonight at seven o'clock, our football team begins its season with a home game against the Elliston Eagles. I want you all to come out and show your school spirit. Let's help the Mighty Hogs *clip* the wings of those Eagles!"

His attempt at wit spurred the thought, *I'm pretty sure that clipping eagles wings is a federal offense.*

Then it seemed the principal swallowed the microphone as his distorted voice bellowed throughout the building, "Go, Mighty Ferrell Hogs!" Mr. Herold's impromptu pep rally was the only one scheduled that day; and unfortunately, he made a lousy cheerleader.

Walking out to the stadium with my players that evening, my stomach was in knots. I fished two antacid tablets from the stash in my pocket and covertly popped them into my mouth. As my band of misfits began their pregame warmups, I surveyed my surroundings. Winston had striped the field that afternoon after giving it a final trim; and it didn't look half bad, although the cow patties now stood out like dozens of reddish-brown Frisbees left randomly lying around some lazy kid's backyard. He hadn't been able to repair the lights, however, and the dimly lit half of the field faded away into the Twilight Zone.

I watched the Elliston players doing their choreographed calisthenics, which only added lightheadedness to my nausea. As a team, they were huge compared to my players, with the exception of the Pugh twins. I counted thirty-two of them. Twice as big and three times as many. I prayed we would make it to halftime alive. Across the field, the Eagles cheerleaders were leading the thirty or forty visiting fans in a cheer:

"Pork chops, pork chops, greasy, greasy!
We're gonna beat ya, easy, easy!"

Attached to the chain link fence was a banner. I squinted to read the words: "We're achin' for some bacon!" Seriously? I turned around and glanced at our own bleachers. I counted nine persons in all, including Reverend and Mrs. Pinckney. We locked eyes for a second; and he smiled, giving me two thumbs up. Their presence buoyed my sinking spirits. One of the nine was a tall, lanky man. It was Avery.

"What's Avery Piggott doing here?" I asked my assistant coach. "I didn't know he was interested in football."

Winston turned to see for himself. "It ain't the football he's here for. He come out to support his wife."

"Support his wife?" I stared at him. "What do you mean by that?"

Just then, the referee blew his whistle, summoning us to the fifty-yard line.

"You'll see," he replied, hustling onto the field.

After we met Elliston's coaches—there were four of them, by the way—the head referee explained a few procedural rules before conducting the coin toss. The Eagles won and elected to receive. We jogged to the sideline to await the playing of the national anthem. My question was about to be answered.

Hermione Piggott, all 450 pounds of her, waddled out to midfield and turned to face the home sideline. She loudly cleared her throat three times and nervously brushed a few wrinkles from her huge tent dress, which, if repurposed, could have adequately housed the entire Ringling Bros. and Barnum & Bailey Circus. Then she inhaled a copious amount of the humid evening air, and, without benefit of a public address system, belted out "The Star-Spangled Banner."

Winston leaned over in the vicinity of my left ear. "She sings 'tween the cracks just enough to make your skin crawl, don't she?" he whispered. I fought valiantly to suppress a grin.

Hermione finished with a flair and bowed theatrically. A smattering of polite applause drifted across the field.

Winston glanced at the bleachers behind the Hogs' bench and shook his head in disbelief. Then he spoke out of the side of his mouth. "Anybody hangin' around o' their own free will after *that* rendition is bound to be a brave soul indeed. Her voice is bluer than the toes on a barefoot field-goal kicker!"

A laugh escaped my lips. "I guess it's true what they say, then. It isn't over until the 'you-know-who' sings. Or in our case, it hasn't *begun*! Either way, it looks like the worst is over now."

A few minutes later, however, the opening kickoff thoroughly disproved that statement.

What do you say to eleven football players who have just had their collective heads handed to them? How do you encourage a team that stinks worse than my second period classroom with both windows shut tight or that has been chewed up worse than Evander Holyfield's ear? Long after everyone had gone home, I sat in the coaching office contemplating those questions. To no one's surprise, the game had been a disaster. I picked up the clipboard with the stats Danny had logged during the lopsided contest, if you could even call it that. Minus eighteen yards rushing, ten fumbles, zero first downs, eight for nine passing. That's not eight completions; that's eight interceptions on nine attempts. I debated whether having a stats-keeper was such a good idea after all. The final score had been zero to seventy, and that's with the Eagles playing their third string the entire second half. They could have played their cheerleaders, and it wouldn't have made any difference. Our opponent had scored a total of ten touchdowns, one every time they touched the ball.

I tried looking for the bright spots. Believe it or not, there were a few. For one thing, we had managed to keep their punt and field goal units off the field for the entire sixty minutes. For another, all our players had remained in the game, playing every single down until the final whistle, although most of them were crawling around on all fours by the end of the third quarter. But Isaiah did have six solo tackles, and Jeremima did knock four of their players out of the game. Following the blowout, I tried to lift their downtrodden spirits by reminding them that they had already come further than any other Piggottsville football team in the past five years. I don't think that helped much.

The next morning, I slept in until almost 11:00. I was so mentally and emotionally drained from the night before that I didn't even feel like getting out of bed. But life goes on. I forced myself to get up; and after moping around for a while, I showered, shaved, and dressed. By then, it was noon. I didn't have the willpower to fix myself something to eat, so I decided to go to the Main Street Café for lunch instead. Maybe a good, hot meal would jump start my motivator, which seemed to be stuck on lethargy that morning.

While walking the four blocks to the little eatery, I passed several side streets that had either bent or mangled stop signs at the intersections. I groaned inwardly. This town definitely had a juvenile delinquency problem.

When I reached my destination, I pushed open the door and found the place almost full. Not wanting to show my face to half the town after the previous evening's debacle, I thought about leaving; but a hunger pang drove me to locate a vacant stool at the end of the counter. I placed my order with the cheerful waitress named Charlene, then picked up a day-old newspaper on the end of the counter and began scanning the headlines.

Some laughter from the booth across the aisle drew my attention away from an article I was reading about sheep and the dangers of Lyme disease. Three men were seated at the table with a large pot of coffee between them. They were Phil Swanson, Mayor Piggott, and his brother, Avery. The mayor caught me looking their way and waved to me.

"Mr. Wisniewski, good to see you!" he called out in his usual jovial way. "How are you adjusting to life in our fair city?"

I couldn't bring myself to tell him how I really felt. "Oh, you know, it's . . . it's going fairly well. I'm settling into a bit of a routine. I've met some very nice people around town, and I'm feeling more at home in the classroom every day."

"Good! Glad to hear it."

There was an awkward silence, which I assumed was because nobody wanted to breach the subject of football. So it fell on me to fill the space. Struggling for words, I turned to Avery and blurted out the first thing that came to mind. "Your wife gave a fine rendition of the national anthem last night, Mr. Piggott."

The lanky farmer stared at me as if I'd just escaped from Nurse Ratched's mental ward. "Are you *deaf*, son? That woman couldn't carry a tune to save her life. The only thing her caterwaulin' is good for is callin' the hogs!"

I had a sudden coughing spell.

Mercifully, Phil Swanson changed the subject. "Mr. Wisniewski, I appreciate you letting Danny be a part of your football team, especially since he's not the athletic type."

I responded with a nervous laugh. "I'm afraid not many of my players are, Mr. Swanson."

He chuckled. "Well, he's excited about it, anyway. I think you'll find that he's very good with statistics."

Avery jumped in. "Don't seem like he had too many to keep track of last night," he stated bluntly. The other men refrained from laughing, probably for my sake.

I decided to keep things light. "You are *so* right about that!" I rolled my eyes. "But like I told my players, even though we lost, we've already played one more game than the past five years combined."

Mayor Wilson Piggott III thumped the table with his beefy hand making the men's coffee cups jump. "Now *that's* the kind of positive attitude this town needs!" He nodded emphatically, looking around the table for confirmation. "I'm confident you're the right man for the job, and you have my full support."

I thanked him for his faith in me and promised to do my best with what I'd been given. Then I spoke without thinking and posed a question I probably shouldn't have asked. "I was a little disappointed that more people didn't show up for the season opener," I complained. "There weren't but a dozen fans in the hometown bleachers, and even *they* all cut out before the end of the third quarter." I took a long swig of my orange juice. "How come no one stayed to the end of the game?"

Avery leaned back against the bench he was sitting on. "The truth is, if a body wanted to hang around and see a team get whupped *that* bad, they'd go over to Nesbitt on a Saturday night and watch the mule 'n' buggy races!"

You get what you ask for.

On Sunday, I made it a point to thank Reverend and Mrs. Pinckney for their attendance at my first game, telling them how much I appreciated and needed their support. They both promised to make every effort to be at all the home games, a commitment that stood in sharp contrast to the support I'd been promised from other members of the academic and civic community. Although I'd been attending their little church for only a month, it already felt like a home away from home, an oasis of calm in a desert of calamity.

As the procession of congregants followed the mayor and his wife into the sanctuary, I spied Emily Davenport ahead of me. I worked my way closer, hoping I might sit next to her. But when she sat down beside Elvira Primrose, I abandoned that plan and slipped into the pew behind them instead. It was a lovely service, although I must confess I don't remember much of what the preacher said. I was too focused on the person in front of me, the one with the long blonde hair no longer tied back but cascading freely across her shoulders like a golden waterfall.

After the benediction, I stood quickly to my feet and waited impatiently for the others to exit my row. I would have liked to hang back and talk with Emily, but I was as eager to avoid Elvira Primrose as she probably was to avoid me. I didn't make it to the aisle.

"Good morning, Mr. Wisniewski," a pleasant voice called out.

I turned to my fellow teacher. "Hello, Miss Davenport. How are you?" That all sounded so formal. It's how Mr. Herold wanted us teachers to refer to one another, but we weren't in his jurisdiction at the moment.

"Now, there we go again, sounding like a couple of business associates at a board meeting. Please, call me Emily." She smiled warmly.

I nodded. "Okay . . . Emily. And you can drop the Mister."

"Okay . . . Wisniewski!" she replied with a devilish gleam in her eye.

The temperature in the room rose a few degrees. "I mean, just call me Jason."

Emily's laugh was a babbling brook. "Okay . . . Jason."

I risked a glance in the direction of Elvira; but to my relief, she was conversing with another parishioner. I turned my attention back to the young lady. "You know, this whole *Who's on First, What's on Second* routine is awfully confusing! At school, I'm expected to address you as Miss Davenport in order to maintain Mr. Herold's proper decorum; but at church, it's Emily, and Mayor Piggott, and Reverend Pinckney. And in town, it's Ezekiel instead of Mr. Pugh, but Mrs. Pugh instead of Naomi! Aaargh!"

Emily grinned. "I see what you mean. It's enough to drive one to distraction!"

"You'd better know it. It's even a problem on the field," I groused. "The kids call me Coach instead of Mr. Wisniewski, and I usually call them by their last names. The problem is, I've got two Pughs and two Piggotts on my team."

"Maybe you could call them Thing 1 and Thing 2 like in Dr. Seuss' *The Cat in the Hat*."

"That may work with the Pugh twins but not with the Piggott cousins."

"Why not?"

I glanced around and lowered my voice. "Are you kidding? Those two would get into a fight over who should be number one!"

Emily's laughter was becoming infectious. She glanced at Reverend Pinckney shaking hands at the back of the sanctuary and changed the subject. "So, what did you think of the pastor's sermon this morning?"

Of all the questions she could have asked, why did it have to be that one? The mercury continued to climb. I cracked open my Bible and peeked at the sermon topic printed on the church bulletin. "I thought it was very interesting. I've always enjoyed listening to preaching on, uh . . . the Beatitudes." Whew! I managed to pull *that* one out of the fire!

"The Beatitudes?" She tilted her head and gave me a puzzled look.

"Yeah. You know, the Sermon on the Mount. Matthew chapter five." I thought that would impress her.

She gave me a look that could only be described as amusement. "Um, I believe that was *last* week's sermon."

"Say what?" I took another look at the bulletin. It was the one from the previous Sunday.

CHAPTER ELEVEN
PIG WARS

I canceled Monday's practice after most of the team members limped into my classes complaining of sundry aches and pains. I honestly felt sorry for them. Besides, Winston and I needed the time after school to review our miserable performance and make the necessary adjustments before our next game, which was only five days away. We met in the coaching office at 3:00.

"Winston, what are your takeaways from our first game?" I asked, handing him the stat sheet.

He studied it for a moment. "Ya mean, aside from the fact that we got skunked seventy to nuthin'?" He removed his cap and ran his hand through his short, curly hair. "Sorry 'bout that!" He grinned and replaced his cap. "One o' my former coaches said that whenever ya critique a player or team, always sandwich the negative 'tween the positives. He called it the Oreo Principle. Start by identifyin' what went right, then address what went wrong, an' end by findin' ways to improve."

"That's great advice. I like that." I leaned back in my chair. "So, what did you see that went right?"

"I was proud o' the kids for hangin' in there to the end," he responded quickly. "They showed a lotta heart an' put in a good effort. Ain't their fault they didn't have no game experience. They's all raw as oysters, but I was pleased with how the Pugh twins played. Them two have the size 'n' strength to excel over time. An' Knox woulda had some completions if he hadn'ta been pressured or sacked on every down."

"I agree. You know, I spent most of the weekend rehashing the game in my mind; and I think our biggest weakness has to be poor blocking and tackling. If those improve, so will everything else."

Winston nodded. "Durin' the second quarter, Jimmy Dean told me he was havin' trouble tacklin' 'cause the other team kept movin' around too much. Said he was only used to stationary targets!" He chortled. "Coach, what we need is some live blockin' 'n' tacklin' drills."

"But we don't have any equipment or enough players," I pointed out.

"I got an idea 'bout that," Winston offered. "Suppose we had 'em go five on six or six on five in practice. That way, they'd get some experience with live opponents. An' I might be able to talk Mr. Swanson into donatin' some feed sacks an' straw from his store. We could use 'em for blockin' pads an' maybe even make tacklin' dummies out of 'em."

I threw up my hands in surrender. "What have we got to lose? I say, go for it! We've already secured two players using your unconventional methods, so who knows? Maybe we can turn this bohemian bunch into a team that can actually block and tackle. Now, wouldn't *that* be something!"

He laughed. "I'd say let's get back to the basics, but we ain't got *past* 'em yet."

"Truth be told, Winston, we may be working on the basics all season. But by making these changes, we just might improve enough to score some points this next game."

My assistant wasn't as optimistic. "Baby steps, Coach, baby steps. Right now, I'd settle for our QB completin' one pass before he gets killed!"

At lunch Tuesday, I sat down at a table with several fellow teachers in the cafeteria annex, including Grady Fuller, who taught math and coached boys' basketball.

"Looks like you've got your work cut out for you with the football team," he said, stating the obvious. "What are you going to do?"

I studied him for a moment before answering. It appeared to be an honest question and not a criticism. "Well, Winston and I are making some adjustments this week that hopefully will improve our performance on the field." I looked around at the others and forced a smile. "Y'all know it can't get much worse." They laughed politely. "Listen, Grady, some of my kids are on your basketball team. How did *you* get them to be successful players?"

He looked slightly embarrassed. "Successful? I don't know how much you know about our sports history at Piggottsville High, but we've only won two games in the past three seasons. The plain truth is, we don't have much natural talent to work with around here."

"What about Knox? I've heard that he's your leading scorer and the star pitcher on the baseball team."

Grady rolled his eyes. "I have a pretty good idea where *that* came from. Yes, he's our leading scorer, but that's not saying much. Last season, the team averaged only twenty-two points per game; and he was responsible for about half of those. As far as baseball is concerned, it doesn't get much better." He winked at the others seated around the table. "Although, he *did* once pitch a perfect game against Jackson County."

I frowned skeptically. "You're pulling my leg! A perfect game? Then why isn't there a trophy outside the gym with his name on it? That's like, what, bowling a three-hundred game?"

Grady glanced around the table again before replying. "It's right there in the record book. You can look it up! We lost that game twenty-three to nothing."

I was confused. "Wait, how can you pitch a perfect game and still lose?"

He let slip a prankish grin. "He walked their entire lineup. Twice!" The others broke into laughter.

I shook my head. "I walked right into *that* one, didn't I?" Apparently, success was a foreign concept to this little community, and it was beginning to look as if it was up to me to introduce them to the word.

I ran into Emily while returning my lunch tray. I was still smarting from making a fool of myself in church over the weekend.

"Hi, Mr. Wisniewski," she said cheerfully. "How's your day going?"

"Better than Sunday," I admitted honestly. "At least, I haven't missed any sermons today. Not that I can recall, anyway!" She laughed at my self-deprecating humor. "And definitely better than Friday night."

She gave me a sympathetic smile. "I heard about the game. I'm really sorry about that. It looks like you've got your work cut out for you."

I placed my tray on the conveyor. "That seems to be the general consensus around here."

"Well, it's only the first game," she encouraged. "I'm sure they'll improve as the season progresses."

"I hope so. We need all the help we can get!"

"I wish there was some way I could contribute to the cause," she mused as we walked out of the cafeteria together.

"Want to join the team?" I asked jokingly. "I could insert you into the starting lineup. Name the position, and it's yours!"

She suddenly turned and placed a hand on my arm as if she hadn't heard me. "Say, I just thought of something. When the players wore their jerseys on Friday, I noticed most of them were ripped or full of holes. If you would like, I can fix them before the next game. I'm pretty handy with a sewing machine!"

I looked into her beautiful blue eyes. "Miss Davenport, that's the best offer I've had since coming to Piggottsville. I accept! I'll collect the jerseys after practice and give them to you tomorrow morning. How's that?"

"Perfect!" She gave me a big smile. "I'll have them back to you on Thursday, so the kids can wear them again on game day." This beautiful lady was full of surprises!

For the past few weeks, my U.S. History classes had been studying the Civil War, including some key events that occurred in Arkansas. On Wednesday morning, I began my summation of the War Between the States by concluding our discussions on the Battle of Gettysburg.

"Today, class, we're going to take a look at an event which occurred on the last day of the Battle of Gettysburg on July 3, 1863. It's considered by many as one of the turning points of the entire war." I pulled up the onscreen map we'd been using that week. "The previous day, the Confederate Army had attacked the flanks of the Union lines; and General Lee felt that an attack on their central position would lead to their defeat, so he ordered a frontal infantry assault against the Union positions held by Major General George Meade."

Grabbing my pointer, I tapped the area I was referring to. "The attack was led by Lieutenant General James Longstreet and three of his Confederate Generals. However, General Meade anticipated the attack and reinforced his lines with infantry and artillery, which resulted in heavy Confederate casualties and ultimately ended General Lee's invasion of the North."

I collapsed my pointer and turned to face the class. "Does anyone know the name given to this decisive skirmish that was the high-water mark for the Confederacy?" All I got were blank stares. It was first period, after all. "Anybody?"

"The Battle of Gettysburg?" The sleepy voice came from somewhere near the back of the room.

"Not exactly. That entire battle lasted three days, remember? This conflict took place on the final day."

Jackson Pressley raised his hand. "The *Final* Battle of Gettysburg?"

I was getting nowhere. "Here's a clue. It's named after one of Longstreet's three generals who led an infantry division into the battle." More crickets. I gave up playing Twenty Questions. "Anyone ever hear of Pickett's Charge?"

"Did he use Visa or Mastercard?" The class erupted in laughter. Oh well, at least they were showing signs of life.

"Good one!" I acknowledged Jackson's wit. "Thank you for waking up the rest of the class. The battle is named after George Edward Pickett, a Virginian who was an officer in the conflict." I put up his picture on the TV screen. "It might interest you to know that George Pickett graduated dead last in his class at the U.S. Military Academy, but he still went on to become a career army officer and a major general in the Confederate Army." I attempted to make a point about the importance of perseverance. "What does that tell you about the man?"

Once again, it was Jackson who answered. "It tells me he was a big loser in school and an even bigger loser in battle!" The class was fully awake now.

"In *this* battle, perhaps, but not through any fault of his own. His story tells me that failure doesn't have to keep you down. By persevering, you can overcome those obstacles and achieve a measure of success. He served successfully in several other wars prior to the Civil War, including one called—get this—The Pig War!" That got their attention.

"Pig War?" Maynard McCoy piped up. "You mean, they fought a war against pigs? I sure hope they won *that* one!"

I waited for the laughter to die down. I usually didn't allow this much freewheeling in class; but since they were engaged now, I decided to let it go. "No pigs in this one unless you count the pork barbecue they ate in the mess tent! The Pig War was a confrontation in 1859 involving the United States and Britain over the border between the state of Washington and what is now Canada. The incident got its name when an American farmer shot an Irishman's pig for eating his crops. He offered ten dollars as compensation, but the Irishman demanded a hundred. The American refused, saying, 'I shouldn't have to pay for a pig that was trespassing on my land and eating my potatoes.' To which the Irishman replied, 'It is up to you to keep your potatoes out of my pig!' When British authorities arrested the farmer, the American settlers asked for military protection. They referred to it as a war, but there were no actual casualties on either side."

"Except for the pig!"

I could only imagine what second period was going to be like.

When I walked onto the field for practice that afternoon, I was met by Winston and a pile of burlap sacks stuffed full of hay. The straws poked out of each like quills on a petrified porcupine.

"Whaddya think?" he asked, holding up one of the sacks.

I took it from him and inspected it. The mouth of the sack had been sewn shut with sturdy jute twine. "Did you make these yourself?" I asked.

"Yep. Stayed up last night stuffin' 'em. I asked for six, but Mr. Swanson gave me a dozen in case they don't last the entire season."

I was humbled by his commitment to our program and told him so. He seemed almost embarrassed by the praise.

When the players arrived on the field, I blew my whistle and gathered them around me. "We're going to put the first game behind us and focus on the fundamentals again this week. The better we are with the basics, the better the outcome will be."

I had Winston explain how we were going to conduct the drills, and then we got down to business. I have to tell you, the pads made a world of difference. Our blocking and tackling improved measurably during those two hours, although I did have to stop the drills once when Jeremima tackled Clay hard enough to knock the wind out of him. With Winston's Oreo Principle in mind, I pulled her aside after practice.

"Jeremima, you're doing great, and I'm very pleased with your effort today. I could tell you gave it everything you had. However, may I suggest that you ease up a bit during practice? If just one of your teammates gets hurt, we won't be able to play Friday night."

The oversized girl looked at the ground. "I'm sorry, Coach. I didn't mean to hurt Clay. Really, I didn't."

"I know you didn't." I phrased my next question carefully. "Is there any particular reason why you play with such . . . aggression? Could you be holding in any hostilities that you can think of?"

"Hostilities?" She looked confused. "You mean, am I mad about something? Or someone? No, not at all, Coach. I just love playing football." She took off her helmet and paused introspectively. "But maybe I'm a little too—what was that word you used—'aggressive' because I'm trying to show my father that I can do everything as good as my brother can. I want him to be just as proud of me as if I were the other boy he wanted."

Now it made sense. I recalled the four players she'd knocked out of the season opener. "Jeremima, I don't think you need to worry about keeping up with the boys. You may very well be the best player on our team."

Her eyes brightened, and she broke into a broad smile. "Really, Coach? You really think so?"

I put my hands on her shoulder pads. "One hundred percent! And I can assure you that your father is every bit as proud of you as he is of your brother. He as much as told me so when I met him last week in the Hoggly Woggly."

"Thanks, Coach! I'll make sure *you're* proud of me, too. See you in class tomorrow!" Having said that, she ran off the field with renewed fire in her eyes. I immediately began to feel sorry for our next opponent.

I was also pleased with Thursday's practice. Most of the players were trying hard to learn their roles on the team, although that led to some bruised egos and a few angry verbal exchanges. In addition, I had to separate Knox and Clay again after a botched handoff. If not held in check, their bitterness toward each other was going to adversely affect the morale of the team, which was already at low tide. On the positive side, Knox's passes were becoming more accurate; and Willard and Nigel were running their pass routes better, although their receiving still needed a lot of work. Henry, Willie, and Clay were running the ball with a little more authority; but they often missed the holes created for them by the O-line.

Even Nigel's kicking was showing some improvement. His kickoffs were now traveling farther than ten yards on a regular basis, and his punts were at least aimed downfield instead of straight up in the air or toward the sideline. His field goal attempts were a different matter. On the rare occasion when the ball became airborne, it drifted far right every time.

At the end of the two-hour session, in an attempt to boost morale, I suggested they come up with a team cheer. Several ideas were bounced around, but the kids finally settled on one. "The few! The proud! The Mighty Ferrell Hogs!" When they ran off the field that afternoon, spirits were no longer wallowing in the mud. That was a good sign.

On Friday, Principal Herold announced the away game against the Mud Butte Mosquitoes. Mud Butte was a farming community not much larger than Piggottsville; and according to Winston, the weakest opponent on our schedule. I secretly held out hope that we would score our first points of the season in this contest. I felt like what a proud parent must feel. My child had crawled; and now, it was time for that child to take its first step.

After my last period class, as I was putting away my notes, Ezekiel Pugh entered the room and marched up to my desk.

"Mr. Pugh, it's nice to see you!" I exclaimed, looking up at the man towering over me.

"You may call me Ezekiel," he reminded me.

I nodded. "Ezekiel." I wondered what he was doing at school and hoped he hadn't changed his mind about letting Jeremima play on the team. "And how is Mrs. Pugh?"

"The missus is doing well, thank you. I have come to offer you a few words of encouragement, Mr. Wisniewski. The twins have kept me informed on the progress of the team, and I must say I am pleased with what you are trying to accomplish with these youngsters."

I was genuinely touched by his sincerity. "Thank you very much, Mr. Pugh—Ezekiel. That means a lot."

"I know you are quite busy, so I won't take up any more of your time. But I did want to leave you with a word of encouragement from the Good Book, if I may."

"By all means, please do."

He raised his right hand as if he were about to swear to tell the truth, the whole truth, and nothing but the truth. *"Humble yourselves in the sight of the Lord, and He shall lift you up.'* James chapter four and verse ten."

Maybe it was because his stiffness made me slightly uncomfortable; but for whatever reason, I chose to respond with a touch of humor. "I know *humble* means 'lowly'; and as a team, we can't get any lower than we already are, can we?" I gave a nervous little laugh, hoping he'd do the same. He didn't, so I stumbled on past the point of no return. "I guess that means there's nowhere to go but up, right?"

I should have known humor was not part of this man's DNA; but then, I've never claimed to be the brightest bulb in the house. I tried my best to salvage the awkward moment by putting on a serious face. "Of course, it will not be by our feeble efforts, will it? It will be the Lord Himself Who lifts us up." It's amazing how the Lord comes to your aid in time of need. I shared the verse that just then popped into my head. *"Not by might, nor by power, but by my Spirit, says the LORD of hosts."⁴*

At that, I detected a twinkle in his eyes and a smile toying at the corners of his mouth. Seizing the moment, I stood quickly to my feet, knocking my chair back from the desk in the process. I shook his hand firmly. "Thank you for sharing that, Ezekiel. I hope I can live up to that truth. I will certainly do my best!"

He nodded his acknowledgment; and without another word, he turned and marched out of the room. I plopped back into my chair and exhaled through puffed cheeks. Lately, I seemed to have begun the undesirable habit of stuffing my size ten-and-a-half-foot into my mouth at the most inopportune times. Whoever said, "Better to remain silent and be thought a fool, than to speak and remove all doubt" sure knew what they were talking about!

At 5:30 that afternoon, I stood beside the rusty, sixteen-passenger bus parked behind the gymnasium and watched my players climb aboard. I had asked Mr. Herold for one of the newer, full-size buses to transport the team and fans to our away games; but he had denied my request, saying it would be a waste of gas to use a larger vehicle when we only had a dozen team members and no fans. He'd even refused to pay overtime for a regular bus driver, so that task had fallen to Winston.

---

4 Zechariah 4:6

I should have known better than to even ask. The school board's purse strings were tighter than the ones on a Victorian woman's corset!

I got on the bus. "Okay, let's roll," I said to Winston. He closed the door and started the motor.

"Hey, Coach!" Willard yelled from the seat next to the open window. "What about Isaiah? He ain't here yet!"

I did a quick head count and realized we were one player short of a football team. Winston opened the door, and I hastily stepped off the bus. As I started toward the building, the door flew open; and the big red-headed man-child lumbered toward me, his helmet in hand. "You're late!" I chastised him. "We almost left without you."

"Sorry, Coach," he apologized.

"What were you doing that was so important, you almost missed the bus?"

He bowed his head. "I just needed a minute alone to kneel down and ask God to help me play my best tonight. Guess I lost track of time. It won't happen again." He hurriedly got on the bus.

I climbed aboard and took my seat, having just been humbled by a six-foot-four, 280-pound, red-headed seventeen-year-old whose dependence upon God put me to shame.

I must have needed further humbling because we lost the game against our weakest opponent zero to forty-nine.

CHAPTER TWELVE
WHOLE LOTTA QUAKIN' GOIN' ON

I had reached my first milestone at Piggottsville-Stuyvesant High School: I had been on the job for an entire month. I know that isn't enough time for a proper evaluation; but if I were to compare the first thirty days of my teaching career to that of an astronaut's, I'd have to say my rocket had successfully launched and achieved orbit. All my classes were going well. I was pleased with how quickly the students had accepted me into their tiny microcosm of the universe and with how well they were responding to my teaching methods and participating in the classroom discussions.

On the other hand, when it came to my coaching career, that rocket had definitely malfunctioned and imploded on the launchpad! We hadn't even managed to get off the ground yet. The team of which I was head coach had been outscored 119 to zero in its first two games. On top of that, we were becoming the laughingstock of the other schools; and they took every opportunity to rub our noses in our own ineptness. During the loss to Mud Butte, I heard some of the derogatory chants from the stands and saw how much that disrespect demoralized my players. After the game with the catcalls raining down on them, my players were barely able to drag themselves back to the bus. On the long ride home, I remember thinking, *It can't get any worse than this!* But like so many times before, I was dead wrong.

When we reached the school, the team filed dejectedly into the locker room, laden with frustration and despair. I could hear the hopelessness in their murmuring and complaining. As I prepared to give my post-game talk, one of the players suddenly slammed his helmet against a locker with a loud bang. All eyes locked on the culprit.

"I can't do this anymore!" Jimmy Dean Tucker growled through clenched teeth. The room fell silent.

I approached him. "What do you mean by that, Tucker?"

He looked straight at me. "I didn't sign up for this. This is stupid!"

"What didn't you sign up for?"

"Being on a losing team that's nothing but a joke," he replied defiantly. "Only it ain't funny at all! Two hours of practice every day and for *what?*"

I fought to find the right words. "Tucker, you can't judge this team or this season just by the final score of our first two games. We started with nothing, but we've already shown improvement. We held our opponent to three fewer touchdowns this week."

"Yeah, so what?" His frustration and anger boiled over. "I know enough math to know that nothing times anything will always be nothing. We're never gonna be any good, never gonna win any games. This is just a big waste of my time!"

"Tucker, you're an important part of this team." I looked each player in the eye. "You *all* are. I need every last one of you. Have you forgotten George Pickett from your history lesson? He was last in his class and suffered many losses, but he still made something of himself. Thomas Edison's teacher said he was too stupid to learn anything. He was fired from two jobs. He failed a thousand times to invent the lightbulb before finally succeeding. Lots of people throughout history experienced frequent failures, but that didn't stop them. Their determination and perseverance paid off in the end."

Jimmy Dean shook his head emphatically. "Well, I ain't like those famous people. I don't feel like putting in all this work for nothing. It just ain't worth it. Besides, I didn't wanna play football in the first place, remember?" He glanced at Jeremima, who was scowling at him. "And I don't care if she *does* beat the snot out of me; I'm done with this gig!"

I felt the growing knot in my stomach. "I can't stop you from quitting if you're determined to go through with it, but that's not being fair to the rest of your teammates. You're not just letting them or your school down, you're letting yourself down, too. Look, why don't you think about it over the weekend, and we'll talk again on Monday, okay?"

"I don't care, Mr. Wisniewski; my mind's made up!" He threw up his hands in disgust. "I just can't do this anymore. I *quit!*" He turned and stomped out of the room, leaving me to pick up the pieces of a shattered football team.

They say when it rains, it pours. If that's true, then I was drowning in rising floodwaters. As a team, we were defeated on so many different levels. Not only had we lost our first two games, but we'd also lost a key player, which meant that unless we found an immediate replacement, we'd have to forfeit the next game. Needless to say, I did a lot of praying over the weekend.

That Sunday, I looked forward to church for a number of reasons. While I usually enjoyed the services and the fellowship, I also needed the shelter that island offered from the raging tempest. But sometimes, storms make landfall. I had no trouble listening to the sermon that morning, most likely because I didn't see Emily Davenport among the congregants. Reverend Pinckney, still in the Gospel of Matthew, preached on the subject of reconciliation.

"*'So if you are offering your gift at the altar and there remember that your brother has something against you, leave your gift there before the altar and go. First be reconciled to your brother, and then come and offer your gift.'*[5]"

I failed to understand how that applied to me personally. As far as I knew, I had no broken fences that needed mending; but I could think of several people in town who did. I glanced across the aisle at Orville and Jolene Piggott with their only child, Knox, sitting between them. Reverend Pinckney had expressed sadness that he had not been able to end the feud between the two brothers, which was affecting their children, the town, and now my football team. It's a funny thing; but when you point a finger at someone else, you tend to forget that three are pointing back at you.

As I shook the preacher's hand at the conclusion of the service, he told me that, Lord willing, he and Mrs. Pinckney would be at Friday night's home game along with several of their friends. I'm pretty sure he said that not so much because he loved football but because he

---

5 Matthew 5:23-24

knew I needed the encouragement. After thanking him, I stepped out of the foyer onto the front stoop, pausing to soak up the meridian sun. Gradually, I became aware of someone standing beside me.

"What a beautiful day!" Emily exclaimed. Closing her eyes, she inhaled deeply and tilted her head to catch the warming rays. With her radiant blonde hair framing her pretty face, she was the express image of an angel! Only without the wings.

"Yes, it is," I replied, finding it hard not to stare. "I didn't see you in the service this morning, so I assumed you weren't at church."

She opened her eyes and looked at me. "Oh, I was just helping with the children down in the basement," she informed me. "One of the regular volunteers is out of town this weekend, so Mrs. Pinckney asked if I'd fill in for her."

"That was awfully nice of you," I complimented her. "I'd like to get more involved myself at some point; but right now, I've got a lot on my plate. You know, being a new teacher and having to deal with all the extracurricular stuff going on."

"I'm sure that hasn't been easy," she responded with feeling. "Especially since you don't have much support at school."

"Or in the community," I added. "When I came to Piggottsville, I expected there to be more interest in football; but I've seen very little so far. If there was just some way to get the students and townspeople to take pride in this team, I'm sure that would bolster the kids' self-esteem and motivate them to play better."

"I'm concerned about that, too," she commiserated, "and I have an idea I'd like to run by you if you're interested. But not here at church. I try not to bring my work into my worship."

I felt a familiar heat rise in my face. "I'm sorry, I didn't mean to hijack the conversation. But yes, I'm definitely interested." I did some quick calculations. "Do you have any free time later this afternoon? Maybe we could meet at the Treat-N-Eat and discuss it over a burger or ice cream." So much for not having the luxury of time or money. But then, can I help it if I'm a sucker for angels?

She hesitated. "Well, I do have to finish my lesson plans this afternoon, but I suppose I could meet you for a little while. How does 4:30 sound?"

"That's perfect. I look forward to seeing you then." I was about to leave when a group of parishioners emerged from the building. Emily glanced over my shoulder at them.

"Oh, wait," she exclaimed, "I'd like to introduce you to my great-aunt!" Before I could reply, she took my arm and steered me toward the group, stopping in front of an elderly woman with silvery-white hair tied up in a tight bun. "Jason, I'd like you to meet my great-aunt, Miss Elvira Primrose."

It's true. In a small town, there really is no place to run and hide.

I silently watched the young lady sitting across from me sip her strawberry milkshake. I could only imagine the look on my face when I'd learned that her great aunt was the same sanctimonious old woman who had so self-righteously disapproved of my public display of plebeian tomfoolery. Whatever it was had made Emily break into laughter. That had only driven Elvira to scold her great niece for succumbing to the bad influences of the crass company she'd been keeping lately. With Reverend Pinckney's words ringing in my ears, I had offered a most sincere apology, hoping to rectify the offense and restore Miss Primrose's insulted dignity. But I don't think it had the intended effect.

Emily read me like an open book. "Are you still fretting about my great aunt?" She paused to wipe her mouth with a napkin. "I told you she's like that with everybody, even me. You saw how she scolded me, didn't you? She's the kind of person who has always spoken her mind." She laughed lightly. "But honestly, I think she's beginning to lose her filter a bit."

"Then how in the world do I get in her good graces?" I asked incredulously.

"Oh, I wouldn't worry too much about that. Once she gets to know you better, she'll come around." A mischievous grin toyed with the corners of her mouth. "As long as you don't react to any more 'Old Fart' jokes in her presence!"

I laughed, grateful for her sense of humor. Then I steered her toward a more comfortable topic. "So, what's this idea of yours that might help with the apathy toward the football program?"

She slurped the last of her milkshake before answering. "What's one thing your first two opponents have that you don't have?"

I grimaced. "Let me guess. A *win?*"

She frowned at my sarcasm. "No, not that. What did they have on their sidelines that we didn't have?"

"Fans?" I wasn't earning any brownie points with her.

"No, silly. Cheerleaders! They both had cheer squads. I'll bet if *we* had a cheer squad, that would boost attendance and inspire your team at the same time."

I couldn't resist. "But I don't know any cheers. And I'm just terrible with routines."

She wadded up her napkin and tossed it at me. "You're impossible!" She scowled playfully. "I don't expect you to know anything about cheering. But *I* do!"

"Really?" I pursed my lips thoughtfully. "You know, the idea has real merit. It's definitely worth considering."

"I think so, too. And I'd be happy to organize that for you. I was captain of my cheer squad in high school, so I know what's involved."

"But what will Mr. Herold say? You know he won't spring for any uniforms. You saw what my players have to wear!"

Emily was undaunted. "Last season, the basketball team had two cheerleaders; so I don't think that will be a problem. They've both graduated, but I should be able to round up a few new recruits. The uniforms and pom poms are stored in a supply closet in the girls' locker room. No doubt, they'll need a little mending, like your jerseys; but I think I can pull it off." She smiled sweetly. "Jason, I believe in what you're trying to do, and I want to help any way I can."

I don't believe in kissing a girl on the first date, but had this been an actual one, I would have seriously reconsidered my theology.

The very next morning, Mr. Herold announced cheerleading tryouts after school in the gymnasium. Emily hadn't wasted any time. Her offer to help lifted my spirits; but that was tempered by the fact that if I didn't find another player, it would all be for naught. I'd determined to talk to Jimmy Dean again, even though he'd made it clear he was finished with football; but he didn't show up for class. It was Isaiah who reminded me of the dilemma during second period.

"Mr. Wisniewski, what good will it do to have cheerleaders if we don't have a team on Friday night?"

"Yeah," Willie Skaggs chimed in, "and what about all the trash-talkin' we hafta put up with? The other schools have been doin' it for years. Do you know what they call our school? *Pig-Sty High!* We don't get any respect. No cheerleaders are gonna change that!" His classmates voiced their agreement.

I surveyed the room full of students, and what I saw was a bunch of deflated kids who all faced a problem that extended far beyond football. While that should have discouraged me even more, for some reason, it didn't. It actually had the opposite effect. It wasn't the team's fault or even my failure as a coach that was to blame for the low morale but rather the long-standing culture of disrespect for the school and the community as a whole. In that moment, I chose to set aside my lesson plan in order to address the deeper issue facing my students. It was a matter of local history; and after all, this *was* a history class.

"I get what you're saying," I began. "I've heard the derogatory chants from the other teams, and I've seen their disrespectful banners making fun of our school. But you're not the first to be treated that way. Let me share some historical examples of that same kind of contempt. I know some of you call yourselves a Christian. Did you know that term was originally meant to be a disparaging name for those following Jesus' teachings? It wasn't a compliment at all. It was a put down." I walked around the desk and stood in front of my students. "Do any of you know what a Quaker is?"

One of the kids raised his hand. "He's the guy on the oatmeal box."

I laughed. "Good guess. The logo features a Quaker because they were known for their honesty. The Quakers are a religious sect called the Society of Friends, which was founded in the seventeenth century in England by a man named George Fox. They were persecuted for their belief that people should tremble at the Word of the Lord and, as a result, were mockingly referred to as Quakers. Did you know that two of our U.S. presidents were Quakers? Herbert Hoover and Richard Nixon were both members of this sect. I'm not one myself, but I grew up in a small town west of Indianapolis with a Quaker influence in its history. Since they were considered to be plain people, the town was named Plainfield. Now, get a load of this! What do you think my high school mascot was?"

Skunk spoke up from the back corner of the room. "A Quaker?"

"Right you are, Willard! We were known as the Fighting Quakers."

Jessie Wilkerson raised her hand. "But I thought Quakers were pacifists."

"They are," I replied, energized by the class's participation. "And that's the irony of it. Who ever heard of a pacifist who enjoyed fighting?"

"So, was your team as bad as ours?" Jeremima asked point blank.

"Well, no. Actually, they were quite competitive when I was there. We were proud of our school and our mascot. But that's not the worst of it. Wait until I tell you about my college!" I had their rapt attention. "You'll never guess what the Wooster football team was called." Tons of hands shot up, but I waved them off. "We don't have time for guesses, so I'll tell you. We were called the Fighting Leghorns."

"What's a leghorn?" From Willie Skaggs this time.

"*We* raise leghorns!" Isaiah interjected. "They're good laying hens."

"Yes, they are, Isaiah. But they aren't exactly known for their aggressiveness, are they? It's kind of like the Fighting Quakers all over again. Wooster College is in a small town near a large facility that raises chickens for their eggs, hence, the Fighting Leghorns." I sat down on the front of my desk. "Can you imagine all the disrespect, trash talk, and chicken jokes we faced with a mascot like that?"

Willie leaned forward on his elbows. "So what did you do about it?"

"For one thing, we didn't let it bother us. Instead, we used it to make us stronger. We embraced who we were and took pride in our school and our mascot all while having fun doing it. The fans started calling themselves the Wooster Rooster Boosters just for laughs! And it paid off. We turned the mocking and ridicule into a motivation to work harder and play harder, and we improved with every game. School spirit shot through the roof. We didn't win any championships while I was there, but we didn't have to hang our heads in shame, either."

It was time to wrap up the lecture and return to the regularly scheduled program; but first, I wanted to make one final point. "Look, no matter what you guys do in life, there will always be someone bigger or better or smarter than you. The goal isn't to be the best in the world, but to be the best *you* can be. Even the army is bringing back its old slogan, 'Be All You Can Be.' Take pride in yourself, your school, your team, and your community. Don't worry about what others think or say about you. You are not Pig-Sty High. You are the Mighty Ferrell Hogs! Go have some fun with that." I took a deep breath and sat down behind my desk. "Okay, now, enough with the pep talk. We need to get back to being the best *we* can be . . . at history!"

Loud groans flooded my classroom and spilled out into the hallway.

CHAPTER THIRTEEN
Home Field Advantage

I blew my whistle and gathered the players around me at the start of Monday's practice. During the day, neither Winston nor I had been able to convince, cajole, or con anyone to join the team. I was counting on Winston to pull another rabbit out of his hat, but his was as empty as mine. So I was prepared to conduct practice a man short. However, I counted only nine heads. Someone besides Jimmy Dean was absent. It turned out to be Willard.

"Does anyone know where Bodkins is?" I asked the assembled players.

Willie Skaggs raised his hand. "I do, Coach. He told me he had to go home after school today."

"Did he say why?"

"Somethin' about his mother bein' upset with him for not gettin' his chores done." He hesitated. "He said he might not be able to be on the team anymore! Coach, I think he didn't tell you himself 'cause he was afraid of what you might say, especially after losin' J.D. and everything."

I glanced over at Winston, who looked as helpless as I felt. Another one bites the dust. I pulled myself together as best I could and put on a resolute face. "Well, we'll have to deal with that later. Right now, there are nine of you dressed and on the field. We'll go with what we've got."

"But what's the use, Coach?" Clay verbalized what all the players were no doubt thinking. "Why bother practicing if we won't be playing?"

I steeled myself for a mass mutiny. "I want all of you to listen to me. Coach Banks and I will worry about the missing players and Friday's game. Right now, I want the rest of you to concentrate on what's in front of you: today's practice." I blew my whistle again. "All right, let's line up for blocking drills!"

In the morning, I had a talk with Willard at the end of second period. From a distance, of course. He still smelled as bad as ever; the stench surrounded him like Pigpen's dust cloud in the *Peanuts* comic strip, only larger. And invisible. I'd toyed with the idea of making him a running back, since nobody in their right mind would want to get close enough to tackle him. I'd also gone as far as to stick a solid air freshener under his seat in the classroom and on the bus. Barely able to look me in the eye, he apologized for not having the courage to tell me himself. I felt sorry for the slight youth with few friends.

When asked if he wanted to be on the team, he replied with an emphatic "Yeah!" That was a pleasant surprise, especially since he'd been dragged to that first meeting under threat of capital punishment. So I determined to pay his mother a visit to see what could be done about the situation.

With Tuesday's practice in the capable hands of my assistant coach, I left school for the Bodkins' farm. Driving out No Name Road, a thousand thoughts paraded through my mind. What would I find when I arrived at their house? What could I say to convince Willard's mother to let him return to the team? What should I do if we were still two players short come Friday? I only had questions, and bouncing across the crumbling, pitted pavement failed to jar loose any answers that might have been lurking in the shadowy recesses of my brain. Three miles outside of town, I turned onto a one-lane gravel road that disappeared over a small knoll. Beyond that, the road passed through a grove of gnarled hickory trees and crossed a narrow, winding brook. About a quarter mile farther, I came upon a rusty, dented mailbox with the name "Bodkins" painted on the side in nearly illegible, faded green letters. There were three bullet holes, one in the center of the letter O. I normally don't think too highly of drive-by shooters; but I'll say this much: whoever was responsible was a crack shot.

I turned onto the narrow dirt drive and navigated the final seventy-five yards to the small homestead, pulling to a stop in front of a weathered, dilapidated old farmhouse. The roof of the veranda porch sagged precariously, and several shutters were askew or missing altogether. One end of the second-story guttering hung away from the house, and the once-white clapboard siding was the same gray color as Skunk's floppy tennis shoes. Across the bare dirt yard, stood a small, out-of-plumb barn with indications of red paint still on the vertical boards. I watched a pigeon fly out of a hole in the roof and disappear over the adjacent field, which was as unkempt as the one behind the school had been my first day in town. A small shed with a lean-to on one side, a galvanized water trough, and an old rusty windmill with several vanes missing completed the landscape.

No sooner had I stepped from my car than the rickety screen door flew open with a loud bang. A gangly youth in a dirty pair of overalls came flying out of the house, his arms and legs flailing wildly like a kid with a sweet tooth and a five-dollar bill chasing after an ice cream truck. He hightailed it across the dirt yard, kicking up tiny eddies of dust and pebbles as he ran, and disappeared through the open barn door. A woman emerged from the house with a rolling pin firmly clenched in one hand. She stopped at the edge of the porch and raised her other hand to shield her eyes from the sun.

"Come back here, you slacker!" she hollered, waving the rolling pin over her head like a club. "Durnell, I'm gonna tan yer hide good!" Clearly exasperated, the woman planted both feet, placed her hands on her hips, and glared at the barn. She was a slight woman with a worn apron tied around her waist and a faded yellow tea towel wrapped around her head and knotted in front like Rosie the Riveter. A wisp of dishwater-blonde hair had escaped the towel and dangled over one eye.

I stood frozen in my tracks, watching the drama play out before me with my mouth as wide open as the car door. Then she saw me. I hastily shut the door and approached the woman, who was now staring suspiciously at me.

"Yeah? What do *you* want?" Her voice bore traces of the vitriol she'd just thrown after the miscreant.

"Excuse me, but are you Willard Bodkins' mother?"

"Who wants ta know?" she asked bluntly.

"I'm sorry. I'm Jason Wisniewski, Willard's history teacher over at the high school. I'm also his—"

"What's he done now?" she cut me off with a scowl.

"Done, ma'am? Oh, he's not in any trouble." I glanced at the barn. "That I know of." Better I should cover all my bases. "I'm also his football coach, and that's why I stopped by. I heard he might not be able to play for the team anymore."

"Ya heard right," she replied firmly. "Willard ain't got no time fer after-school activities. Them rehearsals o' yours is keepin' him from his afternoon chores."

"I wasn't aware of that, Mrs. Bodkins, and I'm sorry to hear it."

The hardness in her voice softened a bit. "It's just Luella. Ain't no 'missus' no more." I noticed the lines on her face and caught the weariness in her eyes. "He promised t' keep up if'n I let him play, so I give him the chance. But he's been neglectin' his responsibilities 'round here since he joined yer team. Says he's too tired t' do any more work."

"I can appreciate your position, ma'am."

"Had ta finally put my foot down," she continued. "Didn't really want to 'cause he seemed ta enjoy playin', but this here farm's all we got. If'n he don't milk them cows an' feed them chickens every evenin', then we don't make it, pure an' simple."

I thought about asking if his brother Durnell might be able to cover for him, but this was one of those rare occasions when I actually listened to the little voice in my head that was screaming *Don't do it!* at the top of its tiny little lungs. "Ma'am, I totally respect your decision, but what if there were some way for Willard to complete all his chores and play football at the same time?"

His mother shook her head. "Don't see how that's possible. He's lazy 'nuff as 'tis. Had a hard 'nuff time getting' him ta do 'em before all this nonsense started." She pulled off her head scarf and tucked the wisp of hair behind an ear. "Look, Mr. Wisniewski, I appreciate ya comin' out here an' yer concern fer my boy, but I don't think ya fully understand. I been raisin' my boys by myself ever since their daddy took off ten years ago. Left me with nothin' but those two rascals an' a pile o' debts. Wasn't easy afore that, neither. Elmer was an alcoholic who thought his pot o' gold could be found at the bottom of a bottle. No sir, I gotta stay on them lunkheads, gotta teach 'em discipline—an' I gotta do it all on my own."

Something the woman said flipped a switch in me. "Mrs. Bodkins—I mean, Luella—I couldn't agree with you more. Your boys definitely need discipline. In fact, all kids need it. *I* needed it, and I'm grateful to have parents who instilled it in me. But I'm here to tell you that you don't have to go it alone. I can help you if you'll allow me. I'm not talking about replacing your disciplinary methods as their parent—just a way to come alongside to help you achieve that goal for your sons."

I thought I detected a glimmer of interest in her eyes, but it could have been curiosity. "An' what way is that, Mr. Wisniewski?"

I smiled broadly. "The football way!" Luella lifted a skeptical brow; but before she could protest, I launched into the best sales pitch I'd ever made for the sport. "Ma'am, the game of football provides a proper, supervised framework in which to develop personal character, discipline, and life principles. It offers a chance for those involved to build a good work ethic through structured practice, to learn social skills through teamwork, and to develop a sense of self-worth through competition that will carry over into their adult lives. Additionally, it fosters a sense of camaraderie and belonging that will create many wonderful memories that will last a lifetime."

When I finished my persuasive speech, I felt as if I could have gone toe to toe with the best motivational speaker in the country. In high school, I'd tried my hand at debate; but when it was discovered that I couldn't argue my way out of a wet paper bag, they'd relegated me to timekeeper. That's akin to riding the bench in football. Now, however, I was not only an invaluable member of the team, but I was also the captain.

Luella pondered my words for a moment, but she didn't look convinced. "Well, I dunno. Willard's been playin' fer most of a month now, an' it's only made things worse 'round here."

"With your permission, ma'am, I'd like to talk with him. He told me he really wants to be on the team; so if I can impress upon him the importance of being disciplined in *all* areas of life, including his daily chores, I think you'll notice a big difference in a very short time. Remember, I'm here to assist you in achieving your goals for Willard."

She resigned with a sigh. "All right, I'll give 'im another chance. But this is it!" She jerked a thumb over her shoulder. "He's in the kitchen peelin' spuds. I hope ya can git through to him, 'cause *I* sure ain't been able to lately." She threw up her hands in defeat. I thanked her for the opportunity and stepped onto the porch. Luella held open the screen door as I crossed the threshold into the dingy interior of the Bodkins' home. "Oh, Mr. Wisniewski, could I trouble ya fer one more thing?"

I turned around. "Certainly, ma'am. What's that?"

She hesitated. "What about . . . what about Durnell? Do ya think *he* could be on yer team, too?"

And just like that, I went from two players down to a full team again.

The Mighty Ferrell Hogs had lived to fight another day; but given the current state of things, that wasn't saying much. After talking with Willard, who agreed to keep up with his chores in order to stay on the team, I'd gone out to the barn to have a "chat" with his brother. I use the term loosely because it was more like a one-sided conversation. Durnell was in my fourth period class, along with Knox and Danny, but he always sat in the back of the room and kept to himself. He never spoke to anyone unless spoken to and only then answered with grunts, monosyllables, or short phrases. And he always avoided eye contact. He was just as unkempt as his brother and even more of a loner—but thankfully, not as repugnant. My initial attempts to persuade him to join the team had fallen short; but when his mother, now keen to the myriad benefits of football, had graciously offered leniency with some of his kitchen chores, he had consented with a careless shrug and a casual, "Sure."

Our newest recruit turned out to be my biggest challenge yet. Durnell was completely ignorant about football and had no discipline or work ethic whatsoever. Additionally, he lacked self-esteem and any sense of self-worth. And we had just two practices to prepare him for the game against our toughest opponent to date, the Belchertown Bulldogs. On a positive note, Winston informed me before practice on Wednesday that he had finally replaced and tested the stadium lights and said to keep my fingers crossed. He also offered some suggestions for Friday night's game plan.

"It come to me as I was up on the lift fixin' the lights this mornin' that we have a home field advantage, an' I think we oughta use it."

I squinted at him. "What home field advantage? We only had a dozen fans compared to four times that many for Elliston. How's that an advantage?"

Winston shook his head. "I ain't talkin' 'bout the fans. I'm talkin' 'bout the field itself!" He crossed his arms. "Whadda we got on our field that the other schools ain't got on theirs?"

"Cows?" I joked. This was beginning to sound like my conversation with Emily.

He chuckled. "Close. Try cow *patties*! Here's how I see it. If ya step in 'em, your shoes get slippery, right? Ya lose traction an' can't cut or tackle very well. The advantage is, we know where they are, an' our opponents don't!"

I stared at him as if he'd played a decade in the NFL without a helmet. "Let me get this straight. Are you suggesting we intentionally run *around* the cow patties while getting our opponents to run *through* them?"

"Why not?" Winston shrugged. "I saw both teams slippin' all over the place durin' the Elliston game. Let's use that to our advantage."

"I'd be willing to bet you didn't learn this trick playing college ball," I retorted. He just stood there with his arms crossed. I took a deep breath. "I can't believe I'm even considering this." I finally grunted and shook my head. "You know you're crazy, don't you?"

He grinned wickedly. "Like a fox!"

The practices Wednesday and Thursday convinced me that Durnell wasn't going to be much more than a body on the field, but that's all we really needed out of him for now. I planned to work with him down the stretch to bring him up to speed with the other players, which, by the looks of things, wouldn't take too long. I talked with Emily on Friday, and she informed me that Savannah Scott and Jessie Wilkerson had agreed to be on the squad and that they even had a new cheer ready for the game that evening.

As if that weren't enough encouragement, Ezekiel Pugh stopped by my classroom again to share another word of inspiration. "'Pray without ceasing,'[6]" he told me before turning and leaving the room without further commentary. Not bad advice for the coach of a team that had been outscored by 119 points in just two games.

Jogging with my players from the school building to the stadium that evening, I noticed how brightly illuminated the field was. Having all the lights working again really livened up the place. They also made the cow patties stand out. While the players ran through their pregame

---

6 1 Thessalonians 5:17, KJV

calisthenics, I turned to look at the bleachers behind the team bench. Emily was lending a hand to her two cheerleaders as they hung a poster on the fence. It read, "Beat the Bulldogs." Behind them, people were starting to trickle into the stands.

My eyes were immediately drawn to a very hefty woman sitting on the front row. It was Hermione Piggott, who stood out in the crowd like a mighty oak amid a forest of Popsicle sticks. She was squirting some throat spray into her mouth from a small pump bottle. Evidently, she was here to provide another stirring rendition of the national anthem, the thought of which set me to rummaging through the first aid kit in search of a pair of earplugs. About halfway up in the stands, in the same spot as before, were Reverend and Mrs. Pinckney. Beside them sat two couples from church I recognized but whose names I couldn't recall. To their right and a few rows back were Mayor Wilson Piggott III and his wife, Mary, along with Jolene and Orville. To the Pinckney's left, I spotted Mr. Swanson and a woman I assumed was Danny's mother; and sitting directly behind them were Ezekiel and Mrs. Pugh. My spirits rose. It was good to see some of the parents and townspeople finally showing support for the team. However, I couldn't help but notice that as most people climbed the steps, they either moved to the far right or the far left, leaving a distinct gap in the middle of the bleachers. That struck me as odd, but I figured the center section might be reserved for the student cheer block.

The Belchertown Bulldogs were warming up at one end; and on the opposite side, their fans of about one hundred strong had gathered in the visitor bleachers. They'd hung two banners on the fence that read, "We're gonna cook your ham hocks good!" and "In your eye, Pig-Sty High!" More disrespect. But for some reason, it didn't bother me. I felt less anxious than I had at the start of the previous two games.

Glancing at my assistants, I observed Winston standing on the sideline reviewing his defensive play card and Danny sitting on the end of the bench preparing his stat sheets. I couldn't help smiling. My Friday night lights vision was finally beginning to materialize. I might not need the antacid tablets after all.

Two achievements worth noting occurred before the kickoff. First, we survived the disharmonious delivery of the national anthem; and second, we won the coin toss. Earlier that day, Winston had informed me that the weather forecast was calling for fifteen to twenty-mile-per-hour winds out of the west by game time, which meant that the Bulldogs would not only have to face a field full of slippery landmines but also a wind bearing the effluvious emissions from Avery's hog farm. We chose to defend the west end zone. After receiving their final game instructions, the players linked arms and gave the team cheer: "The few! The proud! The Mighty Ferrell Hogs!" Then they ran onto the field and lined up for battle.

At the referee's whistle, Nigel kicked off from the forty-yard line. The ball traveled all of eight yards. On the ground. It wasn't supposed to be an onside kick, but that minor detail was irrelevant since the ball hadn't traveled far enough for a legal recovery. The Bulldogs started first and ten on our own forty-eight. They would have scored an easy touchdown on that first possession had it not been for the fact that on one play, their quarterback slipped and was tackled for a loss and on another, their wide-open receiver developed a sudden coughing fit while running into the wind and the ball bounced harmlessly off his helmet.

When they settled for a field goal, I turned to Winston. "I take back what I said on Wednesday. You're a genius!"

He grinned. "What did I tell ya? Home field advantage!"

At halftime, we were only down zero to seventeen. That was real, tangible progress. Isaiah and Jeremima were blocking and tackling phenoms; and had there been a full complement of talent around them, it might have been us with the points on the board and our opponent with the goose egg. Winston and I praised the players for their competitiveness and told them to go out there, do their best, and have fun. Running back into the stadium for the start of the second half, I could hear the cheerleaders leading the thirty or so hometown fans in a new chant.

"We are *(clap clap)* the Hogs! *(clap clap)*

Let's beat *(clap clap)* the Dogs! *(clap clap)*"

We received the ball to start the third quarter. Well, we had it for a second or two; but then, we lost it. In Willie's attempt to pick up the fumbled high, end-over-end kick, he managed to kick it all the way back to the ten-yard line where he was buried under a mound of Bulldog players just as he scooped it up. When the referee cleared the pile, our opponents had the ball first and goal to go. They scored two plays later.

On our next possession, the offense actually moved the ball down the field. Zig-zagging around the landmines, Clay broke off a run of twenty-four yards before finally being brought down by the Bulldog secondary. It was the team's longest play to date, and it brought our fans to their feet. On the next play, Knox was hit as he tried to throw the ball; and it was intercepted, ending the drive. But our defense, anchored by the Pugh twins, kept our opponent from scoring; and we took over on downs.

Once again, we managed to move the ball and picked up a couple of first downs. Near the end of the third quarter, the offense was lining up to run a play when the referee suddenly blew his whistle. I stepped onto the field as he jogged to the sideline.

"What's going on?" I asked, confused by the stoppage of play.

He placed both hands flat on top of his head. "Twelve men on the field, Coach."

"*What?*" I exchanged questioning glances with Winston. "That's impossible, ref! We only have eleven players on our entire team!"

He broke into laughter and pointed toward the twenty-yard line. "Check it out for yourself."

I followed his finger. Grazing their way across the field were three ducks, a possum, and a familiar-looking billy goat. They appeared to be gobbling up small, white chunks that were scattered across the turf. I could see them from where I was standing. I summoned my team to the sideline.

"What's that white stuff they're eating?" I asked once the players had gathered around me. None of them had a clue. None but Maynard, that is. He slowly raised his hand.

"Um, Coach, I know."

"What is it?"

He looked very sheepish. "It's . . . it's bread, Coach."

"Bread?"

"Yeah. I uh . . . I lost one of my foam knee pads last night when I took my pants home for my mom to wash. I think my dog ran off with it 'cause I couldn't find it this morning. I didn't know what to do, so I cut off a hunk of my mom's sourdough bread and stuffed it in there instead. I guess pieces have been fallin' out all over the field."

Now *there's* one for the record books! After a ten-minute delay of game, the field was cleared of all unauthorized participants; and play resumed. We began to move the ball and picked up another first down.

A few plays later, I thought we were going to score our first points of the season. Knox dropped back to pass, and the O-line gave him protection just long enough to unload the ball before getting hammered. Nigel headed straight for a cow patty and cut to his right. The defender slipped and fell down, leaving Nigel wide open. To everyone's surprise, including his own, he actually caught the ball with his hands! Stunned by his success, he stopped dead in his tracks and stared incredulously at the ball. Then he turned toward our sideline and held it high over his head.

"Look, Coach," he shouted exuberantly, "I caught it! I really caught it!"

Eight Bulldogs hit him simultaneously, and he fumbled the ball. A defensive player scooped it up and rumbled seventy-five yards for a touchdown. We lost the game zero to thirty-one.

CHAPTER FOURTEEN

Ineligible

I left my apartment Saturday morning around 9:30 and walked to the barbershop on Main Street for a quick trim. This time, I found Phil Swanson, Virgil Piggott, and Magnus Yokel sitting along the wall, shooting the breeze with Rube Elkins. I'd first met Magnus six weeks earlier when I'd gone into his hardware store to buy the laces and foam for the football uniforms. I was welcomed warmly by the four men.

"Good to see you again, Mr. Wisniewski!" Rube smiled as I sat down in the empty chair. He placed the cape around my shoulders and fastened the collar. "What'll it be today? Just a trim, same as before?"

"Yes, if you please."

He grabbed the tools of his trade and began clipping away. "So, I hear your football team played a really good game last night," he commented casually.

I don't know what news source he got his information from, but that was kind of like saying General Custer put on a really good show at the Battle of Little Big Horn.

"Well, the kids are beginning to make some progress, I'll give you that," I acknowledged honestly.

Phil Swanson spoke up from the sidelines. "I think they've improved quite a bit, Mr. Wisniewski. Danny shared some of last night's statistics with me, and they were much better than those from the first two games."

I nodded vigorously, forgetting for a moment that there was a pair of razor-sharp scissors not an inch from my right ear. "Absolutely! These players have shown wonderful resolve and resilience. Take those Pugh twins, for example. What potential! For a couple of rookies, they had

131

an incredible game. What was it, something like . . . eighteen tackles, three quarterback sacks, and two forced fumbles between them? And that Knox. He threw some great passes, too!"

Out of the corner of my eye, I saw Virgil bristle at the mention of his estranged nephew. "Don't forget that long run Clay had in the third quarter, Wisniewski," he huffed. "He single-handedly faked out the entire Bulldog defense!"

I quickly agreed with the slighted parent. "Right! That was a thing of beauty, wasn't it? I'm sure there will be plenty more like it in the weeks to come." I carefully shot a sideways glance in his direction not wishing to become another Malchus at the hands of a sword-wielding Simon Peter. "Were you at the game, Mr. Piggott? I didn't see you in the stands."

"Of course, I was there," he replied, sounding somewhat offended. "I came to support my boy. And the team, obviously. You probably didn't see me because I was, er . . . ah . . . sitting on the other side of the field."

Those who fail to learn from their mistakes are bound to repeat them. "Why weren't you sitting on *our* side?" I inquired.

An awkward hush settled over the room. Phil and Magnus exchanged knowing looks.

"You want your neck shaved?" Rube asked in a strained, high-pitched voice. I'm sure he noticed how red it was.

"Yes, please." I began counting the tiles on the ceiling.

Virgil tossed his magazine onto the table. "Since you asked, Mr. Wisniewski, I'll tell you precisely why." He uncrossed his legs and leaned forward. "I wasn't sitting on our side because that's where my brother was sitting! I don't know if you're aware of this, but he and I aren't exactly on what you might call speaking terms."

Like a fool, I continued to rush in where angels fear to tread. "Neither were Knox and Clay, but now they're on the same team." You couldn't have cut the tension with a chainsaw.

"You're a newcomer to Piggottsville, Wisniewski," Virgil rather sharply pointed out. "Maybe after you've been here a while, you'll come to understand the way things are around here."

Man, I sure could have told *him* a thing or two! But providentially, my common sense had returned from its brief hiatus.

Every bit the diplomat, Phil Swanson changed the subject. "Coach, how are those feed sacks working out for you?"

"Oh, they're holding up okay," I replied, grateful for the lifeline tossed my way. "We may need some more straw in a few weeks, but they'll do. What we really need is a tackling sled. Then we could get down to some serious blocking drills."

"Tackling sled, huh?" Phil rubbed his chin thoughtfully. "I don't suppose a plow would work, would it? I've got an old International chisel plow with six shanks sitting out in the weeds behind the store. It's been there nigh onto three years. I could stand it on end and make some modifications, so those feed sacks can be attached to the shanks. It's even got wheels, so you could roll it on and off the field."

"That sounds terrific, Mr. Swanson! Thanks. How long before we can use it?"

"Oh, I'd say . . . a week to ten days. In time for the last three or four weeks of practice, anyway." He smiled. "Just call it my contribution to the war effort!"

Magnus Yokel jumped into the conversation. "While we're on the subject of football, did those laces and foam pieces you bought from me at the start of the season do the trick?"

"Yes, and they're holding up quite nicely, thank you. We haven't had to replace a single one yet." I suddenly remembered Maynard's lost pad. "Until last night, that is." For the next five minutes, I regaled the men with the tale of the sourdough bread and the reason for the delay of game. I left the barbershop relieved to have restored the men's conviviality, Virgil's included. As I passed by the front window, I read the sign again. "A Close Shave." It certainly had been!

Mr. Herold always posted his weekly teacher updates every Sunday evening at precisely six o'clock, so one of the last things I did before going to bed at the end of each Lord's Day was check my email. That way, the gist of his discourse would be fresh in my mind for the coming school week. Frequently, he attached messages for individual teachers to his group texts. That night, he sent me a personal note asking me to come by his office sometime during the morning to discuss "a matter of some importance and urgency." I had no clue what he wanted to see me about; but by now, I'd learned that he often resorted to exaggeration in his communiques, so I didn't lose any sleep over it.

My U.S. History classes were beginning a section on America's involvement in the First World War, having plowed through the Reconstruction Era, the Gilded Age, and the Progressive Era the previous week. Since I intended to show a World War I documentary on the classroom TV Monday morning, I had a teacher's aid fill in for me during third period, so I could meet with Mr. Herold regarding his urgent business. Between classes, I made my way down the stairs toward the main office, fighting through the sea of students navigating between their lockers and classrooms. As I approached the office door, I saw Mr. Herold heading toward me and heard three students address him as they passed in the hall.

"Good morning, Mr. Harold!" they said in sing-songy unison.

The principal spun on his heels. "That's *Herold!*" he admonished them sternly. "H-E-R-O-L-D. Herold. Get it straight, young people!" He turned and saw me standing there. "Disrespect!" he muttered, his face full of frustration and heat. "Blatant disrespect! We *must* maintain proper decorum, or our ship will begin to flounder. Don't you agree, Mr. Wisniewski?"

I agreed. I mean, what else could I do? I followed him into the office and stopped at the counter. The principal continued marching across the room and disappeared into his inner chamber, closing the door behind him.

Claudine Cooper glanced up from the stack of papers she was collating on the desk next to the copier. "I'll be with you in a jiffy," she called out.

I took a seat against the wall. A minute later, she approached the counter. "Good morning, Mr. Wisniewski. How are you?"

"Fine, thank you. Mr. Herold asked me to come by his office this morning." I glanced at the closed door. "I guess I don't need to ask if he's in."

The secretary laughed politely. "He's in, all right. In one of his moods, that is. Something must have happened to upset him."

I told her about the verbal exchange I'd just witnessed.

She chuckled. "So that's it." She glanced back at the closed door and then leaned forward and spoke in hushed tones. "Whenever the kids call him by name, he's convinced they're using his *first* name instead of his surname; and he's probably right. They both sound the same. It's become a running joke to some of the students, especially since there's no way to prove they're being disrespectful."

I noticed the twinkle in her eyes and let slip a grin. Piggottsville-Stuyvesant High School was governed by an insecure headmaster, who was also a self-doubting disciplinarian. We had a paranoid principal on our hands.

"Enter!" Mr. Herold bellowed in response to my knock. I turned the handle and opened the door.

"You wanted to see me, sir?" I asked, peering into his office.

He waved me inside. "Yes, I do. Please close the door and have a seat." I complied and sat down in the ugly orange chair facing the massive mahogany desk. The principal leaned back in his black leather throne and folded his hands across his stomach. "I understand that you had a new addition to the football team this past week who participated in Friday's game. Is that correct?"

"Yes, we had a player leave the team—two players, actually—but we were able to convince one of them to come back, along with his brother, Durnell Bodkins. Are you referring to him?"

"I am. And therein lies the problem. For your information, Mr. Wisniewski, Durnell Bodkins is not qualified to participate in extracurricular activities. According to state high school regulations, in order to be eligible, a player must maintain passing grades in a minimum of five courses each grading period."

"I'm aware of that, Mr. Herold. I acquainted myself with those regulations before the season began. But the first grading period isn't over yet. I don't see how he can be deemed ineligible until then. I can't speak to his other subjects, but he's on track to pass history. Not by much, I'll grant you. He's a very disengaged pupil with very little motivation or self-esteem, but I believe the discipline he develops through football will transfer into the classroom."

"Be that as it may, Mr. Wisniewski, the fact is that Mr. Bodkins failed to maintain passing grades in five subjects last year, which means that until he does for one grading period *this* year, he is ineligible to play sports."

I pleaded my case. "I can appreciate your position, Mr. Herold; but since there are only two weeks left in this first grading period, couldn't we postpone that decision until then? I can ill afford to lose him for those two weeks. We won't have enough players to field a team."

Mr. Herold did not like to be challenged. But then, I did not like to lose players, either. He placed his palms flat on the desk. "We simply cannot bend the rules, Mr. Wisniewski. The state regulations are crystal clear, and we must follow them to the letter. Perhaps you can recruit another student to replace Mr. Bodkins, at least until his grades are official. However, I wouldn't hold your breath. He appears to be on the same track as last year. Besides, if you found *him*, surely you can find someone else."

I continued my oral arguments. "Coach Banks and I have tried everything we can think of to get more students to join the team." I didn't go into detail, for obvious reasons. "There just isn't any more interest among the student body."

"I am not unsympathetic to your plight, Mr. Wisniewski, and I do wish to assist you in any way possible." He paused and pursed his lips. "I'll tell you what. Tomorrow, I will make an announcement that you are in need of at least one more player. That will surely make an impact. After all, I do have significant influence among the student body."

I stared at the nameplate on his desk and fought hard to keep a straight face.

As frustrated as a mosquito on a rhinoceros, I left Mr. Herold's office and headed down the hall to the cafeteria. I went through the line, made my selections, and found a corner table in the teachers' annex. I wasn't up to engaging in idle conversation with so much weighing on my mind. After praying over my food, I began to eat what felt like the last meal of a prisoner on death row. I was in the middle of my pity party when Emily pulled out the chair across the table from me and sat down. I quickly buried my feelings and put on a mask. "Hello, Miss Davenport."

"Hello yourself, Mr. Wisniewski!" She was more than her usual cheerful self today. "I've got some good news for you. I was able to persuade another girl to join the cheer squad this morning. Isn't that awesome?" she gushed, looking all happy and excited about it. "Now we've got enough for a proper pyramid!"

I tried my best to mirror her enthusiasm. "That's great. I'm really happy for you." I must not have been very convincing.

Her smile faded. She cocked her head and studied me. "But what? Something's bothering you; I can tell."

I can't fully explain it, nor do I claim to understand it; but intuition has got to be the true sixth sense in this world—and apparently, only women have it. "I'm glad you found a third cheerleader; honest, I am," I insisted, trying to sound more upbeat. "It's just that they may not get a chance to cheer for another two weeks, if not longer."

She offered a compassionate look. "Did you lose another player?" she asked gently.

"Well, yes, but I don't want to burden you with my troubles," I replied honestly. Then I tried to deflect her by injecting humor into the conversation. "Besides, I see no reason to ruin *both* our lunches, do you?"

"Mr. Wisniewski, have you forgotten the biblical admonition that we are to 'bear one another's burdens'⁷?" Emily crossed her arms and frowned at me; but that quickly morphed into a sly grin, which completely ruined my party.

"'And so fulfill the law of Christ'?" I responded, returning her grin.

She quirked her eyebrows. "Why, Mr. Wisniewski, what a firm grasp of Scripture you have. I'm quite impressed!" Then I caught the gleam in her eyes. "I'd be even more impressed if you had that same grip on Reverend Pinckney's sermon topics!"

I don't know the technical name for the deepest possible shade of red, but I'm pretty sure my face was covered with it. Her familial ties to Elvira Primrose were obvious. Nevertheless, it was her empathy, coupled with her laughter, that reminded me how truly blessed I was to have her as a friend and confidante. I surrendered with a sigh. "All right, I'll share my burdens with you—since you asked!" I laid out the details of my dilemma and how frustrated I was. She commiserated with me for a while, even telling me she would pray for a resolution. Then she smiled warmly.

"I hesitated to share this with you, but I think it might be of some encouragement. Last Friday, I spoke with Mr. Masters about the possibility of having some of his music students play their instruments at our home games, and he said he'd ask around today. Wouldn't it be great if we had a pep band show up for our home games?"

I forced a crooked smile. "It would also be great if we had a *team* show up for our home games."

---

7 Galatians 6:2

She waggled her index finger at me. "Aha! I see you haven't lost your sense of humor, Mr. Wisniewski. That's a very good sign!"

The longer I was around Emily Davenport, the brighter things seemed to become. She had a way of chasing away any lingering clouds with her cheerful disposition and glass-half-full outlook, which only made my Eeyore-ish world view all the more ridiculous and petty by comparison.

"I'm sorry I rained on your parade," I apologized. "When you told me the good news, I should have rejoiced with you. Who did you get as your third cheerleader?"

"Lexi Rae Brannigan!"

"Lexi Rae? Isn't she kind of stuck on herself? In fifth period, the other kids refer to her as 'Lexi Rae Brag Again' because she thinks she's better than everyone else."

She grinned. "No comment on that, Mr. Wisniewski, but I *will* tell you that she only agreed to be on the squad so long as she could be the captain. And the top of the pyramid!" We shared a laugh.

When I left the lunchroom, vestiges of Emily's upbeat spirit were still clinging to me. I needed her edification because I had a rather difficult afternoon. I'd been given the unpleasant task of telling Durnell that he would not be able to play football until his grades improved. I assured him the decision hadn't been my call and urged him to give due diligence to his schoolwork over the next two weeks, so he could rejoin the team at that time. "I'm awfully sorry about this, Durnell; really I am."

For the very first time, he looked me in the face. "So 'm I," he replied softly.

I broke the news to the rest of the team at the beginning of practice and told them we would push on in hopes of finding a replacement for Durnell before Friday. When I finished, I asked if they had any questions or comments.

Isaiah spoke up. "Coach, remember what you said in class about taking pride in ourselves and our school and not worrying about what others think or say?"

I nodded. "Yes, I remember. I said you should embrace the ridicule and have some fun with it."

His eyes lit up. "We've been thinking about that all week, Coach." He looked around at his teammates. "We know we're the Mighty Ferrell Hogs and not Pig-Sty High; but as long as the other schools are going to make fun of us, we might as well make fun of ourselves. Just to show them they can't get us down by putting us down!" The other players voiced their agreement. "So, we talked it over, and we decided to lighten things up a bit."

I'd only been teaching in an official capacity going on six weeks, but it's amazing how quickly you pick up on things when you're around teenagers all the time. "What exactly do you have in mind?" I asked, ready to nix any foolhardy or inappropriate notions.

"We came up with some nicknames we want to use from now on," he announced. "You know, to make things more fun around here."

I turned to Winston. "What do you say, Coach? Think we ought to give them a listen?"

He grinned. "Why not? I'd like to hear it. Might be good for a few laughs."

"All right." I turned back to the team. "You have the floor, Isaiah."

The hulking young man pulled a folded piece of paper from his helmet and handed it to me. "Here's the names we picked for ourselves. And we're hoping you'll let us use the names we chose for you and Coach Banks."

I took the paper and unfolded it. With Winston looking over my shoulder, I read the list. I must say, the names showed creativity and humor:

Isaiah Pugh:	Porky—as in Porky Pig
Jeremima Pugh:	Petunia—as in Petunia Pig
Knox Piggott:	Goldie—for his long blond hair, short for Goldi-Knox
Clay Piggott:	Pigeon—he likes to trap shoot using clay pigeons
Maynard McCoy:	McNerd—no explanation necessary
Jackson Pressley:	J.P.—ditto
Willie Skaggs:	Billy Bob—short for William Robert
Henry Panke:	Hanky—short for Hanky Panky
Willard Bodkins:	Skunk—what else?
Durnell Bodkins:	Leonardo—as in da Vinci

Nigel Oglethorpe:	Bender—he keeps "bending" his kicks around goalposts instead of through them.
Coach Wisniewski:	Coach Wiz
Coach Banks:	Coach Bang

I looked up from the sheet. "Where did you guys come up with these names, anyway? *Petunia?* I seem to recall you threatening to whup the fire out of Willie for calling you that in class."

Jeremima dismissed it with a laugh and a wave of her huge paw. "It's okay, Coach. I decided to have fun with it instead. Besides, I like it a lot better than 'Big Red.'"

I read down the list. "These are good, real good. But this one for Durnell, this. . . . 'Leonardo.' What's *that* all about?"

It was Knox who replied. "Uh, Coach, you probably ought to ask *him* about that. He chose that name for himself."

"What do you say, Coach?" Jackson insisted. "Will you call us by our nicknames?"

"Well, I suppose so," I replied hesitantly. "It might be a little confusing if I keep calling you by your last names, since I've now got two Pughs, two Piggotts, and two Bodkins on my team." The kids laughed.

"Can we call you and Coach Banks by those nicknames, too?" Nigel wondered, pointing to the list. "I know they're a bit bonkers, maybe even cheeky; but we thought they'd be great fun."

I held up the paper and looked at Winston. "Are you down with this?"

He shrugged nonchalantly. "Sure, I'm down. It's like Bender said, might be great fun."

"Okay," I agreed with a chuckle, "but we keep these to ourselves—and only when you're in uniform. No nicknames in school. There I'm still Mr. Wisniewski, and he's Mr. Banks. Got it?"

"Got it," the players answered as a team.

I blew my whistle and pointed to the field. "All right, then, you pork chops! Let's get out there on that field and have some more great fun!"

We had the best practice of the season that afternoon.

CHAPTER FIFTEEN
The Letter of the Law

Tuesday after lunch, I walked down to the first floor music room at the far end of the building. Munro Masters, the music teacher and band director, was sitting in his tiny office adjacent to the large band room sorting sheet music. I rapped lightly on the open door.

Munro glanced up from the scores on his desk. "Oh, hi, Wisniewski," he called out. "I suppose you're here about the pep band."

"Yes, can you spare a few minutes?"

"Sure." He motioned to a chair against the wall. "Miss Davenport said she planned on talking to you about it."

"She mentioned it at lunch." I sat down and surveyed the tornadic mess on his desk. "So, how do things look?"

He pushed his glasses back onto the bridge of his nose with an index finger. "Look? Not too good, I'm afraid. I asked for volunteers in all my periods; but the only commitments I got were a trumpet, a tenor sax, a clarinet, and a bass drum."

"Well, that's a start, anyway. Are they any good?"

He stared at me like I was a few quarter notes short of a measure. "'Good' is a relative term, Wisniewski. Two of them are first-year music students if that tells you anything. The other two are a little better, but good? I wouldn't go that far. They try hard, though. They don't keep good time, and they don't stay in tune. But they're loud; I'll give you that."

I pictured them in the stands Friday night for the start of the game. "Do any of them know how to play 'The Star-Spangled Banner'?" I asked, hoping against hope that we had found a "cover band" for Hermione.

"I don't think so, but I could have them practice that . . . if I can find the sheet music." He gave a nervous little chuckle and shook his head. "I wouldn't expect too much. They'll do their best—I can promise you that. Only, their best may not be good enough."

"Have you seen my football team?" I laughed, sensing a common denominator. "Mr. Masters, I'd be happy if they just showed up and made some noise. Anything to let us know they're there."

"Oh, you'll know they're there, all right! In any event, I'll keep you posted on their progress this week."

I thanked him for his cooperation and left for my fourth period class. We'd come a long way since the start of school. First a team, then a cheer squad, now a pep band. What more did we need? How about a football player?

I was clearing off my desk at the end of the day and was about to head to the coaching office when I glanced up and saw Ezekiel Pugh standing in the doorway. I waved to him. "Ezekiel, come in! Nice of you to drop by. I didn't expect you until Friday."

The lanky farmer ambled across the room and stopped in front of my desk. "I sensed the good Lord prompting me to come by today," he declared, towering over me. "The children told me your team is without a player again, and I thought you might need some encouragement now rather than later."

I smiled up at him. "I really appreciate that, Ezekiel. I'll admit to being frustrated and discouraged of late, but I'm at a loss as to what I can do at this point."

"Have you been around farming much?" The question came out of left field.

"I can't say that I have. There were corn and soybean fields scattered across the county where I grew up, but I spent my youth in suburbia."

"One thing all farmers agree on is that they have no control over the weather. Since the amount of rainfall determines the yield at harvest, all a farmer can do is cultivate and plant his fields and then pray for the right amount of rain." A faint smile manifested itself on his usually stoic face; and for the first time, he called me by my given name. "Jason, prepare your field. Keep on practicing just like you are doing, and let the Almighty supply what is lacking, which, in this case, is a player. He will provide in His good time."

I was humbled once again. I stared at my desk, unable to look him in the eye. "Ezekiel, I've tried to follow the advice you gave me to 'pray without ceasing,'[8] but I'm afraid my faith has been sorely tested this week."

"That is to be expected." Compassion tinged his voice. "Testing forces us to become more dependent on the Creator, but it also makes us stronger. The apostle James said, 'The trying of your faith worketh patience,'[9] and patience produces a maturity through which all our needs are supplied."

I stood up and extended my right hand. "Thank you for sharing that verse with me this week. I will definitely take it to heart."

Ezekiel grasped my hand firmly. "Oh, that was just a bonus," he explained. "The word I wanted to leave with you this week is found in Proverbs chapter seventeen and verse twenty-two: 'A merry heart doeth good, like a medicine.'"

I laughed out loud. "That's exactly what I've been trying to impress on my students and players lately! But I'm curious. Why did you select that particular verse this time?"

I hadn't seen Ezekiel Pugh grin before, but his leathery face broke into countless tiny wrinkles. "Suffice it to say, the idea came to me last night . . . when Porky and Petunia got home from practice!"

Ezekiel's words rang like a clarion bell in my head for the next two days; and as a result, I focused on preparing my field while having fun doing it. A new lightness hovered over practice and classroom alike; and spirits, in general, seemed to be running higher. There was even an air of expectancy throughout the school as if Rip Van Winkle had yawned and stretched for the first time in twenty years. But he wasn't awake yet. Since Mr. Herold's announcement had not produced its intended results, I was still down one player, and I dreaded informing the team that we would have to forfeit Friday's game. My latest goal was to finish the entire eight-game season, and we had been on track to accomplish that. But now I was faced with modifying my expectation yet again.

---

8 1 Thessalonians 5:17, KJV

9 James 1:3, KJV

Thursday night, I lay sprawled on the sofa with a bowl of cheese puffs in my hand, waiting for the 10:00 news. My mind flashed back to the meeting in which I learned of Durnell's ineligibility. The principal had been adamant that there was no way around the rules, which were, as he'd emphatically reminded me, so crystal clear that "we must follow them to the letter." *To the letter.*

Something about that phrase forced me off the sofa and into the kitchenette. I sat down at the table and flipped open my laptop. Scrolling through my saved files, I came upon the state requirements for high school athletic eligibility and clicked it open. I carefully read through the document just as I'd done a dozen times before. Mr. Herold was correct in saying that the wording was crystal clear—so clear, in fact, that in my attempts to understand the spirit of the law, I'd passed over a single word that, if read in the *letter* of the law, might provide us with the answer we were looking for.

Sleep did not come easily that night—not so much from anxiety but from excitement. I was at school early the next morning, printing out a copy of the precious paragraph containing the evidence which would hopefully overturn the court's previous ruling. As soon as Mr. Herold entered the building, I followed him into his office without troubling his secretary for an appointment.

"What is it, Mr. Wisniewski?" he asked, bypassing the most perfunctory of greetings. He placed his burgundy briefcase on the credenza.

"I believe I may have found a way to keep Durnell Bodkins on the team, sir!" I jubilated.

The principal shot me a disparaging look before opening the window blinds. "Mr. Wisniewski, I'm a very busy man," he declared, glancing at the wall clock, "and I have an appointment in ten minutes. Besides, I thought we'd settled that issue on Monday. There's nothing more that can be done about it."

"With all due respect, Mr. Herold, I believe there is. I've found what you might call a 'loophole' in the state's regulations." I waved the evidence in my hand. "I have a copy right here that I'd like to show you."

"I am quite familiar with that document, thank you," he huffed. "I fail to see the need to review it again." He plopped down into his executive chair and powered up his computer. "I made the announcement for Mr. Bodkins' replacement on Tuesday; and if nothing has come of that, then we have no recourse but to call off tonight's game. I'm as disappointed about that as you are, but it cannot be helped. I'll call the principal at Montgomery North High School and inform him of the cancellation."

"But, sir," I pleaded, "I don't think we need to do that! Please, before you make the call, just indulge me for two minutes. If you still disagree, I'll drop the matter completely."

Mr. Herold sighed impatiently. "Oh, very well. But make it brief."

I handed him the copy, which he quickly scanned. I pointed to a highlighted sentence. "The regulation states that those academic requirements must be met 'in a grading period in which the student would *otherwise* be eligible to participate in the sport.'"

He glanced up from the paper in his hand. "And what is your point?"

I delivered my closing argument. "My point is, Mr. Herold, Durnell Bodkins was not otherwise eligible to play football last year because there *was* no team! He wouldn't have been able to play, even if his grades *were* good enough. Since there has been no team for the past five years, this is the first qualifying grading period that can legally be used to evaluate his eligibility. And *that* cannot be determined for another two weeks!" I rested my case.

The principal scowled, then closed his eyes and leaned back in his chair. He twiddled his thumbs and breathed so deeply that his nose whistled. "Mr. Wisniewski, your interpretation of the rules is what some might call splitting hairs."

"I prefer to call it following the letter of the law, sir," I parried.

I could only imagine what was going on in that steel trap of his. The hard truth was, one of his subordinates had refused to accept his edict, had challenged his authority, and had questioned his judgment. I grew aware of the faint ticking of the wall clock as I awaited his decision.

Mr. Herold's eyes abruptly popped open, parting his brows like two boxers disengaging from a clinch. He sat up straight. "On the other hand, it *does* follow the exact wording of the regulation—technically speaking, of course. So, by interpreting it that way, if our football team is allowed to remain intact . . ." He paused thoughtfully before making the call. "I say, let's *go* with it!" He resolutely thumped a fist on the desk and bellowed, "Go, Mighty Ferrell Hogs!" so loudly that a startled Claudine Cooper came flying into the office to see what I'd done to upset her boss.

When I walked out of Mr. Herold's courtroom, I felt like Perry Mason after winning a difficult case. If only my debate team could see me now.

At the end of fourth period, I asked Durnell to hang back for a few minutes. Once the other students had cleared the room, I informed him of Mr. Herold's decision. He responded with a monosyllabic "Good," but I thought I detected a hint of a smile. I was about to dismiss him when I remembered something I'd been meaning to ask.

"Durnell, the other day, when your teammates requested permission to use their nicknames, they said you chose Leonardo. Is that what you want to be called?" He nodded. "That's fine by me, but I'm just curious. Why did you choose that particular name?"

The quiet youth shuffled his feet. "I like ta paint things," he mumbled, staring at the floor.

"You mean, like the artist Leonardo da Vinci?" He nodded again. "Really? That's great, Durnell! I'm pleased you have a passion for something. Are you taking an art class this semester?"

"Yeah."

"Super! Then let me encourage you to keep pursuing that interest. And take every opportunity you can find to develop your painting talent, okay?"

He shot me a quick glance. "Okay, I will."

I dismissed him before he wore himself out talking.

That evening, with Durnell reinstated to the team, we traveled west to play the Montgomery North Tigers, the smaller of two county schools about an hour from Piggottsville. During the trip, Winston had to pull over twice because the rusty, old bus kept overheating; and as a result, we almost missed the start of the game. Emily and her three cheerleaders followed us in her car; and even though no Piggottsville fans showed up, the squad did their routines anyway in front of empty bleachers. I was grateful for their show of support. However, the team had to take the field without the benefit of warming up, and it showed from the opening kickoff. The Tigers scored easy touchdowns on their first two possessions.

Early in the second quarter with frustrations running high, Knox and Clay fumbled an exchange, which the Tigers recovered. The cousins got into a shouting and shoving match which resulted in an unsportsmanlike conduct penalty against the Hogs. The referee was going to eject both players; but when I explained that we had no substitutes, he conferred with the other referees and the Montgomery North coaches. They agreed to let the boys remain in the game, so long as it didn't happen again. Winston and I were able to calm down the cousins, and play resumed.

Right before halftime, we had a rare chance to score. Playing side by side, Isaiah and Jeremima opened up a gaping hole that even Henry couldn't miss this time. He darted through and headed downfield behind a blocker. But suddenly, he slowed and stopped. Winston and I watched in stupefied wonder as he pulled out the huge handkerchief he kept tucked in his football pants and blew his nose loudly enough for me to hear all the way from the sideline. Before he could put it away, he was tackled and dropped the ball. Fortunately, Willard, who was supposed to be on the other side of the field, happened to be loitering in the neighborhood and fell on the ball. The drive stalled, however, and Nigel got his first crack at a field goal. He missed the right goal post by at least twenty yards.

In the second half, the Tigers scored another touchdown and added two field goals while holding the Hogs scoreless; and the game concluded with us on the short end of a score of zero to twenty-seven.

On the long bus ride home, Winston and I praised the players for their good effort. They'd been competitive the entire game; they'd forced the Tigers into two field goals instead of the usual touchdowns; and they'd put themselves in a position to score for the second game in a row. I think we all went home that night feeling a little better about ourselves. We hadn't just shown up as a complete team; we'd come to play.

Late Saturday morning, I left my apartment around 11:30 and hotfooted it down to the bank before it closed at noon to deposit a check from my parents. After completing the transaction, I was heading across the lobby when I heard someone call my name.

"Mr. Wisniewski!" Orville beckoned me from inside his office. I stepped through the open door and saw that he had company. It was his rotund father, Mayor Wilson Piggott III.

"Do come in and sit a spell," the bank president suggested graciously. I acknowledged the two town leaders and complied.

The mayor held up a copy of *The Piggottsville Daily Scoop.* "The paper had some very nice things to say about the game," he began.

"Is that so? I'm afraid I haven't gotten around to subscribing yet," I confessed. "What does it say?"

He made a great show of shaking the folds out of the tiny, four-page newspaper before reading from it. "'Piggottsville-Stuyvesant High School enjoyed its third consecutive football game of the season when it tackled Belchertown on Friday night. Relying heavily on the accurate throwing arm of Knox Piggott, the star quarterback, and the powerful legs of Clay Piggott, the star fullback, the Mighty Ferrell Hogs put up another valiant effort against the Bulldogs but came up just shy of a victory in the hotly-contested battle, which was attended by a plethora of Piggottsville fans.'"

Orville interjected like an embarrassed child. "Da-ad, that was last Friday's game. The coach thought you were talking about last *night's* game!"

"I know that," his father retorted defensively, "but last night's game won't be in the paper until *next* Friday."

"I'm afraid I don't understand." I pointed to the paper in the mayor's hand. "When did that edition come out?"

"Yesterday," he replied, as if I should have known.

"Yesterday? Why would the paper wait a whole week to print a write-up on a seven-day-old game?"

It was Orville who tried clearing up my confusion. "That's because it's only published once a week. It comes out every Friday morning without fail."

"Then why is the paper called *The Daily Scoop?*" I couldn't seem to leave well enough alone.

"It used to be a daily newspaper back in my granddaddy's day," Mayor Piggott clarified. "But it became unprofitable to print it every day, so he scaled it back to three times a week. And with the advent of the internet and the proliferation of cellphones, the circulation dropped off significantly. So about ten years ago, I decided to . . . er, ah . . . the *publisher* decided to make it a weekly. Kept the name, though, to honor the paper's history."

That explained a lot of things. I altered the course of our conversation. "Well, anyway, I appreciate the exposure given to the team. I view the football program as more than just a school function, and I'm thrilled about the growing interest in the community as a whole."

"Oh, you'll find this community backs you 100 percent!" Mayor Piggott stated emphatically. I'd heard *that* before. "Of course, it wouldn't hurt if you won a game sometime soon." He must have picked up on his son's frown. "But you have the town's full support, no matter what!" he quickly added.

"Speaking of support, I've been meaning to ask about the concession at the stadium. If that were opened up, I think it would bring in more of a crowd. There were over thirty people in the stands last week, and I expect even more next Friday. If you include the visiting fans, that's well over a hundred people in attendance. Think of the profits the concession might generate from a crowd that size!" I could see the wheels of commerce beginning to turn.

"Not a bad idea," Orville concurred. He turned to his father. "Do you think we'd have the votes if we brought that up at Monday's council meeting?"

The mayor grunted. "We might, if you can convince that brother of yours that it was *his* idea."

"Da-ad!" There it was again. Was there *nothing* in this town unaffected by this petty feud?

CHAPTER SIXTEEN
GETTING TO KNOW YOU

On my short walk to the little white church at the other end of E Street, I noticed that the large shade trees had already begun changing into their colorful fall clothing. Once in the foyer, I looked around for Emily. I was bound and determined to sit next to her today, Elvira Primrose notwithstanding. I spied them off to one side conversing with Nancy Pinckney and Jolene Piggott, so I bade my time. A moment later, the mayor and his wife made their entrance; and after working the small crowd like the politician he was, Wilson Piggott III marched into the sanctuary. As the rest of the congregants followed him in, I made my move and positioned myself so that when Elvira and Emily stepped into a pew, I was right behind them.

After taking her seat, Emily noticed me standing in the aisle and motioned for me to join her. "Jason, would you like to sit with us?" She didn't have to ask twice.

My pulse quickened as I sat down next to her. "Good morning, Miss Daven... I mean, Emily." I leaned forward to acknowledge the elderly woman sitting on her other side. "And a good morning to you, too, Miss Primrose."

"It *was*," Elvira responded under her breath.

"Auntie El!" Emily scolded her relative. Then she whispered in my ear, "I'm so sorry, Jason. She didn't really mean that."

Elvira addressed the church bulletin in her hands. "I know you think there's something wrong with my mind, dearie, but there's nothing wrong with my hearing!"

Emily and I laughed with our eyes. "I'm still getting used to calling you Emily," I confessed, diverting the conversation. "I guess that comes from seeing you in school more frequently than anywhere else."

She contemplated my explanation for a moment. "Well, then, what do you suppose we should do about that?"

My heart skipped a beat. Was that another invitation? Before I could think of a reply that wouldn't scar me for life, the service began. It was never my intention to minimize the details of the services; but the plain truth is that as wonderful and engaging as the minister's sermons were, they often went on for quite some time. It's been said that the Bible is an inexhaustible book, and I believe the Reverend Norbert Pinckney took that literally. The apostle John closed his gospel by referencing Jesus' many works, stating, "Were every one of them to be written, I suppose that the world itself could not contain the books that would be written."[10] The same could be said for Reverend Pinckney's sermons.

At the conclusion of the service, Jolene Piggott tapped me on the shoulder as we were leaving the sanctuary. "Mr. Wisniewski, my husband tells me you want to reopen the concession stand at the high school, and I think that's a wonderful idea! I know it may be premature, but I would be happy to volunteer with that undertaking. As you may know, I am head of the Women's Missionary League here at the church, and we frequently hold bake sales for a number of charities. I'm certain I could recruit a few ladies who would be more than willing to work in the concession on game nights."

"That would be most appreciated," I replied, greatly encouraged by her offer. I turned to Orville. "I guess your father was right when he said the community supports us."

He smiled at the compliment. "Oh, I meant to ask you, what brought you into the bank yesterday?" He winked and elbowed me in the side. "Deposit or withdrawal?"

"Orville!" Jolene grabbed his arm in a mild rebuke.

"What? I was just curious, that's all." He placed an arm around my shoulders and laughed awkwardly. "Deposit, I hope."

"Have no fear, it was a deposit." I returned his laugh to assure him I'd taken no offense. "My parents sent me a check for my birthday."

"How nice of them," he replied. "Was it your birthday yesterday? If I had known that, I would have given you a birthday greeting right then. And a lollipop!" He sure was in a jolly mood.

"Actually, *today* is my birthday," I corrected him.

---

10 John 21:25

"Well, then, happy birthday, Mr. Wisniewski!" He gave me a slap on the back so hard that had I been given a choice, I would have picked the Heimlich maneuver instead.

"Thanks!" I spat out the word as if it had been a grape lodged in my windpipe.

A soft hand touched my arm. "I didn't know it was your birthday today," Emily chimed in. "Happy birthday, Jason!"

"Thanks!" This time, the word came out almost normal.

Orville was on a roll. "Since we're on the subject of banks and deposits, do you know what kind of banks vampires use?" Before I could answer, he blurted out, "Blood banks, of course. But they only make withdrawals!" He guffawed and slapped his knee.

"Orville!" Jolene scolded him again. She apologized for her husband's behavior before steering him out the door. If only I could have been a fly on the wall of the Piggott household when they got home . . .

"Why didn't you tell me it was your birthday?" Emily rebuked me.

"Because I'm not the kind of person who makes a big fuss over birthdays anymore." I grinned at her. "Or haven't you noticed that I'm all grown up now?"

"Now, that's just plain silly!" she admonished me. "Not making a big fuss over your birthday, I mean. Of *course* you need to celebrate it. What are you doing this afternoon?"

"This afternoon? Well, um . . . not much, really."

"Then why don't you let me take you to the Treat-N-Eat for a banana split or whatever else you like. We can't let your birthday go to waste."

She didn't have to ask twice. I glanced at Elvira, who was standing quietly next to her great niece pretending to be disinterested in our conversation. But I knew she was listening. I just wondered how long it would take for the news of our "date" to make the rounds before returning to me. When it comes to gossip, small towns are like boomerangs.

"Miss Primrose," I heard myself say, "would you care to join us for some ice cream this afternoon? You're quite welcome to celebrate my birthday with us. In fact, I would count it an honor."

The prickly octogenarian's eyes widened at my invitation. I was rather surprised myself that I had asked her to join us. Then again, I was quite adept at speaking before thinking.

"Thank you for asking," she replied in a civil tone, "but I usually don't approve of such indulgences. Besides, I'm trying to keep my weight down." I observed the diminutive, one-hundred-pound woman and wisely said nothing.

"Auntie El, Jason is just trying to be polite," Emily gently scolded her great aunt. "Surely, one ice cream sandwich won't hurt."

"No, you two go on without me," Elvira insisted. "I don't want to be a fifth wheel."

I think she meant *third* wheel, but there was no way I was going to correct her. I may not be the sharpest crayon in the box, but I'm not *that* dull!

Emily and I agreed to meet at 4:00. As they began to walk away, Elvira turned around. "Mr. Wisniewski, as long as you're going there anyway, could you send Emily home with a pint of pistachio?" Emily frowned her disapproval. "Oh, don't look so hoity toity!" the old woman chided her great niece. "You know it's not for pleasure. The cream helps my complexion."

I wondered if she planned on applying it to her face. I couldn't speak to that; but if it stopped her from complaining, I would have gladly bought her an entire gallon of pistachio.

She must have read my mind. "Just a pint, now," she insisted, raising an index finger. "I still have to watch my figure, you know!"

"Auntie El! Really!" Exasperated, Emily rolled her eyes and shook her head. Then she escorted Elvira out of the building. Reverend Pinckney would have done well to have preached from James chapter three that morning on the subject of taming the tongue.

"I'm so sorry for my great-aunt's inappropriate comments at church," Emily apologized once we'd gotten our ice cream and taken a booth. "Like I told you before, she might be losing her filter. Poor Auntie El. I don't think she even knows what she's saying half the time."

"Don't give it another thought," I reassured her. "At first, I didn't know what to make of her; but now, it doesn't bother me." I took a bite of my birthday banana split.

"Thank you for understanding." She smiled gratefully.

"You're welcome." I gave her a wonky grin. "Besides, she wasn't the *only* one dispensing unsuitable comments in church this morning."

"So I noticed," Emily laughed. "What was up with Orville today? I've never seen him like that before. He sure was in a good mood."

"I have no clue. He was fine yesterday when I talked to him at the bank. Maybe he took too much cough syrup, or maybe he's on pain meds or something." I watched her enjoying her treat for a moment. "So, where did you go to college?"

"*The* Ohio State University."

"Ohio State? That's a really big school. And what a great football program—one of the best in the country!" I was quite impressed. "Am I right to assume that your degree is in the English field?"

"Yes, I have a Master of Ed in English Education and Integrated Language Arts. How about you?"

I suddenly felt like a bantam rooster. "I have a BS in History from Wooster College." That was kind of like pulling up alongside a Mercedes in a Ford Pinto. "I also have a minor in Sports Management," I added, hoping to salvage some of my self-respect.

"Wooster?" Her look said it all.

I grinned to hide my embarrassment. "Yeah, Wooster is a tiny Division Three school in northeastern Indiana. And don't feel bad, nobody else has heard of it either."

She laughed lightly. "Okay, I won't. Yet here we are working side by side in little, old Piggottsville. Life's funny that way, isn't it?"

I nodded in agreement. "It sure is."

Emily played with her ice cream for a while. "Oh, by the way, I meant to tell you on Friday, but I completely forgot. The girls have come up with a name for the cheer squad."

"A name?"

"Yes. The word's been going around that the players want to turn the tables on the other schools for saying disrespectful things about us. So they came up with a name that plays along with that."

I squinted at her. "Do I really want to know?"

She grinned. "Oh, it's fine. They voted to call themselves the Hogettes."

"Hogettes?" I thought about that for a moment. "Well, if the team can be called the Mighty Hogs, then I guess the cheerleaders can be called the Hogettes. It fits. Was the vote unanimous?"

Emily sighed. "We-ell, not exactly. It was two to one."

"Let me guess. Lexi Rae?"

She scrunched up her nose. "Yep! No surprise there. She thought Hogettes was too undignified, so she wanted us to be called the Rockettes instead, but she was outvoted. I'm afraid she might quit over it, though. At least, she threatened to if we don't reconsider." She sighed wearily. "I'm not sure what I can do to keep her on the squad."

My brief experience with how to handle these types of situations came into play. "Do you know if she likes donuts?" I went on to explain about the magical powers of powdered sugar and maple syrup. She agreed to give it a try.

"So . . . how long do you plan on teaching at Piggottsville High?" I asked, returning to the previous subject.

She stared thoughtfully into her dish of peppermint ice cream. "Well, I'm in my second year of a two-year contract with the school board, so I'll have to see what happens at the end of this year. I do like the community, though, in spite of that silly feud going on." She looked up from her treat. "But what small town doesn't have things like that, right? As for the school, I think it's a much more relaxed environment than the one where I did my student teaching, even with Mr. Herold's firm-handed disciplinarian approach to everything. And the kids are friendly and cooperative." She grinned. "With a few exceptions, of course. I'm sure you know the ones I'm referring to."

I grimaced. "I've got a pretty good idea."

She continued, "The climate here is a little warmer than I'm used to; but at least, it doesn't fluctuate as much as it does back in Elyria. We have a saying in Ohio: 'If you don't like the weather, wait a few minutes, and it will change.'"

"The same could be said for Indy," I replied, enjoying even the smallest of commonalities between us. "Is Elyria a very big place?"

"I'd say it's a medium-sized town. I think the population is around fifty thousand or so. It's definitely bigger than Piggottsville!" She licked her spoon.

I scooped some hot fudge back onto the top of my banana split. "Well, at least you knew one person when you moved here. That's more than I can say. And you're blessed to be living with family."

"I suppose I am." She waved the spoon at me. "But if you think it's a walk in the park living with Elvira Primrose, then you'd better think again, Buster!" We laughed together. "Still, I'm grateful to have a place to stay. She won't even let me pay rent, which allows me to save a little money for later."

"But why Piggottsville?" I wondered. "Graduating from such a prestigious university, you could have had your choice of any number of teaching positions in much larger school corporations."

"I did my student teaching in a huge urban high school in Columbus and didn't much care for the atmosphere at all. I felt the experience of teaching in a very small school might broaden my perspective some. Besides, I'd been praying about where God wanted me to teach; and not long after that, Auntie El called to let me know about the opening here." She watched me spill hot fudge down the front of my shirt.

Here was a young woman who, in spite of her superior intellect and educational background, had received a Divine calling to this Podunk community very similar to mine. I sensed a growing connection between us. The more I got to know her, the more Emily just kept getting better and better.

CHAPTER SEVENTEEN

Cousins

The feuding between Knox and Clay Piggott could no longer be ignored. Their latest skirmish during the Montgomery North contest was a painful reminder that I needed to address the problem as soon as possible and definitely before our next game. However, it was a very delicate situation that had to be handled with kid gloves. If I angered or upset the cousins, both might quit, in spite of Winston's unorthodox methods for keeping them on the team.

So I gave the matter considerable thought and prayer. If Mayor Piggott had not been able to resolve the animosity between his two sons after all these years and Reverend Pinckney had to admit defeat in his efforts to end the standoff, then what could I possibly achieve that they could not? My youthfulness and newness to the community made me the most unlikely candidate. Obviously, I couldn't talk to Orville and Virgil about it, as they were my elders. But I could talk to their sons. After all, I was their teacher and coach; and as such, I not only had the authority but also the responsibility to address the conflict, which was detrimental to the academic learning environment and the football team alike.

Monday morning before the start of school, I approached Mr. Herold, seeking his permission to pull the boys out of class for a meeting in the coaching office. To my mild surprise, he was amenable to the idea.

"I agree that the issue needs to be addressed," he affirmed, "and I admire your bravery for attempting such a feat." His use of the term "bravery" did not help my trepidation in the least. "The conflict between those two has flared up from time to time here at school during the

PIGGOTT FAMILY TREE

past several years, and now you're telling me it threatens to derail the entire football program." He grew resolute. "We must try and put a stop to it!" His commitment to assist gave me hope. But that was short lived. "I wish you the best of luck. I hope you can get through to those boys."

I promised to do my best. Then I thought of another issue facing the team. "Mr. Herold, about Durnell Bodkins—he's promised to work very hard to remain eligible, but I'm afraid that may not be enough. Is there anything we can do to help him, academically speaking?"

"I'm glad you brought that up, Mr. Wisniewski. I gave that some very serious consideration over the weekend; and in my staff emails last night, I asked a number of his teachers to tutor him in the subjects he's most likely to fail. I've asked Mr. Fuller to help him with math, Mrs. Calhoun with science, and Miss Davenport with English. With your assistance in history, we just might be able to pull him through over the next two weeks."

"That's wonderful, Mr. Herold," I replied. "But even if he fails to maintain his eligibility this grading period, I hope the tutoring will continue beyond that for his sake as a student and not just as a football player."

"Absolutely!" Mr. Herold responded firmly. "Academics before sports. I must say, you have managed to elicit signs of life within that young man that I thought were all but impossible. Congratulations, Mr. Wisniewski. Each week that passes is further confirmation that my decision to hire you was the right one."

"Thank you, sir. I appreciate that vote of confidence." I was about to leave when a totally different matter crossed my mind. "Oh, by the way, I still don't have that new nameplate for my office door. Do you have any idea when it will arrive?"

The principal scratched behind his ear. "The last time I checked, I believe the manufacturer said it was on back order. Something about supply chain issues." He must have picked up on my disappointment. "Now, don't you worry," he interjected quickly. "I'm staying on top of the situation!" Of *course* he was.

At 10:55, I sat in the coaching office, along with Winston, waiting for Knox and Clay. I'd asked my assistant to join me, not only as a witness but also for support. Additionally, he had some kind of influence on the cousins, which I lacked. A few minutes later, Knox rapped on the door and stepped into the small room.

"You wanna see me, Coach?" he asked, looking back and forth between me and Winston.

"Yes, have a seat, Knox," I replied, pointing to two folding chairs facing my desk.

He sat down in one of them. "What's this about, anyway?"

Just then, Clay walked in. "I was told you wanted to see me." He spied his cousin and recoiled. "What's *he* doing here?"

Knox's face clouded over. "I didn't know *he* was going to be here. I don't wanna be in the same room with him!"

"I'm sorry you feel that way, but I called this meeting on account of you both." I turned to Clay and pointed to the empty chair. "Please sit down."

"If I have to be here, I'd just as soon stand," Clay retorted. "I won't sit next to him."

"Neither will I!" Knox added defiantly.

Winston turned to me in mock amazement. "Well, whaddya know, Coach? They both finally agree on somethin'!" Then he addressed Clay in a tone I'd never heard before. "You'll sit down 'cause you was *asked* to by your head coach." He pointed to the chair. "Now, sit down!" Clay stared at him as if assessing his resolve and then complied with a scowl on his face. I really needed to find out what leverage Winston had over that boy.

"Thank you, Coach." I nodded to my assistant before settling in my desk chair. I silently clasped my hands together and raised my index fingers to my lips. After giving the boys time to adjust to each other's presence, I began. "We've asked you here because we need your help, without which the team is doomed to fail. But the problem is not limited to football. It goes way beyond that. I think you both know what I'm referring to."

The cousins remained silent, but I caught their sideways glance. "Boys, having been a part of this town longer than I have, you're much more aware of the longstanding disrespect coming from the other schools and from our opponents on the football field. I admire you for wanting to turn that around in our favor by loosening up a bit and having fun with it. However, with all the animosity directed at us from *outside* our little community, do we really need more of it coming from *within?*" I paused, waiting for an answer. "Well, do we?"

Knox finally spoke up first. "But, Coach, you don't understand. *His* old man wrote me a ticket for speeding and reckless driving for no reason at all! That's unforgivable."

Clay pointed to his cousin. "*His* old man rejected an application for my auto loan. We had to go all the way to Ransomville to get one, and it has a higher interest rate. That's unforgivable, too!"

"Yes, so I heard. Your father stole the wheels off his father's pickup truck, and his father threatened to have your father arrested. Is that how it all started?" Both boys nodded. I turned to Winston. "There's something else they agree on, Coach!" Winston grunted. I turned back to the boys. "I'm aware of the hard feelings between your two families. But there is one key fact you both have omitted about this longstanding feud."

"What's that?" Knox wondered. "Everything we said is the honest truth."

"I'm sure it is," I replied, "but what you two seem to have forgotten is that neither of you did those things to each other. Knox, Clay didn't steal the wheels off your truck, did he? *He* didn't give you that ticket. And, Clay, Knox didn't threaten to throw you in jail, did he? *He* wasn't responsible for turning down that loan. You're both angry and bitter with each other for something your fathers did, something that started before you were even born. What you're doing now is carrying *their* grudge. You've taken up *their* offense."

I looked both boys in the eye. "As far as I'm aware, neither of you has done anything directly against the other, am I right?" Silence hung heavily over the small room. "Well, am I?"

Both boys nodded reluctantly. I turned to Winston again. "In the five minutes we've all been sitting in this room, that's the third time they've agreed on something."

He grinned wryly. "I'm beginnin' to see a pattern here, Coach. These two knuckleheads have more in common than they thought, outside o' havin' the same granddad, that is."

"You're right," I replied, "they actually have more in common *with* each other than they have offenses *against* each other." I turned to the cousins. "Boys, from where I sit, I can see no benefit whatsoever for you two being on the outs like this. In fact, all I see are negatives. You've dragged a lot of innocent people into your feud. This grudge you hold against each other doesn't just hurt the two of you, it hurts your team, your school, your town, and your church. You're so bitter over something that others have done that you don't want to play on the same team, or sit in the same room, or attend the same church service."

I paused to let the weight of those words sink in. "Since we're in school, I may get into trouble for saying this; but I'm going to say it, anyway. Jesus said that anyone who is angry with his brother without cause is liable to judgment. He said if you're going to offer 'your gift at the altar, and there remember that your brother has something against you, leave your gift . . . and . . . First be reconciled to your brother, and then come and offer your gift.'[11] All you two are doing by continuing this offense is to pile up judgment against yourselves. You see that, don't you?" Both boys stared at the floor. "Well, don't you?"

It was Clay who answered. "Yeah, I guess so."

Knox gave a slight nod of his head.

"Then why not put a stop to it right now? You can't control what other people do, but you can control what *you* do about it. Who knows, maybe your decision to end it will challenge the others to do the same."

Knox raised his head. "But it's not that easy to just let it go, Coach. Not after all this time."

"Yeah, not after everything that's happened," Clay added.

I studied their faces. "You both have heard Reverend Pinckney preach on the Sermon on the Mount." I arched an eyebrow. "Unless you were sleeping in church." Both boys grinned. "Jesus went on to say that if we forgive others their trespasses against us, then our heavenly Father will forgive us, but if we are unwilling to do that, then He will not forgive us.[12] You don't want *that* to happen, do you?"

"No," both boys answered in unison.

"Coach, if I might add somethin'," Winston chimed in. "Ain't no reason at all for these two to be mad at each other. Like you said, they're carryin' their daddys' grudge, not one o' their own makin'. Seems kinda ridiculous 'n' petty to hold that against each other, don't ya think?"

"I agree." I put it to the boys once again. "So, what will it be, guys? Do you want to hang on to the bitterness and anger, or will you let it go

---

11 Matthew 5:23-24

12 Matthew 6:14-15

and forgive one another? Your decision will not only affect you but also everyone else around you, for good or for evil. It's up to you."

I caught the glance Knox and Clay gave each other and waited, praying silently.

Finally, Clay spoke up. "I guess I shouldn't have gotten mad at *him* for what Uncle Orville did to my dad."

I witnessed the struggle on Knox's face. "Um . . . I guess I shouldn't have gotten mad at *him* for what Uncle Virgil did to my dad." He hesitated. "Maybe we should let them fight their own battles."

Clay nodded. "Yeah, we got enough battles of our own to fight without getting involved in theirs." He suddenly turned to his cousin. "Truce?"

"Truce!" Knox responded.

I was greatly encouraged. "That's a big first step, guys, and I appreciate you reaching that agreement. But knowing something about history, let me remind you that a truce and true forgiveness aren't the same thing. A truce is a temporary suspension of hostile actions which can resume once the truce ends. The offense is still there. What you boys need is true forgiveness. Forgiveness ends the hostilities *and* permanently removes the offense. It can never be brought up again. Are you both willing to do that?"

The cousins sat pensively for a moment. Then Clay wet his lips. "I'm not sure I'm ready to do *that* just yet. Saying the words now when I'm not sure I mean them wouldn't really count for anything."

"Yeah, that's how I feel about it, too," Knox joined him. "But you don't need to worry, Coach. We won't give you any more problems on the field. After all, isn't that what you were after?"

"That's part of it, yes. But I want you to forgive one another completely and permanently, just as God forgives us when we ask Him. When that happens, the offense is removed forever, never to be brought up again; and you will be truly free. Until then, you've just buried the hatchet. The trouble is that you both know where it's buried should you ever decide to dig it up again."

"We get what you're saying, Coach," Clay acknowledged, "and we don't mean to disagree with you." He tugged on his earlobe. "I guess what we're trying to say is . . . we just need more time to think it over. Right, Knox?"

"Yeah," Knox replied, nodding his head in agreement. "What Clay said."

I sensed my appeal had run its course. "Well, then, we'll leave it at that for the time being. But I think we've made real progress today, and I'm proud of you both for agreeing to be civil to each other and to work together for the good of the team." I reached into my desk drawer and pulled out my bag of candy. "I think that calls for a celebration, don't you?" I held out the bag to the boys. "Goldie, Pigeon, help yourselves!" The cousins laughed and reached simultaneously for the open bag.

Winston rose and walked over to the small locker where he kept his coat and work boots. He opened the door and removed a white box, which he placed on my desk. "Allow me to contribute to the festivities," he added. His eyes sparkled behind his wire-framed glasses as he opened the lid. Inside were a half dozen maple glazed donuts from the Piggotty Dough Boy.

"Ya sure your degree ain't in psychology 'stead o' history?" Winston quipped once we'd sent the cousins back to class.

I returned the candy to my desk drawer. "I could have benefited from a few more courses in the subject. I'm not sure how long this truce of theirs will last. To be honest with you, I was hoping to resolve the matter once and for all. As it stands, I'm afraid I've failed in my objective for this meeting."

Winston placed his hands on his hips. "Ya kiddin' me, Coach? Ya got through to them two knuckleheads. I heard things comin' outa their mouths I never heard before!" He waved a hand toward the two empty chairs. "Why, ya heard it yourself just a minute ago. 'We won't give ya any more problems; we get what you're sayin'; we need more time.' That's the first time I ever witnessed 'em stand together like that." He shook his head. "No, sir, Coach, don't sell yourself short. You accomplished a lot more today than ya think. An' I'd be surprised if they don't come around like you're hopin' for. Just give 'em some time."

The team scrimmaged that afternoon without Durnell. For the next two weeks, he would be staying after school for tutoring. While he certainly needed the practice time, his academic needs came first.

At least I could count on him to be a body on the field for the next two games. However, I couldn't help wondering how this additional pressure might affect his home life. If he began to neglect his chores, Luella might just pull him off the team, even if he maintained his eligibility. But there I was again, looking for trouble where none might exist. It's a fine line between foresight and fear, and I must confess that I'm not very good at spotting it or knowing when I've crossed it.

During practice, I observed Henry Panke stop again to blow his nose, a maneuver that had cost us a touchdown against Montgomery North. I beckoned to him. "Henry—I mean, Hanky—I've noticed you've been blowing your nose a lot lately. Do you have a cold?"

He stuffed the damp, wrinkled cloth back into his waistband and sniffled. "No, it's allergies, Coach. They get really bad this time of year."

"Have your parents ever had you tested to see what you're allergic to?"

"No, but I know what it is. Any time I'm around freshly cut grass or hay, I sneeze my head off, especially during harvest season. How come you're asking?"

"It seems to be affecting your play a bit," I understated the obvious. "Do you take anything for it?"

"If you mean store-bought drugs, then no. My parents are down on Big Pharma and big on home remedies. I take some of my mom's own recipe but only as needed. We believe that less is more when it comes to medicine." He sniffed again and swiped the back of his hand across his nose.

What do you say in a situation like that? I fought for the right words. "Well, uh . . . whatever it is your mom prescribes, do you think you could take a double dose of it before the game this Friday?"

"What for?" The boy was clueless.

"Well, for one thing, you don't want the rest of the team catching what you have, do you?"

"Oh, you don't have to worry about that, Coach Wiz. Allergies aren't contagious."

"That's true. But when you cough and sneeze all the time, you're spreading germs. We can't afford for anyone to get sick on this team, can we? Besides, don't you think it would be nice if you didn't have to *stop* next time on your way to the end zone?"

It finally dawned on him what I was driving at. He grinned sheepishly and adjusted his glasses. "Okay, Coach, I'll double up before the game. I sure don't want to let the team down again."

When practice was over, I approached Isaiah and Jeremima. "Porky, Petunia, I've got a question for you."

"Sure, Coach, what is it?" Isaiah removed his helmet and wiped the sweat from his eyes.

"Coach Bang and I are very pleased with how well you're both doing. For two rookies, you play at an exceptionally high level, better than most third-year starters. I don't think I've seen either of you miss a blocking assignment or a tackle, and you seem to have an agility and a confidence that the others on the team lack. You've even forced our opponents to run plays away from your side of the line just to avoid you. Why is that? If you've got a secret, I'd sure like to know what it is!"

Isaiah looked at his sister. "Well, we watch a lot of games on TV," he offered.

"And I've read some books about football," Jeremima added.

"I know you both love the sport, and it's obvious you understand the game; but that knowledge alone doesn't account for your ability to anticipate your opponents' moves and chase them down like you're doing." I was puzzled. "You've never played football before, so where did that talent come from? That can only be acquired through experience."

Jeremima removed her helmet and tucked a loose strand of red hair behind one ear. "I don't know, Coach. Maybe it comes from chasing down the hogs and chickens."

"Hogs and chickens?"

"Yeah," Isaiah tag-teamed, "twice a year we round up all the livestock to tag them or give them their medication and shots. We have to catch the chickens one by one and chase the hogs into their pens. Sometimes, they don't cooperate, so we have to wrestle them."

I held up my palm. "Wait a sec. Are you saying that chasing chickens and wrestling hogs might account for your ability to chase down and tackle football players?"

"Sure!" Jeremima crossed her arms. "I haven't met a football player yet who's harder to tackle than Bo!"

"Bo? Who's that?"

"He's our largest hog. Last time father weighed him, he tipped the scales at nearly a thousand pounds!" Jeremima's eyes widened. "Is he ever hard to chase down and tackle! Gives me a good workout every time."

My mind began spinning like a clothes dryer during a power surge. The maelstrom in my head spat out a crazy idea that made Winston's unconventional methods look like standard operating procedure. I dismissed the twins and headed to the office to make a very important phone call.

CHAPTER EIGHTEEN
FiELD TRiP

"Good morning! May I have your attention, please?" Mr. Herold's authoritative voice filled every classroom in the building. "This is your principal speaking." As if every student within a ten-mile radius didn't already know that by now. "Today is Tuesday, October 17. As a reminder to all PSHS students, the first grading period ends one week from this Friday, so I want us to work hard and push through to the very end. Let's all buckle down and put our shoulders to the wheel, shall we?

"I am pleased to announce that the town council has approved the reopening of the concession stand for the remainder of this season's home football games. If anyone would like to help members of the community clean-out the building this week or help prepare and serve food during our games, please stop by the office and leave your name with Mrs. Cooper. In conjunction with that, we are holding a contest to name the stadium and concession stand! Turn in your suggestions to one of your teachers before the end of the school day tomorrow, and the winning names will be read during Thursday morning's announcements. You will *not* want to miss Friday's home game against Nimrod High. The concession will be open, and the new Hogettes cheerleaders and Mighty Hogs pep band will be entertaining the crowd. Let's all come out to support our team and show our school spirit, shall we? *Go, Mighty Ferrell Hogs!*"

Mr. Herold's voice returned to its previous decibel level. "Today's lunch menu is chicken fried steak, creamy mashed potatoes, fresh peas, and hot apple cobbler."

For the remainder of the day, the school was abuzz with talk of the contest and the game against Nimrod High. By the end of last period, I'd received nearly two dozen contest entries, which I turned in to Claudine Cooper before going to football practice. In spite of Durnell's absence, we had a pretty good scrimmage. Knox and Clay were civil toward each other; and the team as a whole put in a great effort, although I thought Willard seemed a little more lethargic than usual. I hoped he wasn't coming down with something. Just in case, I kept him as far away from Henry as possible. After the final drills, I blew my whistle and gathered the team around Winston and me.

"Good practice, you guys! Take a knee." I waited as they removed their helmets and knelt on the turf. "Okay, I've got a surprise for you. Tomorrow, instead of our normal practice, we are going on a little field trip!"

"Field trip?" The players all began talking at once.

I held up my hands. "Whoa, wait a minute! Just listen, and I'll fill you in. Tomorrow after school, I want you all to meet here at the usual time but no helmets or shoulder pads, got it? I want you to change into the oldest clothes you've got, clothes you don't mind getting dirty or torn. If you've got an old pair of tennis shoes or work boots, wear those as well." I turned to Winston. "Am I leaving anything out?"

"Might wanna bring an old towel or two along," he suggested.

Jackson raised his hand. "Where are we going, Coach?"

"Yeah, and what's with the old clothes?" Willie wanted to know.

I smiled coyly. "You'll all find out tomorrow. But you won't want to miss this. We're going somewhere to do something that should really improve our play for the rest of the season. Plus, I guarantee it'll be a blast!"

Danny Swanson raised his hand. "Do you want me to come, too, Coach?"

I looked at our small statistician. "Of course, I want you to come! You're part of the team, aren't you?"

"Well, yes, but I just wanted to make sure, since I'm not one of the players."

"This activity is for all of you." I blew my whistle to drown out the endless questions. "That's all, folks. Practice is over. C'mon, you guys, hit those showers!"

In my three U.S. History classes on Wednesday, the students deluged me with all kinds of questions about the contest, the game, the cheerleaders, even the pep band. Their participation was so enthusiastic and universal that I began to suspect it was an orchestrated plot to postpone the big quiz I'd scheduled for that morning. While I was sorely tempted to spend the entirety of each period discussing my love for all things football, I limited the question-and-answer sessions to the first fifteen minutes of each class, which left plenty of time for administering the dreaded exam. To be an effective teacher of teenagers, one must have a sense of humor. Of course, having a healthy dose of skepticism and suspicion doesn't hurt, either. Without that, it's only a matter of time before you lose control and your tight ship slips into the depths faster than the *Titanic*.

I ate lunch with several other teachers that day, including Emily, Grady Fuller, and Munro Masters. Munro surprised me with the news that he'd managed to secure another trumpet player for the pep band. I believe the actual word he used was "coerced," but I chose not to go there. When I inquired about Durnell's tutoring, Grady informed me that there was no two ways about it; the boy was going to be a challenge, not so much because of his lack of effort or desire but because of his lack of ability. He promised to do all he could. Emily's report was disappointingly similar.

Their prognoses did nothing to ease my anxiety. If they could not guarantee a passing grade in math or English after working with him daily, then what could I expect to achieve in history? I had no time for tutoring outside the classroom. I would either have to make time later in the evenings to tutor him myself or find another student willing to work with him during school. However, if he was already struggling in a normal school setting, too much tutoring could lead to burn out. Then there was the matter of his chores at home. When would he have time to do those? Feeling the weight of the situation, I did the only thing I could do—pray.

"I tried your idea of offering donuts to Lexi Rae," Emily reported as we placed our trays on the dishwasher conveyor belt.

"Please tell me it worked," I bemoaned. "I'm not sure how much more bad news I can handle today."

She tilted her head. "Do I detect a note of discouragement?" She placed a gentle hand on my arm. "Jason, don't be too hard on yourself. I know you've been under a lot of pressure since you arrived in Piggottsville, but cheer up. Things are starting to change. Can't you see what you've been able to accomplish since the beginning of school? You started with nothing; and now, look what you've got!"

We walked out of the cafeteria together. As we headed down the hallway, I finally responded. "Emily, you're right. You're absolutely right. I have no business being discouraged. God has done some amazing things since that first day when I discovered what I was up against. I shouldn't be complaining. In fact, I should be grateful for the trials. Who was it who said the trying of our faith works patience?"[13]

"That would be the apostle James." She gave me a wry look. "Why, Mr. Wisniewski, I thought you knew that."

I couldn't help but grin. "I did. I just wanted to see if *you* knew it!"

"Yeah, right!" She playfully punched me in the arm.

"No, really, I did!" I pleaded my case. "James chapter one, right? Verse two or three, somewhere around there."

Emily laughed. "Okay, I'm convinced. You're off the hook."

"So, getting back to the subject of donuts, did Lexi Rae go for it?"

She shook her head. "No. I discovered she doesn't eat donuts. But I found something else that did the trick."

"What's that?"

"I promised to sponsor her for homecoming queen."

I stared at her. "You did what?"

"I promised to sponsor her for homecoming queen. Every candidate has to have a faculty sponsor. Besides, I know she's dying to get elected. She's tried for the past two years but didn't get enough votes."

I was bewildered. "Wait, how could there be a homecoming queen if there was no football team? For that matter, how could there even be a homecoming?"

"There's always been a homecoming. Of sorts. They elect a king and queen and have Spirit Week and all that. Just no game."

"Sounds kind of dull," I stated honestly. "I thought the game was supposed to be the climax of it all."

---

13 James 1:3

Emily chuckled. "Oh, the week has plenty of excitement and drama—just not on the football field. There's never a dull moment when Lexi Rae stumps for votes, believe me."

"Desperate times call for desperate measures, huh? Hippocrates said that, by the way."

"Oh, so now you can remember Hippocrates; but a minute ago, you couldn't remember James!" I caught the twinkle in her eye. "Just teasing."

As we climbed the stairs to our classrooms, we were giggling like a couple of giddy schoolchildren.

Mr. Herold approached me as I erased the whiteboard following fifth period. "Mr. Wisniewski, I'd like to ask a favor of you, if I may." I'd been in his employ for about eight weeks, yet this was the first time he'd ever requested something of me. The principal was used to giving orders and issuing commands, so this was nothing short of a five-star general asking a private if he wouldn't mind running an errand, providing he felt up to it. Whatever the request was, it had to be a doozy.

"Of course, Mr. Herold," I heard myself reply. "What can I do for you?"

"I'd like you to be responsible for a booth at the Ferrell Fall Festival on Saturday next week."

I put down the dry eraser and turned to face him. "Ferrell Fall Festival? What's that?"

"It's our annual community celebration commemorating the founding of Piggottsville and is held the last Saturday in October. On that day, Main Street will be blocked off, so the local businesses and civic organizations can set up their booths and games. The school usually has a booth; but this year, I'd like to have a separate one promoting the football program. What do you think about that?"

I envisioned my busy schedule with its lesson plans, daily practices, football games, and ongoing efforts to keep my eleven players eligible and motivated. "Well, to be honest with you, Mr. Herold, I have quite a lot on my plate right now. I don't see how I could possibly take on anything more at this time."

Mr. Herold was not accustomed to being denied. "It requires very little preparation, Mr. Wisniewski, and it certainly won't take up much of your time. Besides, it's on your day off. All I ask is for a visible presence at the festival, a simple table set up to generate community interest. I'm sure you won't mind being a goodwill ambassador for the football program. After all, that's one of the responsibilities of coaching, is it not?"

While I was not in danger of being thrown into the slammer or facing a court martial for refusing his request, how could I say no to my superior officer? Hadn't he already acquiesced to several of *my* requests? I caved with a sigh. "Very well, I'll do what I can."

"Excellent! I knew you'd see it my way." The principal waxed enthusiastic. "Perhaps you could encourage Miss Davenport to have the cheerleaders there, as well as some of your players, for visual impact. Since homecoming is a mere two weeks after the festival, I'm confident your participation in this endeavor will have a positive influence on our game attendance . . . and our concession sales!"

The more I thought about it, the more I was inclined to agree with him. The broader support we had from the community, the better. I made a mental note to run the idea by Emily at lunch the following day. I even considered asking Munro about having the pep band play at the festival; but after reflecting on the band's status, I wasn't so sure we needed that kind of attention.

After school, Winston had the team bus waiting at the curb behind the gymnasium. Once everyone was aboard, we started on our field trip. All the windows were wide open—not because it was hot but because Skunk was more pungent than usual that day. I noticed he was still wearing his grungy school clothes, which likely doubled as his newest and oldest outfit. As the small, rusty transport rattled and bounced along No Name Road, the players began guessing our destination.

"I think we're gonna scrimmage another team," I heard Maynard suggest to his teammates. "Somebody we haven't played yet. Maybe Nimrod or Jackson County."

"Without helmets and pads?" Willie countered. "Naw, I bet we're goin' on a hike. We're goin' to that trail runnin' alongside Copper Creek."

"A hike?" Maynard turned around in his seat. "Coach said this would improve our play. How's a hike gonna do that?"

"Maybe we're going to that exercise gym in Ransomville," Jackson chimed in. "The one with all those sophisticated workout machines."

"No way!" Maynard snorted. "You don't get your clothes all dirty and torn at a workout gym. Sweaty, maybe, but not dirty and torn. And you don't wear work boots there either!" The players argued back and forth for a while. Finally, Nigel grabbed the seat in front of him and pulled himself forward.

"Hey, Coach Wiz. We're all kind of befuddled. Be a good sport and give us a clue!"

I glanced into the large mirror from my front row seat. "You'll find out when we get there!" I turned and looked at Winston.

"Keep 'em guessin', Coach!" he said with a grin.

As the bus squealed to a stop at the intersection of No Name Road and County Road 44 East, there was a loud metallic "clunk" from somewhere near the front of the vehicle. Winston put the gear shift into neutral and applied the parking brake. Then he opened the door and climbed down to see what it was. I saw his head disappear below the hood for a moment and then reappear as he straightened up. He removed his worn cap and scratched his head. After instructing the players to stay in their seats, I joined him. He was staring at the front bumper. One end had broken loose and was resting on the pavement.

"What are we going to do?" I asked. "Should we call a tow truck or see if we can get another bus?"

He shook his head. "Nope, that ain't necessary."

"But we can't continue driving with that bumper scraping the ground like that."

Winston didn't reply. Instead, he walked around to the back of the bus, opened the rear door, and pulled out a tool kit from beneath the back seat. He removed a small roll of baling wire and held it up for my inspection. "Oh ye o' little faith," he chastised me. Ten minutes later, we were back on the road again.

"Now that's what I call being prepared," I complimented our driver as we cruised along the comparatively smoother asphalt of County Road 44 East.

"Just chalk it up to experience."

"Experience? You mean, it's happened before?"

Winston nodded. "Three times. Figured I oughta get ahead o' the game for once!"

About three miles later, the bus slowed and turned into a long, winding dirt lane. Ahead lay a good-sized farm consisting of a simple but neat white house, a large red barn, two livestock barns, several other outbuildings, and a maze of fenced pens and paddocks. I turned to face the kids behind me. They were all craning their necks out the windows.

"Is *this* where we're going?" Clay asked, his head completely outside the bus.

"Where are we, anyway?" Henry had a puzzled expression on his face.

"Hanky, you might want to ask Porky and Petunia that question," I suggested.

The bus came to a squealing stop, and Winston opened the door. "Okay, ever'body off the bus! An' don't forget them towels." The kids stepped down single file, talking among themselves.

Once they had all disembarked, I waved my hand in a broad arc. "All right, you Mighty Hogs! This is where the fun begins! Welcome to the Pugh farm."

"We already know what farm animals look like," Willie complained.

"Yeah, what does all this have to do with football?" Knox asked, surveying the grounds.

I addressed my team. "Guys, this afternoon we are going to try some new agility and tackling drills. We will be chasing chickens and wrestling hogs!"

With the exception of Isaiah and Jeremima, the teens stood there gawking at each other with eyes and mouths wide open.

Ezekiel Pugh stepped off the porch of his trim farmhouse and strode toward the stunned group. He shook my hand firmly and then Winston's, welcoming us to his homestead. Then we followed him across the yard toward one of the livestock barns, where a dozen or so chickens were milling about pecking and foraging for food. The tall farmer instructed my team on how to chase down a chicken without hurting the bird.

"What do I do after I catch one?" Maynard didn't look at all sure of himself.

"Just bring it back here and release it," Ezekiel told him. "But they are harder to catch than you might think. They don't run in a straight line. They zig and zag much like your opponents on the football field."

"For each chicken you catch, I'll give you one piece of candy," I promised. Then I turned to Danny. "Do you have your stat sheet ready?"

He held up his clipboard. "Ready, Coach!"

For the next thirty minutes, the team members took turns chasing chickens. To say it was a comedy of errors would have been an understatement. Maynard, who was slow on his feet, lunged for one several times and fell face first in the dirt, evoking howls of laughter from his teammates. He never did catch one. After repeated tries, a number of other players managed to bring back a bird; and Danny dutifully recorded each catch. But it was Willard who amazed me. I should have known he would be familiar with this kind of thing. He was a natural, and being small and lightweight gave him an advantage. He captured four hens in four tries. When our time expired, the score was Mighty Hogs ten, Elusive Chickens twenty-nine.

After a water break, Ezekiel led the group to the other barn where the hogs were kept. Inside was the largest swine I'd ever seen. The players crowded around the stall and stared at the huge beast. Clay pointed to the floppy-eared, reddish-brown monster who was warily eyeballing his admirers. "We're not gonna tackle *that*, are we?"

Ezekiel chuckled. "No, son, he is too big for anything like that. He weighs upwards of 975 pounds."

"*I've* wrestled him before!" Jeremima announced proudly. "Even pinned him once!" I could think of no reason to doubt her.

"His name is Bodacious," Isaiah informed the group, "but we call him 'Bo' for short. He's quite friendly most of the time, but he gets riled when we give him his shots or force him into the hog hauler."

"This is a mature Duroc boar," their father continued, "and like Isaiah said, he is not very aggressive. The danger is that he could step on your foot or crush you against the fence by accident. But don't worry, you will be tackling the juvenile American Yorkshire pigs outside. They are only about two hundred pounds right now." I saw looks of relief all the way around.

We left Bo and followed Ezekiel outside to one of the pens. Three very dirty pigs were rooting amid the thick mud. A fourth was sleeping on its side against the far fence that provided a narrow stripe of shade.

"Now you know why we had you wear your old clothes and bring a towel." My statement was met with wry looks.

Willie snorted. "Huh! They don't look too hard to catch!"

"They are a bit easier to grab onto than the chickens," Ezekiel admitted, "so that is why I am going to grease them first." He picked up a can of lard sitting near the fence and opened the gate. Then he and the twins entered the pen. As his children cornered and held the pigs, Mr. Pugh rubbed a light coat of lard onto the back and sides of each one. When they were sufficiently lubricated, he addressed the boys lined up along the fence. "Now, who wants to try first?"

"I do!" Willie grabbed the top rail and climbed into the pen. He gleefully rubbed his hands together and turned to his teammates. "This oughta be easy! Watch and learn, fellow Hogs, watch and learn!" He started confidently toward the nearest pig; but his right shoe got stuck, and he pitched forward full-length into the thick mud. When he stood up, he was minus both shoes and covered from head to toe in black ooze. Hoots and howls echoed across the barnyard.

Willie wiped the mud from his beet-red face. He stepped back into his shoes with a grimace and tied each in a double knot. Then he charged the nearest pig. He got his hands on it; but it slipped from his grasp with a squeal, and he fell again. After three more attempts, he gave up and climbed back over the rail. "It's harder than it looks!" he acknowledged, breathing heavily.

Nigel volunteered to go next. He crept up on the pig like an Indian stalking a buffalo; and before the animal could react, he wrapped his arms around its middle. The pig squealed and began running, dragging the exchange student across the pen until it wriggled loose and left him face down in the mud. More hysterical laughter followed. He bounded to his feet and shook himself like a dog, flinging mud everywhere. "Wowzer, that was bonkers! Can I give it another go?"

Mr. Pugh nodded. Nigel gamely went for another pig, but this one was a little wiser and faster; and try as he might, he couldn't get a hold of it. Exhausted, he stumbled over to the fence and leaned against it.

"I'm plumb knackered!" he gasped before breaking into a grin. "But that sure was wicked fun!"

Our tackling drill continued for another forty minutes. At one point, I asked Danny if he wanted to give it a try, but he shook his head emphatically. "No way! Those pigs are bigger than me . . . and twice as heavy. They'd kill me!"

When everyone had taken all the turns they wanted, Ezekiel led the kids back to the barn, where they hosed each other off. Then we thanked the Pughs for their hospitality and climbed aboard the bus. On the ride home, there was very little conversation, probably because everyone was, as Nigel had put it, "plumb knackered." And even though the windows were closed, not a single person complained about Skunk. I guess a little water goes a long way.

CHAPTER NINETEEN
Super Bo and the Mighty Ferrell Hogs

During his Thursday morning broadcast, Mr. Herold announced the winners of the contest. "I know all you students have been eagerly awaiting the results of the 'Name the Stadium' contest. There were many excellent suggestions; but unfortunately, there can be only one winner. I must tell you it was a very difficult decision. After careful consideration, the winning entry was submitted by . . . Henry Panke! And the new name of your stadium is—drum roll please—the 'Pigskin Palace'!"

From my class's reaction, I gathered most of the students approved of the choice. I thought it was rather clever myself. The principal continued. "Other suggestions given serious consideration were the 'Hog Arena' and the 'Piggottsville Pavilion.' But now, let's not forget the 'Name the Concession' contest. The winner is . . . the 'Heavenly Hog,' submitted by Jessie Wilkerson. Other considerations were the 'Slop Shop' and the 'Boar Store.' Congratulations, Henry and Jessie! You will each receive a coupon for 10 percent off any item purchased at the concession stand." Such a lavish display of generosity with the school board's money was sure to jeopardize Mr. Herold's reputation as a tightwad.

There was a lot of chatter about Friday night's home game throughout the student body that day. Even the teachers were discussing it in the cafeteria. Emily was excited about a new cheer the squad was going to introduce, and Munro assured me the pep band was as prepared as it would ever be for its debut—whatever that was worth.

Later in the day, a very animated pair of redheads buttonholed me in the hallway with the news that the team had decided to make Bo their official mascot. They wanted to call him Super Bo and asked if he could be on the sidelines during the Nimrod game.

I mulled over their request. "We-e-ell, I'm not so sure having Bo at the game is such a good idea. What if the crowd upsets him, or the pep band spooks him?" We'd already had to pause one game on account of a small menagerie. Having a rampaging one-thousand-pound Duroc boar tearing around in the middle of a large gathering didn't exactly fit my definition of public safety.

"But, Coach, Bo won't be a problem," Isaiah assured me. "He's used to crowds. We take him to the county fair every year, and he enjoys all the noise and attention."

"We promise to keep him tethered," Jeremima added.

I was still reluctant. "There's the matter of responsibility and liability and things like that. Who would watch him while you're on the field?"

"Our father will," Isaiah promised. "He'll see that Bo gets to and from our remaining home games, too."

"The U of A has Tusk at all *their* games," Jeremima argued, "and they don't have any problems with him. Besides, having Bo at our games will bring out more fans. I'm sure of it!" My best player could be very persuasive. And persistent.

Isaiah clasped his hands. "Please, Mr. Wisniewski, please! You told us we could have fun with this."

I succumbed to their pleas. Sort of. "Well, the decision is not up to me. You would need to clear this with Mr. Herold first. If he approves, then I guess I'm okay with it."

The twins looked gleefully at each other. "Great! Thanks, Coach. See you at practice." They galloped off toward the school office like a pair of hungry Clydesdales heading for the barn at supper time. As I fought my way through the crowded hallway, Winston flagged me down.

"Coach, I'm takin' the team bus over to Ransomville Saturday mornin' to have the brakes worked on," he informed me. "Wanna tag along?"

"I thought I heard them squealing on the field trip. Do you need my help?"

My assistant shook his head. "Not really. Just thought ya might like to pick up that load o' tires I was tellin' ya about earlier."

I mentally checked my Saturday schedule. "How early do you plan to leave?"

"Oh, 'bout 10:30. I made the appointment for noon."

"But it only takes forty-five minutes to drive to Ransomville," I pointed out, calculating how much sleep I'd have to forfeit.

He grinned. "Figured we might need the extra time case the ol' gal decides to act up again."

I couldn't argue with that logic; and since I didn't have any other plans, I agreed to meet him at the school.

During that afternoon's practice, Winston was called away to fix a wiring problem in the concession stand. I'd been skeptical that the derelict structure could be converted into a functioning concession in less than a week. But a contingent of ladies from the community, led by Jolene Piggott, along with volunteers from the high school, had been cleaning out the building for the past three days; and it was beginning to look as if they might have it ready by game time. I had grossly underestimated the resolve and tenacity of the Piggottsville Community Church Women's Missionary League. It was definitely a force to be reckoned with.

Willard had been acting tired and run down all week; and on Friday, I caught him sleeping during second period. I went easy on him, figuring his lethargy was either the result of his gallant efforts on the field trip or because he was coming down with something. That thought prompted me to remind Henry to double up on his mom's homemade allergy recipe as soon as he got home from school.

During lunch, Isaiah and Jeremima came up to me while I was going through the food line and informed me that Mr. Herold had granted permission for Bo to be at the home games. I couldn't believe he had approved the idea, especially with all the liability associated with having such a large animal in the stadium and with his propensity for caution and keeping things close to the vest. I hoped Bo's presence would not cause any distractions or problems on the sideline. We already had enough of those on the field.

As was his weekly custom, Ezekiel Pugh stopped by after my last period class with another word of encouragement for me. This time it came from the book of Psalms: "'Delight thyself also in the Lord, and He shall give thee the desires of thine heart.'[14]" Pretty good advice.

When Winston and I led the team into the stadium Friday night, we were greeted by a most unusual sight. There were people in the stands! At our previous two home games, we had conducted pregame exercises in front of empty bleachers. No one had bothered to show up until the start, and most of those had skedaddled long before the end of the fourth quarter. Now here we were, half an hour before kickoff, and already thirty or forty people were in the home stands . . . but still sitting on opposite ends.

As the players jogged onto the field for warmups, I looked around. Emily and the Hogettes were off to one side practicing a pyramid—with Lexi Rae on top, of course. In the lower middle section of the bleachers, Munro was busy dishing out instructions and sheet music to his patchwork five-member pep band. Stretched across the top railing was a ten-foot-long banner bearing the words "Pigskin Palace" in black letters outlined in red. My gaze swept across the bleachers to the newly opened concession stand.

The exterior of the block building, while still needing a good coat of white paint, had at least been washed clean of the five years of accumulated dust and dirt; and the boards had been removed from the serving window, which was now open for business. A temporary sign made from what looked like a white sheet hung above it. Behind the counter, Jolene Piggott and several other ladies and students were busy taking and filling orders. I could smell the fried food and hot buttered popcorn all the way out to where I stood at the fifty-yard line. A queue was beginning to form, and I spied our oval-shaped mayor and heralded principal animatedly shaking hands and working the lineup. While I couldn't quite make out the individual items listed on the menu posted beside the order window, I had no trouble seeing the dollar signs in both men's eyes. They seemed to be in hog heaven.

Across the field, good-sized delegations of Nimrod fans were climbing the stands or making their way around the end zone toward

---

14 Psalm 37:4, KJV

the concession. The Mighty Hunters pep band of about twenty strong was warming up while the opposing players were preparing to take the field for their pregame drills. Winston and I counted forty-two of them. Forty-two against eleven. Not exactly what you would call even odds, but I wouldn't have traded a single one of our players for a dozen of theirs.

I gradually noticed that people throughout the stadium were stopping and pointing to the far end zone. Entering the arena along the cinder track was a tall, thin man and the largest animal I'd ever seen that wasn't either behind a safety fence or the handiwork of a taxidermist. It was Ezekiel Pugh leading his prize pig, Bodacious—all half-ton of him! As the pair crossed in front of the home bleachers, a spontaneous smattering of applause broke out. Ezekiel walked the imposing porker to the grassy area in front of the concession, where he tethered him to an iron stake driven into the ground.

When I checked back a few minutes later, people were taking pictures of our new mascot, who seemed to be enjoying the attention . . . and the carrots periodically fed to him by his owner.

At that moment, the most awful discordant din split the early evening air. I spun around to locate the offending source. It came from the center section of the home bleachers. Waving his arms like a deranged octopus, Munro was attempting to lead the Mighty Hogs pep band in what I could only assume was some sort of musical composition. It was hard to tell what it was. A fight song maybe? However, the only fight in the song was the battle between the different instruments. I'd heard of the Battle of the Bands before, but this was more like the Battle *within* the Band! The cacophony of unrelated sounds was enough to set a person's teeth on edge. If it was true that Hermione sang between the cracks, then the pep band most certainly played in the chasms. Munro had said they couldn't keep time, didn't stay in tune, and were loud. Unfortunately, he was right on all counts.

To preserve my sanity, I began searching for familiar faces in the gathering crowd. Directly behind the band, a concentration of students was forming. Reverend and Mrs. Pinckney and their church friends occupied their usual spot further up in the stands; and Orville and Avery Piggott, along with a number of my fellow teachers and most of the players' parents, were scattered among the other townspeople. Their support really bolstered my confidence. When the pep band's musical mayhem ground to a merciful stop, the Hogettes introduced the new cheer Emily had told me about. The small student section started getting into it.

> "We are the Ho-ogs, Mighty Ferrell Ho-ogs!
>
> We wanna betcha we're gonna getcha!
>
> Soo, soo-wee, soo, soo, soo-wee, yeah,
>
> Soo, soo-wee, soo, soo, soo-wee, hey!
>
> We are the Ho-ogs, Mighty Ferrell Ho-ogs!
>
> Get on the bus; don't mess with us!
>
> Soo, soo-wee, soo, soo, soo-wee, yeah,
>
> Soo, soo-wee, soo, soo, soo-wee, hey!"

Not to be outdone, the visiting fans responded with a cheer of their own. Or rather, it was a disrespectful taunt like those we'd heard from previous opponents. It sounded like a drill sergeant's cadence used to keep his platoon in step.

> "Hogs are losers; they can't play!
> (Hogs are losers; they can't play!)
>
> We can beat them any day!
> (We can beat them any day!)
>
> Hogs are stupid; they can't think!
> (Hogs are stupid; they can't think!)
>
> We are great, but they sure stink!
> (We are great, but they sure stink!)"

Several Nimrod students held up large posters, adding insult to injury: "It's Nimrod High time for a Hog roast!" and "It's a fine time to dine on swine!"

My players stopped their warmups and stared as the verbal abuse continued. Even the opposing players joined in mocking our team and school. Not wanting to risk an altercation, I summoned my team to the sideline.

Knox angrily yanked off his helmet. "Coach, do you hear that? They're disrespecting us!"

"Yeah, we can't let them get away with that!" Jackson spat on the ground.

The other players voiced their agreement.

"We've got to do something, Coach," Jeremima pleaded. "We have to fight back!"

I held up my hand. "We will, guys, we will. Just as soon as the game starts. Then you can let your play do all the fighting for you. Don't let them rattle you. That's what they're trying to do. Stay focused on the task ahead."

My players stood shoulder to shoulder on the sideline, listening to the jeers and ridicule. Suddenly, without warning, Willard broke rank and ran onto the field. I started after him, fearing a stampede. But he stopped and planted his feet. Then he cupped his hands around his mouth and shouted, "Y'all are nothin' but a bunch of . . . of . . . of *Nimrods!*" He was shaking from head to toe, barely able to contain himself.

Nigel ran to his side. "Yeah, that's right!" he shouted, mimicking his teammate. "The whole bloomin' lot o' you are merely a cluster of *Nimrods!*"

I wasn't sure whether a reprimand or a laugh was in order. Winston sidled up to me. "We gotta work on our trash-talkin' a skosh, don't ya think, Coach?"

I buried my head in my hands and choked back a laugh.

We managed to calm the players down as Hermione waddled out and began to sing the national anthem. After hearing the pep band, she sounded like an opera singer. I must confess, I was glad for the distraction. When she finished, I turned for a final look at the home stands. There were sixty or seventy people there, and more were filing in. A slightly built woman wrapped in a shawl caught my eye. She climbed the steps at the far end of the bleachers and sat down in the very top corner away from the rest of the fans. She looked familiar, and I strained to identify her. It was Luella Bodkins! Pleased that she had made the effort to support her two sons in their quest for personal discipline, I turned my attention back to the field.

My warriors gathered in a tight circle around Winston and me. I looked each one in the eye. "Are you ready for this?" I asked. Their responses ranged from animated nods to "Let's kick some Hunter heinie!" Then they gave a loud team cheer and started onto the field.

I grabbed Henry by the jersey and pulled him back. "Hanky, did you remember to take something for your allergies?"

He nodded. "Sure, Coach, I did just like you said. I took some of my mom's home remedy." He seemed to be having trouble focusing on me, but I dismissed it as pregame jitters. I slapped him on the back and sent him out to join his teammates, who were determined to defend the honor of their team, their school, and their hometown.

From the opening kickoff, it was obvious that our players were on a mission. They wanted to make a statement, and they had a score to settle. On the very first play from scrimmage, Jeremima broke through the Nimrod offensive line, tossed players aside like rag dolls, and sacked their quarterback for an eight-yard loss. The Piggottsville fans erupted in cheers and whistles. The Hogs stood their ground and forced a punt.

A few plays later, Knox dropped back and lofted a pretty little throw to Nigel, who caught the ball and ran for thirty yards before finally being brought down. On first and ten, the quarterback handed off to Henry. Isaiah and Jeremima opened a huge hole on the right side of the line, but Henry missed it completely and ran smack dab into Isaiah's back. He fumbled the ball, and a Nimrod player scooped it up and returned it for a touchdown.

I threw up my hands in disbelief. "How could he miss that hole?" I turned to Winston. "You could have driven a Mack truck through that gap! Two of them in fact. Side by side!"

He shrugged. "Don't know what to tell ya, Coach. Just be patient. Maybe he'll come around." A sly grin tugged at the corners of his mouth. "Even a blind pig finds an acorn ever' now an' then." Winston had his own unique way of calming me down.

At the end of the first quarter, I approached Henry. "Hanky, you seem a little dazed. Are you feeling all right?"

My running back looked at me with glassy eyes and smiled broadly. "I feel great, Coach. Never felt better in my life!"

I sent him back into the game. I mean, what choice did I have?

At halftime, we were down ten to nothing; but the team was playing at a higher level and with a greater intensity than I thought possible for this bunch. They had handled the disrespect and had responded in a way that made me proud, and I told them so. As the second half commenced, they continued their gallant efforts; but as had been the case in our previous four games, playing every down without substitutions began to take its toll.

Halfway through the third quarter, they were running out of gas; so I called a timeout to give them a much needed breather. As Danny passed out water bottles, the Nimrod pep band began playing. They sounded good enough for the Rose Parade compared to our quarrelsome quintet. Then the taunts started up again, and I wished I could protect my players from the demeaning and disheartening jeers. Gathering my weary warriors around me, I opened my mouth to give them a pep talk.

But at that very instant a loud, shrill cry rang out, flooding the stadium and spilling across the open, rolling fields beyond. "SOOOO-EEEE! PIG, PIG, PIG! SOOOO-EEEE!"

All heads within a half-mile radius turned in unison. Right behind the Hogs pep band and cheering section, Hermione Piggott stood with feet firmly planted wide apart, head tilted back, and hands cupped around her mouth. Fans sitting nearby had their hands over their ears.

The call rose again, drowning out the mocking chants and even the Nimrod band. "SOOOO-EEEE! PIG, PIG, PIG! SOOOO-EEEE!" As she drew a third ample breath, you could feel the air being sucked out of the stadium. She belted out one final ear-splitting call, followed by a fist pump and a "GO MIGHTY HOGS!" before sitting back down next to her dumbfounded husband, Avery, who was pretending he didn't know her.

I'm not sure how long I stood there, but the referee's whistle brought me back to my senses. The time-out had expired. Figuring Hermione's rallying cry had accomplished more than any motivational speech I could have given, I had the players huddle up and give the team cheer again. "The few! The proud! The Mighty Ferrell Hogs!" Then they rejoined the fight with renewed vim and vigor.

They seemed to have found some hidden inner strength and played with the passion of Tom Brady, Reggie White, and Jerry Rice all rolled into one, with a little Hulk Hogan thrown into the mix. That would be Jeremima. On defense, they forced two fumbles, intercepted a pass, and blocked a punt, keeping our opponent out of the end zone. They also moved the ball well on offense, completing a dozen passes and churning out some good yardage on the ground.

I think it was about five minutes into the fourth quarter when it happened. We had just taken over the ball on downs and were starting from our own thirty-yard line. I called for a rare screen pass to Willard. At only five foot five and 125 pounds, he was our smallest player. No one expected him to do anything other than fill the position. Knox lined up under center and received the ball from Maynard. He faked a handoff to Clay, who had been running exceptionally well; and the defense took the bait. Meanwhile, Willard took a few steps back, and Knox lofted the ball over an opponent's raised arms and into the wide receiver's hands.

Willard took off like a scalded dog. He darted this way and that, dodging defenders and cow patties. Several players slipped and went down hard. Only one Mighty Hunter stood between him and the end zone—Nimrod's all-star safety, who was a lean, mean, hitting machine. He never missed.

As he bore down on Willard for the sure tackle, he suddenly hesitated. I saw him place a hand over his nose and mouth and turn his head away. Willard scooted around him and ran in for the Mighty Hog's first score of the season! Just as he crossed the goal line, the nearest bank of lights blew with a loud "POP!" sending a shower of sparks raining down onto the ground below.

The local fans were on their feet screaming and cheering. The rest of the Hogs raced down the field to celebrate with the new hometown hero. Munro frantically tried to jumpstart the band; but they couldn't get their act together, and he finally gave up in a fit of frustration.

Winston stood beside me with arms crossed, nodding silently. Then he turned to me, grinning from ear to ear. "Notre Dame's got their 'Touchdown Jesus.' I guess we got *us* an angel in the end zone!" He uncharacteristically gave me a high five.

The brouhaha subsided, and the game resumed. The team lined up for the extra point try; but Nigel's kick was so low, it hit Maynard in the seat of the pants. The Nimrod players were upset at becoming the first team to be scored on by the Hogs; and they took out their anger on the next drive, marching down the field in just six plays and scoring a touchdown on a double reverse. But the Hogs weren't through yet.

The adrenaline rush from Willard's touchdown carried the exhausted players through the next series of downs. Knox completed passes to Nigel and Willie, and Clay broke out for a twenty-five-yard run. On the next play, Henry got the ball again; and he managed to find his acorn.

As he plowed through the hole, a defender hit him and spun him around several times. Somehow, he stayed on his feet and kept his legs churning. It turned out to be the longest run of the season. Unfortunately, it was in the wrong direction. Dazed and confused, he bounced like a pinball off his own teammates, who were yelling and trying to turn him around. Evading them all, he ran into his own end zone and spiked the ball, giving the Nimrod Mighty Hunters a two-point safety. Then he pulled out his yellowish-green hanky and waved it in the air while doing a ridiculous celebration dance.

When he staggered to the sideline, he had no idea what he'd just done. I looked into his eyes and saw that the boy was as loopy as a moonshiner's sow. "Whaddya think o' *that* run, Coach?" he exclaimed, all out of breath and slurring his words. "Purdy good, huh?"

I grabbed his shoulder pads to steady him. "That was a mighty fine run, Hanky, mighty fine. Now all you need to do is work on your directional skills!" He stared at me with bleary eyes and grinned. "Hanky, just how much medicine did you take before the game?"

"Medicine?" Henry scrunched up his nose. "Oh, ya mean my aljury remedy . . . *allergy* remedy! Well, ya said ta double up, Coach, so that's 'zactly what I did. An' ta make sure I didn't letcha down again, I took a third dose." He held up four fingers, then tried to hold down his pinkie. Giving up on that, he rolled his eyes melodramatically. "Guess that was a li'l too much, huh?"

I was not about to let Henry continue to play in his condition, so I called a time-out and conferred with Winston. My assistant reminded me that there were only three minutes left on the clock; and if we didn't finish out the game, we would have to forfeit. A million things ran through my mind in that moment, but I had to put the welfare of my player first. I gathered the team around me and explained what I had to do.

Jeremima looked worried. "Coach, if we forfeit now, will the game count as an incomplete or just a loss? We can take a loss, but we can't take an incomplete."

"The rules state that if the forfeiting team is losing at the time the game is stopped, the score stands as is." I glanced at the scoreboard. "That means this game will be recorded as a twenty-six to six loss. However, there will be an asterisk beside the score indicating it was achieved by forfeit."

"But that means we didn't finish the game, Coach," Isaiah argued. "There goes our perfect season!"

"Yeah, we gotta finish out the game," Maynard insisted.

I looked around at the other players in the huddle. "Are you all in agreement with that?" Each replied with a very intense affirmative. "Okay, then," I acquiesced, "but I want you to keep their players away from Hanky, got it?" I patted the top of Henry's helmet. "And I want *you* to keep away from the action. On every single snap, just jog off to the side and stay out of the way, you hear me?"

"Yessir, loud 'n' clear, Sarge!" Henry saluted me with a goofy grin—and promptly fell over. We helped him to his feet, and he staggered back onto the field with his teammates. Somehow, he managed to stay alive and out of trouble until the clock ran out. That's how game five of the Mighty Ferrell Hogs' crazy inaugural season ended.

If someone had told me eight weeks earlier what I would have to deal with during my rookie coaching season, I would have immediately packed my bags and headed straight back to central Indiana, where this sort of thing could never happen. I'm so grateful that God doesn't tell us what's around the next bend or over the next hill until we get there. If He did, we just might be tempted to turn back.

CHAPTER TWENTY
Unexpected Competition

The worn gears uttered a metallic, teeth-grinding growl as Winston downshifted and turned onto State Road 44 East toward Ransomville. Sitting in the right front passenger seat, I listened as the rusty old bus offered its running commentary on the state of the county highway system. There wasn't a part on that vehicle that didn't have something to complain about. The transmission whined; the brakes squealed; the suspension groaned; and the bumper rattled incessantly. We would have been better off leaving that heap at the scrap yard instead of the brake shop; but we had one more away game, and this was the only transportation available to the team. Besides, Winston seemed to have developed a love-hate relationship with the thing. He'd nurtured that bus for years; and I think it would have broken his heart to hasten its demise, although he never would have admitted it.

"How many tires ya think we need, Coach?" Winston's question pierced my meandering thoughts.

"Tires? Oh, I don't know. Eight or ten maybe. It sure would be nice if we could get a couple of larger ones for strength building."

He nodded without taking his eyes off the road. "Uh-huh. Oughta be able to find somethin' for that. Couple o' old tractor tires might do."

I studied the man in the driver's seat. The school custodian/grounds maintenance/assistant football coach was someone I'd grown to respect in the short time I'd known him. There was a quiet strength about him and an imperturbable confidence upon which I'd come to rely. He kept me grounded as head coach. Although a man of few words, his wisdom and knowledge were an invaluable asset to me; and I decided to tell him so. "Winston, I've been meaning to thank you for all you've done for this team. There's no telling where we'd be right now without you."

"Don't sell yourself short, Coach," he replied, shifting uncomfortably in his seat. "Most woulda turned tail an' run weeks ago. You stuck it out."

"I almost *did* run when I first saw what I was up against! Several times since, for that matter. But your calmness and support have been instrumental to our success." I chuckled. "Not to mention your unconventional methods!" That evoked a grin. "Hey, speaking of that, what did you say to Clay Piggott that's kept him on the team this long? I've been dying to know."

Winston took his time answering. "Um . . . I don't mean to be disrespectful or mysterious or nothin'; but sometimes, things are best left unsaid."

I frowned at him. "You know you're killing me here, Winston!"

He grinned. "Don't worry, it's nothin' you'd disapprove of. Just somethin' I picked up keepin' my eyes 'n' ears open, that's all." He stared straight ahead for a while. "Tell ya what. Ask me again at the end o' the season, an' I'll reconsider. How's that?"

I threw up my hands. "Fair enough." We drove in silence for a while. "So, do you have family here in Piggottsville?" I immediately regretted the question. Winston had been very tight-lipped about his personal life. He'd hesitated even when asked about something so innocuous as his football experience.

My assistant glanced at me and then looked away. "Used to."

"I didn't mean to pry," I backtracked. "It's just that I don't know much about you outside of football. Anyway, that's your business. I apologize."

"No need," he replied, keeping his eyes on the road ahead. "Guess if I'm *too* mysterious, ya might get the notion I'm a fugitive or somethin'." He shook his head. "Ain't nothin' like that. I told ya I played two years for Ole Miss, but I didn't graduate. Grades weren't good enough. Dropped out an' got married instead. High school sweetheart. Worked a couple o' odd jobs in Mississippi an' Louisiana, started a family, then moved to Piggottsville in '98. My kids graduated from here."

"I didn't know that! Are they still in this area?"

"No. My oldest lives in Huntsville with her husband an' my two grandkids. She's a nurse. Got a boy up in Little Rock. He's an auto mechanic." Winston took a deep breath. "My youngest . . . well, I ain't sure where he's at right now. Might say we're estranged. Got into some trouble an' left town 'bout eight years ago to go live with my sister in New Orleans. Last I heard, he was dealin' drugs somewheres down there."

I didn't know how to respond. But that had never stopped me before. I figured if I just kept on talking, that would somehow prove better than remaining silent. "I'm so sorry, Winston. I had no idea. I know what you mean about the grades, though. I was turned down by a dozen different schools before being accepted at Wooster. Even then, it took me five years to earn enough credits to graduate." I tried to lighten things up a bit. "And don't ask me where I ranked in my class. I'm embarrassed to say!"

A smile creased Winston's face. "An' yet, here ya are, livin' your dream o' teachin' 'n' coachin'."

I stared at him. "My dream? This isn't exactly how I envisioned the start of my career! But I believe God has me here for a reason. I just don't know what it is yet. I *do* know that 'all things work together for good'[15] to those who love Him, though."

Winston was silent for a moment. "That's a purdy good way o' lookin' at life. Kinda takes the worry 'n' fear outta things, don't it?"

I laughed awkwardly. "You'd think! Yet somehow I keep forgetting that God's in control. Did you know the Bible tells us not to be afraid 365 times?"

My assistant quirked an eyebrow. "No foolin'? Guess He figured we need the remindin'. That's one a day for a whole year. Kinda like takin' vitamins."

I nodded silently and stared pensively out the windshield as Winston took the next exit and turned onto the two-lane road leading into Ransomville. "So, have you ever thought of moving closer to your grandkids?"

"Thought about it lotsa times. Go to visit 'em at least twice a year." He shook his head. "But I can't leave. Been here twenty-six years. This is my home. It's where I belong." He sighed deeply. "Besides, it's . . . it's where my wife is."

"Oh, I see. Is it because she doesn't want to leave?"

Winston turned his head away but not before I saw the moisture in his eyes. "Well, truth is, she can't. She's buried in the Piggottsville Cemetery."

---

15 Romans 8:28

It never ceases to amaze me how we can interact with people on a daily basis and yet not know much about them. When we leave the safety and comfort of our homes, we often put on a mask, sometimes unintentionally, to make a good impression on others. We want them to see us as we *want* to be seen, not necessarily as we really are. We want them to think well of us. I guess that's just human nature. The problem comes when we place too high a value on others' opinions. That often becomes a snare, and we fall into the trap of trying to please people instead of God.

I'm not saying we should air out all our dirty laundry—just that we shouldn't be afraid to show our flaws and cracks and failures. And we shouldn't put on a facade. This world needs more people who are genuine and humble. We don't have to be perfect. That's a trait belonging only to God. I felt very blessed.

This little side trip had given me a new understanding of my assistant coach. He had feelings and hurts like everyone else yet had graciously allowed me a glimpse into his vulnerability. As a result, my compassion and appreciation for Winston grew by leaps and bounds.

Once the brakes had been repaired, we swung by the scrap yard to pick up the tires we needed, cramming them into the empty seats and aisle of the tiny bus before heading home. When we arrived back at the high school, I helped him stash them under the bleachers. I couldn't wait for Monday's practice so we could try them out.

It was close to 4:00 when we parted ways. I hadn't had anything to eat since breakfast; and with the workout I'd just had wrangling those tires, I was famished. Since no frozen dinner or mac-n-cheese out of a box would satisfy such a craving, I decided to eat supper at the diner. After parking my car on the street in front of my apartment, I ran upstairs to take a quick shower and change clothes. Then I walked down to the Main Street Café a few blocks away. I entered the eatery and took a seat at the counter, not wanting to tie up an entire booth or table.

"Welcome back!" Charlene, the waitress, set a glass of water in front of me. "Do you know what you want, or do you need a menu?"

I returned her smile. "Better let me see the menu. I haven't made up my mind yet."

She reached under the counter and pulled out the single, laminated page and handed it to me. "Take your time. No rush." I looked over the options and made my selection.

After placing my order, I picked up Friday's edition of *The Piggottsville Daily Scoop* from the end of the counter. I turned over the folded, four-page rag, curious to see what had been written about last week's game against Montgomery North. Much of the narrative appeared to be cut-and-pasted from the previous week's article: "Piggottsville-Stuyvesant High School enjoyed its fourth consecutive football game of the season when it tackled the Montgomery North Tigers on hostile turf Friday night. The accurate arm of Knox Piggott and the powerful legs of Clay Piggott put the Mighty Ferrell Hogs in position to score the team's first points of the season. However, due to a series of unfortunate miscues, namely a fumble and a missed field goal, the team once again came up just shy of a victory in the hotly-contested battle. On a positive note, the crowd was entertained by the newly-formed Piggottsville cheer squad, which put on quite a show."

There had been no crowd for the cheerleaders to entertain, so I'm fairly certain the reporter hadn't even been at the game. I glanced up from the paper. Charlene was leading a group of four to an empty table next to the front window. The place was already about half-full.

As I searched the room for familiar faces, I spied Emily seated in the booth closest to the kitchen. Feeling a sudden urge to go say hello, I started to get up off my stool; but I froze. She was not alone. Seated across from her was a young man I'd never seen before. I hesitated. Should I leave them alone or just mosey over and say hi anyway? I decided to sit back down and study the situation further.

Her booth mate was a fairly good-looking guy in his mid-to-late twenties with sandy-brown hair. He was maybe six-feet tall with a muscular build. I watched as the pair engaged in animated conversation; but due to the chatter from the other patrons, I couldn't hear what they were saying. Was he a local or an outsider? Either way, what was he doing having dinner with her? Were they just friends, or were they on a date? After all, that would be normal, even expected, for a girl as nice and as pretty as she. So *what* if she went out with other guys. I had no claims on her!

I know; I know. I should have stopped that train of thought right there, but I couldn't help myself. Our friendship had been growing steadily, and I have to admit I'd been hoping it might progress into something more serious at some point down the road. Something the guy said made Emily laugh, and I felt a twinge of jealousy. *I* should have been the one sitting opposite her making her laugh, not him! Who was this interloper, anyway?

The young man accidentally dropped his fork onto the floor. My heart soared. This macho dude was nothing but a klutz. I still had a chance! When he bent over to pick up the utensil, I saw some printing on the front of his red sports shirt and recognized it instantly. It was the Ohio State logo. So this guy was someone she must have known from her time at the university. An old acquaintance or friend, perhaps? An old boyfriend? Or maybe a current one.

I couldn't take my eyes off the pair. I had to know. Their eyes locked as he said something to her. My stomach knotted up. Trying hard not to stare, I watched him reach into his pocket and take out a ring. *Nooo! Not a ring. Anything but that!* He took one of her hands and slipped it onto her finger. Emily gazed rapturously at it for a moment. When she looked up, her face was glowing.

"Here you are, sir!" The clank of the heavy ceramic dinner plate snapped me out of my trance. Charlene was standing in front of me. "Is there anything else I can get for you?"

I stared blankly at the plate and then at her. I must have had the strangest expression on my face because she tilted her head to one side with a worried frown. "Are you okay?"

After one more sideways glance at the two lovebirds, I looked up at her. "Um . . . would it be possible to get a take-home box? I don't feel so good."

"Of course, sir. I'll be right back."

As soon as she returned, I packed up my meal and paid the tab and then crawled back to my apartment like a whipped pup with its tail between its legs.

My alarm clock aroused me from a troubled sleep. I hit the snooze button and flopped back onto the bed, hoping against hope that what I'd witnessed the night before would somehow turn into the stuff dreams are made of and magically evaporate into nothingness. But there was no denying it. I knew what I'd seen, and there was nothing to do but face reality. Drawing on every last ounce of willpower, I forced myself out of bed and into the shower.

After a light breakfast, I began dressing for church, all the while trying to talk myself out of going. I did not want to face Emily and learn the awful truth about her relationship with the mystery man. And yet I couldn't let it go.

As I walked the short distance to the little white church, it dawned on me just how fond I'd become of my fellow teacher. In spite of not having the time or money to pursue a proper romantic relationship, my feelings for her had slipped in under the radar. They were very real and much deeper than I'd led myself to believe. It had just taken some competition to bring them to the surface. But now it was too late to do anything about it.

I dawdled the last two blocks, hoping to sneak into the service at the very last minute. However, Reverend and Mrs. Pinckney were in their usual spot on the front stoop greeting parishioners, and I couldn't avoid them.

"Good morning, Jason!" the pastor greeted me pleasantly, shaking my hand. "Nice to see you, as always."

Feeling like a total hypocrite, I put on my cheerful mask and nodded to the couple. "Reverend. Mrs. Pinckney. It's nice to be here."

We chatted briefly, but I honestly can't recall the conversation. My mind was on what to do if I ran into Emily. Mayor Wilson Piggott III chose that moment to arrive, and the worshipers began filing into the sanctuary. I lagged behind and slipped into the back pew as the service started.

When everyone stood to sing a hymn, I spied Emily and Miss Elvira in the third row from the front. And standing between them was the guy from the diner! Not only was he still in town but he was also standing right next to Miss Elvira as though he were part of the family. Then it hit me—hit me hard enough to stop me from singing. He was still here because he had come to propose to Emily. He *was* about to become part of the family!

A wave of nausea swept over me, and I wrestled with the idea of ducking out of the sanctuary and going home. The nausea eventually passed and with it the thought of leaving. However, I decided I wasn't up to facing Emily and the painful truth. In spite of my burning curiosity, I had no desire to meet Mr. Right. So I refocused on the hymnal in my hand and somehow made it through the service.

At the conclusion, I headed for the exit. The only thing standing between me and freedom was the Reverend Norbert Pinckney, who grabbed my hand and wouldn't let go. He leaned in and lowered his voice. "If you could just give us about forty-five minutes, that would be ideal."

I had no idea what he was talking about. I stared at him blankly. "Forty-five minutes?"

"Yes, that will allow Nancy and me time to get the meal ready before you and the others arrive."

The meal? So that must have been what they'd talked to me about earlier. They'd invited me to Sunday dinner again. And I must have said yes. I forced a smile. "Oh, of course, Pastor. No problem." I glanced at my watch. "I'll be there around noon, if that's all right with you."

"Noon it is!" he replied, finally letting go of my hand. "Nancy's making her chicken casserole this time. I'm sure you'll like it as much as I do."

"I'm sure I will." I hastily retreated and walked to the corner of Main and Cross Streets, where I sat down on a public bench outside City Hall. I really wanted to be alone, but how do you turn down an invitation you've already accepted? What was it that he'd said? "Before you and the others arrive." What others? I didn't recall them saying anything about others being invited. But then, I didn't recall them saying anything about me being invited, either. Oh well, it was just one meal. I could get through that. Besides, some of Mrs. Pinckney's delectable dishes would be good for me, even if it meant sharing the table with a few other folks from church.

Just then, a familiar four-legged animal moseyed past. I tipped my invisible hat. "And a good day to you, too, Mr. Billy Goat!" He rolled his eyes in my direction before continuing on his merry way. I was jealous. The creature didn't seem to have a care in the world.

"Come in!" Reverend Pinckney smiled and held open the door to the parsonage. As I stepped across the threshold, the aroma of baked chicken greeted me. I was suddenly glad I'd agreed to come. "Dinner will be ready in a few minutes. Please, won't you join the others in the parlor?" He ushered me into the adjacent room. "I believe you know most everyone here."

Three people were seated in the room. An elderly woman sat erect in the high-backed Queen Anne chair. Elvira Primrose! The other two sat cozily on one end of the sofa. I blinked. It was Emily Davenport and . . . *him*! In all my life, I've never had a stronger flight impulse than I had at that moment. I wanted to bolt. But I just stood there . . . like a *dork* in the headlights!

Emily broke the silence. "Hi, Jason! I was hoping you'd come." She sounded so cheerful. But then, why wouldn't she? She'd just been proposed to. "I didn't see you in church this morning." She motioned me toward her. "Come here, I'd like for you to meet someone." I couldn't move. My feet were nailed to the floor. She gave me a quizzical look. "Jason?"

I snapped out of my funk. "Oh, sorry." I managed to break free and crossed the room to where the happy couple was seated. I could feel the heat in my face. Mr. Right got to his feet, grinning from ear to ear. Of *course* he was. Why wouldn't he be?

Emily smiled warmly. "Jason, I'd like for you to meet Ronnie."

The victor extended his hand. "Hi, Jason. Nice to meet you! I'm Ronnie, Emily's cousin."

I mechanically reached out and fumbled for the hand offered me. "Uh, it's nice to uh . . . wait! Did you say . . . her *cousin*?"

It was Emily who replied. "Yes, he called me up Friday afternoon to say he was driving down for the weekend. Isn't he a character? I was so surprised!"

"That makes two of us," Elvira said bluntly.

Actually, that made three of us. I finally located my manners, which had disappeared into the witness protection program. "It's nice to meet you, Ronnie." I shook his hand as vigorously as if it were a pump handle. "You have no *idea* how nice it is to meet you!" My face was burning hot now. I made a feeble attempt at conversation. "Uh, where did you come from?" I stammered.

"Cincinnati. I had no plans this weekend, so I thought I'd surprise Auntie El and cousin Em."

"I figured you were from Ohio. I saw the OSU shirt you had on in the diner last night."

Emily looked surprised. "You were at the diner? Why didn't you come over and say hi, silly? You could have joined us!"

I don't know at what temperature a person spontaneously combusts, but I'm sure I was awfully close to it. "I, uh . . . I didn't want to bother you. It looked like you two were having such a . . . a good time." I thought of the ring he'd placed on her finger and stole a glance at her hands. It was still there. A billion questions swirled in my brain, but I wisely kept them at bay. Sometimes, my self-control amazes me—on those rare occasions when I show some.

"Dinner is served!" Reverend Pinckney announced from the doorway. I was never more eager for a meal in my life. When we sat down at the table, I noticed my hands were shaking. As I reached for my napkin, I knocked over my water glass; and in my haste to mop up the spill, my fork clattered onto the floor.

Awkward! *Now* who was the klutz?

"You didn't seem yourself yesterday at the Pinckneys'," Emily stated, looking straight into my eyes.

I wiped my mouth with my napkin and glanced around the lunchroom to stall for time. How was I supposed to respond to that? I was weary of beating around the bush, so I chose to be straight up. "You noticed, huh? I guess I *was* a bit out of sorts, wasn't I?" I laughed nervously. "To be perfectly honest with you, when I saw you at the diner with your cousin, I didn't know what to think. I figured he was someone you knew from college. Then when he put that ring on your finger, well, I just assumed . . . " I let my words trail off, too embarrassed to continue.

"Ring? Oh, you mean this thing?" Emily held up her hand and showed me the antique opal ring. "This is a keepsake that belonged to my grandmother. Mom gave it to Ronnie to bring down to me the next time he came for a visit. She promised I could have it after Grandma passed." She paused. "And you assumed it was an engagement ring?" She held up her hand again and smiled. "It's on my *right* hand, not my left. See?"

"I . . . I didn't notice," I stuttered, feeling like a total bozo.

"Then you must have thought Ronnie was my fiancé!" She cocked her head to one side. "Was *that* what was bothering you?"

"Well, not exactly. I just thought that . . . " I heaved a sigh. "Okay, yes, it *was* bothering me! I've been hoping that I might . . . I mean, that *we* might explore the possibility of, you know, developing a deeper relationship. At some point in the future, that is." I threw up my hands. "But when I saw the ring, well, I figured that idea was out the window."

Emily didn't reply for the longest time. But the silence was not embarrassing or uncomfortable at all. It was pleasant. She gazed at me with a tenderness that melted my heart into one big puddle of mush. She took a sip of her bottled water and smiled at me like no other girl ever had. "Why, Mr. Wisniewski, I do believe that is just about the sweetest thing I've ever heard. And I just might be open to exploring that possibility with you!" She gathered her belongings and got to her feet. "At some point in the future, that is." She grinned and winked playfully at me. Then she pushed in her chair, picked up her tray, and walked away, leaving me to find my own way back down to earth from Cloud Nine.

CHAPTER TWENTY-ONE
THE RAIDERS

I felt lighter than air that week. My spirits were higher than they'd ever been since arriving in Piggottsville. The days seemed brighter, the nights sweeter, and the air fresher. That is, as long as the wind wasn't blowing from the west. On those days, I shut my classroom windows and took my chances with Skunk in an enclosed environment.

When Winston and I went out to the field Monday afternoon, we saw Danny's dad, Phil, unhitching our new tackling sled from the back of his pickup truck. We helped him roll it to the sideline and stand it upright. The re-purposed plow was perfect. Winston said he'd attach the blocking pads to the frame after practice so we could begin using it the following day.

During first period the next morning, J.P. told me his dad was having some fliers printed up for us to hand out during Saturday's festival, compliments of his insurance agency. And at practice, Knox informed me that Orville, ecstatic over his son's first touchdown pass of the season, had ordered two hundred pig snouts for the fans to wear at our remaining games. I was thrilled with the news. We'd come a long way since the start of the season when hardly anyone gave a hoot about football. School spirit and town pride were beginning to grow, in spite of the mocking which continued from those outside our little community. In fact, that unpleasantness reared its ugly head again that very evening.

On my way home from practice, I stopped at Yokel's Hardware on Main Street to buy some spray paint for our scuffed-up helmets. Earlier in the day, I had asked Mr. Herold for the money; and to my utter amazement, he reached into his desk drawer and forked over the school credit card. But true to form, he stressed the need to limit the purchase to twenty-five dollars or less. No matter. We only needed to repaint eleven helmets.

I entered the old, hardwood-floored establishment and went straight to the paint aisle at the back of the store. But instead of finding rows of different-colored spray cans, the shelf was completely bare. Mr. Yokel had taped up a handwritten sign: "For Spray Paint Purchases, See Owner."

I located Magnus near the cash register. He was wiping down a glass display case with an old rag. "What happened to all your spray paint?" I inquired. "You used to have quite a selection."

"Had to move it all behind the counter," he replied with a look of disgust. "There's been a rash of thefts the past two weeks. Funny thing is, they've only gone after spray paint. I've seen some new graffiti around town lately, so I reckon it's just a bunch of local kids. But you can be sure Virgil's looking into it, though!" He bent down and put the cleaning rag under the counter. "Why'd you ask? You need to buy some?"

"Yes, I need four or five cans of gloss black, if you have them. I'd like to repaint the football helmets before Friday's game against Ransomville."

Magnus grunted. "Black seems to be the color of choice among those thieves, but I think there's enough left for what you need." He disappeared into the back room for a moment and then returned with several cans in his arms. "You're in luck. Had exactly four left." He plunked them down on the counter.

"How much will that be?" I asked, pulling the credit card out of my pocket. "Mr. Herold gave me a budget of twenty-five dollars."

Magnus grinned crookedly. "Last of the big-time spenders, huh? Did you say this is for the football team?"

"Yes, the kids' helmets are in awful shape; and after all the hard work they've put into this season, I wanted to give them something they'd be proud to wear."

"You're doing a fine job with those kids," the proprietor mused. "They're improving every week. Town's getting behind the team, too. The wife and I have been to the last two home games ourselves. You should be mighty proud of them." He began placing the cans into a paper sack.

"I am. They've overcome a lot. So, how much did you say the total was?"

Magnus waved a dismissive hand. "No charge. Just call it a donation to the team." He winked. "Besides, it sounds like Mr. Herold needs that twenty-five dollars more than I do!"

I laughed and thanked him for his generosity. Then I left the store. As I opened the door of my sedan, which was parked at the curb, the sounds of honking horns and shouting captured my attention. I glanced up to see five cars driving single file right down the middle of Main Street. Pedestrians stopped on the sidewalks to gawk, and people appeared in doorways and windows as the noisy parade approached. Teenagers dressed in Ransomville Raider colors hung out of the car windows waving and shouting wildly.

"Piggottsville is nothing but a suburb of Podunk!"

"Come to the Raiders' Friday night Hog roast!"

"We're gonna fry your bacon good!"

"Pig-Sty High stinks!"

Then the eggs and tomatoes started flying. I instinctively ducked behind my car as the missiles rained down around me. I heard the splattering as well as an occasional yelp as they found their targets along the street.

Once the rowdies had passed, I stood up thinking the excitement was over. It wasn't. The visiting marauders apparently didn't realize that Main Street was a dead end. Three blocks away, the caravan did a U-turn and roared back through town but this time a little faster. The invaders lobbed a few more hand grenades before racing out of town the way they'd come.

As the shouting and honking faded, I looked around. The facades of the businesses on both sides of Main Street were covered with egg and tomato residue. Several unfortunate pedestrians were wiping the stuff off their clothes. Business owners and customers emerged from doorways to take stock of the damage. I inspected my car, which had taken several direct hits. Opening my trunk, I retrieved an old towel and began to wipe off the mess as best I could before it dried and damaged the faded maroon paint.

I was working on my car when I heard a siren start up about two blocks away. A black and white patrol car with the Piggottsville Police Department shield on the side came screeching around the corner with lights flashing and siren blaring. As it roared past, I caught a glimpse of

a very-determined Virgil at the helm, trooper's hat tilted low, mirrored glasses covering his eyes, jaw tightly clenched, and hands firmly gripping the wheel at ten and two. He raced up Main Street after the perps, who were probably out of his jurisdiction by now. It seemed a fitting finale to the big show.

I tossed the towel into the trunk and then drove straight to the single bay, do-it-yourself car wash on A Street, figuring it would be getting a lot of business over the next few hours. Approaching the facility, I noticed that one block wall was covered in new graffiti. There was nothing bad about it—no vulgar or gang-related symbols—just words and pictures—and funny ones, at that. The vandals had spray painted "HOG WASH" on the wall, along with the slogan, "Clean the sloppy off your jalopy!" Under that was a cartoon pig shaking the mud off its back. I laughed out loud . . . and snapped a picture of it.

After washing my car, I turned onto 6 Street to go home and observed several more bent and mangled stop signs. I glanced up at the water tower, which stood in the middle of the next block hovering over the surrounding houses. It was also covered in artwork—artwork that wasn't there when I'd first driven into town nine weeks earlier. Some kids bravely—if not foolishly—had climbed the four-legged, 130-foot-tall, galvanized structure. A large hog was painted underneath the word "Piggottsville," standing upright with its front hooves resting defiantly on its haunches. It sported a red Superman-style cape along with the words, "Home of the Mighty Ferrell Hogs." So this was where all the spray paint had gone! Piggottsville definitely had a juvenile delinquency problem. I wondered what Virgil was doing about it.

Back in my apartment while nuking a frozen dinner, it occurred to me that the artists were likely students at the high school, perhaps even in my classes. Pretty brazen if you ask me. But they showed real talent, I'll give them that. And a penchant for pigs. New York had its *Starry Night*. Paris had its *Mona Lisa*. Now Piggottsville had its *Mighty Hog*.

The scuttlebutt at school on Wednesday centered around the raid by the Ransomville teens. The students were angry about the disrespect shown by our rivals. There was even talk of revenge, which prompted an unprecedented public announcement by Mr. Herold during fifth period.

He assured the student body that our capable sheriff was conducting his own investigation and instructed them to keep out of the way and let the authorities do their job.

Skunk fell asleep in U.S. History again, making this the fifth day in a row. He'd also been uncharacteristically lethargic during the last few practices. Determined to learn the reason, I asked him to remain after class. Once the room cleared out, I sat down on the front edge of my desk and addressed the droopy-eyed boy in the back row. "Willard, I've noticed you've been really tired the past few days. You haven't been able to stay awake in class, and you haven't been yourself at practice. Are you not feeling well?"

The boy shifted uneasily in his seat and chewed his lip. "Naw, I ain't sick or nothin' like that."

"Are you not getting enough sleep at home?"

He stared out the window before answering. "Ain't that, neither."

I studied him for a moment. "Willard, I wouldn't be asking if it wasn't affecting your schoolwork and practice. First quarter finals are Friday, you know, and I'd hate to see you do poorly. Besides, I really need you at your best for the game against Ransomville. As your teacher and coach, I only mean to help. I don't mean to pry."

He picked absentmindedly at a chip in the corner of his desk. "I know that, Coach Wiz . . . I mean, Mr. Wisniewski." He drew a deep breath. "I'm tired 'cause of all the chores."

"Chores? I thought we had that sorted out. You've been doing fine with your chores since your mother said you could keep playing football."

He looked up at me. "It ain't *my* chores makin' me tired. It's Durnell's."

"Durnell's? You're doing Durnell's chores as well as your own?" He nodded. "So that's it. But why are you doing his? Are you being punished?"

Willard shook his head. "Naw, I'm doin' his so's he can study some more when he gets home from tutorin'. He don't have time to do both."

His explanation floored me. "You mean, you *volunteered* to do your brother's chores so he can pass enough classes to remain with the team?"

He nodded as if embarrassed. I suddenly choked up, then put my palms together and touched my fingers to my lips. I stared at the ceiling, blinking back tears. Finally, I got to my feet and walked back to where he sat, not caring how bad he smelled. "Willard?" He looked up at me. "Willard, that is the most unselfish act of kindness I have heard of since coming to Piggottsville. You're making a huge sacrifice for your brother and the team. I'll bet your mother is really proud of you." He nodded self-consciously. "I'll tell you what. Why don't you skip practice today and tomorrow and rest up for Friday's game? Do you think that will help?" He nodded.

"Good. Then we'll leave it at that." I placed a hand on his slight shoulder. "But I want you to know one thing. *I'm* mighty proud of you, too!"

A broad smile spread across his face. "Thanks, Coach Wiz!"

"No, thank *you*, Skunk!" That's the first time I ever heard him laugh.

At lunch, I spoke with the teachers who had been tutoring Durnell to check on his progress. They all told me the same thing. He was making an effort, but whether it would be enough was anybody's guess. That night, I found myself praying that Willard's selfless act would be the difference.

During my Thursday classes, I encouraged the students to attend the Ferrell Fall Festival on Saturday and invited them to stop by the football team's table for a photo op with Bo, the Mighty Ferrell Hog.

"It should be a lot of fun," I raved. "The festivities begin at noon with the firing of an old cannon, followed by a short speech from our mayor." Knowing snickers tittered across the room. I looked at my pupils. "What? Did I say something wrong?"

"You said the mayor will give a *short* speech," Danny blurted out. "Everybody knows he's long-winded. Last year, he rambled on for twenty-seven minutes. I know, I timed him myself!" The others laughed.

Knox took issue with Danny's comment. "Hey, watch what you're saying! Boss Hog's my G-Pop."

I stared at him. "Excuse me?"

"Boss Hog's my G-Pop!"

I shook my head. "You're not making sense. Could you speak English this time?"

Knox spelled it out slowly for me. "Boss. Hog. Is. My. G. Pop." He rolled his eyes and held up both palms. "You know . . . the mayor is my grandfather."

"Oh, okay. *Now* I get it!" I laughed. "At first, I thought you were speaking hip-hop, or Be-Bop, or some such claptrap."

"Huh?" Knox shot me a quizzical look. "Now *you're* the one not making sense." The class cracked up. Although only seven or eight years younger than me, my students were quite adept at making *me* feel like a G-Pop.

Testing began Friday morning. As I passed out the exams to my first period class, I couldn't stop thinking about Willard and Durnell, and I offered up a quick prayer for both. While my students concentrated on the three pages of questions, I silently walked up and down the rows of desks, fully cognizant that the temptation to cheat often loiters in a classroom like a penniless teenager on a Saturday night. Convinced that the class was well in hand, I sauntered past the windows and looked outside. The small parking lot was full of teacher and staff vehicles with Mr. Herold's car in the reserved space closest to the main entrance. Adjacent to the paved lot was the grass lot reserved for students with their own transportation. I spied Knox's now infamous pickup truck parked among the dozen or so student vehicles along with a couple of farm tractors. Several kids living in outlying areas occasionally drove them to school, but that was only permitted if they missed the bus or had to stay late for extracurricular activities and had no other means of getting to or from school.

On the front lawn next to the sign, Bo, the school's new mascot, lay contentedly in the cool grass, soaking up the sunshine. I smiled to myself. Mr. Herold had granted the Pugh twins permission to have him staked out front on game days as a means of generating school spirit and game attendance. And concession income, of course.

During lunch, Emily assured me the cheerleaders were ready for a big crowd, and Munro informed me he'd convinced another student to join the pep band.

"That's great!" I exclaimed. "What instrument?"

"Trombone! He should add a lot of volume to the band."

I had learned by now to be optimistically cautious in my expectations. "How much experience does he have?"

The band director grimaced. "Not much, I'm afraid. He just started this year." Then his face brightened. "But while I was hunting for some trombone music, I stumbled upon the old school fight song."

"I didn't know the school had its own fight song," I commented.

"Neither did I," Emily interjected.

"We don't." Munro took a sip of his soda. "Leastways, not since the turn of the last century. This one dates back to 1909, I think."

"How does it go?" I asked out of curiosity.

Munro's eyes bugged. "Oh no, you don't! Don't ask me to sing it in here! But the lyrics go something like, 'Go, ye mighty Ferrell Hogs / Ever raise thy standard high / Onward press at ev'ry turn / Fight, for vic'try is well nigh.' Something to that effect."

"That sounds rather archaic," Emily observed.

The music teacher made a comical face. "It does, doesn't it? So I'm going to try and come up with some new words. Maybe the pep band will even have the tune ready in time for homecoming." He paused and adjusted his glasses. "How's *that* for optimism?"

Fifth period World History began the same as my other earlier classes. I handed out the test and after giving a few basic instructions, had the students begin. About twenty minutes in, Henry, who sat next to the window, happened to look outside. He suddenly jumped to his feet and shouted, "Hey, they're kidnapping Bo!"

The rest of the class rushed to the windows, the test all but forgotten. Had we been in a boat, the stampede to the port rail would likely have capsized the vessel. I hastily followed them. A couple of cars and a pickup truck were idling at the curb. Two young men were placing a ramp against the truck's open tailgate while ten or twelve other teens formed a circle around Bo, who was eyeing them warily as they inched closer. We watched in mesmerized disbelief as the kids, all dressed in Ransomville Raider colors, untied our mascot and tried enticing him toward the truck with carrots and potatoes.

Nigel broke the stunned silence. "Well, if that don't take the biscuit!"

Henry turned to me with pleading eyes. "Mr. Wisniewski, we can't let them steal Bo!"

Clay pressed his face against the wire screen and yelled down at the kidnappers. "Hey, get away from our mascot!" The teens glanced up and made several inappropriate gestures. "If you don't leave, I'm calling my dad. He's the sheriff, and he'll throw you all in jail!"

He was met with ridicule and a few choice words.

He turned to me, his face red with fury. "Coach, are we gonna stand here and let them steal our mascot? We gotta stop those scumbags!"

"Yeah! Let's go down there and chase 'em off!" someone suggested. The idea met with unanimous approval, and most of my class rushed headlong for the door.

I quickly cut them off, fearing that a physical confrontation might turn into a full-blown rumble. I held up both palms. "Whoa! Hold on. Nobody is leaving this room!"

"But, Coach, we gotta stop them!" Clay argued.

As I racked my brain for some rational course of action, Lexi Rae Brannigan, who was still watching out the window, yelled, "Hey look, Bo's fighting back!"

When the mob rushed back to the windows, I whipped out my cell phone and called Mr. Herold's hot line, a number given to current teachers only to be used in dire emergencies. I figured these circumstances met that criterion. He was already aware of the situation, having just been informed by a teacher on the first floor, whose classroom also faced the front of the building. I slipped the phone back into my pocket and joined my students at the windows.

I'll never forget what happened next. The raiding party had managed to entice Bo over to the back end of the truck, but he was balking at going up the ramp. So three muscular guys climbed into the bed and pulled on his rope while the rest pushed from behind. That didn't go so well. Bo let out a squeal that expressed irritation in any language, human or animal. He lowered his head and began swiping it from side to side. Then he arched his back and raised his hackles.

From our vantage point, I could see the hair on his back standing straight up like a Mohawk. Then he lunged. The three boys in the pickup's bed tumbled backward, then scrambled over each other in their haste to get to safety atop the roof. Satisfied that he had run off those in front of him, Bo turned his ire onto the others. He chased them around the cars until they dove through open windows or climbed onto hoods and roofs to get away from the rampaging giant. Our agitated mascot then body-slammed the vehicles several times, leaving huge dents in a couple of doors and fenders. Satisfied that he had run off all his attackers, Bo gave one final snort and returned to feasting on the discarded vegetables as if nothing had happened.

Suddenly, the air was filled with catcalls and taunts. However, this time, they came from *our* side, not theirs! As their teacher, perhaps I should have tried to stop them; but for some reason, I didn't. These kids had taken so much abuse lately, I thought it might be therapeutic to let them vent for a change.

With the mocking calls raining down on them, the Ransomville students warily climbed down from atop their vehicles and clambered to get inside, fighting each other in the process. You could see the dents they'd left in the roofs and hoods and trunk lids. Bo had crumpled one car's door so badly that it wouldn't shut, and the passengers had to hang on to keep it from swinging open. The other car had a flat tire, and it made a "ka-thump, ka-thump, ka-thump" sound as the entourage retreated down the road. Cheers and shouts erupted from the windows of all the front-facing classrooms, and my students began to high-five each other. I hate to admit it; but in some strange way, it was all so satisfying. The Mighty Hogs had emerged victorious over the visiting Raiders without so much as a single student getting involved! Now, if Bo could only learn how to play football . . .

At that moment, Winston and several teachers emerged from the main entrance, followed by Jeremima and Isaiah. The twins gently guided Bo back to the stake, where they securely tethered him again. Then they gathered up the vegetables and placed them within his reach. When a sense of normalcy returned to the classroom, my students resumed their testing. However, I was fairly certain that their history exam wasn't going to be the main topic of conversation around their dinner tables that night.

Ten minutes before school let out, Mr. Herold broke in with another special announcement. "May I have your attention, please? This is Mr. Herold. By now, I'm sure most of you are aware of the incident which occurred outside the building earlier this afternoon. Let me assure each and every one of you that the proper authorities have been notified, and an investigation has been launched concerning this egregious disruption of the academic process by a few agitators from outside our community."

The principal cleared his throat. "That being said, let me make one thing perfectly clear. Under *no* circumstances should any thought be given, or action taken, to exact revenge upon those responsible. Any attempt at retribution will be dealt with swiftly and severely. May I suggest instead, if you feel compelled to respond, that you do so legitimately, lawfully, and loudly at tonight's game against Ransomville.

Let's all come out and support our football team, so we can show those Raiders what Piggottsville High pride really looks like. Go, Mighty Ferrell Hogs!"

Once the building emptied of students and the buses all departed, I packed up my messenger bag and left the room. I was a little surprised that Ezekiel hadn't stopped by. After all, it was game day; and I had come to warmly anticipate his weekly words of wisdom. In a way, his brief visits had become a part of my pregame ritual. However, when I stepped out of the building, I discovered the reason for his absence. He was busy coaxing Bo into his short, lowboy hauler parked next to the curb. I waited at a safe distance on the chance that our mascot had any further notions of defending his turf. Once the boar was safely inside, Ezekiel closed and locked the tailgate. Then he leaned against the hauler, pulled out a handkerchief, and mopped his brow. I waved to get his attention.

"Jason! I didn't see you there," the farmer acknowledged. "I am sorry I did not drop by your classroom; but as you can see, I have had my hands full."

"I understand. I assume you've heard about the kidnapping attempt?"

He nodded. "Yes, the twins called me right after it happened. So did Mr. Herold. Those pranksters were very foolhardy. They could have been badly hurt. But I thank the good Lord there were no injuries."

I decided not to mention their damaged vehicles. "You're still bringing Bo to the game tonight, aren't you?" I asked. "I'd sure hate to lose our biggest sideline attraction."

Ezekiel wiped his brow again and tucked away his handkerchief. "I gave the matter some very serious consideration, but I don't foresee this happening again. He's really quite docile, you know. Stubborn at times, but manageable. I assured Mr. Herold that as long as I stay with him and he remains tethered when people approach, there won't be any problems. Besides, the children begged me to let him come tonight. They have a surprise planned that involves him."

"They do? They didn't say anything to me about that," I confessed. "Anyway, I'm grateful that you're doing this for the team and the school. It must be a lot of extra work for you."

Ezekiel was gracious in his reply. "I don't mind. And neither does Bo. The truth be told, you have done wonders with this team; and I am happy to be a part of it, if only in a small way." He glanced at his watch. "I had better get this animal home. It's close to his suppertime, and he gets a might grumpy if he's not fed on schedule. But I will have him at the stadium, you can count on that."

I thanked him and started heading for my car.

"Oh, Jason," he called out. "I almost forgot. I have a word for you. 'Moreover, it is required in stewards that a man be found faithful.'[16]"

I smiled. It was going to be a great night.

CHAPTER TWENTY-TWO
THE AEROSOL ARTIST

The air in the Pigskin Palace was charged like the atmosphere before a thunderstorm. You could feel the energy from inside the locker room. As I began my pregame talk, I heard the pep band start up under the capable leadership of Munro Masters. They were, indeed, loud—but still awful. When I concluded, the players jogged from the school to the stadium and gathered outside the end zone gate, eager to get onto the field and respond to the disrespect our opponents had shown the community and school.

As was my custom, I appointed one player who had gone above and beyond that week to lead the team onto the field for warmups. That night, I chose Skunk. With one fist in the air, the diminutive wide receiver and cornerback led the charge. The team's freshly painted black helmets glistened under the glare of the stadium lights. Many of the hometown fans were already in their seats on both sides of the center section, and more were streaming in. The concession stand was doing a brisk business. Mr. Herold would, no doubt, be happy with the night's take.

While the team ran through calisthenics, I conferred with Winston on the sideline. He had a perplexed look on his face. "What is it?" I inquired.

He pointed to the field. "See anythin' different?"

I scanned the playing surface. "No. Should I?"

"The cow patties are gone! Thanks to the Women's Missionary League."

I stared at him. "What does the Women's Missionary League have to do with the cow patties?"

"While that business with the pig was goin' on out front o' the buildin' this afternoon, they had some volunteers cleanin' up the field. When I went out to stripe it 'bout an hour later, they was just finishin' up." He looked at me and shook his head. "Don't ya get it? We lost our home field advantage!"

"Oh, I see." I shrugged. "Well, it was bound to happen sooner or later." I watched the team warming up for a while. "At least, we still have Skunk as a secret weapon."

He grinned. "That kid's kinda like a trick play, ain't he? Can't rely on him too often, though, or the surprise'll lose its potency."

"Fat chance of that!" I retorted.

Winston laughed heartily. Then he looked out across the field again. "Hey, notice anythin' else missin'?"

"What do you mean?"

"No opponent! Where's the Raiders?"

The Ransomville team was nowhere in sight. In fact, there were only four fans on the visitor's side. "That's strange. Their team should be on the field by now." I looked around. "I don't even see their bus. I wonder if they had a breakdown or something."

"I doubt it," Winston replied. "Ever see their buses? All of 'em are no more'n two or three years old." He shook his head. "No, somethin' else musta happened. Should be more o' their fans here by now, too. They're a purdy big school."

I glanced at my watch. "It's almost seven o'clock. You know what that means, don't you?"

He dished up a sly grin. "Yeah, it means if they don't show in the next five minutes, they forfeit the game." He chuckled. "Maybe we'll get our first win o' the season tonight, Coach!"

I scowled. "I don't want to win that way. I want us to earn it. Besides, our fans have come to see a football game, not a forfeit." I located the referees and ran out to where they were huddled at the fifty-yard line. "Do any of you know why Ransomville isn't here yet?"

"No, we don't," the crew chief admitted. He pointed to the small pocket rule book in his hand. "We were just reviewing the forfeiture rule." He read from the book. "'If a team fails to appear by the agreed-upon starting time, or following the optional grace period, the referee in charge shall declare the contest forfeited to the team ready to play.'" He looked at his watch. "If they don't show in exactly . . . two minutes, do you want me to declare tonight's game a forfeit? Or do you want to extend a grace period?"

I was familiar with the ruling, but I never thought I'd be involved in a forfeit that was the result of the *other* team not showing up! I glanced at our stands. There were probably a hundred people there, not counting the pep band and the cheer squad. They'd be mighty disappointed if the game was forfeited. So would my players.

Out of the blue, a Bible verse popped into my head: "An athlete is not crowned unless he competes according to the rules."[17] While it was not against the rules to be declared the winner by default, where was the glory in accepting victory without fighting for it? I looked at my players, who had gathered a few yards away with their helmets in their hands. It would be a hollow victory indeed if they didn't get the chance to at least compete against their rivals.

"What's your call, Coach?" the ref asked impatiently.

"Something beyond their control must have delayed them," I suggested, "because their fans haven't shown up yet either. Maybe an accident has traffic backed up, or they were forced to take a detour."

"Are you saying you want to give them a grace period?" he pressed.

Winston came up alongside of me. "What do you think?" I asked him. He shrugged impartially. I responded to the ref. "Yes, can we give them fifteen more minutes? Even if they arrive now, they'll need time to warm up."

"That's fine with me." He turned and walked back to his crew.

"What's the problem, Coach?" Knox asked as the players crowded around us.

"Yeah, did the Raiders turn chicken on us?" Willie blurted out. The others laughed. I ushered them to the sidelines and explained the situation.

"Why show them any grace at all?" Maynard argued. "After what they did to us, they don't deserve any!"

It has never ceased to amaze me how God puts thoughts in your head and words in your mouth when you least expect them but need them most. I grinned at my center. "That's a good question, McNerd. And you're absolutely right—they *don't* deserve any grace." I looked around the huddle. "But then, neither do any of us. I have it on the highest authority that we are all sinners; and were it not for the grace that God has shown us, we who don't deserve it would remain unforgiven and without hope. If God extends grace to us, shouldn't we extend grace to others?"

---

17 2 Timothy 2:5

The group fell silent. Then Isaiah spoke up. "Coach is right, y'all. If God did that for us, then we should at least do the same for the Raiders." He looked around at his teammates. "Shouldn't we, guys?" Most nodded reluctantly.

"Speaking of the Raiders, look who just showed up!" Jackson muttered under his breath. A long, yellow bus with "Ransomville High School" on the side came to a stop just outside the end zone gate. As the blue-and-gold-clad players ran into the stadium, one of their coaches met with the refs at midfield. Then the crew chief jogged over to our sideline.

"Their head coach says they got hung up near the intersection of Highway 44 and No Name Road," he informed us. "Something about a bunch of farm equipment in their way. Anyway, he's requesting a fifteen-minute warmup period. Is that okay with you?"

"Sure," I told him, "no problem."

Out of the corner of my eye, I spotted Mr. Herold motioning me toward the fence. I walked over to him.

"What's going on? Why the delay?" the principal demanded, a mixture of confusion and concern in his voice. After I explained the situation, he heaved a sigh. "Oh, is that all? Well, then, there's no need to worry, is there? The delay will allow more time for sales!" He pointed toward the concession stand. "Do you see how long that line is? And how many people there are in the bleachers? This is the largest crowd I can recall since becoming principal!" he exclaimed, barely able to contain his ecstasy.

As he walked away, I stood at the fence and surveyed the stands. People were still flowing into the stadium. In addition to the faithful few, I saw many new faces, including most of my players' families and a contingent of students dressed in school colors sitting directly behind the pep band. Just then, I spied Virgil patrolling in front of the home crowd. He cut quite a figure. He was smartly dressed in his sheriff's uniform with his trademark mirrored glasses covering his eyes, even though the sun had disappeared behind Avery's barn twenty minutes earlier. He tipped his hat to me as he passed. Trailing behind him was one of his deputies. Virgil usually ran the town single-handedly; but on certain occasions, he would swear in a temporary deputy or two to assist with parking and crowd control and the like. I got the impression he was trying to make a statement by letting everyone know there was a police presence at the game—no doubt due to the tomfoolery and bad blood our opponents had evoked that week.

Suddenly, people began pointing to the far end of the track. I turned to see Ezekiel Pugh jogging toward us, leading our beloved mascot, Bo. The huge hog sported a red cape across his massive shoulders and back with the words "Super Bo, The Mighty Ferrell Hog" on the sides. As he got closer, people stood up and began laughing and clapping and cheering. I did a double take. Attached to Bo's broad snout was a pair of fake tusks! Two students with feed bags slung over their shoulders followed behind, throwing objects into the crowd. I assumed they were snacks or rolled-up T-shirts. Then I witnessed several fans slip them onto their faces. They were pig snouts! Orville must have had them shipped express in time for tonight's game. I turned back to the field with a smile on my face. At last we had some decent support from the school and the community. It was going to be a memorable night.

From the opening kickoff, it was evident that my players were fired up. On their first possession and with the home crowd solidly behind them, the Mighty Hogs marched downfield to the Raider's thirty-two-yard line behind the excellent blocking of Isaiah and Jeremima. On third and three, Knox handed off to Clay, who slipped between the twins and dodged three defenders, beating the last one in a footrace to the end zone. Piggottsville had scored first!

The fans erupted, shouting and waving and stomping the bleachers. I fully expected a section or two to collapse under the force of the exuberant celebration. Even Munro managed to crank up the pep band, but the tune they played was unidentifiable. However, nobody seemed to care. We had just scored against our archrivals and had taken the lead for the first time that season.

Above the din, I heard a familiar shrill cry. "SOOOO-EEEE! PIG, PIG, PIG! SOOOO-EEEE!" No trouble identifying *that* one!

Nigel's extra point attempt bounced off the back of Maynard's helmet this time. At least, his aim was improving. Our defense then rose to the occasion as well, holding the Raiders to a couple of field goals.

At halftime, we went into the locker room tied six-all. The kids were ecstatic, and Winston and I had nothing but praise for the way they had played. Even Durnell had two tackles. I told them to keep up the effort and to go out and have fun in the second half.

When we ran back into the stadium, the Raiders fans started up with the taunts and jeers we'd grown accustomed to. They'd hung two large banners on the fence in front of their cheering section: "Slaughter the Hogs!" and "Rout the Snouts!" Some of their players were pointing to them and mocking our team.

Turning to Winston, I joked, "I don't think there's going to be a rout here tonight, do you, Coach?"

My capable assistant shook his head. "Not if we keep on playin' like we did the first two quarters!"

The referee blew his whistle, summoning the teams for the start of the second half. But before my players took the field, I gathered them together for the team cheer.

Just then, Knox spoke up. "Hey, Coach Wiz, where's Leonardo?"

I counted helmets. There were only ten in the huddle. I glanced at the bench; but the only person there was Danny, who sat hunched over his clipboard. I scanned the crowd. Maybe he'd gone over to the fence to speak with his mother. No Durnell. I turned back to my players. "Did any of you see him come out of the locker room with us?"

"Yeah, Coach," Willie responded. "He was right next to me when we ran onto the field."

Now I was really stumped. Earlier in the season, I'd lost a player or two in practice; but I'd never actually lost one during a game before!

The referee jogged over to us. "What's the holdup, Coach?"

I threw up my hands. "I seem to have misplaced a player!"

That must have sounded as ridiculous to him as it did to me because he tossed a rather odd look my way. Then he glanced at his watch. "Well, your team needs to take the field in the next sixty seconds, or I'll charge you with a delay of game." He turned and walked back to the other referees.

In desperation, I turned to Winston. "What do we do now?"

Before he could reply, Henry pointed to the end zone and shouted, "Here he comes!"

We all turned in unison as Durnell ran up to the team.

"Durnell," I scolded him, "where have you been?"

He stared at the ground. "I had ta do somethin'," he mumbled.

"You had to do something?" I then noticed the can of spray paint in his hand. "What are you doing with that paint? Is that the can from the equipment bag?"

Durnell shuffled his feet nervously. "I . . . I had ta borrow it."

Winston jumped into the conversation. "Boy, you got exactly ten seconds to explain yourself!"

I'd never seen Durnell show any emotion before; but in that moment, a fire flared in his eyes that took me completely by surprise. He pointed to the opposite sideline. "I couldn't stand it no more!" he exclaimed in a shaky voice fraught with anger. "They was mockin' us. So's I got *back* at 'em!"

I looked across the field at our opponent's banners. One was missing altogether. The other had been altered . . . with black spray paint. Much like the sign on the wall of the bank. It now read, "Root 4 the Snoots!"

As I stifled a laugh, Winston grabbed my sleeve. "Coach, we gotta get 'em out there. Time's up!"

I hastily sent the team onto the field with a trillion questions racing across my mind. How in the world had Durnell managed to steal one banner and alter the other without being caught? Was this why he wanted to be called Leonardo? Could he be part of the group responsible for the graffiti around town? I had to shove those questions aside as the game resumed.

The Mighty Hogs continued their excellent play in the third quarter; but they began to tire, and the Raiders scored a touchdown to take the lead. Halfway through the fourth quarter, the offense got close enough for Nigel to attempt a field goal. He finally found the distance but not the direction. The ball sailed so far wide right, it landed in the next county. After that, the players sputtered and ran out of gas; and in spite of a heroic defensive stand, our rivals scored another touchdown with a few seconds left on the clock. The final tally was six to twenty. Another loss but another contest completed in our march to a full eight-game season. It was by far the best game we'd played all year.

As a reward for their herculean efforts, I canceled Monday's practice. After the team was dismissed, I asked Durnell to come to the coaching office for a minute. When we were alone, I confronted him.

"Durnell, I want you to know that I do *not* approve of what you did at halftime. I understand your frustration, but you had no right to tear down their poster or deface the other one. Do you understand what I'm saying?"

He nodded silently.

"Then it won't happen again?"

He shook his head.

"Good. Then we'll let it go at that. But before I let you leave, I'd like to ask you something else. There's been a rash of graffiti in town recently. I've seen it at the car wash and on the water tower, and I've been made aware of a few other places as well. Would you happen to know anything about that?" I held my breath, half-expecting a nonchalant shrug or a full-blown denial. But the boy was full of surprises that night.

"I done it," he confessed to the floor.

I let the air escape my lungs. "*You* did it? All by yourself?"

He nodded.

"So then, it wasn't a group of kids who defaced those properties?"

He shook his head.

"Durnell, I'm not going to ask how you managed to climb the water tower or how you found the time to do all those murals by yourself. I just want to know why."

Durnell lifted his head. "'Cause ya tol' me to!"

My mouth dropped open. "*I* told you to? When?"

"After class that one day."

"What did I say?"

"Ya tol' me ta pursue my int'rest."

I tried to sweep the cobwebs from my brain. "I said that?"

"Yeah. Ya said I should take ev'ry opportunity ta develop my paintin' talent."

It was beginning to come back to me. "Now I remember. But, Durnell, when you said you liked to paint things, I just assumed you meant bowls of fruit or landscapes like in Miss Godwin's art class—and on paper or canvas, not on the car wash and water tower!" I paused. "Or the wall of the bank."

Our eyes met briefly, and I caught the faintest hint of a grin before he turned away. "So, where did you get the paint? Did you steal it from Yokel's Hardware store?" He thrust his hands deep into his pockets and hung his head. "Well, did you?" I pressed.

"Yeah," he answered in a barely audible voice.

His admission did not come as a surprise. "Durnell, I really appreciate your honesty. But I have to ask you one more thing. Do you ever use the spray paint for any other illicit or . . . or *harmful* purposes?"

A puzzled expression clouded his face for a moment. Then he crinkled his nose in disgust and glanced up at me.

"Why would I do that? That'd be wastin' good paint!"

His answer satisfied my concerns. Then his eyes widened. "Are ya gonna kick me off the team?"

I stared at him. For all the trouble he was in, *that* was what he feared most? I pointed to a chair, and he sat down. I sat in my desk chair and pondered my answer. "I'll have to think about that. But you know you're going to have to pay for what you stole."

"I know," he replied softly. Then he placed his head in his hands, and the self-loathing I'd observed at the beginning of school emerged. "I messed up. I always mess up. I don't mean to, but I always do. I ain't no good. I ain't worth *nothin'*!"

I gazed compassionately at the slack-shouldered boy. "Durnell, you're not nothing. You have value! You're worth something, especially to God."

He displayed a long face. "God? What would God want with me, anyways?" He squirmed in his seat. "I ain't got nothin' He wants."

I looked him straight in the eye. "Yes, you do, Durnell. You have a soul—a soul worth dying for! God loves you so much, He gave His Son, Jesus, to die on a cross for you. He paid for your sins, for my sins, and for the sins of the whole world so that we could be forgiven and have eternal life."

Durnell stared pensively into space for the longest time. "But . . . I ain't got nothin' ta give *Him*."

His simple sincerity touched me deeply. "That can be said of all of us. But never underestimate the Potter, Durnell." I smiled warmly at him. "When placed in His skillful hands, even the most useless lump of clay can become the most valued piece of treasure! Besides, you matter to me. You're one of my students and one of my players."

"Yeah, but I'm bad at learnin' an' even worse at playin' football. I ain't *good* at nothin'!"

"You're good at painting," I heard myself say. "Very good, in fact."

He looked surprised. "Ya think so?" His eyes brightened. "Ya oughta see the back of our barn. It's covered with my stuff!"

"I'd like to see that sometime," I replied honestly. "So, how did you get the paint for *that*?"

"I worked at Mr. Piggott's hog farm some." Suddenly, words began to pour out of the non-communicative youth. "But I didn't have no time ta earn the money for the other ones. I just wanted ta do somethin' ta show how proud I am ta be a Mighty Hog. Paintin's all I know how ta do. I couldn't help myself—'specially after all the grief we been gettin' lately. I'm sorry, Coach. I didn't mean ta hurt the team. I'll do *anythin'* ta make it right. Jus' don't kick me off the team. I can't let the rest of 'em down!"

I studied the trembling boy. For a non-verbal social misfit who wasn't used to expressing himself, he was doing a remarkable job. At last, he was beginning to show a sense of belonging, a sense of being part of something larger than himself. I thought of the possibility of losing him due to his grades, the results of which I'd learn early next week. For the moment, though, I was pleased that he was showing concern for others and that he was trying so hard at his schoolwork and his football skills. I decided to give him a break.

"Durnell, I'll tell you what. I'll let you stay on the team as long as you agree to do three things. First, you need to tell your mother what you've done. Second, you need to go to Mr. Yokel and apologize for the thefts and offer to make restitution for what you took. Third, you need to go see the sheriff and admit everything to him. Will you do that?"

His eyes widened, and fear seemed to grip him. Then he let out a long, low sigh and nodded. "All right." His fear turned to pleading. "But will ya come with me?" he asked pitifully.

"Of course, I will, Durnell. Taking responsibility for your actions isn't an easy thing. I'll be glad to help you face up to Mr. Yokel and the sheriff."

"It ain't them I'm afraid of. It's my ma! When I tell her what I done, she's gonna tan my hide good! Then she's gonna tell me I can't play football no more."

I patted his shoulder to reassure him. "I think you might be wrong about that, Durnell. Anyway, Monday after school, we'll go see her together."

CHAPTER TWENTY-THREE
CROSSING THE GREAT DIVIDE

BOOOOOM! The percussion from the small cannon rattled windows up and down Main Street, signaling the start of the Ferrell Fall Festival. Adults and children alike removed their hands from their ears, and several babies began to wail simultaneously. Right on cue, Mayor Wilson Piggott III ascended the raised platform set up in the intersection of Main and Cross Streets followed by his wife, Mary. The two were polar opposites in every way imaginable. The mayor was round, loud, and grandiose. His wife was petite, quiet, and demure. He made sure he was front and center at every public function, whereas she always kept in the background, content to live in his shadow—which was immense in every sense of the word. Even at high noon.

As the townspeople inched closer to the platform, I observed a most unusual sight. The crowd parted with half gathering on the west side of the platform and the other half on the east. Reverend Pinckney had warned me about what to expect. Those taking Virgil's side in the feud always set up their booths on the City Hall side of Main Street, whereas those loyal to Orville set up theirs on The Old Fort Bank side. Even though no line was painted down the center of the street, the Berlin Wall might as well have been there because the divide was that obvious.

Mayor Piggott pulled out his pocket watch and confirmed the hour. Then, with most of the townspeople segregated on either side of the platform, he slipped it into his vest pocket and silently surveyed the crowd, much as a king gazes down upon his subjects before delivering his state of the kingdom address.

"Good citizens of Piggottsville," the center of attention bellowed, his commanding voice needing no microphone, "it is my distinct privilege and pleasure to welcome each and every one of you to the seventy-first annual Ferrell Fall Festival, inaugurated by my grandfather, Wilson Piggott, our beloved third mayor. Each year, on this final Saturday in October, we Piggottsvillians pause our busy lives to celebrate the founding of our fair city in 1878 by my industrious ancestor, Ferrell Piggott."

The town's beefy boss began to wax eloquent regarding the history of the municipality and all the improvements his predecessors had made since its inception. I tried valiantly to remain focused on his loquacious discourse; but by the time he got up to his great grandfather, Simeon Piggott, I had already failed miserably. To keep from going bonkers as the mayor meandered through the accomplishments of his forebears, I studied those gathered.

Seated on the platform behind him were most of the town council members: Orville Piggott, Darryl Pressley, Phil Swanson, Magnus Yokel, and Mr. Herold. Conspicuously absent was Virgil Piggott. The fact that he was not on the same platform as his brother was certainly no surprise to anyone. The two were still not on speaking terms, although seeing Virgil on the same side of the field as his brother during the Ransomville game showed a considerable thawing of the icy stalemate, in my humble opinion. Surely, he was around somewhere. I scanned the area and spotted his wide-brimmed hat and mirrored glasses at the back of the crowd on the police station side of Main Street.

When the insufferable address finally came to a merciful end, the mayor pulled out his handkerchief and wiped his perspiring brow. Then he waved it over his head and announced,

"Ladies and gentlemen, boys and girls, let the Ferrell Fall Festival fun begin!" A truer statement was never uttered. No matter what transpired next, it *had* to be better than what we'd just been subjected to. Out of the corner of my eye, I saw Danny Swanson look at his smartwatch. Spotting me, he hurried over and pointed to the touchscreen.

"It's a new record, Coach!" he exclaimed excitedly.

"What is?"

"Boss Hog's speech. It lasted twenty-eight minutes and thirteen seconds!"

I shot him a fake frown but couldn't help laughing. Then I headed for the football table, which had been set up in front of Darryl Pressley's insurance agency adjacent to the bank. Several of the players' mothers had gotten together and sewn a cover for it in the school colors. As I straightened the stack of fliers, which featured a caricature of a hog and the team's schedule, I felt extremely thankful for the show of support, even though there were only two games left in the season. Better late than never.

In short order, I was joined by several members of the team, Emily and one of her cheerleaders, and Ezekiel Pugh with our decked-out mascot. The crowd fanned out along the street, stopping to visit the booths, sample the food, and play the games. Soon, people were coming by our table to pick up a flier and have their picture taken with Bo. The players began handing out pig snouts to anyone interested. Many commented on how pleased they were that the town had a football team once again, and several thanked me for all I was doing for the school and the community. That was very gratifying. But what really touched me was when I witnessed several children approach two of our players and ask for their autographs. That made it all worthwhile!

When we hit a slight lull, Emily suggested we walk around and see the other booths; and I accepted her invitation. Leaving Knox in charge of the table, we sauntered down Main Street toward the barbershop. The Piggottsville-Stuyvesant Consolidated School Corporation had a booth, as well as the chamber of commerce and a number of community businesses. The Women's Missionary League had a colorful canopy set up over two long tables filled with all sorts of delicious-looking baked goods. They were doing a brisk business. There were the usual ring toss and free throw games, a dunking booth, and two shooting galleries, one using Nerf guns and the other squirt guns.

When we reached the end of the block, we crossed the street and started back up on the other side. The first booth we stopped at was called Big Boar Bingo, run by the Piggottsville Garden Club. I picked up one of the cards. It was a map of the town. The vertical lines were A to F Streets, and the horizontal lines were 1 to 6 Streets with the letters and numbers scrambled on each card. The intersection of Main and Cross Streets was in the center marked with a star, indicating that it was a freebie. The caller would announce "D-4" or "A-2" or "Main-C" and the players would put an "X" on that intersection. I showed it to Emily, and we shared a laugh.

As we made our way up the street, I became aware of people staring at us as we passed. I turned to her. "Is there something wrong with the way we look? People are giving us the eye."

Emily shook her head. "It's that silly feud," she replied, not bothering to hide her disgust.

"What about it?"

"Haven't you noticed? We're part of the small minority in town impartial enough to cross over to the other side."

I looked up and down Main Street. She was right. There were plenty of people milling about, but they all stayed on their side of the street. I stood still and watched for a while, but not a single person crossed over to the other side. Not one!

"Come to think of it, I don't recall any of the people on this side of the street stopping by our table."

She scowled. "That's because we've got our booth set up on Orville's side. Those on Virgil's side won't have anything to do with us."

"That's ridiculous!" I blurted out, feeling totally frustrated. "Something needs to be done about this."

Emily frowned. "I feel the same way, Jason. It was like this last year and, from what I've been told, for the past fifteen years or so." A sigh escaped her lips. "I guess we'll just have to make the best of it. There's nothing we can do."

Something rather strange occurred at that instant. I had an epiphany. Now, I'd had inklings and ideas many times before, but nothing had ever hit me quite like this. To use Nigel's vernacular, it was not only cheeky and bonkers; it was also bloomin' brilliant! "Oh, yes there is! And we're going to do something about it right now." Before Emily could protest, I took her arm and steered her across the street toward our table.

She gave me a half-quizzical, half-apprehensive stare. "What do you have in mind?"

My adrenaline-charged words shot out in rapid-fire succession like bullets from a Gatling gun. "Do you remember what I told you about how we handled Knox's and Clay's animosity toward each other? How we got them to set aside their differences for the sake of team unity?" She nodded. "Well, if those two can come together for the good of the team, then the team can come together for the good of the town!"

She cocked her head. "I'm not sure I'm following you."

We reached our table, where half a dozen townsfolk were gathered taking pictures of Bo and talking with the players and the cheerleader. I still can't believe what I did next. I'm not a very assertive person by nature, but I'd had just about enough of this petty feuding that had our town split right down the middle. The Bible says, "a house divided against itself cannot stand,"[18] and I, for one, was not going to stand for it any longer. I grabbed the fliers and handed them to Emily. Then I addressed the two players taking their turns at the display. "Knox, Jackson, give me a hand with this table, will you?"

Jackson looked bewildered. "What are you doing, Coach?"

"I'm moving our display into the center of the street!"

Both boys hesitated. "Uh . . . you think that's wise?" Knox asked with some trepidation.

"Wise or not, we're doing it." The three of us carried the eight-foot table out to the middle of the street and set up shop again. Ezekiel brought Bo out as well. Just then, Clay walked up.

"What's going on, Coach?" he inquired before biting into the caramel apple in his hand.

Without replying, I grabbed his shoulders and parked him beside his cousin. Then I climbed atop the table and stretched out my hands like Moses facing the Red Sea. What came out of my mouth next didn't sound at all like me.

"May I have your attention?" I shouted. "Your attention, please!" People up and down the street stopped what they were doing and stared. A hush gradually settled over the festival. I continued, unabashed. "Friends and neighbors, I'm told that the Ferrell Fall Festival is supposed to bring the people of Piggottsville together in celebration. But as you all know, we are a divided community. Your football team was also divided at the beginning of the season; but we found a way to set aside our differences and come together for the sake of our team, our school, and our town." I pointed at the two cousins. "Now we stand shoulder to shoulder, united as one. We are one team; and we play as a team, knowing that we represent this entire town, not just half of it. We invite all of you to join us! Join us as one town, one community, and one people. Folks, we are *all* on the same team!"

---

18 Matthew 12:25

As I paused to catch my breath, an authoritative voice bellowed from among the throng, "Go, Mighty Ferrell Hogs!"

There was a smattering of applause.

Then a shrill cry arose from somewhere near the mayor's platform. "SOOOO-EEEE! PIG, PIG, PIG! SOOOO-EEEE!"

That sent the crowd into hysterics, and more applause followed. Greatly embarrassed, I climbed down off my soapbox. *Did I really just do that?*

Ezekiel Pugh offered me a look of respect. "That was well stated, son!"

Emily grabbed my arm and squeezed it tightly. Her eyes were sparkling, ten-carat diamonds. "Oh, Jason, that was awesome. I'm so proud of you!"

Quaking visibly, I heaved a sigh. "I sure hope I didn't ruin the festival. I feel a bit like that Civil War soldier who put on Union britches and a Confederate coat in hopes of surviving the war. He ended up getting shot by *both* sides!"

Then an amazing thing happened. The Women's Missionary League ladies began moving their canopy and tables from the Old Fort Bank side of Main to the middle. Several other organizations followed suit. From *both* sides of the street! However, the transition was not without some drama. I witnessed a husband and wife in a tug of war over moving their display. She was trying to drag their table into the middle of the street, and he kept pulling it back to the curb. I watched the conflict for a while, then posed a question to Emily. "Who do you suppose is going to win *that* argument?"

Her eyes twinkled impishly. "*She* will, of course. Just wait and see."

She was right. With a frustrated sigh, the husband finally surrendered to the will of his wife. Before long, over a dozen booths lined the middle of Main Street. Gradually, the festival attendees began frequenting the neutral displays. At first, some were reluctant to leave their side; but as the flow of traffic increased, the crowd became so intermingled that you couldn't tell an Orville supporter from a Virgil supporter if you offered a $500 reward for one in their daddy's newspaper.

Twenty minutes later, I spotted Orville standing on the sidewalk outside his bank, hands on his hips, shaking his head. I think the man was in shock. Glancing across the street, I spied Virgil stoically surveilling the scene from the steps of City Hall. I would have given my entire salary to know what was going on behind those mirrored glasses of his.

"Good morning, Reverend." I smiled as I shook Norbert Pinckney's hand outside the Piggottsville Community Church building. Instead of his usual warm reply, the pastor lowered his voice.

"Could I have a word with you, Jason?" he asked in a somewhat subdued tone.

"Of course." He took my arm and guided me to one side. I imagined that someone—perhaps Elvira Primrose—had informed him of my shameless public display of defiance at the festival and figured he was about to chastise me for my rash behavior. Boy, was I wrong.

"Jason, I want to thank you for taking a public stand at the festival yesterday. That must have taken a lot of courage."

I was stunned. "You mean, you *approve* of what I did?"

"I most certainly do!" he replied with conviction. "I believe the Lord used you to address a long-standing problem in a positive and effective way. And you led by example by using the unity your team has achieved as a road map for all of us to follow." He gave me a plaintive look. "Lately, I'm afraid I've lost sight of the goal. Instead of dealing with the issue and seeking a resolution, I've settled for merely keeping the peace and maintaining the status quo. I've done that by allowing the two factions to attend on alternate Sundays and by seeing that our church booth is on opposite sides of the street every other festival so as not to ruffle any feathers. In doing so, I've unwittingly encouraged and prolonged the problem. However, you changed all that yesterday when you attempted to resolve it."

I made a face. "I'm not sure it did much to resolve the initial feud, although I have to admit I was surprised by how many people broke ranks and joined us in the middle."

Reverend Pinckney placed a hand on my shoulder. "Jason, it may not be fully resolved yet; but by stirring things up, you started the ball rolling. In time, we may come to see the fruit of your good deed."

I laughed nervously. "I'm holding my breath that it turns out to be good fruit, Pastor, and not bad!"

When the congregation stood for the opening hymn a few minutes later, I glanced around the little sanctuary. On the other side of the center aisle, Virgil, Ruby, Clay, and his younger sister, Claire, stood in the row directly behind the mayor and his wife. That wasn't surprising. After all, this was their Sunday to attend. As we began the second verse, I turned and looked behind me and nearly dropped the hymnal I was holding for Emily. In the very back row stood Knox Piggott! We made eye contact for a second, and he gave me a thumbs up. Then I noticed the man to his right. It was Orville, dressed in his Sunday finest, with Jolene beside him. The entire family was here. And it wasn't even their Sunday! They must have slipped in after the service started. The brothers were still not talking to each other and not sitting on the same side of the aisle; but at least, they were in the same building. I smiled inwardly and returned to the hymnal. When God begins to work, He sure doesn't waste any time, does He?

After church, I asked Emily if she would like to go out to dinner with me and suggested a popular restaurant in Nesbitt. She thought for a minute and then accepted my invitation. After the scare with her cousin, I'd come to the conclusion that my meager teacher's salary was more than adequate for a little romance, after all.

I gave her time to take her great-aunt home and then swung by their house and picked her up. We animatedly gabbed all the way to and from the restaurant and enjoyed a wonderful meal together. We talked about our lives growing up in small towns, how things were going in our classrooms, whether or not Durnell would pass five subjects and be able to stay on the team, and Reverend Pinckney's interesting but lengthy sermon. This time, I was fully prepared to discuss the latter. Once burned, a lesson learned! Even for a knucklehead like me.

When we got back to Miss Elvira's, Emily invited me to sit on the porch with her for a while; and I wasted little time accepting her offer. Enjoying the company of Emily Davenport was rapidly becoming my favorite pastime. Did I mention that by now, I'd also come to the conclusion that I had some *time* for romance as well? It's amazing how one's perspective can change so quickly. We walked up the sidewalk to the veranda porch and sat down on the swing suspended from the ceiling.

"Thank you for inviting me to dinner," she said pleasantly as we gently rocked back and forth. "I really enjoyed the meal. And our conversation."

"Same here. And I enjoyed your company." I paused to gather my thoughts. "Emily, I've been meaning to thank you for standing by me all this time. When I first came to Piggottsville and saw what I was up against, I felt pretty alone and helpless. I really needed your support in the beginning. Still do, obviously! Ever since we first met, you've provided a listening ear, encouraged me when I was down, challenged me when I was out of sorts, and helped me wherever possible. That means a lot to me."

"You're welcome, Jason. I'm glad I've been able to help. Besides, I believe in what you're trying to do." She smiled sweetly and placed a gentle hand on my arm, sending a zinger throughout my body. "And I want you to know that I believe in *you*." She blushed self-consciously.

I felt myself returning her blush, but I'm sure it looked better on her than me. We moved on to less personal topics; and soon, we were laughing and joking like two giddy teenagers on a first date.

"I've got an English teacher joke for you," she suddenly announced.

"An English teacher joke? Okay, let's hear it."

"What's the difference between a literalist and a kleptomaniac?"

I thought for a minute and then shook my head. "I have no clue. Literally!"

She giggled. "A comma."

I scowled playfully. "A comma?"

"Yes. A literalist takes everything literally. A kleptomaniac takes everything, literally!"

Our laughs mingled. "Good one!" I replied. "And may I say, I certainly appreciate your grasp of grammar and punctuation!"

Emily batted her eyes coquettishly. "Why, Mr. Wisniewski, thank you for that lovely compliment. I'm so glad you feel that way about my proficiency with the English language."

A shot of boldness flowed through me. "Well, if you want my honest opinion, Miss Davenport, it's really not English I'm feeling right now."

"No?" She tilted her head to one side, swishing her blonde hair out of the way in the process. "Then what subject *are* you feeling?"

I made sure our eyes locked before answering. "I'm feeling...*Chemistry!*"

She fought hard to keep a straight face. "Is that so? And would you say that feeling is based on scientific fact or mathematical probability?"

That girl had a sense of humor to die for. I let slip a grin. "Well, I'd like to think it's a scientific fact, but I'll settle for a mathematical probability." I tell you, in that moment, Emily's eyes were shining, and my heart was beating louder than the bass drum in Munro Master's band. Like the drum, I think it even skipped a beat or two. Then the magical moment was completely shattered by a familiar, crotchety voice that burst through the open front window.

"English. Chemistry. Science. Math. Humph! If that young man doesn't stop with the Biology lesson and behave himself, he's going to end up being *history*!"

We both lost it. In that moment, our laughs not only got engaged; they also said their "I do's."

CHAPTER TWENTY-FOUR
CRIMINALS AND CONVOYS

Monday morning, I got the good news that Durnell Bodkins had passed five of his subjects. Just barely. While that meant the wait was over regarding his status with the team, I hoped the ongoing tutoring would help him achieve graduation at the end of the school year. When I talked with him following fourth period, he seemed relieved that he would be able to stay on the team. I think that meant more to him than the grades. After school, I drove him home for the first stop on his confession and apology tour. As predicted, his mother was not happy with the news, to say the least.

"What was you thinkin', ya lunkhead?" she scolded him. I cringed as she cuffed him upside the head in exasperation. "An' after all the trouble yer teachers done went to ta see that ya passed yer subjects. While they was givin' o' their time, *you* was runnin' around paintin' up the town. An' all the while, yer brother doin' yer chores for ya!"

Durnell hung his head, unable to look his mother in the eye. I came to his defense. "Mrs. Bodkins—I mean, Luella—he knows what he did was wrong. Don't you, Durnell?" He stared at his feet and nodded. "He's even agreed to make restitution. Do you remember what I said about football being good for your boys? He didn't do this for his own sake; he did it to defend the honor of his teammates. And football was his motivation for studying so hard. That's also why Willard offered to do Durnell's chores—so we could keep the team going. They both have worked hard and made sacrifices for the good of something greater than themselves. Wouldn't you say that shows some wonderful growth?"

Luella tucked a wisp of hair behind her ear and paused to consider my words. "I s'pose so. Hadn't really thought of it thataway." Then she turned to her oldest son. "Boy, if you make good on them promises of yourn an' do whatever Mr. Yokel an' the sheriff tell ya to do, I guess I'll let it go with just a warnin' this time." She grabbed his collar and got in his face. "But if I *ever* hear o' you doin' anythin' stupid like this again, so help me, I'm gonna tan yer hide good! Ya got that?"

"Yes'm," he mumbled softly. Then he met his mother's withering glare. "Does this mean I kin stay on the team?"

Luella stared hard at her son for a moment before turning to me in amazement. "Mr. Wisniewski, that there game ya play is doin' wonders fer my boys. An' I thank ya kindly fer all ya done for 'em." That was the best compliment I had received since becoming a coach.

Next up was Yokel's Hardware Store. Magnus listened patiently as Durnell, with a little coaching and prompting, confessed to the thefts. The store owner then gave him a stern lecture and agreed not to press charges if he would work at the store on Saturdays until the debt was paid off. When we walked out the front door, I quietly breathed a sigh of relief, grateful for Magnus' generous display of mercy. So far, so good.

We weren't so fortunate on the final stop of our tour. As Durnell stumbled through his confession, the sheriff's face grew redder and redder. I thought he was going to blow a gasket. Smoke was coming from his ears. When the teen finished explaining everything, Virgil gave him a withering stare for the longest time. I didn't know if he was trying the "scared straight" tactic or if he was simply furious with the boy. But when he finally spoke, that question was answered in a heartbeat.

"You're in a peck of trouble, boy!" the sheriff stated forcefully. "I don't tolerate disrespect or put up with any shenanigans in this town. You ought to know that by now. I haven't forgotten that little matter of the fireworks burning down the old schoolhouse or the problem with those delinquents shooting up our street signs and mailboxes. And don't think for a minute that I'm through investigating the vandalism on Main Street the other day by those thugs from Ransomville. I'll have you know, I'm on top of things in this county; and I come down hard on lawbreakers!" He jerked a thumb toward a door in the far wall of his office. "I've a great mind to toss you in a cell and let you cool your heels for a week!"

Once again, I went to bat for my penitent student and player. "Sheriff, I agree that Durnell needs to be held accountable for what he did. He knows that as well. But isn't that a little harsh for his first offense? Besides, he came in here of his own free will." My efforts as a defense attorney fell on deaf ears. If I ever change professions, I hope somebody reminds me not to take up law.

Virgil scowled. "You're forgetting that I'm the sheriff *and* justice of the peace here, Mr. Wisniewski. I have every right to hold him for a week. Besides, I've been investigating these malicious acts for over a year, and it was only a matter of time before I made an arrest. His coming in here only expedited that process. Perhaps if I make an example of him, the other troublemakers around here might think twice about breaking the law!" He shook his head resolutely. "No, holding him for a week will send a clear message and put the kibosh on this town's wanton delinquency problem."

"But he's not responsible for those other acts of vandalism," I argued, "only for what *he's* done." Virgil's eyes narrowed. He did not like having his decisions called into question. I redirected my line of reasoning. "What about his schoolwork?" I pleaded. "If he's in jail, his grades will suffer. He's worked very hard of late by missing football practice for after school tutoring and studying at home every evening."

"Even so, he still found time to skulk around in the dead of night vandalizing the town!" the lawman retorted. He frowned at Durnell. The boy's shoulders sagged, and he was unable to look Virgil in the eye. "As for his schoolwork, he can do that in here just as easily as he can at school or at home." He paused, then sighed deeply. "However, since he *did* come in on his own, I guess I can cut the boy some slack. He can go home to his mother tonight, and he can go to school tomorrow. But as soon as school's out, he'd better turn himself in right here to begin serving his seven-day sentence." He gave Durnell an icy stare. "If you fail to show tomorrow afternoon, I'll pick you up and throw the book at you faster than I can write out a speeding ticket. Then, your stay behind bars will make these seven days seem like a nano-second. Do I make myself clear, boy?"

Durnell swallowed hard and nodded meekly. "Yes, sir."

"I plan to keep you busy and out of trouble for those seven days. Call it community service, if you like. If you have time to paint up the town, you have time to *clean* up the town!"

Feeling that I'd pushed the sheriff as far as I could, I rested my case. On my way home after dropping off Durnell, a familiar knot began to grow in the pit of my stomach. Once again, I'd lost a player. Would this week's game against Jackson County finally be the one we had to forfeit?

I did not relish the thought of informing my team that we would be without Durnell on Friday. The players were sure to pepper me with all sorts of questions about his absence, so I decided to be proactive. As we gathered at the beginning of Tuesday's practice, I broke the news.

"Okay, guys, today we begin preparation for our game against the Warriors on Friday night. We'll be on their turf, in another hostile environment. You've all played very well on the road this season, so don't let anything distract you from our team goals. Stay focused." I looked around the semi-circle of helmeted players. "Unfortunately, we will be without Leonardo for this game." Loud groans emanated from the group.

"How come, Coach?" Willie asked. "Was it his grades?"

"No, he worked very hard and passed all his classes; so academically, he's still eligible for the remainder of the season."

"Then why won't he be playing Friday night?" Maynard pressed.

Not wanting to say too much, I chose my words carefully. "Well, this week, he's . . . um . . . he's doing some community service instead."

Clay frowned. "Is he in trouble for the graffiti?"

My eyes widened in surprise. "You guys know about that?"

"Sure, Coach," Jackson admitted freely. "Everybody in school knows he did it."

"Everybody but me, apparently." I turned to Winston. "Did *you* know it was him?"

Winston shrugged. "Had a purdy good idea. I keep my eyes 'n' ears open, remember?"

"What are you going to do about the game, Coach?" Nigel wondered. "We're a mate down again."

Isaiah spoke up before I could answer. "We plow our field and prepare for rain, right, Coach?" I could see a lot of Ezekiel in him.

"That's right, Porky," I replied emphatically. "We've weathered this storm before. Nothing new here. We do our part and leave the results up to God."

At the end of practice, I overheard some of the players express concern for Durnell. I was pleased that they were finally accepting him as one of their own. He was a teammate, a comrade in arms, one of the Mighty Hogs. They really cared about him. This team was beginning to gel into a cohesive unit, much like the apostle Paul's description of the body of Christ. The body functions best when all members are doing their part; and when one member suffers, the whole body suffers. My players were actually hurting for one of their own.

As they trudged to the locker room, Clay told me his car was in the shop and asked for a ride home.

Knox, who was directly behind us, overheard the request. "You need a lift?" he interjected. "I can drop you off on my way home."

Clay stared incredulously at his cousin. "You'd do that for me?"

"Sure, why not?" Knox replied nonchalantly. "You're my teammate, aren't you? And teammates stick together."

Clay still wasn't sure he'd heard right. "You're willing to take me home? In your *truck*?"

"Yeah," Knox replied. "You can even drive if you like!"

Clay's eyes bugged. "*Seriously?* You'd let me drive your new truck?"

Knox shrugged. "If you want to. Only keep under the speed limit. I wouldn't want your dad to give you a ticket for speeding and reckless driving!"

Gobsmacked, I watched the two cousins enter the building together. They were animatedly laughing and talking to each other. Winston came up alongside me with his mouth hanging open. "Will miracles never cease?" he marveled. "If I hadn'ta seen it an' heard it, I never woulda believed it!"

I grinned at him. "This team is finally coming together, isn't it, Winston?"

He slapped me on the back. "In more ways than one, Coach. In more ways than one!"

I was interrupted in the middle of Wednesday's first period lesson by a student messenger dispatched from the school office to deliver a note addressed to me. It read, "Please come to my office immediately after class." No signature, no explanation. My first thought was, *Oh no, not another crisis!* Although Mr. Herold often made mountains out of molehills, I'd learned to take his instructions seriously. They were not meant to be requests. They were demands. So I secured a stand-in for second period and scurried down to the first floor.

"You can go straight in," Claudine Cooper said as soon as she saw me. "He's waiting for you." I thanked her and walked back to the principal's closed door and knocked.

"Enter!" he bellowed.

I could tell before I even opened the door that he was in one of his "all business" moods. When I stepped into his office, I saw a student sitting in the ugly orange chair with his back to me. "Close the door, Wisniewski," the principal barked, dispensing with his proper decorum for addressing teachers. I complied, and he promptly got down to brass tacks. "Are you aware, Mr. Wisniewski, of the reason *why* our most recent opponent nearly missed the start of Friday night's game?"

The question was a total curveball. "The reason? Well, um . . . the head referee told me they got hung up behind some farm equipment— or something to that effect."

"Not just *some* farm equipment," he huffed. "Not just *any* farm equipment. They were delayed by a whole *convoy* of farm equipment! A whole convoy meant to be a blockade, organized and executed by Piggottsville High students!"

I stood there like a doofus who'd played hooky the day they handed out brains. "Seriously?" I replied, sounding just like one of my students.

Mr. Herold scowled. "If you doubt the facts, why not ask the mastermind himself?" He pointed to the student cowering in front of him. I angled to the side for a better look. It was August Riggins, one of Avery Piggott's grandsons, and a student in my fourth period World History class. The boy looked as guilty as a third monkey caught sneaking aboard Noah's Ark. "Go ahead," the principal urged the junior, "tell Mr. Wisniewski why you organized the blockade. Go ahead!"

A bead of sweat trickled down the side of August's greenish face. "W-w-we wanted to do something to show our support for the football team," he explained in a shaky voice, looking as if he might barf at any moment. "The other schools make fun of us and call us losers all the time. So, um . . . a bunch of us got together and came up with a plan to keep the Raiders from showing up. We figured if they had to forfeit, then maybe the Hogs would be declared the winner for once."

An exasperated Mr. Herold jabbed his finger at the boy. "See, what did I tell you? They deliberately interfered with an official, duly scheduled, extracurricular school activity. This attempt at sabotage was nothing short of a hostage situation!" He glared at me as if I were the culprit. "What do you have to say about *that*, Mr. Wisniewski?"

How does a young rookie teacher respond to a furious principal who's over twice his age? I fought for the right words, knowing that anything I said could and probably would be used against me. "Mr. Herold, this is all news to me! I was totally unaware of this incident until now. And I want to make it crystal clear that I do *not* condone what happened in any way, shape, or form." I grabbed a breath. "May I address Mr. Riggins?"

"You may," he granted with a wave of his scepter-less hand.

Winston's Oreo Principle came to mind as I turned to the trembling teen. "August, I know you meant well, and I appreciate your team loyalty and school pride." The veins on Mr. Herold's neck were popping out, and he began perspiring as if he were about to have a stroke, so I hurried on. "But you showed it in the wrong way. You see, we all have to play by the rules. If a student cheats on a test, then their grade means nothing; and they might get expelled. If a cross-country runner takes a shortcut, then the race means nothing; and they might get disqualified. And if we win a football game by trickery, then that win means nothing; and the school might get into trouble.

"Even the Bible tells us we must win by following the rules. If my players are going to win a game, I want them to do it fair and square by outplaying their opponent on the field." I glanced at my boss. He seemed to be retreating from the brink. "August, if you really want to help your team and school, then why don't you encourage more students to come out for the games or make posters showing your support and school spirit? Something positive like that?"

With the fate of the misguided teen yet to be determined, Mr. Herold dismissed me from his office. I left at least knowing that my boss's blood pressure had returned to near-normal levels.

Right before lunch, Jimmy Dean Tucker stopped me in the hall. That in itself came as a surprise. Since quitting the team, he hadn't spoken to me outside the classroom and was only minimally cooperative in class.

"Mr. Wisniewski, I heard Durnell isn't gonna play against Jackson County on Friday. Is that true?"

"Um . . . yes, that's true," I replied, careful not to add more fodder to the rumor mill. "Why are you asking?"

"I'd like to rejoin the team."

I wasn't expecting that. Certainly not from him. "We-e-ll," I hesitated, "I appreciate the offer, J.D., but why do you want to come back now?"

"So, I was thinking, Coach. If we don't have a full team, the game's gonna get canceled; and we won't complete all eight games, right? I'd sure hate to see that happen. The team's worked too hard to lose out this late in the season. Besides, they're doing real good now. The school's getting behind them, and so's the town. I'd like to be a part of it again."

"Hmmm. I'll have to think about that. Let me mull it over, and I'll get back to you, okay?"

Jimmy Dean shrugged nonchalantly. "Sure, no problem. Just thought I'd ask." Then he spun on his heels and disappeared into the cafeteria.

The former player's offer was on my mind for the rest of the day, and it followed me home that evening. When I climbed into bed around 10:30, it was still haunting me. Jimmy Dean had let the team down when it needed him most, forcing me to search for a replacement. But I was desperate for a player, and he was the only student in school with any playing experience. Did I really have a choice? I decided to sleep on it before making the call.

Early the next morning, I tracked down Winston and found him in the electrical chase replacing some blown fuses. When I told him about Jimmy Dean's offer, he lifted his worn cap and scratched his graying head. Then he adjusted his glasses. "You familiar with the children's book, *The Little Red Hen?*" he asked. "She tried gettin' all the other animals to help her make the bread, but they refused. Then, when it was ready, they all wanted to help her eat it. Know what she told 'em?"

I knew exactly where he was going with this. "She said, 'No, you won't. I will eat the bread myself.'"

"An' she did!" he replied with conviction. "Our team's like the hen, an' J.D.'s like the other animals. He refused to help when the team needed him. But now that they're near the end o' the season an' gettin' a lot of attention, he's wantin' in on it." He shook his head resolutely. "If *I* had a vote in the matter, I'd say, 'No way, José!' But, it's your call, Coach."

Winston's words of wisdom made the decision easy for me. Jimmy Dean was definitely out. But then, who was in?

CHAPTER TWENTY-FIVE
Senior Prank

"Good morning, PSHS students!" Mr. Herold vociferated at the start of Thursday's announcements. "Today is the final day for submitting nominations for next week's homecoming king and queen. All candidates must be sponsored by at least one member of the faculty. Tomorrow, the ballot box will be placed in the hallway outside the main office, and student voting will commence at seven o'clock and end promptly at noon. Your king and queen will be announced during last period and, as in the past, will serve their terms throughout Spirit Week, which will culminate this year with a homecoming football game between the Mighty Ferrell Hogs and the Montgomery South Wolfpack. This is sure to be a memorable homecoming, so let's all get involved in the activities as we carry on this long-standing, hallowed tradition at Piggottsville High." The principal cleared his throat. "As a final reminder, there is to be *no* stuffing of the ballot box this year!"

I popped into Miss Godwin's art room right before lunch and asked to see some of Durnell's recent work. She was more than happy to oblige and commented on what a talented artist he was, a fact with which I was already somewhat acquainted. And yet, I was still impressed, to say the least. He was really good, especially with media such as acrylic on canvas. Mostly *spray* acrylic on canvas.

Looking at his creative talent, a plan began to formulate in my brain; and when I left her room, I hurried to the office and caught Mr. Herold just as he was about to go out for lunch. I sought permission for Durnell to paint a mural on the wall of the concession stand.

Aware by now of the trouble the aerosol artist was in, the principal's first question was, "Why?"

I'd anticipated that response and quickly explained how the project would serve a three-fold purpose. It could count toward his community service requirements; it might allow for an expeditious release in time for Friday's game, and it would provide a huge stimulus for concession sales at next week's homecoming game, which, I reminded him, would be attended by the largest paying crowd in recent Piggottsville history. Just as I'd anticipated, that last one sealed the deal for our fiscally-tightfisted administrator.

With those details out of the way, I texted Winston and informed him of my plan. He thought it was worth a shot, since the only other alternative was to call off the game in the morning. It seemed like we'd been down this road a hundred times before, yet God had always provided a way when there seemed to be none. What would He do *this* time?

After school, with Winston covering practice, I drove to the police station to once again plead my case before Virgil. I was secretly hoping he might have softened in the last seventy-two hours. But truthfully, I wasn't counting too heavily on that.

Upon learning the reason for my visit, the sheriff stated that he was rather busy at the moment. I noticed the open travel magazine, the half-eaten donut, and the cup of coffee sitting on his cluttered desk but wisely kept my mouth shut. He finally capitulated and listened impatiently to my little spiel.

"I'm not opposed to him doing the mural, per se," he admitted, taking a sip of his tepid coffee, "but it can wait until next week, after I'm finished with him here. If I were to release him early, what kind of message do you think that would send?" He stood up and ushered me toward the door. "Look, I know what your angle is, Mr. Wisniewski, and I'm not unsympathetic to your dilemma; but you'll just have to find someone else to take his place. I don't want to see the game canceled any more than you do. After all, I have a son who's going to be greatly disappointed if he doesn't get to play tomorrow night, and so will I. But as sheriff, I have a job to do. The town comes first. Forfeiting a game or two might just show those other delinquents there are serious consequences for this kind of behavior. My goal is to put an end to this epidemic of lawlessness in our town once and for all."

"But my players aren't responsible," I argued. "Except for Durnell, of course. Yet they're the ones being punished the most."

Virgil stiffened. "You're forgetting that *I'm* not the one responsible, either. That falls squarely on the Bodkins boy." He held open his office door. "I'm sorry, Mr. Wisniewski, but I have no other choice. I do hope you find another player, though."

Disheartened, I stepped through the doorway and ran smack into Clay. He was still in his practice uniform. "What are you doing here?" I asked.

"Coach Bang told us why you weren't at practice, so I came to see if you were able to get Leonardo released in time for the game tomorrow."

Virgil beat me to the punch. "That's not your concern, son," he asserted, with a frown.

"But, Dad," Clay pleaded, "if you don't release him early, we'll have to forfeit the game. Then there goes the whole season down the drain!"

His father attempted to placate him. "Clay, I'm as sorry about that as you are, but I have a job to do. If I don't come down hard on these delinquents now, things will soon get out of control in this town."

"Why can't you let him out just for the game? He could make up the time at the end of his sentence."

"No, son. That would send the wrong message," Virgil replied firmly. "Besides, I've been after these kids for over a year. This is not the time for leniency."

"But Dad—"

"The matter is closed!" his father cut him off sharply.

Clay looked at me in desperation, but there was no way I was going to get between father and son. Frustrated, he expelled the air from his lungs and held out his hands. "Then in that case, I'm turning *myself* in, too!"

Virgil raised an eyebrow. "What in the world are you doing?" he demanded.

"If you're gonna put Durnell in jail, then you're gonna have to put *me* in jail, too!"

The father stared at his son. "What for?"

The son met his father's gaze. "'Cause I'm the one who shot up all the signs and mailboxes!"

Virgil's jaw hit the floor. Mine followed shortly thereafter. "You . . . you . . . *you're* the one responsible?" he stammered. "When did that happen? And where did you get the gun?"

I saw fear creep into Clay's eyes. "I was riding around with some friends a while back, during the summer. We got bored, so I stopped by the house and . . . and took my .22 out of the safe while you were at a town council meeting."

The sheriff's face turned the color of a boiled lobster. I think it was a combination of rage and embarrassment. He cast a sideways glance in my direction before addressing his son. "Clayton Jeffrey Piggott! You're in a lot of trouble. A *whole* lot of trouble! I want you to go straight home and wait for me. I'll be there in an hour. Then we're going to sit down and have a talk. A very *serious* talk."

"Yes, sir," he replied obediently. When he reached the front door, he turned to me. "Coach, I'm sorry I let you down. Real sorry! But I couldn't let Durnell take all the blame when I'm just as guilty." Then he pushed open the door and walked out of the police station.

I drove home a few minutes later. My head was buzzing with a gazillion unanswered questions, but at least one had been answered. I now knew what information Winston had been holding over Clay's head to keep him on the team.

Sheriff Virgil Piggott was in a quandary. He'd been chafing at the bit for over a year to catch the delinquents who had vandalized his town, and now he finally knew the identity of two of them. The problem was that one happened to be his own son! What was he to do? If he treated Clay differently than Durnell, it would be an obvious show of favoritism and would set the precedent for a double standard. If he treated his son the same, Clay would have to sit in his own father's jail for the next seven days.

I would have loved to have been a fly on the wall of the Piggott family home that evening, but I had my own problems to worry about. Only nine players were still available for tomorrow's game. What's more, if I couldn't find a replacement for one, how in the world was I supposed to find replacements for *two*?

I was too upset to eat supper that night. I even went to bed early. But I couldn't sleep. All I could think about was how hard my players had worked to reach this point in their season, and I did not relish the thought of giving them more bad news. They didn't deserve this. For that matter, neither did I. Right there I should have turned the situation over to the Lord; but being the yo-yo that I am, I decided to attend a pity party instead. The moment I walked through the door, I blended right in with the rest of the crowd. I chatted with Worry and Doubt and even flirted with Fear and Anger. I moped, and complained, and felt sorry for myself for over an hour. Needless to say, I was the life of the party.

But then Somebody crashed the party, and the music stopped. I'm convinced it was the Holy Spirit, Who'd let me have my own way just long enough to show me how miserable that can be. Then Truth bounced the other guests. This was no way to behave! Hadn't I been in this fix before, when both Jimmy Dean and Willard left the team? Hadn't God provided a way?

Then it struck me. This was not just about football! It was far more important than that. This was about me teaching and guiding and nurturing the young people whose lives had been entrusted to me. Maybe they needed to learn this vital life lesson about actions and consequences more than they needed to play football. So how was I doing with that? At the moment, not very well, I'm afraid. I couldn't do this on my own. I needed God's strength and wisdom if I was ever going to make a lasting difference in these kids' lives.

I asked the Lord to forgive my heart of stone and my feet of clay, and claimed the promise of Psalm 37:5, "Commit your way to the LORD; trust in him, and he will act." Then I turned out the light and went to sleep.

When I awoke on Friday morning, I texted Mr. Herold and asked him to call off the game against Jackson County. It was the only thing left to do. Shortly after that, I left for school, feeling deeply saddened for my dedicated players. You can imagine my shock when the principal promoted the game during his morning announcements. He hadn't responded to my text, so my first thought was that he hadn't received it or read it.

I made a beeline for his office. He was standing behind the counter questioning Claudine Cooper about a missing shipment of copy paper.

In my haste, I interrupted their conversation. "Mr. Herold, didn't you get my text this morning? We need to cancel tonight's game!"

"Oh, that won't be necessary, Mr. Wisniewski," he replied calmly. "The game will be played as scheduled."

So he's finally lost it, I thought to myself.

The principal offered a rare smile, as if he'd read my mind. "I received a call from Sheriff Piggott just after school started, informing me that the students involved in the vandalism will be available for tonight's game. In fact, they're both at school today."

I couldn't believe my ears. So Sheriff Piggott was not the Tin Man after all. He really *did* have a heart behind that shiny badge of his! Of course, Clay's confession had absolutely nothing to do with it. "Did he say what changed his mind?" I pressed, unable to resist the temptation.

"No, that's all he shared with me. If you want more information, you'll need to contact him. Oh, by the way, I'm aware that a number of students are planning to attend tonight's away game. So, in appreciation for what you've done with the football program this season, I've secured one of the regular buses for the team and fans to use tonight when you travel to Jackson County. I've even included a driver to relieve Mr. Banks of that responsibility."

I was dumbstruck. One of the school board's purse strings must have snapped! I left the office feeling as if my team had just been reborn from the ashes, and I soared back to my classroom with visions of tackles and touchdowns dancing in my head.

Something was going on among the student population at Piggottsville High. I'd noticed it ever since Mr. Herold's homecoming announcement Thursday morning. Nothing overt, mind you. More like an undercurrent. But there were all the telltale signs: groups huddled in the hallways, lowered voices, surreptitious glances, and lots of tittering and snickering. I shared my observations with the other teachers during lunch, and most said they'd noticed the same thing. The consensus was that a senior prank was in the works. None of us had a clue what it was, but the possibility put us all on high alert. And, I might add, on edge.

When Mr. Herold came on the intercom later that afternoon to announce the results of the vote, we all simultaneously found out what the prank was. "May I have your attention, please? Your votes for homecoming king and queen have been received and tabulated, and I'm sure you all are eagerly awaiting the results. Well, I have those results right here in my hand." The speakers made a rustling noise. "The person you have elected to represent the student body as this year's homecoming queen is . . . drum roll please . . . Lexi Rae Brannigan! Let's all give Lexi a round of applause, shall we?"

My students looked at each other and stifled snickers and laughs. So Lexi Rae finally got enough votes this year. Or could it be something else? It turned out to be something else.

The principal continued. "And the person you have elected to represent the student body as this year's homecoming king is . . . drum roll please . . . Willard Bodkins! Let's hear it for Willard!"

The school broke out in an uproar. The ruckus from the other classrooms swept down the hall and mingled with the laughter of my own students. I sat at my desk and watched them high-five each other. Lexi Rae and Willard? Seriously?

Before I could think of anything to say, the final bell rang. The kids shot out of their seats and rushed for the door, chattering boisterously among themselves. I grabbed the last one to leave. "Hey, Dylan, what was *that* all about?" I asked.

The boy couldn't keep the grin off his face. "Good one, huh, Mr. Wisniewski? Lexi Rae thought Colt Pennington was gonna get elected king, and she wanted to be queen real bad 'cause she's got a wicked crush on him. So we got together and voted for her. But since she thinks she's all that, we all decided to vote for Skunk instead of Colt. Pretty funny, huh?"

I bit my tongue until I tasted blood.

On my way down the stairs, I ran into Ezekiel. "I apologize for being late," he said, "but I had trouble navigating against the stampede. The students seem a bit wound up this afternoon."

"You have no idea!" I exclaimed with a chuckle. "Have you come to share another verse with me?"

The farmer smiled. "Of course." He then grew serious. "Mr. Wisniewski, you have had to face a lot of adversity this season, and I know it has not been easy. That is why I have chosen Isaiah 40:31 as your encouragement today. 'But they that wait upon the LORD shall renew their strength; they shall mount up with wings as eagles; they shall run and not be weary; and they shall walk, and not faint.' Keep waiting on the Lord, Jason, and good things are bound to happen."

I thanked him and went home for a quick bite to eat before the game.

Per Mr. Herold's promise, one of the regular buses was waiting outside the gymnasium that evening. It was a real treat riding to the game in style. Not only did Winston get to sit with the players, but I also got to sit with Emily, who had come along with the cheer squad and about two dozen student fans. However, the longer vehicle bounced its riders so much higher than our shorter version that I offered my players' helmets as protection against the possibility of head trauma. But at least this bus didn't rattle; the brakes didn't squeal; and the bumper stayed put the entire trip.

It began raining when we reached Warrior Stadium; but other than that, the arena was no different than the other hostile environments we'd faced. There were the usual signs of disrespect: "BBQ the Hogs!" and "We're gonna fry your bacon!" But my players seemed impervious to the insults that night. I think they were grateful to be playing at all, thankful for the show of support, and happy to have Leonardo and Pigeon back with the team. As a result, it showed in their performance.

In spite of the downpour, the Hogs scored two touchdowns in the contest, one on a long pass from Goldie to Pigeon and the other when Petunia caused a fumble, which Billy Bob scooped up and ran back for the team's first defensive score of the year—if you don't count Hanky's wrong way run a few weeks earlier. On top of that, Bender finally found the distance and accuracy to make one of two extra point attempts. Even though we ended up on the short end of a thirteen-to-twenty-four score, the soggy ride home felt more like a victory lap.

Earlier that week, Mayor Wilson Piggott III had declared Saturday as "Pigskin Palace Day" in Piggottsville. Many students and townspeople came out to beautify the stadium for the season finale homecoming game. They painted the center section of the home stands in the school colors and cut down the weeds underneath. Winston and several helpers rewired the lights to prevent any more electrical mishaps. And as part of their community service, Durnell and Clay worked together painting the mural on the wall of the concession, which was open and serving the volunteers. It was gratifying to witness all the support. What a transformation from the beginning of the school year when nobody cared. But the best was when Chuck McCoy, Maynard's dad, showed up carrying a large cardboard box.

"I've got a little something for the team, Coach," he said, setting the box down on the front row of the bleachers. "Something to show my appreciation for what you've done for Maynard and the school and the community at large. I was afraid they weren't going to arrive in time." He opened the flaps and pulled out a brand new football jersey. "I ordered two dozen of them just in case you pick up a few more players next season!"

I hadn't cried since the fifth grade when my pet frog died, and I fought hard to keep that record intact.

On Sunday, the surprises kept on coming. Not only were Orville and Jolene in church, so were Virgil and Ruby and Claire. They even sat in the same row this time but on opposite sides of the center aisle. I scanned the sanctuary for Knox and Clay. They were several rows from the back with some of their friends. I smiled. They were sitting next to each other. Reverend Pinckney preached on the subject of perseverance that morning. I very distinctly remember the topic because he kept smiling at me throughout his message. I got the impression I'd somehow given him the idea. When the service let out, I found myself walking out the front door with Virgil.

"It was good to see you in church today, Sheriff," I said pleasantly.

Virgil stiffened and scowled. "And why shouldn't I be? If my brother can come on *my* Sunday, then why can't I come on *his*?"

Old habits die hard.

CHAPTER TWENTY-SIX
THE RUNT OF THE LITTER

It was the beginning of Spirit Week; and the entire student body was in a real state of excitement, except for Lexi Rae Brannigan, who was in a real snit because she'd been denied the chance to be Colt Pennington's queen. Students hung banners in the hallways showing their school pride, and many dressed in the school colors. Some wore pig snouts to class, but I had to ask the kids to remove them. Have you ever tried to teach a class with a bunch of pig faces staring at you? Believe me, it's next to impossible.

I had just begun the second period lesson when a pungent scent hit me smack in the face. It came from the back corner of the room where Willard sat and was every bit as overpowering as his usual emissions but vastly more pleasant. I stopped teaching and called him up to my desk. When he approached, my eyes began watering.

"What's that stuff you've got on?" I asked, coughing in the process.

Willard smiled. "It's Old Spice, Mr. Wisniewski. Since I'm gonna be the homecomin' king, I figured I oughta act 'n' smell like one. So I took a bath an' put on some cologne."

I've never been close enough to a king before to know what one smells like, but I'm pretty sure they don't smell that strong. "That's fine, Willard, just fine. But tell me, did you *splash* on some of that cologne; or did you *bathe* in it?"

He grinned broadly. "I used a whole bottle o' the stuff. Economy size! Just ta be sure." He lowered his voice so only I could hear. "Ya think Lexi Rae will notice?"

I coughed a few more times. "Willard, I can pretty much guarantee that."

He looked relieved. "Good, 'cause I want her ta like me. I know the other kids did this for a joke, but I got a crush on her."

I tried to sound encouraging. "Well, Willard, all I can say is, this is one small step for man!" Actually, it was more like one giant leap for mankind. I sent him back to his seat and did my best to resume the lesson. But I couldn't help thinking that we'd lost our secret weapon.

During lunch, I inquired about Lexi Rae; but Emily didn't seem overly concerned. "Oh, don't worry about her," she assured me. "She'll pout for a day or two, but she'll get over it. She knows she's not going to get another chance like this to be in front of such a large crowd. She'll be her usual self come game time, both as homecoming queen and top of the pyramid!"

As I left the cafeteria, Grady Fuller stopped me in the hallway. "Hey, Wisniewski," he called out, "got a minute?"

I turned to the math teacher. "Sure, what's up?"

"I've been meaning to ask you. Have you ever coached basketball before?"

"Basketball?" I shook my head. "No. I tried out for my high school team once, but the other players wiped the floor with me like I was the janitor's favorite mop. Why do you ask?"

"Well, after seeing the success you've had with the football program, I was wondering if you'd consider being my assistant coach come basketball season!"

I stared at him. "Success? You *do* know we haven't won a game yet, right?"

He laughed. "I know. But you've done more this year than anyone expected, myself included. And I sure could use your motivational skills. You have a real knack with these kids."

I was honored. "I appreciate the offer, Grady. I don't know what I'd be able to contribute, but I'll definitely think about it. Let me finish out the season and take a few weeks off before I give you an answer. How's that?"

"Sure. No problem." He grinned and did his best principal imitation. "Go, Mighty Ferrell Hogs!"

Practice went extremely well Monday afternoon. Every player was focused like never before. We had finally reached the pinnacle of our inaugural football season, and our goal of completing all eight games was within reach. After scrimmaging, Winston and I let the players share their thoughts and feelings about the season. I was amazed how close the team had grown. Their comments were very insightful and inspirational, to say the least. I went home feeling very good about the rest of the week.

The next morning, however, the bumper fell off the bus. Not only did the bumper fall off but also the wheels came off, and the motor blew up. I was laying out my notes for first period when Maynard and Jackson burst into the room all out of breath.

"We're in trouble, Coach!" Maynard exclaimed, his cheeks puffing like a blowfish.

"Yeah, *big* trouble!" Jackson tag-teamed, his sides heaving.

The color drained from my face into a puddle at my feet. "What in the world did you guys do?" My imagination spun faster than the *Looney Tunes* Tasmanian Devil.

"Not us personally, Coach," Maynard corrected me. "The *team's* in trouble. Skunk is out for homecoming!"

I took a deep breath. "Okay, then, what did Skunk do?"

Jackson grimaced. "He went and broke a bone in his foot! Last night, he was milking their cow and got stepped on."

"How bad is it?" I asked with a tremor in my voice.

"He came to school in a walking boot. Doc says he's gotta wear it for at least four weeks."

"What are we gonna do, Coach?" Maynard looked as worried as I felt.

Jackson answered him before I had a chance. "We do our part and leave the results up to God. Right, Coach?"

Wham! There was that heavenly two-by-four again. I managed a pained smile. "Right, J.P.!" He was preaching my own message back at me, and I needed the reminder big time.

News of Willard's injury spread throughout the student body faster than a prairie fire in a drought. The electricity that had been building suddenly developed a short, and the lights began to flicker. I was asked Maynard's question so many times that by the end of school, I thought of taking out an ad in *The Piggottsville Daily Scoop*: "WANTED: One football player. Immediate opening. No application, experience, or talent needed. Must be able to stand on two feet for sixty minutes. Uniform provided. If interested, see Coach Wisniewski. Please hurry!"

Over the next two days, Winston and I buttonholed nearly every boy in the school—and about a dozen girls, to boot—in our search for a player willing to fill Willard's jersey. We came up empty. But I refused to give up. I even called Reverend Pinckney for encouragement, and he promised to start the church prayer chain in response to the need.

On Wednesday during lunch, Munro tried to cheer me up with some good news. "The pep band is up to seven players!" he announced triumphantly. "We picked up a flute this morning."

"That's great," I replied. "Every little bit helps."

"Of course, I don't have any flute music," he confessed, "but it doesn't really matter. Nobody can hear a flute, anyway. I just told her to make it up as we go." He laughed awkwardly. "Most of the others do that, anyway, even *with* music!" Then he added proudly, "But I did finally rewrite the lyrics to that old fight song."

"That's wonderful!" Emily interjected. "Can we hear them?"

Munro beamed. "Sure. I'll give you a little preview now, but I'm saving the entire thing for the pep rally on Friday. That's when we're going to teach it to the whole school!" He pulled a folded paper from his shirt pocket and spread it out on the table. "'Fight, you Mighty Ferrell Hogs / Let the stampede now begin. / Trample ev'ry single foe / Root for Piggottsville to win!'" He looked around the table for approval.

"That's very good!" Emily complimented him.

"Yes, much better than the old lyrics," I added hastily.

"I think so, too," he replied, looking rather pleased with himself. "Now if I can just get the band to play it right . . . "

He and Emily fell to discussing how to coordinate the cheers with the pep band, so I struck up a conversation with Herman Bean. Herman was the social studies teacher as well as the lone Driver's Ed instructor in town.

"Wisniewski, you're lucky to be only one player short," he said in response to my comment about homecoming. "I heard the sheriff arrested two of your players for vandalism." Then he expressed what everyone else in town was no doubt thinking. "It's a good thing one of them was his own son! Otherwise, you'd be up a creek without a paddle. Or a canoe!" He laughed at his own joke. "I taught Clay how to drive a year and a half ago; taught most of the kids in this town how to drive. But not that Bodkins boy. For some reason, he never enrolled in Driver's Ed."

I chose not to comment on the release of my players. "Well, at least the sheriff has resolved two of the four delinquency problems in this town. Now, all that's left is for him to discover who was behind last year's fire and who vandalized those stop signs."

Herman looked puzzled. "What vandalized stop signs? I wasn't aware there was a problem with that."

I squinted at him. "You mean to tell me in all your driving around town you haven't noticed the bent and damaged stop signs?"

Herman began to laugh. "Oh, that's not vandalism. You can thank Daisy May Harper for that!"

"Daisy May Harper?"

"Yeah, she's a sixteen-year-old student I've been trying to teach how to drive for over a year now. Keeps flunking her driving test. Failed seven times so far."

"What seems to be the problem?"

"Every time she comes to a stop, she jerks the wheel to the right. Sometimes, she jumps the curb and runs right over those stop signs." He grunted. "You ought to see the Driver's Ed car. Right front fender's mashed in pretty good! Mr. Herold says he isn't going to file any more insurance claims, so I just have to deal with it the best I can. Even the town council got tired of replacing the signs. They claim there isn't any money left in the budget."

I laughed. "I guess that's one less headache for the sheriff, then."

He rolled his eyes. "And one more big one for me! For the life of me, Wisniewski, I can't get that girl to break the habit. I'm at a total loss as to what to do about it."

An idea suddenly popped into my head. "Have you ever considered bribing her with donuts from the Piggotty Dough Boy?" I asked.

The team continued to practice without Willard and prepared for homecoming as if they were actually going to play. However, late Thursday afternoon, Mr. Herold stopped by my room between classes to inform me that he was going to call Montgomery South at the end of school and cancel the game. I begged him to hold off until morning. At first, he saw no reason for the delay; but when I reminded him of all the revenue that would be lost, he finally caved and gave me until 8:00 a.m. to come up with another player. He was about to leave when he remembered something.

"Oh, by the way, Mr. Wisniewski, I have a bit of good news for you. I'm sure you could use some right now. I received an update regarding your office sign. I'm pleased to inform you that the order shipped this morning, and you should have it on Monday—Tuesday at the latest! Isn't that great?"

What perfect timing. Go figure.

After our final practice of the season, I huddled with Winston in the "Coach's Closet" for one last powwow. We were at our wit's end, having exhausted all options in our search for Willard's replacement.

"There's always J.D.," Winston suggested after a long, melancholy silence. "Course that'd mean havin' to set aside our principles."

I shook my head resolutely. "No, Winston, as tempting as that sounds, we just can't go there. An old Southern preacher once said, 'Don't sacrifice the permanent on the altar of the immediate.' We have to stick to our guns, come what may."

"But there *ain't* no other way," he bemoaned, lifting his cap and scratching his head. "We're dead in the water. Unless . . . unless we can convince Danny boy ta suit up."

I gave him a long, skeptical stare. "Danny? You've got to be kidding!"

"Why not? He's been with the team since the beginnin'. Knows the game, knows how things work. Prob'ly knows most o' the plays by now, too. He's a sharp kid."

"Yeah, but he's way too small!" I argued. "I'll bet he's not even a hundred pounds dripping wet."

"Willard ain't much bigger," Winston countered. "Maybe four inches taller an' twenty-five pounds heavier is all. An' don't forget, he scored our first touchdown!"

"But Danny told me he's afraid to play."

"All we need is a live body, Coach. He could run to the sideline on every down, kinda like ya had Henry do when he had them blind staggers."

I tried to think of a reasonable rebuttal but failed. "Winston, all I can say is, you've come up with some real doozies this season, what with your unconventional methods, your home field advantage, even your MacGyvering of the bus." I grinned crookedly. "I have to hand it to you; they've all worked so far." I hesitated. "But *Runt*?"

My assistant shrugged in resignation. "What other choice've we got?"

That evening after supper, I drove across town to the Swanson residence on A Street. I don't mind telling you, I had the same butterflies in my stomach that I had when running onto the field for my first game.

As I walked up to the house, I said a quick prayer. This was our last hope. If my visit failed to secure a player, the Mighty Hogs' season was over.

Phil Swanson greeted me at the door with a smile and a handshake and then ushered me into the family den where Danny and his mother were waiting on the sofa. Phil introduced me to his wife and then pointed to a recliner. "Please, have a seat, Coach." After I was seated, he sat down next to his son. "When you called to say you needed to talk to our family, I figured it had to do with football and not history. Danny tells me he got an A in your class this first quarter."

My laugh sounded forced. "Yes, he did. His schoolwork is exemplary, Mr. Swanson, and so is his help with the team. He's been an invaluable asset to Coach Banks and me, and an integral part of the football program."

"That's very kind of you to say," Phil acknowledged, glancing at his son. "Isn't it, Danny?"

Danny looked a bit embarrassed but nodded. "Yes. Thanks, Coach."

"So, if this isn't about his schoolwork or his record-keeping, what did you want to see us about? You made it sound rather urgent over the phone."

With trepidation, I began my prepared pitch. "It is, actually. I'm sure Danny has informed you that we're short one player for tomorrow's season finale. Mr. Herold is going to call off the game at eight o'clock in the morning if we don't come up with number eleven by then."

Phil frowned deeply. "That's what I've heard. Now *that* would be a crying shame, wouldn't it? Especially after all the hard work the players have put in and after everything the team's gone through this season. But what exactly is it that *we* can do to help?"

I took a deep breath to steady myself. "I've come to ask Danny to suit up for tomorrow night's game." The whites of Danny's eyes grew so large that had he been a British soldier in the Revolutionary War, he'd have been the target of every colonial musket by now.

"You want *Danny* to play on the team?" Mrs. Swanson queried as if she hadn't heard me correctly.

I nodded. "He's our last hope, Mrs. Swanson. We've asked just about every other kid in school."

Phil exchanged glances with his wife. I could see the cogs turning in their minds. Then he looked at his son. "Well, I think that decision will have to be up to him. But whatever he decides, I'll support him."

"So will I," Mrs. Swanson added, patting her son's knee.

"What do you say, Danny?" I asked my sideline assistant. "We really need your help *on* the field this time."

Danny's voice quavered. "But I've never played football before, Coach."

I was ready for that one. "Well, if you recall, neither had any of the other players when we first started. And even though you haven't played, you've been observing the entire season. You know the game as well as anyone. In chess, not every man has equal abilities or strengths; but every piece, including the pawn, is important to the game. The same could be said for football."

"Well . . . I don't know." He fidgeted in his seat and wrung his hands nervously. "I'm not very big. What if I get hit?"

"I've got that all figured out. We just need you on the field. You won't have to block or tackle or anything. Just step out of the way on every play. Besides, you'll be wearing a helmet, shoulder pads, and everything else you need for protection." He still didn't look convinced. "I'll ask your teammates to watch out for you," I promised. "I could even put you behind Porky and Petunia. *Nobody* gets through them!"

The corners of Danny's mouth curled up at the thought. Then the frown returned. "And if I don't say yes, the game's canceled; and our season's over?"

His father jumped in. "Son, no one is going to hold it against you if you say no. Whatever you decide, you've got our full support."

"That's right," I added hastily, "and mine, too. In fact, only Coach Banks knows I'm here. No one else will ever know if you choose not to play."

There was a long silence. I witnessed the battle raging in Danny's mind. Finally, he shook his head as if to dispel any lingering doubts and sighed deeply. Then he looked me straight in the eye. "Okay, Coach," he agreed, his voice surprisingly steady. "I'll play!"

Friday morning dawned like no other in Piggottsville history. Well, at least since *I* came to town, anyway. The excitement in the air was palpable. Maybe it was only the anticipation coursing through my veins, but it had to be more than that. As I left the apartment, my neighbor across the hall stuck his head out the door to wish me good luck and promised to be at the game.

Ten minutes later, when I turned onto the long, straight lane leading to the high school, I saw homemade signs dotting both sides of the road, which had been dubbed "Mighty Hog Drive." Inside the building, the halls were a riot of color with more student-generated artwork hanging on the walls above the rows of lockers. Posters of pigs and football players were everywhere. One in particular caught my attention and made me smile. It had a drawing of Super Bo, the Mighty Ferrell Hog, poking a wolf in the face, along with the words, "Pig-Sty High says, 'in *your* eye!'" A red and black paper chain hung from the ceiling and snaked the length of the hallway.

I climbed the stairs to my classroom and found the second-floor corridors equally awash in colorful banners, all proclaiming Piggottsville pride and support for the Mighty Hogs. But when I reached my classroom, I received the most wonderful, if not totally unexpected, surprise of all. Sitting on my desk was a small bouquet of flowers. The attached card read, "Jason, congratulations on a fine season! You have achieved wonderful things, and I'm sure there will be many more successes to come. I'm so proud of you! Go Mighty Ferrell Hogs! ~ Emily."

I'd never had trouble teaching before; but I found it next to impossible that day, in part because my mind was on the game but also because my students were not in a learning mood at all. The football players wore their brand-new jerseys, and most of the other kids wore the school colors and sported pig snouts. Several rascals had curlicue pig tails stuck to the seat of their pants, and one brave student even had the nerve to show up in a pink pig costume. Everyone seemed to be fired up about homecoming, so I dispensed with the lesson plan and discussed the game and the benefits of discipline and perseverance instead. But I managed to weave in a few historical examples in the process, just to keep things legit.

Mr. Herold was in rare form when it came time for announcements. "Attention all you Mighty Ferrell Hogs out there! This is a historic day in Piggottsville, and one in which we should all take a great deal of pride. Today is not only Homecoming Friday, but tonight is also our first homecoming football game in five years! To celebrate that achievement, there will be a school-wide pep rally in the gymnasium at two o'clock this afternoon in place of your last period classes."

Cheering erupted throughout the building. I'm fairly certain the spontaneous outburst had more to do with the dismissal from class than the actual pep rally itself.

The principal continued. "Tonight's historic game starts later than usual at eight o'clock sharp, so come early to get a good seat and show your Piggottsville pride. You don't want to miss this! Your king and queen will be presented to the crowd, and . . . drum roll please . . . every student showing their school ID will receive a 20 percent discount at the Heavenly Hog!"

As the anemic applause subsided, Mr. Herold concluded his pep talk. "In honor of this momentous occasion, today's lunch special will feature your choice of a delicious barbecue pork sandwich or pigs-in-a-blanket, tater tots, fresh farm vegetables, and root beer. And speaking of root beer, I'll see you tonight at the Pigskin Palace, where we're all going to *root* for our team!" My class groaned at the bad pun. "Go, Mighty Ferrell Hogs!"

At noon, I thanked Emily for the flowers and sentiments. She smiled sweetly. "You're welcome, Mr. Wisniewski." Then she leaned over and whispered in my ear, "I meant what I said, Jason. I'm really proud of you!"

Throughout the lunch period, many of my fellow teachers congratulated me and wished the team success. Most said they were planning to be at the game.

Munro scanned the room in awe, his head swiveling like an owl's. "I haven't seen this much buzz in town since Hermione Piggott got stuck at the top of the Ferris wheel during the county fair six years ago!"

Like I said, the atmosphere was palpable.

The gymnasium was packed that afternoon. First, Willard and Lexi Rae were escorted across a red carpet to their makeshift "thrones" under one of the baskets. One moment, the queen was waving to her subjects with a smile plastered on her heavily made-up face; and the next, she was scowling at her king, who returned her scornful glances with rapturous smiles. Next, the other two cheerleaders led the students in several cheers. Following that, as Mr. Herold read off their names, the football players ran onto the basketball court and lined up—all twelve of them. I'd made sure to include Danny in the lineup. Standing shoulder to shoulder with Isaiah—or should I say, shoulder to stomach— he looked like a Danny DeVito next to a Shaquille O'Neal.

After the introductions, the principal had me come out and say a few words to the student body. I thanked them for their show of support and told them they had every reason to be proud of their team. Then several students put on a skit about how eleven little Hogs defeated the big, bad Wolfpack. To conclude the rally, Munro taught his new lyrics to the students, after which the pep band attempted to play the fight song. It was nearly unrecognizable, but they were definitely loud. Except for the flute. I actually thought they sounded better than ever, which still wasn't saying all that much.

On my way out of the gym, I ran into Ezekiel and invited him into the coaching office to escape the murmuration of raucous students in the hallway. I closed the door behind us for some privacy and offered him a seat, which he declined.

"I won't take up your time," he promised, "as I'm sure you have plenty to do before the game. But on behalf of the missus and myself, I wanted to thank you for what you have done for our children this season. You have been a positive influence on them and a true blessing." He extended a huge paw, which I grabbed the best I could.

"The blessing is all mine," I insisted. "You have every reason to be proud of them both."

"Proud?" A shadow clouded Ezekiel's face. "Pride is a sin, Mr. Wisniewski! The Good Book says, 'Pride goeth before destruction, and an haughty spirit before a fall.'[19]"

I stood there, uncertain how to respond. Surely, *that* wasn't the verse he meant to share with me, was it? Had my reference to pride upset him? He must know I meant no offense. Or was this intended as a warning? Then I caught the twinkle in his eyes and the slight upturn at the corners of his mouth.

Suddenly, the skyscraper of a man broke out into a loud guffaw and slapped his knee so hard, I cringed. "I'm just joking with you, Jason!" he chortled. "I heard you told the team to lighten up and have some fun, so I figured it wouldn't hurt for me to do the same." You could have bowled me over with a ping pong ball. "The truth is, I *am* mighty proud of them, and I told them so over supper last evening. In fact, when I said goodnight to Jeremima, I told her I was glad God had given me

---

19 Proverbs 16:18, KJV

her instead of another son." He grinned broadly, scattering the creases across his face. "I have never been hugged so hard in all my born days!"

We shared a hearty laugh together. I really was growing to like this man a lot.

Ezekiel pulled a small Bible from his overalls. "Coach, I would like to leave you with one final verse, if I may." He flipped through the gossamer pages. "I am reading from Second Samuel chapter twenty-three and verse twelve. Take this with you into the battle tonight." He straightened, like a soldier standing at attention. "'But he stood in the midst of the ground, and defended it, and slew the Philistines: and the Lord wrought a great victory.'" With that, he turned and marched out of the room.

CHAPTER TWENTY-SEVEN
When Pigs Fly

My Friday night lights vision was no longer a dream. It had finally come true. From inside the locker room, I could hear the pep band warming up and the whistles tweeting as Virgil and his deputies directed traffic. Winston and I gathered the players around us for our final pregame talk.

"When we first started this journey, did any of you imagine that we'd be where we are tonight?" I began. They all shook their heads, including Winston. "I'll be honest with you, neither did I! When I came to Piggottsville, I had a dream. But after seeing what I'd been given to work with, that dream seemed impossible. Over the course of the past ten weeks, we have faced innumerable odds and immovable obstacles, both on and off the field. Yet here we are, ready to play our eighth and final game of an improbable season and your first homecoming game in half a decade!

"Do you remember what I told you after that first game? I said you'd already come further than any other team in the past five years. But you've come even further than that. I'm not talking about games or statistics now; I'm talking about personal growth—not just as football players but as human beings. We began with eleven individuals . . . well, only two if you want to get technical about it!" The players looked at Porky and Petunia and laughed. "Individuals who were, in many ways, vastly different from one another but who all had one thing in common. Inexperience! But now that's no longer true. You are *all* experienced." I smiled at Runt. "And you set aside those differences to come together as teammates." Goldie and Pigeon exchanged fist bumps. "I no longer see eleven individuals kneeling here. You know what I see? I see one team. One team that makes me proud to be called 'Coach.'"

I paused and looked around the circle. "You all will remember this night for the rest of your lives, so I want you to go out there and make some great memories, okay? But have fun doing it! Oh, and one more thing. Never *ever* forget this truth: you are *not* Pig-Sty High." I raised my fist in the air. "You are the Piggottsville-Stuyvesant High School Mighty Ferrell Hogs!"

The Mighty Hogs made a grand entrance into the Pigskin Palace that night. Instead of running onto the field from the end zone gate, we all climbed aboard an enclosed hog hauler attached to one of Avery Piggott's tractors. Then, on cue, Avery drove onto the cinder track as the band played the new fight song. At least, that's what it was supposed to be. When the hauler came to a stop in front of the home stands, the rear gate flew open; and our caped mascot was escorted down the ramp and past the crowd to where he would be tethered for the evening.

As the noise from the band reached a crescendo, I watched my players burst from the hauler, helmets held high. With Runt leading the charge, they broke through a paper banner held by the cheerleaders and ran onto the field to the applause of the home fans. I breathed a sigh of relief. The night before, I'd dreamed Runt had bounced off the banner, causing the players behind him to pile up like the Keystone Cops.

As my team began warming up, I took a moment to drink in the scene. The stadium was impressive. Under lights blazing like the sun, the field looked sharp wearing its coat of green trimmed in white. The Heavenly Hog had a permanent sign over the serving window, and the colorful mural on the side wall sparkled with fresh paint. Tantalizing aromas filled the air, and two lines of hungry customers snaked out onto the track. But the most wonderful sight of all was the stands. They were nearly full! The Piggottsville fans already outnumbered the Montgomery South fans four to one with more arriving every minute. Many even sported pig snouts.

I spotted our rotund, little mayor and his wife in their usual seats behind the cheer block, which tonight occupied most of the center section. Reverend and Mrs. Pinckney and about half the church congregation were there as well. So were all the players' families and many members of the community, including Mr. Yokel and Rube Elkins, the barber—make that barber *and* sheep-shearer. The cheerleaders were forming a pyramid—with Lexi Rae on top, of course—under the watchful eye of their amazing squad leader, Emily Davenport. I chuckled when I saw the banner hanging on the fence: "Newsflash: Little Pigs Defeat Big, Bad Wolf!"

Turning my back to the spectators, I watched my players run through their calisthenics in unison for a minute or two and then glanced at our opponents. They were big, and there were a lot of them; but I didn't bother counting this time. Numbers no longer mattered. A good-sized contingent of Wolfpack supporters had shown up, filling three quarters of the visitor bleachers. Two signs hung on the fence: "Pork: the Other Dead Meat!" and "Time to Kick Some Pork Butt!" I pursed my lips and groaned inwardly. *Still no respect!*

"The field looks terrific tonight, Winston," I complimented my assistant coach and groundskeeper.

He smiled. "Don't it, though!" Then he jerked a thumb over his shoulder. "Crowd looks purdy good, too, don't ya think? In all my years in Piggottsville, I can't ever recall seein' it packed like this before. Gonna be standin' room only tonight. School's finally behind us. So's the town!" I nodded, too awestruck to answer. "An' it's all 'cause o' you, Coach."

His accolade broke my spell. "Me?"

"Yeah. I don't think anybody else coulda taken this team as far as *you* have. An' ya managed to unite the town in the process." He placed a hand on my shoulder. "'Bout time ya gave yourself some credit, Jason!" he exhorted.

Humbled, I shook my head. "It wasn't me, Winston. I'm just a rookie coach who has no idea what he's doing." I pointed to the heavens. "It was God. *He* should get all the credit."

"Amen to that, Preacher," my friend responded with conviction. "Amen!"

Five minutes later, the homecoming king and queen were introduced to the local fans. Along with his crown, Skunk wore his new football jersey to show his team loyalty, while Lexi Rae wore her crown and cheerleader uniform. Both appeared to be over the moon. I even witnessed the queen toss a smile at her king, Colt Pennington notwithstanding. Following the presentation of the flags, Hermione Piggott sashayed out onto the field and turned to face the overflow crowd. She smoothed the wrinkles from her dress and cleared her throat. Then she sucked in oxygen like a jet engine on takeoff and launched into "The Star-Spangled Banner." Like the pep band, she still wasn't very good; but she was loud. When she finished, she bowed to the polite applause and made her way back to her front row seat.

Winston leaned over and whispered in my ear, "Some things never change, do they, Coach?"

I just smiled.

After receiving last-minute instructions, the players huddled for the team cheer. Then they ran onto the field, ready for battle. Montgomery South won the coin toss and elected to receive. Bender laid into the ball; but like the Wright Brothers' first flight, it only flew a short distance—twelve yards, to be exact. A Wolfpack player attempted to field the one-hopper; but Petunia knocked the stuffing out of him, and he fumbled. With the home crowd on its feet, Billy Bob pounced on the ball, and the play went down in the books as a successful onside kick, although that was not the intention at all. The Hogs then gained several first downs but stalled on our opponent's twenty-two-yard line. Facing a fourth and seven, I signaled for a field goal try, which Bender shanked far right—as usual.

On their next possession, the Wolfpack marched down the field and scored. Early in the second quarter, they added another touchdown to take a fourteen-to-zero lead. But the Hogs fought back. On the ensuing kickoff, Leonardo caught the ball, bobbled it for a second, and then returned it thirty-four yards behind the blocking of Porky and McNerd. As he got to his feet, his teammates pummeled him joyously. Jogging back to the huddle, he turned and waved toward the home stands. I assumed that was for his mother's benefit.

After gaining two first downs, Goldie found Pigeon on a crossing pattern; and the former juvenile delinquent outran two defenders into the end zone for the Hogs' first score of the contest. The Piggottsville stands erupted in cheers as the pep band jumped on the fight song. For a second, I thought I heard the flute; but I think that's because she was playing an entirely different tune. Bender actually made the extra point try; and at halftime, we went into the locker room down seven to fourteen.

During the break, I asked Runt how he was doing. He gave me a sheepish grin. "Staying out of trouble, Coach."

After a brief rest and pep talk, the Hogs ran back into the stadium for the second half. Behind us, the cheerleaders were leading the student section in a cheer.

"Who's afraid of the big bad wolf?

Big bad wolf? Big bad wolf!

Who's afraid of the big bad wolf?

Not the Mighty Hogs!"

As the team jogged to the sideline, I saw Leonardo turn and wave toward the stands again. "You played extremely well the first two quarters," I praised him. "Your mother must be awfully proud of you right now."

He nodded inside his helmet. "So's my pa!"

"Your pa?" I stared at him. "You mean, your *father's* here? At the game?"

"Yeah! I found out he's been livin' up in Pine Bluff all these years, so's I asked him ta come watch me play." He proudly pointed to the far end of the bleachers. "That's him sittin' up there in the last row."

I'd never seen Durnell so happy. I slapped his shoulder pads. "That's wonderful, Leonardo! I'm sure *both* your parents are proud of you. And so am I! But not just because of football."

His face beamed. "Thanks, Coach. An' ta show ya how grateful I am, I'm gonna go out there an' help *win* this thing for y'all!" As he ran onto the field with his teammates, I used my sleeve to wipe the moisture from my eyes.

The Hogs received the ball to start the second half. Behind the line's solid blocking, Billy Bob, Hanky, and Pigeon chewed up decent chunks of yardage, good enough to take them down to the Wolfpack's eight-yard line. On fourth and two, since I didn't have much confidence in Bender's leg at this point, I chose to have them go for it. They came up short by inches, and Montgomery South took over on downs at their own six.

I was second-guessing my decision when Petunia shut down that line of thinking in a hurry. On the very next play, upset that we hadn't scored, she steamrolled through the Wolfpack line like a bowler throwing a strike and sacked their quarterback in the end zone for a safety. The crowd went wild.

With twenty seconds to go in the third quarter, Montgomery South kicked a field goal to increase their lead to eight points. Early in the fourth, the Hogs once again began moving the ball; but a missed block led to Goldie rushing a throw, and the ball was intercepted. The Wolfpack maintained possession and marched down to our eighteen-yard line. At 3:30 left on the clock, I called for a time out.

Winston grabbed my sleeve as the players gathered around. "We can't let 'em score, Coach! We gotta get the ball back if we're gonna have any chance at all o' winnin' this thing."

I agreed. We sent the defense back out with the instructions to blitz on every down. Two plays later, Leonardo slipped through a gap created by Porky and McNerd and knocked the ball out of the quarterback's hand. J.P. pounced on it for a fumble recovery. The hometown fans were getting a good workout tonight. Even Munro's arms were showing signs of tiring.

The Hogs offense moved the ball to the forty-eight; but the Wolfpack defense asserted itself, and we lost yardage on two consecutive plays. I called another timeout with 1:45 left in the game.

"What do you think, Coach?" I asked my assistant, as our spent players limped to the sideline. "We're running out of time."

"We gotta go with a trick play," he insisted. "Time to use our secret weapon again!"

I frowned. "What secret weapon? We lost Skunk, remember?"

He chuckled. "We got us a *new* secret weapon."

"What's that?"

"We got Runt! Other team's paid him no mind all game. They'd never suspect *him*."

I dropped my voice to a whisper. "I can't do that, Winston. I promised his folks we'd keep him away from the action."

"He's our best option, Coach," he pushed back. "We need a big play right now. Can't afford to turn the ball over again. Besides, their defense is on to us. Can't fool 'em with the reg'lar stuff no more."

I looked at our miniature player and sighed. "Runt, did you catch what Coach Bang just said?" He nodded. "Do you think you could carry the ball for us one time?"

His eyes grew as big as flying saucers. "But I've never carried the ball before, Coach!" he exclaimed, his voice trembling. "What if I drop it? Or get hit?"

"I have every confidence you won't drop the ball," I assured him, not being totally honest. "Don't let fear get the best of you. When you're playing that video game you like so much, do you let the fear of getting hit by an asteroid stop you from playing?"

"No, but video asteroids don't hurt. Getting tackled *does!*"

I took him by the shoulders and pointed to the field. "Do you see those eleven Wolfpack players out there? I want you to imagine them as giant asteroids in your video game. All you have to do is hold onto the ball, follow your blockers, and dodge the asteroids when they come at you. Think you can do that just this once?"

"We won't let them lay a finger on you, will we guys?" Porky promised emphatically. His teammates voiced their agreement.

Runt glanced nervously around the huddle and took a deep breath. "Okay, Coach. I'll do my best!"

I diagrammed the trick play and sent the team back into the fray. I was sweating like a hippie at a barber convention. "I hope I'm doing the right thing," I confided to my assistant, while nervously chewing my nails.

"As Bender would say, that was bonkers, Coach," he replied. "Bonkers, but brilliant!"

I leaned forward with both hands on my knees and my eyes riveted on the ball. Goldie took the snap from McNerd and then spun to his right and handed off to Pigeon, who ran parallel down the left side of the line, drawing the linebackers with him. At the last second, he handed the ball to Runt, who was standing stationary at the edge of the play. Runt scampered to his right and darted through the huge hole created by Porky and Petunia. He followed his two lead blockers, J.P. and Billy Bob, until they were knocked to the ground.

By now, he was in the backfield all alone with three Wolfpack players in front of him. Runt easily sidestepped the first one but then slowed drastically as the other two barreled in on him from converging angles. Aware of Winston's grip on my arm, I held my breath. Would he drop to the ground to avoid contact, or would he get creamed off the map? I was tempted to shut my eyes. Suddenly, he lowered his head and leaped forward like a shot, and the two defenders collided with each other. Churning like a windmill in a hurricane, Runt's short legs propelled him down the field and through the end zone. He kept on going until he bounced off the fence on the other side of the track.

The hometown fans were on their feet, yelling and screaming. Rising above the celebratory noise, I heard Hermione's famous call. The other players raced to the ball-carrier with such jubilation that I feared Runt would be crushed under the weight of his own teammates. There was no question in my mind about what to do next. With the score fifteen to seventeen, I called for a short jump pass to Pigeon. The Hogs lined up for the two-point conversion and the chance to tie. It nearly worked, too, but a diving Wolfpack defender got a finger on the ball and tipped it away at the very last second.

On the ensuing kickoff, I told Bender to drill the ball as deep as he could. He obliged with his best tee-off of the season, a twenty-five-yarder, which was promptly returned the same distance. I glanced up at the scoreboard. One more first down and Montgomery South could simply run out the clock. Facing a fourth and two just outside their field goal range, the Wolfpack went for it. This was it. With the game on the line, the Mighty Hogs held!

I summoned my players to the sideline. "I know you're all exhausted. You've played your hearts out for fifty-nine minutes. Coach Bang and I are incredibly proud of you. Whatever the outcome of this game, you have every reason to hold your heads high. You've reached a goal nobody thought possible, a complete eight-game season. And you did it with only eleven players!"

"Twelve, Coach," Leonardo corrected me. "We wouldn't be here if'n it wasn't fer my brother. And Runt." He patted Danny on the top of his oversized helmet.

I smiled. "You're right, Leonardo. Every last one of you has been an indispensable part of this team. There are no superstars here—just teammates who've got each other's backs. But now you have a chance to win your first game! Can you all give me just sixty seconds of your best football of the season? Just *one* more minute? Can you?" After roaring their affirmation, my lionhearted players ran back out to write their own ending to an impossible season.

Mixing running plays and play-action passes, the Hogs picked up a quick first down. Then another one. My players were competing with a sense of urgency and were giving it everything they had. As the saying goes, they were leaving it all on the field. These kids were playing to win! The Hogs reached the twenty-yard line before I called our final time out with just three seconds left.

"What do you think, Winston?" I asked my dependable assistant. "Screen pass, Hail Mary, or field goal try?"

Winston took off his ball cap and rubbed his head. "Hail Mary's too iffy. That'd be my last choice. I'd say either a screen pass an' hope for good blockin' or a field goal try, an' pray for a miracle. It's your call, Coach."

"Well, a screen pass *is* the higher percentage play, but Bender's been kicking pretty well this game."

"Course, he ain't made a field goal yet," Winston pointed out, as if I needed the reminder.

I grinned at him. "Then he's about due for one, don't ya think?" I grabbed the exchange student's face mask. "Bender, I'm giving you another chance to put one through. I know you've never made a forty yarder before, but will you at least give it your best shot?"

He saluted me like a navy seaman salutes a four-star admiral. "Aye, sir! You can count on me to give it a proper go!" He turned to look at the distant goalpost. His shoulders sagged, and his bravado melted. "Forty yards? Wowzer!"

"Just do the best you can," I told him. "That goes for all of you. Win or lose this game, you're already winners! Now, chin up, old chaps! And let me hear that team cheer one final time!"

The players put their hands together in the center of the circle. "The few! The proud! The Mighty Ferrell Hogs!" Then they lined up for the last play of the season.

I'd never asked God to give me a win before. He doesn't play favorites. Besides, I honestly don't think He's too concerned about things like that. What He *is* concerned about is that we do our best and give Him the glory while doing it. But I'll admit, I was tempted. These kids deserved to win. They had earned it.

You've probably seen it in movies and on TV where the action scene at the climax of the show plays out in super slow motion. Well, that's what seemed to happen just then. I glanced at the stands behind me. The crowd was on its feet, applauding slowly and holding its collective breath. But I don't remember any noise at all. It was as if the sound had been turned off. The cheerleaders' pom-poms were making lazy circles over their heads, and Munro's baton seemed frozen in mid-air. I glanced at the faded pink scoreboard.

HOME: 15, VISITORS: 17. TIME REMAINING: 0:03.

Then the sound of the referee's whistle shattered the silence.

McNerd hiked the ball to a kneeling Goldie, who caught it in mid-air and lowered it to the turf, the end pointed upward and tilted back slightly. The offensive line surged forward as one in an effort to hold back the horde of unwelcome invaders. I saw one of the opposing players slip around the left side and raise both arms over his head as he charged toward the ball. Leonardo lowered his shoulder in an attempt to block his advance. Bender took three steps and swung his leg in an arc, making contact with the elliptical ball. It rose slowly from the grass, just ahead of the intruder's outstretched fingertips. Clearing McNerd's helmet by mere inches, it continued its trajectory toward the goal post . . . and its drift to the right. I faintly recall using a little body English to aid the path of the ball, which was lazily turning end over end and heading for no man's land again.

Then it hit me. This was the end zone where the goal post tilted. To the *right*! With all the repairs made to the stadium in recent weeks, nobody had bothered to square it up. I watched the ball sail toward the right vertical. I leaned as far to the side as I could without falling over. The ball hit the upright and glanced off . . . and over the crossbar. The head referee paused for an eternity, then slowly raised both hands over his head, making the kick official. It was good! The Mighty Hogs had won!

The Pigskin Palace erupted in pandemonium as my players buried Bender under a jubilant dog pile. I glanced at my assistant coach. Winston was pumping his fist in the air and shouting, "Yes! Yes! Yes!" I looked behind me. Students who earlier in the season couldn't have cared less about the team were streaming from the bleachers and pouring onto the field like a tsunami. Other fans were jumping up and down with such seismic exuberance that they must have registered at least a 4.0 on the Richter Scale. I spied Mr. Herold among them, his proper decorum completely abandoned, hopping up and down like a kid in a bouncy house and high-fiving everyone in sight.

I caught Reverend Pinckney's eye. My pastor smiled and gave me an enthusiastic two thumbs up. A few rows away, a beaming Mayor

Piggott was vigorously shaking hands with all those around him; and Orville was proudly pointing to the tangled pile of players and shouting, "That's my boy!" to anyone who would listen. A euphoric Hermione Piggott was clinching her husband in a tight embrace, and Avery was struggling to breathe. On the track, the three cheerleaders were dancing like woodland nymphs in a circle around their squad leader. Emily was looking in my direction and gleefully clapping her hands. Our eyes met. I smiled and waved. She smiled back and blew me a kiss.

Amid the sea of maniacal motion, I spied a lone, stationary figure, a frail woman in a blue floral-print dress. She seemed impervious to the frenzied frivolity surrounding her, almost offended by it. I blinked. It was Elvira Primrose. Then I stared in open-mouthed disbelief. She was wearing a pig snout!

The joyous celebration was not without its casualties, however. In his wild delirium, the pep band drummer beat the head of his bass drum to smithereens, and six people were sent plummeting to the ground when one board of the bleachers broke under the pounding of myriad feet. Fortunately, they emerged unscathed, as it was only the second row. But one unsuspecting student was injured when the trombonist, who was sitting directly behind her, got carried away during the playing of the school fight song, forcing her to make an unscheduled trip to Doc Halliburton's house for three stitches to the back of her head.

Suddenly, there was a loud "POP" overhead, followed by a shower of sparks. At first, I thought the lights had blown again. But when I looked up, I saw the spreading multicolored canopy of lights and heard the distinctive crackle of fireworks. Someone was setting them off in the field adjacent to the stadium. The crowd roared its approval and began to "ooh" and "aah" at each successive starburst. I smiled, allowing myself a congratulatory moment—a homecoming victory followed by a fireworks show! What a fitting end to the season.

"Out of the way! Coming through!" I instinctively turned in the direction of the shout. A very determined-looking Sheriff Piggott ran up to the fence, grabbed the top rail with both hands, and hurdled over.

"What's going on?" I inquired, as he sprinted past me onto the field.

"It's those pyromaniacs who burned down the school!" Virgil yelled over his shoulder. "I've got 'em now!"

Like I said, what a fitting end to the season.

CHAPTER TWENTY-EIGHT
All's Well That Ends Well ... ?

I overslept the next morning. That was to be expected considering the previous night's emotional victory and celebration. I lay in bed for a while, reliving the magical moment. I had received a plethora of congratulations and accolades following the game, some from people I'd never even met. Mr. Herold had informed me that this was the school's first football victory in twenty-two years, and the mayor had said he was going to declare next Saturday "Mighty Hog Day" in Piggottsville and have the town council organize a parade down Main Street with me as the grand marshall. I recalled thinking, That shouldn't take too long. But what pleased me the most was seeing Knox and Clay embrace after the win, their feud a thing of the past, and witnessing the town come together after so many years apart. Maybe this was one of the reasons why I had been called to this little corner of the world in the first place.

I finally found the energy to get up. I showered, shaved, and dressed and then went to the diner for a very late breakfast. So many people came up to me that I never got around to finishing my meal. It was nearly 11:00 when I crossed the street to the barbershop for a quick trim. As I stepped into the little establishment, I saw that Rube was busy with a customer. Seated along the wall were Wilson Piggott III, his brother Avery, and his son Orville.

The barber glanced up from the mop he was working on. "Be with you in a jiffy," he called out, waving his scissors dangerously close to his client's left ear. I nodded and took the remaining seat. "The team played a whale of a game last night, Coach," Rube began without taking his eyes off his masterpiece.

The mayor replied for me. "They sure did at that!" he interjected loudly. "Most exciting game I've seen since I took over this here . . . er, ah . . . since I was elected mayor of this here town. Never saw anything quite like it. And the townsfolk really showed their support, didn't they? Had them outnumbered four to one!" He slapped his knee gleefully.

"Yes, they did!" I added quickly before I lost the chance. "I don't think there was an empty seat in the house."

Avery tossed in his two cents' worth. "Sure sent that Wolfpack home with their tails 'tween their legs." I nodded and smiled, happy to see that he'd survived his wife's embrace without apparent injury.

Rube finished with his customer. After the man paid him, the barber turned to me. "You're up, Coach!" I climbed into the chair. "The usual?" he asked, fastening the cape around my neck.

"Yes, please."

Just then, the door opened; and Virgil stuck his head into the room. "You got time for me this morning, Rube?"

The barber glanced nervously at Orville lounging against the side wall. "Um . . . sure, Virgil. Right after I'm done here."

Virgil spied his brother and the empty seat next to him. He stiffened. "I think I'll come back when you're not so busy," he said curtly, turning to leave.

"Oh, don't be such a party-pooper!" his father blurted out. Then he softened a bit. "Have a seat, son. We were just talking about the big victory last night."

"This won't take long," Rube promised. "Just a quick trim's all."

Virgil hesitated. "Oh, all right. But if you don't mind, I'll stand." Everyone stared at him. "Well, I've been *sitting* all morning!" he explained with a scowl.

An awkward hush descended upon the barbershop. Nobody knew what to say with both Orville and Virgil in the same space. It was too shocking . . . and risky. But of course, that didn't stop me. "Did you catch those kids shooting off the fireworks last night?" I inquired of our sheriff.

Virgil's eyes narrowed. "I *almost* did. Only, they got away on a four-wheeler. I confiscated a good bit of contraband, though. Probably averted another tragedy. Might have burned down the school if I hadn't stopped them!" Everyone in the room quickly voiced their agreement.

I wasn't done putting my foot in my mouth. "I've been meaning to thank you for letting Durnell and Clay off so they could play the final two games. If it weren't for you, there would have been no complete season and no homecoming win."

Virgil's face reddened. He glanced uncomfortably at the others in the room. "Don't think twice about it," he replied, acting all casual-like. "After giving the matter a lot of consideration, I decided that jail time wasn't necessary after all. Since this was both boys' first offense, I felt that community service would be punishment enough and still send the clear message that I will not tolerate that kind of behavior in this town!"

The others nodded in unison like Bobbleheads lined up in the rear window of an automobile.

"And what a game!" Rube exclaimed, his voice an octave higher than normal.

Orville picked up on Rube's cue. "Did you see that touchdown pass my boy threw in the second quarter? Perfect spiral. Thing of beauty! And so was the way he snagged that ball out of midair and held it for the game-winning field goal." He proudly looked around for confirmation. "Knox is a gifted athlete, all right. Yes, sir, that boy is as good as gold!"

Not to be outdone by his older brother, Virgil pushed himself away from the wall he was leaning against. "What about Clay?" he argued pointedly. "*He* was involved in two scores, too, you know. He was the one who *caught* that touchdown pass. Then he faked out the entire Wolfpack defense on that trick play that scored the second touchdown!" He looked triumphantly at Orville. "Yes, sir, *my* boy's got sure hands and quick feet, all right!"

Avery leaned back in his chair and thrust his thumbs under the straps of his overalls. "Seems to me he's got a purty good *eye*, too."

Virgil stared at his uncle. "What do you mean by that?"

"Oh, nothin' much. Just that he hit the letter 'O' on my mailbox dead center is all. One shot!"

I began counting the tiles on the ceiling again.

"Good morning, Jason!" Reverend Norbert Pinckney greeted me at the door of the Piggottsville Community Church.

"Yes, it is!" I responded cheerfully, vigorously shaking his hand. "God is good."

"All the time," he replied with a twinkle in his eye. Then he leaned in. "Congratulations on the win Friday night, Coach. That was some game!"

I smiled. "Wasn't it, though! I'm so thrilled for my kids. They sure deserved it. They've come such a long way since the start of the season, both on and off the field."

Mayor Piggott arrived at that moment; and after shaking hands with everyone within a five-mile radius, he made his usual regal entrance into the sanctuary. Standing next to Emily and Miss Elvira during the singing of the hymns, I let my eyes wander over the congregation. In the second row from the front on the opposite side of the aisle, I saw Wilson and Mary Piggott sharing a hymnal. To their right stood Orville and Jolene and next to them, Knox and Clay, shoulder to shoulder. I smiled. The two cousins were acting like family again.

Then, like a complete schlub, my mouth dropped open; and my singing faltered. To the mayor's left were Virgil and Ruby and Claire! All three Piggott families were in attendance today. On the same Sunday. In the same *pew*! I nudged Emily and pointed them out. She smiled and gripped my arm.

"Hallelujah!" she whispered in my ear.

As we stood on the front stoop after the service, I turned to Miss Elvira. "I saw you at the game Friday night. Thank you for coming out to support the team and for joining in the victory celebration."

The spunky octogenarian furrowed her brow. "I came out to support my great-niece is what I did, young man. And I was *not* celebrating. I don't approve of such wanton displays of unrestrained emotion!" She huffed self-righteously. "I believe self-control to be a virtue."

I thought back to our first encounter outside the bank. At least she was consistent.

When Miss Elvira assumed a rectitudinous posture, I just couldn't resist the temptation. "Well, now, if you weren't celebrating, then *why* were you wearing that pig snout?" Emily choked on a laugh.

Elvira scowled deeply. "I was merely protecting myself from that Cupid virus," she replied defensively. "I heard it might be coming back, and I was just taking precautions is all." I'm pretty sure she meant to say "that *Covid* virus"; but who was I to judge whether it was a simple slip of her tongue or a sample of her sharp-tongued wit?

Later that evening, having just returned from dinner at an Italian restaurant in Nesbitt, Emily and I sat side by side on the well-worn white porch swing on the veranda of Mary Piggott's rental house. We swung silently for a while as we watched the sun settle behind the distant undulating hills. Then I turned to her and held out a thin, rectangular jewelry box.

"Emily, I hope you don't mind, but I'd like you to have this little token of my appreciation for your support and friendship these past few months."

Emily stared at the box and then at me. "You didn't have to get me anything, Jason."

"I know, but I wanted to. Besides, you gave me those flowers. And as they say, turnabout is fair play!"

She laughed lightly. "Okay, you convinced me." She took the box and opened it. Inside was a friendship bracelet with her birthstone attached. "This is beautiful, Jason. Thank you so much!"

I helped her fasten it around her wrist. She held it up to catch the last horizontal rays of the sinking sun and smiled sweetly. "I think I'm going to call this my 'Arkanstone.'"

I scrunched up my nose. "Your *what?*"

"My 'Arkanstone.' You know, 'The Heart of the Mountain': the 'Arkenstone' in *The Hobbit*. Only this is spelled with an *a* instead of an *e*. For Arkansas."

"That's very clever. I like it!" I watched her admire the bracelet. "I'm sorry it has such a small gemstone, but it's all I could afford on a Piggottsville-Stuyvesant Consolidated School Corporation salary." I grinned self-consciously. "Maybe you should call it your 'Little Rock' instead!"

She laughed, her eyes sparkling like the stone on her wrist, only bigger—and brighter. "Why, Jason, I think that's a *'capitol'* idea!" She settled into the swing and gave a happy, little sigh.

My arm floated out across the back as if it had a mind of its own. She responded by snuggling closer and laying her head on my shoulder.

I inhaled slowly and deeply, enjoying the ambrosian scent of her flaxen hair. Stoked about the prospects that lay ahead, I turned and gazed into Emily's beautiful blue eyes. She gazed into my green ones. Time stood still. The distance between us narrowed. I was convinced I would remember this moment for as long as I lived. Was I ever right.

Our eyes closed . . .

Our lips touched . . .

And we both *gagged*!

The wind had suddenly shifted out of the west.

EPILOGUE

Danny "Runt" Swanson graduated from Piggottsville High and eventually took over his father's Feed-N-Seed. He started three branch stores, and most of his older siblings now work for him.

Henry "Hanky" Panke went into the medical profession and became an ENT specialist. He no longer carries a hanky.

Nigel "Bender" Oglethorpe returned to England and became a highly successful youth soccer coach. A number of his players went on to have careers in the Premier Leagues.

Isaiah and Jeremima "Porky and Petunia" Pugh enrolled in the University of Arkansas, where they both tried out for the Razorbacks football program as walk-ons. Neither made the team, although Jeremima *did* make it to the second round of cuts.

Willard "Skunk" Bodkins ended up having a successful career with a large manufacturing conglomerate and was credited with inventing a dozen new air freshener scents. He also married Lexi Rae Brannigan and now showers regularly.

Durnell "Leonardo" Bodkins graduated and found employment at the railroad repair facility in Montgomery. By day, he works on boxcars as a welder; and by night, he decorates them as a graffiti artist. Most of his income goes toward spray paint.

Winston Banks moved to Huntsville to be near his family. He took a custodial position at his grandchildren's elementary school and enjoys being their janitor. Make that janitor *and* G-Pop.

Jason and Emily had their contracts renewed at the end of the school year. Jason, along with his new assistant coach, Grady Fuller, went on to lead his teams to multiple-win seasons and was named Conference Coach of the Year three times. Jason and Emily married and began raising their own litter of future Mighty Ferrell Hogs. Both continue to teach at Pig-Sty High.

The Piggottsville-Stuyvesant Consolidated School Corporation school board, in an unprecedented display of optimism and generosity, unanimously approved the purchase of a larger trophy case. *Go, Mighty Ferrell Hogs!*

So you see, my friends, miracles can happen. Miracles do happen. But not all miracles are "big" ones like someone being raised from the dead, walking on water, or being cured of cancer. Some are right under our noses or in front of our faces, yet we're often too farsighted or blind to see them. Sometimes, we're too busy or distracted to even notice. I'm not just talking about the miracle of resurrecting a high school sport and leading an improbable group of misfits to a one-win season. I'm talking about miracles such as a failing, defeated young man with low self-esteem seeing himself for the first time as valuable in the sight of an Almighty God. I'm talking about two cousins setting aside their differences for the benefit of their team and learning what it means to forgive. I'm talking about two brothers who haven't spoken to each other in decades realizing that their feud has divided an entire community and finally humbling themselves enough to work on putting things right between them. And I'm talking about a naïve, young teacher and coach who thought he was facing the impossible but discovered that *"'with God all things are possible.'"*[20]

The next time you're asked to do the impossible, to make something out of nothing, remember this: you will never have nothing to start with because you will always have *you*! Start by giving yourself to God. Give Him your heart, your soul, your life. Let Him use you to accomplish something outside of yourself, beyond yourself, greater than yourself. That's what miracles are all about: God doing something in us and through us that we could never do on our own—always for our good and ultimately for His glory.

So, when life gives you lemons, don't try making lemonade. Give those lemons to God. Then faithfully plant and water the seeds

---

20 Matthew 19:26

and patiently watch Him grow that meager offering into an entire orchard, plum full of abundant fruit trees. That's what I did and look what happened!

Oh, and never forget one other thing: pigs really can fly!

ABOUT THE AUTHOR

David Mathews was born in the small midwestern town of Friend, Nebraska, a community of eleven hundred people once listed in *Ripley's Believe It or Not* for having the world's smallest police station—a tiny tool shed previously used by highway construction crews. He grew up in small towns in Kansas and Indiana before settling in Indianapolis.

Now living in Xenia, Ohio, David and his wife, Donna, have six children between them, along with a son-in-law, three daughters-in-law, and six grandchildren. He enjoys home remodeling, woodworking, bicycling, camping, and writing. He also serves in their local church, loves being a grandfather, and never grows tired of watching *Andy Griffith reruns*.

For more information about
DAVID MATHEWS
please visit:

www.davidjmathews.com
www.facebook.com/davidmathews.author
davidmathews.author@yahoo.com
@davidmathewsau1

Ambassador International's mission is to magnify the Lord Jesus Christ and promote His Gospel through the written word.

We believe through the publication of Christian literature, Jesus Christ and His Word will be exalted, believers will be strengthened in their walk with Him, and the lost will be directed to Jesus Christ as the only way of salvation.

For more information about AMBASSADOR INTERNATIONAL please visit:

www.ambassador-international.com
@AmbassadorIntl
www.facebook.com/AmbassadorIntl

Thank you for reading this book!

You make it possible for us to fulfill our mission, and we are grateful for your partnership.

To help further our mission, please consider leaving us a review on your social media, favorite retailer's website, Goodreads or Bookbub, or our website, and check out some of the books on the following page!

Abandoned as infants, Tovi and her twin brother were raised by an eclectic tribe of warm, kind people in a treehouse village in the valley. After her brother's sudden disappearance Tovi questions her life and her faith in an invisible King. Ignoring her best friend Silas' advice, she decides to search for her brother in the kingdom on top of the mountain. Amidst the glamour of the kingdom above the cloud Tovi is torn between her own dark desires and unanswered questions.

When Ari finds herself with a job offer to work undercover and find her purpose again, she can't resist. But as her undercover case deepens, she discovers that the voices in her head aren't as imaginary as she thought.

After department layoffs and an increase in crime, Crime Scene Specialist and Bloodstain Pattern Analyst Renee' McKenzie develops her own crime scene team of junior interns, including her own daughter, Bailey. The team arrives to their biggest crime scene yet, and Bailey's father, DEA Agent Liam McKenzie, is brought in to help with the investigation as the "players" of this case appear to be connected to something bigger than a local narcotics investigation.